Praise for Sara's Sacrifice

"Flo Parfitt offers a colorful cast of characters steeped in their time, a period of history and a movement we don't see covered nearly enough in fiction. Parfitt made early twentieth century Milwaukee come to life in this story of the hard work and sacrifice of Wisconsin's forward-looking suffragists. Readers will want to find out what happens to Tillie, Catherine, Ruby, and others, especially Sara, as they struggle to win the most basic right to vote in *Sara's Sacrifice*. These women seem real and remind me of women like my mother and aunts and so many of our modern feminist icons. I thoroughly enjoyed it."
—Virginia McCullough, Award-winning author of romance and women's fiction novels

"*Sara's Sacrifice* is a read that keeps you turning from one page to the next wondering how the protagonist is going to survive. Made me feel like I was there, wanting to know what's next? Hard to put down to the very end."
—Heidi Gillis, Life Wellness Coach

"*Sara's Sacrifice* takes the national fight for women's votes and takes it to a personal level, showing the grassroots efforts of the suffragist movement in one small Wisconsin town and the sacrifices the women of that time made in order to create a better future for their daughters. It's a book every voter should read."
—Dorothy St. James, Author of *The Broken Spine*

"If Louisa May Alcott had been born in modern day, she would be most impressed with this work of Flo Parfitt's, both for its reflection of an era in writing style and tone, and for giving us something to connect with in today's societal challenges."
—Paul Lisnek, Emmy-award winning TV anchor

"You will laugh, cry, and love as you read the story of this heroic woman."
—Arlene Bourgeois Molzahn, Retired teacher and author of twenty-four books

"*Sara's Sacrifice* is a beautifully written testament to the women who pioneered women's rights as Sara risks both status and stability in her determination to create a better world of opportunity for her children. The author stirs a fury of emotion set against a backdrop of smooth, descriptive writing, leaving the reader appreciative of both the women's rights movement and the writing style of the author."
—Callie J. Trautmiller, Author of *Becoming American,* a young adult historical fiction

"The 19th Amendment to the U.S. Constitution didn't "just happen." In this fast-paced novel, set in Wisconsin, Flo Parfitt depicts the period of the suffragettes. The main character embodies the passion, courage and actions of women determined to secure their right to vote."
—Jacklyn Lohr Burkat, Retired Librarian

SARA'S SACRIFICE

Vote Proudly

Flo Parfitt

Publishing Editor: Brittiany Koren
Editor: A.L. Mundt
Copy-editor: B.A. Koren
Cover Art Designer & Interior Layout: The Killion Group, Inc.

Category: Women's Historical Fiction
Description: In 1912, as women are lobbying for the 19th Amendment, many
hardships happen to a Wisconsin woman suffragette who must make a sacri-
fice to insure her daughters' future.
Hard Cover ISBN: 978-1-951375-05-8
Paperback ISBN: 978-1-951375-04-1
Ebook ISBN: 978-1-951375-06-5
LOC Catalogue Data: Applied for.

First Edition published by Written Dreams Publishing in September, 2019.

Green Bay, WI 54311

*I dedicate this book to my husband, Gary Cichocki.
Gary was highly supportive and encouraging through
my long hours of writing. Although he had not read
even an excerpt from my book he would often ask,
"How is the book coming?"*

*Unfortunately, Gary passed away before I finished
the book and never got a chance to read it.*

Chapter One

T he sky lit up as fire roared into the valley. Flames reached like devil fingers to the heavens above, as if screaming out to God Himself. The blaze engulfed the lone log cabin. The west winds swirled over the valley, fueling the fire.

Jedediah Adams awoke to find flames licking at the walls of his home. "Mandy, Mandy, wake up!"

His wife was sound asleep beside him. He shook her frantically as he jumped from the bed. "We need to get out. The house is afire. I'll get Sara."

Amanda Adams began to choke on the smoke, which ate up the oxygen in the room. She struggled to get up while Jed ran to Sara's room.

"Sara, Sara, come quickly!" Jed said.

Sara coughed.

Jed wrapped his nine-year-old daughter in a blanket and carried her out into the brisk fall air. Sara coughed harder as the smoke burned her lungs.

Jed looked around but did not see Amanda. He panicked. "Sara, stay here. I need to get Mama." He placed Sara beneath the old oak tree some distance from the side of the house where she would be safe. Jed ran back into the flames.

"Papa, Papa!" Sara screamed as he disappeared into the burning homestead. She stared at the house, now a skeleton in the dark. She shivered, partly from the frosty air and partly from the fear welling up inside of her. Her eyes widened as sparks flew high into the sky.

Neighbors heard the sounds and smells of the fire, a nightmare for a logging community that was always on alert. The commotion outside built as neighbors grabbed their buckets and gear to come to the rescue.

"It's Jed Adams's house," a voice called out in the darkness.

"Buckets ain't gonna help," one of the neighbors yelled. "The creek is dry." A recent drought had left the creek a mere mud hole.

A next-door neighbor saw Sara shaking at the trunk of the tree. She wrapped Sara in a blanket and pulled her to her breast. "There, there, Sara. Where are your mama and papa?"

"Mama didn't come out and Papa went to get her." Tears welled in her eyes.

Later, Sara learned that her father never made it to her mother. It was evident Mama had succumbed to the smoke. Her charred body lay outside their bedroom door with what appeared to be the family Bible clutched in her arms. A fallen rafter must have struck her father, as the neighbors found him under remnants of wood. Now Sara was all alone.

***

Thinking back on the years, Sara remembered details from long past. Jed had been the owner of the logging company for more than a decade. He'd treated his workers well and built up a small fortune for the times. That was in 1887. The company was sold to his long-time competitor.

Sara went to live with an elderly aunt, her mother's older sister. Sara's inheritance was held in trust at the local bank since she had no male heir or guardian. Women were not to be trusted with money or property. Except for her living expenses, which were doled out on an as needed basis, the money would be held until Sara married when her husband could manage her estate.

Sara's aunt was kind and wise and raised Sara to be strong and independent. She would often tell Sara, "It is a difficult road you have to travel, but it will make you stronger."

Having decided to become a teacher, at seventeen Sara went away to college in Milwaukee. But while she was away, her aunt died, leaving Sara all alone in the world.

She grew up to be intelligent and proud, and learned how to take care of herself. She knew how to keep gentlemen callers in their place and spent her money wisely. She kept abreast of local politics and she taught the children in her school with love and discipline. Her mother had instilled in her a strong faith in God, and she turned to him in moments of sadness.

Sara thought she might never marry. She found most men self-centered, incapable of intelligent conversation, or useless at managing their own lives, much less that of a family. But then one day, she came upon the handsomest man she had ever seen—Henry Dewberry—and he stole her heart.

Henry was clearly head over heels in love with Sara Adams. He had important plans for his life, recently taking a position with the First National Bank of Milwaukee. He loved children and the work Sara did at the school. They didn't always see eye to eye, but Henry could carry on an intelligent conversation. He listened to her opinions and ideas.

In June of 1898, at the age of twenty, Sara became Mrs. Henry Dewberry, and Sara's life changed dramatically. She was a stunning woman, small in stature with auburn tresses, brilliant blue eyes, and a zest for life. Much to her chagrin, Sara had to quit her job when she married Henry. By law, married women were not allowed to teach.

But family was very important to Sara and Henry. They immediately began a family. Their daughter Ella was born in 1900, soon followed by Thaddeus. After a miscarriage, Elizabeth came next, and three years later, Adam was born. Although she was expected to live the life of a socialite, Sara chose to spend her time raising her own children, volunteering at the poor house, and spending time with her friend Catherine, whom she had met at the university.

The children grew quickly, and Sara was quite content being a wife and mother. Her volunteer work and her conversations with Catherine, who had never married, made her realize that outside of her beautiful, seemingly perfect world, women had a hard life. They were unfairly treated by the laws of the land and had no rights or voice of their own. Sara's sense of justice told her there was an answer.

***

Alone in the parlor in their house on Astor Street, Sara sat on her old bentwood rocker beside the fireplace. The fire was growing dim. Sleet splattered on the window. She shuddered and pulled a wool plaid shawl tighter over her shoulders. Was there a chill in the air this damp March morning in 1912, or was it her anxiety?

This evening, Sara planned to attend her first meeting of the Wisconsin Suffragettes. It was well known in the community that her husband was not an advocate for the movement. She did not want to imagine what Henry might do if he found out.

Maybe I should wait. Henry is a good man. He provides everything our family could possibly need. But he can be so pig-headed and set in his ways. Just yesterday, he summed up women's suffrage in a few words: "A woman's place is in the home. They should know their place."

Know their place indeed.

Claudia entered the room with her always-present feather duster. "Would you like anything, Mum?"

"No, thank you," Sara said, and cleared her throat. Then, she took a deep breath. "Claudia, would you mind watching the children this evening? Henry has a meeting at town hall and I need to go out."

The woman nodded. "Certainly, Mum. Will you be late?"

"I hope to be home before Henry. Thank you so much." Sara took another deep breath and exhaled slowly. She had set the wheels in motion. There was no turning back.

She tried to concentrate on the muffler she was knitting for Henry, but her mind was busy thinking of her decision and the difficulties of carrying out her plan. Sara hated the deceit, but she had no choice. Henry would never understand.

Giving up on her needlework, Sara dropped her knitting on the table next to her, stood, and paced in front of the fireplace. If Henry arrived home first, what would Claudia tell him? What if the children asked where she was going? Sara sat down again and wrung her hands.

The suffragettes' cause is important. Women are given no credibility. They can't own property, even if they pay for it. If they work, their paycheck goes to the men in their lives—their husbands, brothers, or fathers. It isn't fair. Men have ownership over their wives and their children. Women have no voice. If they protest, the laws of the land are such that their voices are not heard. It is high time things changed.

Sara was startled when Adam awoke from his nap and called out, "Mama, Mama!"

She hurried up the stairs to his bedroom.

Adam reached out his pudgy hands, a wide smile on his face. Sara gathered him into her arms and savored the warmth of her toddler's clutch.

Although Adam was almost three, he was still her baby. She knew at thirty-four, her child-bearing days were almost over, but if all indications were correct, another was on the way.

She got Adam dressed and took him downstairs. "Come, Adam, it's almost time for the children to come home from school."

Soon eleven-year-old Thaddeus and twelve-year-old Ella clamored into the house, each vying to get Sara's attention first.

Ella blurted out, "Thaddeus and the other boys found a snake behind the school, and they chased the girls with it to make them scream."

"But we was just funnin'," Thaddeus protested. "B'sides, it was only a grass snake."

Sara frowned at Thaddeus. He put his head down and shuffled his feet.

"That may very well be," Sara said, "but it was not a very nice thing to do. Where did you find a snake? Aren't they still hibernating?"

"The school had a terrarium with snakes," Ella explained. "They woke up early, and the teacher wanted to release them into the wild."

"We dumped them in the brush behind the school," Thaddeus cut in. "It was so fun to see them slither away."

Sara gave him a stern look. "And you were not satisfied just to see them slither?"

Ella smiled smugly while her mother took charge.

Thaddeus wouldn't meet her eyes. "We just wanted to have some fun cuz the girls were all squeamish about them."

"I hope you apologized," Sara said.

Thaddeus looked at her and nodded. "Teacher made us."

"Okay, then. Don't do it again." Sara shook her finger at Thaddeus. "And where is Elizabeth?"

Ella ran to the window. "Here she is now. She walked behind us with her friend, Kate. She didn't want to have Thaddeus anywhere near with his snakes."

Thaddeus ran to the door and faced his younger sister. "Sssssss," Thaddeus hissed.

"Young man, that will be enough out of you," Sara reprimanded. "Tell Elizabeth to come in...and be decent about it."

Thaddeus gulped. That was the end of his "funnin'," or he would be in deep trouble. He opened the door. "C'mon, Liz, I won't do it no more."

Treats were routine when the children returned home from school.

"There are cookies and milk in the kitchen," Sara said. "I'm sure Claudia has them ready."

Elizabeth ran to the kitchen with Thaddeus at her heels.

Sara turned her attention to Ella. "And what about you, my pretty damsel? What did you learn today?"

"Teacher says girls don't have to be smart because they will have husbands to take care of them someday." Ella rolled her eyes.

"Oh, he did, did he?" Sara had to work to keep the anger from her voice. "What else did he say?"

"He said girls should learn how to read and take care of babies, but boys should study hard because someday they could be president. Then I asked him, 'What if I want to be president?' He laughed, and then said something about pigs flying."

All of Sara's uncertainty melted away. She was going to that meeting.

Dinner was a pot of stew with hot biscuits and cold, fresh milk. The smell of fresh baked biscuits drew everyone to the table.

"Claudia, please join us for dinner this evening," Sara said. "Henry won't be home until later."

"Thank you, Mum. Don't mind if I do."

They sat down and bowed their heads.

"Dear Lord," Sara prayed, "thank you for blessing us with this wonderful meal. We pray you will always watch over us and keep us safe." She hesitated. "Also, please watch over Tillie and help her be strong and overcome her trials. We ask this in Jesus' name. Amen."

Sara filled the bowls for the children, and Claudia passed the hot biscuits and butter.

"Is Tillie not well?" Claudia asked.

"She's having difficulties," Sara explained. "Hopefully, she will be out and about soon. I thought it would be nice if I looked in on her."

Sara hadn't lied. The fact that Tillie served as the local leader of the suffragette group didn't need to be mentioned. No, she didn't exactly lie, but the deceit had begun. Sara was entering a whole new world.

Chapter Two

After dinner, Thaddeus and Elizabeth played checkers on the gaming table in the parlor, and Ella sat on the bentwood rocker embroidering a sampler. Adam amused himself with a toy truck. Sara paced from child to child while peeking out the window to the circular drive in front of the house. It was nearly six o'clock when Catherine's carriage pulled up into the driveway.

"Claudia," Sara called out. "Catherine is here to pick me up."

"Children, be good and mind Claudia." Sara hugged her children, then grabbed her long wool cloak and fur muff, tying her bonnet as she dashed to the carriage.

Sara's long-time friend, Catherine, lived a couple of blocks from Sara. It was Catherine who had first introduced Sara to the suffragette movement. Catherine, an intelligent single woman, had opened Sara's eyes to the various facts concerning the single women's plight. Catherine could never own property. Job opportunities were limited. She was dubbed an old maid and a thing to be pitied.

"Hurry, it's so cold," Catherine shouted to her friend.

Sara climbed aboard. "Catherine, you always dress so smart, even in this cold." Catherine wore a full-length fur trimmed coat with a matching hat and collar.

Once in the seat of the one-horse carriage, Sara pulled the wool blanket over her legs and tightened her cloak to fend off the chill of the Milwaukee winter. Despite the cold, it was a beautiful star-studded evening. The remaining snow of the season crunched under the wheels of the buggy, and the bells on the horse jangled as they trotted away. They moved swiftly toward Tillie Morgenson's home, a short distance away on State Street.

"How did you manage to pull this off?" Catherine asked. She was quite aware of the circumstances in the Dewberry household.

"I think the devil has his hands on me. You know Tillie is having a difficult time and would appreciate my looking in on her. In fact, she is having such a difficult time, she's going to need the attention of many of her friends. Don't you agree?"

Catherine shouted, "Bravo! A magnificent performance! This is so unlike you, Sara. I am surprised you pulled it off."

Sara grinned. "I feel so guilty yet at the same time exhilarated. What has come over me?"

"I completely understand. It is the Susan B. Anthonys and Carrie Chapman Catts of this world who will receive recognition when this fight is over, but it is the Sara Dewberrys who are the real heroes. The ones who hide in the shadows but are the heart and soul of the movement."

"Pshaw." Sara ducked her head in embarrassment. "Don't be silly. I am no one."

"You're wrong, Sara. You are one of the faceless, voiceless participants who can't come to the forefront because they might lose everything. The only armor these women have is deceit, and isn't that sad? They do it so one day they can stand proud knowing they have done the right thing for the good of their sisters and daughters."

"And it is the Catherine Livingstons who will light the way."

"Ha! But since I have no husband, I deceive no one, but being part of the movement makes me more diligent. Being in the shadows is far easier than openly shining light on the issues."

Catherine pulled the steed around to the back of Tillie Morgenson's home to avoid attention. Several carriages were already there, though none of the porch lights were burning to greet guests. The house was dark as they entered through the service door to the kitchen, where other suffragettes showed them to the living room.

Sara had anticipated being in a room full of strangers but was pleasantly surprised to find she not only knew Tillie and Catherine, but also Reverend Reinhart's wife, Ruby, and Martha Thompson and Gertrude Roland from the Presbyterian Church. About fifteen women had arrived. Sara soon learned most of the people present had husbands who were not aware of their activities.

Martha and Gertrude handed out leaflets.

"Sara!" Gertrude exclaimed. "Fancy seeing you here. Henry is a known vocal opponent to the cause. How did you manage to get away?"

Sara placed a finger to her lips. "Shhh, Sara isn't here," she whispered.

Gertrude and Martha laughed heartily.

"Neither are we," Martha said and winked.

Sara took the pamphlet, found a seat next to the fireplace, and took in the warm glow. Tillie's home was well-appointed with beautiful furniture of the time. The ceilings in the house were high, and a rich oriental rug nearly covered a hardwood floor. The furniture was rich brown leather, with ladderback chairs brought in to accommodate the number of women attending.

Tillie raised her hand. "Ladies, ladies. We need your attention."

The room quieted.

Tillie was tall and thin and wore an engaging smile. Her gray hair was tied back in a bun. "We're happy to see some newer faces here, as well as the many loyal women who have long been dedicated to our cause. Tonight, we have a new guest, Sara Dewberry, who is a friend of Catherine Livingston and me."

The group applauded.

Tillie continued with a warning. "I must caution you all to never reveal the location or attendees of our meetings. We face a desperate populace out there who would like nothing better than to shut us down...or worse."

Ruby, the pastor's wife, stood. "I am fortunate to have a husband who is sympathetic to our cause, but there are many in the church, including the deacons and elders, who would have us run out of town if our activities were to become public. It's our right to meet, but it's also a matter of safety that we be discreet."

She continued, "Just this morning, this poster was tacked to our church door." Ruby raised a poster with large red letters for all to see.

DANGER!
WOMEN'S SUFFRAGE WOULD DOUBLE
THE IRRESPONSIBLE VOTE!
IT IS A MENACE TO THE HOME,
MEN'S WORK, AND TO ALL BUSINESS.

The room came alive with incredulous protests.

A woman in the back stood. "They think we are the problem. What rubbish. Listen to this." The woman turned the pages of a book and read:

"Would men but generously snap our chains and be content with rational fellowship instead of slavish obedience? They would find us more observant daughters, more affectionate sisters, more faithful wives, more reasonable mothers—in a word, better citizens. We should then love them with true affection, because we should learn to respect ourselves; and the peace of mind of a worthy man would not be interrupted by the idle vanity of his wife."

Sara soon learned the meetings were quite informal. People spoke when they had an item to address. Tillie kept things moving and introduced issues for discussion.

"Here, here," shouted Gertrude.

"Who wrote that?" a woman in blue asked.

"Mary Wollstonecraft," the woman said. "It's called A Vindication of the Rights of Woman." She raised it high for all to see. "This book is from 1792. It is quite clear women's suffrage is not a new idea."

The excitement in the room was palpable. Sara was sure she wanted to be part of this.

Women gave status reports for future rallies, progress reports from past events, and gave assignments for signs and banners. Sara was in awe of all that was happening, all she could be a part of without divulging her activities, particularly to Henry.

Before they knew it, the huge grandfather clock in the corner chimed eight o'clock. Tillie's stable boy entered via the kitchen, handed Tillie a note, then made a quick exit.

Sara was about to motion to Catherine when Tillie said, "For those ladies whose husbands are attending the town meeting, word has arrived they will soon be adjourning, so we had better do the same."

There was rustling as attendees gathered their things and prepared to leave.

"Thank you all for coming. I hope you'll all attend next week's meeting here. We'll have posters for you to distribute regarding the march to the courthouse in Racine in three weeks. We hope there'll be a good turnout. It will be on April ninth to coincide with the spring primary election."

Sara and the other ladies put on their cloaks and mufflers for the cold ride home.

Tillie's coachman was on hand to help the ladies make a safe exit to the main road through a back trail hidden by the trees. As Catherine and Sara got into their carriage, he cautioned them, "I skidded the trail with the sled, so you won't get stuck, but be careful of the sides. There are some big ruts."

One by one, the carriages followed the trail and escaped to the main roadway undetected.

They'd been traveling a few minutes when Catherine broke the silence. "What did you think?"

"I'm so excited and overwhelmed and scared. I want to do this. I must do this, but how? Henry may think Tillie is sick today, but she can't possibly stay ill forever." Sara tugged on her coat with anxious fingers.

Catherine patted her hand. "It won't be easy, but we'll find a way."

They pulled into the drive at Sara's home. "Good-bye, Catherine. I can't tell you what an exciting evening this has been."

"We'll talk more later. You'd better hurry. Henry could arrive any minute."

Sara entered her parlor. She removed her cloak and placed it on the hall coat stand, then warmed her hands by the fireplace.

Claudia greeted her with a hot cup of tea. "How is Tillie?"

"Tillie is amazing." Sara smiled. "We had a wonderful conversation, and she's already making plans to travel soon."

Claudia sighed. "I certainly am glad to hear that, Mum. Tillie is not one to lay around. Some say she's one of them suffragettes."

"Oh, don't listen to gossip," Sara said. "It only brings trouble. Tillie is a lovely lady."

If only you knew the truth, Claudia, if only you knew.

Chapter Three

Early the next morning, Sara reflected on Claudia's comments. If her housekeeper had heard Tillie was involved in the suffrage movement, then the rumors were out there. Suspicions were one thing, but if anyone truly knew Tillie was a suffragette, her home was no longer a safe place to meet. Vengefulness against suffragettes ranged from exposing the members to burning down the place where they met. She must warn Tillie.

After the children were off to school and Claudia left for the market, Sara bundled up Adam and put him in his pram. Then, she hurried to Tillie's house. It was a pleasant day, so the walk would be invigorating.

Margaret, Tillie's maid, greeted her. Margaret could be trusted with any confidential matter since she was very much in sync with Tillie's politics and practices.

"I am here to see Tillie. Is she in?" Sara asked.

"I believe she's in the library," Margaret said. "I'll tell her you're here. What a cute little boy you have." Margaret tweaked Adam's cheek. "May I take your cloak and muffler?"

Sara removed her coat and handed it to Margaret, who disappeared down the hall.

A few moments later Margaret scurried back, breathless from carrying the bulk of her hefty frame. "Miss Tillie will see you in the library," she huffed. "I'll be back in a minute with tea—" she focused on Adam "—and milk for you, my sweetie."

With Adam in her arms, Sara followed Margaret to the library.

"Sara, how nice to see you! Did you enjoy our meeting last night?" Tillie sat behind the big mahogany desk that had belonged to her late husband, Senator Morgenson. She rose and motioned for Sara to take a seat on the large leather chair in the corner by the coffee table.

"Oh, yes," Sara said as she sat, seating Adam on her lap. Sara squeezed her hand in a fist and placed it over her mouth. She closed her eyes, then quickly opened them before she dropped her fist to her heart. She took a deep breath. "It was amazing, Tillie, and my visit today is about that. I want to be involved in the cause, but I'm afraid my husband is in strong opposition to the movement. I must keep my activity under cover at least for a time."

"Certainly, my dear." Tillie came around the desk and took a seat next to Sara. She patted her hand. "There are many women in the movement who share your dilemma. There's still plenty for you to do behind the scenes, and we appreciate any time you can dedicate to the cause."

Margaret came in carrying a silver tea service and placed it on the table between the ladies. She poured tea into the delicate Royal Dolton china cups, then she hurried out of the room.

Tillie continued, "Most of the women involved in the cause are highly educated and economically well positioned in the community. Many pour a lot of money into the movement, and most are well versed in the issues of the State and Nation. We need more women like you, Sara."

Margaret returned with a plate of warm molasses cookies.

"Margaret baked these this morning," Tillie said. She took a plate off the coffee table and held it out to Sara.

"I like to bake early to take the chill out of the morning air," Margaret said.

"Mmm, they certainly smell tempting," Sara said.

Margaret smiled proudly. "Help yourself, Ma'am."

Sara took a cookie for herself and another for Adam.

The sweet treats were delicious. The cookies' toasty, spicy smell permeated the room and provided a warm, inviting atmosphere.

Margaret turned to Tillie and asked, "Will there be anything else, Ma'am?"

"No, Margaret, thank you."

Margaret exited the room.

"So, my dear," Tillie said, "what brings you here this morning? I'm guessing you must have more on your mind than tea and cookies."

"I'm very concerned. My housekeeper has heard gossip, and it seems many people in the community suspect you have connections to the suffragette movement. I fear your home as a meeting place is compromised."

"I see." Tillie looked beyond Sara, pressing her lips together. "I am quite aware my involvement is questioned and under observation. My late husband was an active proponent, and at that time, I openly shared my views. Since his death, I have not been at the forefront of the movement, choosing to recruit in secret instead. Since so many face the opposition of husbands, fathers, and brothers, I knew it would better serve the cause to remain in the shadows for a time."

Adam wiggled to the floor with a toy truck Sara had brought to amuse him.

"Now that the Milwaukee Suffragettes are well established," Tillie said, "they can move forward on their own. My involvement will no longer be suspect after our Racine rally—it will be common knowledge. I had hoped we could keep our location under wraps until then."

"Do you think we will be safe meeting at your house in the meantime?"

"I'm not sure, but I don't think we should take the chance. The group has already discussed various alternate meeting sites. Catherine has volunteered her home."

"Catherine?" Sara asked, surprised. Her friend hadn't mentioned it to her. But then, why would she? Until last night, Sara had not been a part of the movement, and to tell anyone, even her best friend, would have made the meeting place less secure.

"She lives a few houses away from you, correct?"

Sara was bewildered. "Catherine lives across from the town hall. She has no place to hide carriages or to keep a meeting secret."

"Exactly!" Tillie smiled. "That is the general idea. We would be hiding in plain sight. We will spread the word that Catherine is hosting a baby shower. We will, of course, bring gifts so it will appear authentic. And, it will be a real baby shower, but the main conversation will not be on birthing but on voting."

"What a fabulous idea," Sara said, clasping her hands together. "But we can't have a baby shower every week."

"We'll be changing locations for a while. The next meeting site will be on our agenda for discussion at the shower."

Children were taught early to be seen and not heard. The truck Sara had brought along kept Adam busy, but he was becoming a bit restless. Sara stood. "I really must be going. Thank you for your hospitality."

"Thank you for informing me of word on the street. It isn't a surprise, but it does accelerate what we'd planned. Stop by anytime. I enjoyed our visit."

Margaret scurried in with Sara and Adam's wraps and showed them to the door. "You take care of that baby now." She winked. "And take care of business."

Sara laughed. Margaret was part of the sisterhood.

Sara put Adam in the pram and headed back home in time to find Claudia in the kitchen preparing dinner.

"Did you have a nice walk, Mum?" Claudia inquired.

"It was wonderful. It feels like spring. Could you watch the children next Tuesday evening? I have a baby shower to attend at Catherine's house."

"Who's having a baby?"

For a moment Sara faltered, her heart pounding. She had no idea whose baby was being showered. "Ah...no one you know."

"I'd be happy to watch the children. You enjoy the baby shower, Mum. It is good to see you getting out."

Sara hurried off to change Adam. She needed to be more careful. She'd almost blown their secret already. This deceit game was new to her.

***

During the week, Sara knitted frantically to finish an afghan for the new baby. She had learned from Catherine that their friend, Marilyn Thomas, was expecting in June. This was her first.

Henry was pleased his wife was finding new friends and activities to keep her busy. He liked the idea of women knowing their place, concentrating on family and babies. Sara had always made her children a top priority, and although she was cordial with all of Henry's associates, she had never adapted to the life of a socialite.

Henry was now vice president at First National Bank in Milwaukee. He was well-known and well-liked in the community, and a handsome gentleman. He wore his dark hair slicked back, he sported a full mustache and was always impeccably dressed.

On Tuesday evening, Henry sent Sara to the shower with much

enthusiasm. Spring was still in the air, so Sara walked the two blocks to Catherine's home.

As she stepped on the path, Sara recalled a conversation she'd had with Catherine.

"I live in a row house that I rent," Catherine said. "When my parents died, I received a substantial inheritance, but was not allowed to buy my own property as a single woman. I thought it would be good to invest it in property. I tried to buy a house, but I was refused. I could put it in the name of a brother or an uncle, but I could not purchase it on my own."

Sara had understood since she had also received an inheritance when her parents died. She had never attempted to purchase a home on her own, but when she had married Henry, the property had been listed in his name, although it had been paid for with her money.

"The inheritance was substantial enough to allow me to live in comfort, but it's the principle of the thing," Catherine had told Sara with an annoyed sniff. "That was why I joined the movement two years ago."

Sara arrived at Catherine's home. There was a front porch with a swing. Catherine often sat on it and greeted friends and neighbors who were out for an evening stroll in the neighborhood. Her home was modest, but it had many modern conveniences, such as running water and electricity.

Sara knocked on the door and Catherine greeted her. "Hello, my friend. Come in, come in."

Others arrived behind her, and Catherine continued her greetings as Sara took wraps.

The ladies began to gather in Catherine's living room, laden with gifts. Catherine had chairs enough for nine, and with the aid of a small utility stool she kept in the kitchen, she was able to seat everyone. The ladies placed their presents on a side table in her living room.

Catherine went to the kitchen for refreshments.

"Let me help you with that," Sara said, and helped Catherine distribute cups of punch for the guests.

Marilyn opened the gifts. She had many hand-sewn diapers, and a couple of hand-knit sweater sets and booties. Sara's knitted afghan was a big hit. Marilyn also received several purchased gifts of layettes, bottles, lotions, and other supplies. All received the customary ohs and ahs, but everyone, including Marilyn, was anxious to get on with the real purpose of the gathering.

Marilyn thanked everyone for their generous gifts. "Now let's move on to the meeting. We need an update on the Racine rally."

"Yes, let's do it." Tillie gathered her papers and reminded everyone yet again of the importance of secrecy. "We have two important items to discuss. Besides the rally, we also need to discuss the location of our next meeting. Racine has provided the parade route and the agenda for the day. As you know, the ninth is election day, and the streets will be crowded. Racine is less than two hours south of Milwaukee by train. We'll catch the train out of Milwaukee at eight in the morning on April ninth and return at three in the afternoon to be home before dinner. We'll march from the train station to the courthouse, where we'll hold a rally on the courthouse steps at noon. Noon is the busiest time in Courthouse Square, with workers scurrying around for lunch and running errands as well as getting to the courthouse to vote. We'll work out the final details at our next meeting."

The meeting moved swiftly.

"Unless there are further things to address about the rally, we need to get to the business of our meeting location," Tillie said.

Ruby rose to speak. "Martha and I have been discussing the problem of a place to meet, and we think we have a solution. We have a nice meeting room in the church that's available on Tuesday evenings. However, meetings held at the church are listed in the church bulletin, and for the most part, are open to all congregants. We can't call ourselves suffragettes. Typically, ladies' meetings are for quilting or ladies' aid. Either of those meetings might draw outside interest, and we certainly don't want a wife of a church elder deciding to check out our group. We need to find a group name that would not draw attention, such as a boring finance group."

Sara suggested, "How about the Women's Educational Research Fundraising Group? Our purpose can be to raise funds for educational research. No one wants to be part of fundraising, nor do they want to open their purse strings for anything that doesn't affect them."

Several women nodded in agreement.

Sara said, "Educational Research is vague enough yet intellectual enough to scare some away."

This drew more laughter.

Catherine liked the idea and expounded on it. "We are in the business of education for women and researching ways to secure the vote. We cannot raise too much money for the cause, so if someone interpreting this incorrectly wants to throw funds our way, we would be most happy to take it."

Excited chatter permeated the room.

"Ladies, ladies." Tillie clapped her hands. "Your attention, please."

The room quieted.

"All in favor, say aye!" Tillie called out.

A resounding cheer went up when the vote passed unanimously.

"Are there any other concerns?" Tillie asked when the women had quieted once again.

"Is the room private?" came a question from the back of the room.

Another voice called, "Who else has access to the space?"

"It is possible other people could be in the building," Ruby said. "The pastor, the choir director, the janitor. We'd have to keep the door closed for privacy."

Ruby made the arrangements, and the permanent site of the Women's Educational Research Fundraising Group was born. The first meeting would be held the following Tuesday, the last gathering before the trip to Racine.

Sara wanted so much to go to Racine, but how would she pull it off?

Later in the week, at dinner, Sara approached the subject with Henry, twiddling her fingers nervously. "There is a new organization I want to join at the church. You know I am concerned about education, and this organization could provide an opportunity to ensure an education for everyone, including those who have no funds."

"I think that is a wonderful idea, Sara," said Henry. "I'm glad to see you involved further with education. I'm very proud of you."

Sara almost squealed with joy. She couldn't wait for next Tuesday.

Chapter Four

March ended. The snow melted, and the grass turned green. Trees budded, and tulips poked their heads out of the cold winter soil.

Ladies headed to the church for the first meeting of the Women's Educational Research Fundraising Group. Some came by carriage, and some took advantage of the warm weather by getting out their bicycles, which had become a popular mode of transportation, especially among suffragettes. The often-opposed mobility of the bicycle phenomena had become a symbol of the suffragettes' independence.

Sara and Catherine decided to ride their bicycles, too.

"Catherine, you have a new safety bicycle. Aren't you glad it is 1912? In the late 1800s, your bicycle would have had a large wheel in the front, and you would've had to climb up to the seat." Sara chuckled as they mounted their bicycles and headed toward the church.

"You wouldn't have found me on one of those contraptions. Some gentlemen drove like drunkards and took wild tumbles," Catherine recalled.

"Catherine, some of those men *were* drunkards." Sara chuckled.

"I tip my hat to the French for designing the safety bicycle."

"Tip your hat to Pierre and his son Ernest Michaux, so the tipsy do not tip. *Merci beaucoup.*"

They soon reached the church, parking in the church lot.

"That was invigorating," Catherine said.

They entered the church, greeting the other ladies cordially. Everyone felt confident they could meet here without fear of their true cause being discovered. After all, churches and clergy in general were some of their biggest opposition, so who would suspect a meeting at the Presbyterian Church as anything but a noble undertaking? Besides, every member had been introduced and supported by someone already involved and active in the organization.

The door shut, Tillie began the meeting. After her usual opening remarks, her tone turned grave. "Ladies, you must be aware our cause is best served by our rallies and our numbers. Because our faces are not known in Racine, we can be openly active in supporting the cause without fear of reprisal. Because of our anonymity, we are hoping to have a large turnout. We will be leaving town on the train as the Women's Educational Research Fundraising Group, but we will be exiting the train in Racine as the Milwaukee division of the Wisconsin Suffragettes, complete with banners. At the depot, the other suffragettes across our state will meet us. Racine has alerted us there will be a Madison contingent and a new group from Eau Claire representing western Wisconsin. A Northeast Wisconsin contingent will already be on the train when we board. You'll recognize your sisters in this cause. We'll pass out sashes for everyone to wear in Racine." Tillie raised up a sash for all to see. The sash said in clear large letters, WISCONSIN SUFFRAGETTES.

"Now, how many of you ladies will be joining us?" Tillie asked.

Hands went up throughout the room.

"Impressive," Tillie exclaimed. "Now maybe it would be better if I ask who *cannot* make it. Please don't feel obligated."

Two hands went up, but Sara's was not one of them.

"Excellent. It looks like we will have eighteen from here," Tillie said, counting heads. "Northeast Wisconsin has about sixteen, Madison will top twenty, and Eau Claire believes they have six. We will be sixty strong representing our state."

Applause rang throughout the room. Catherine leaned over to Sara and squeezed her arm. "Woman, I am so impressed. I didn't think your support would be so strong. Welcome aboard."

Sara beamed.

"I need to inform you all that I am going to be a strong voice in the movement," Tillie said, "and I will have to dissociate myself with this group to not cause problems for those of you who need to remain anonymous. I wouldn't want you to be presumed guilty by association. I will be one of the speakers at the courthouse in Racine."

The room buzzed with emotion. They didn't want to lose their leader, and though they admired her courage, they feared their loss.

"What will you do?" someone from the back of the room called out.

"What will *we* do?" another woman asked.

"I'll be spending time in Washington and New York," Tillie explained. "I have connections with people who were associated with my late husband, Senator Morgenson. I'll be lobbying for our cause. Also, Carrie Chapman Catt has asked me to be a part of the activities in New York, where there is still much to do. We are fortunate our state legislature and our governor are, for the most part, supportive. Other states have a much bigger struggle. I hope to be of assistance to them as well. As for what you will do?"

Tillie looked around the room. As she did so, she seemed to grow taller with pride. "I have no doubt you'll find a strong leader amongst you. I hope Catherine or Ruby will take up the reigns."

She met each of their eyes individually and assured each woman: "You are an amazing woman, you are strong, you are committed, and you will prevail." Her smile was warm, her eyes filled with enthusiasm, her confidence contagious.

Nods and smiles to each other ended in loud applause of approval.

"Voting on a new leader should be the first topic on the agenda at the first meeting after the Racine rally," Tillie said. "Obviously, I will not be there."

The room buzzed again.

"Go get 'em in Washington," Catherine shouted.

Tillie made a little bow. "I'll give it my all, but now we must move on. Our time is running short. For those who are willing to go public, there will be a rally in Milwaukee in August. I was pleased to see so many bicycles outside, because this will be a bicycle rally on Wisconsin Avenue in downtown Milwaukee. It will begin at the Pfister Hotel and continue downtown to the Marquette Campus. Neither place supports the cause, so we will use those sites as markers. Think about whether you want to join us."

The meeting ended in an excited flurry, and all the focus was on the Racine rally the following week.

When Sara arrived at home, the children were in bed and Henry met her at the door with a hug and a fetching smile. They had been married for fourteen years, but her heart still skipped a beat when he smiled at her that way.

"So, my lovely wife, how was the first meeting of the Women's Education Funding, or whatever it's called?"

"It was very productive," Sara said as she removed her hat and gloves. She didn't quite meet his eyes.

Henry reached out to help her with her short black velvet jacket. "You know, my bank could serve your group with funding issues and investments."

"How sweet of you to offer, Henry. I think it'll be some time before we're ready for financial guidance, but I'll let you know when the time is right. I am sure the money will be handled by someone else. Finance is not my area of expertise."

"And what would be your area of expertise?"

"Harrumph!" Sarah rolled her eyes. "Are you insinuating I have none?"

"My dear, I would say you are a very talented lady," Henry teased as he nuzzled her neck. "The children are all asleep. Maybe you could show me how talented you are." He tilted his head and raised his eyebrows, then winked.

"You are incorrigible." Sara giggled.

Henry took Sara's hand and they headed up the stairs. Since Henry appeared to be in a good mood, now was as good a time as any to tell him. "Our group is going to Racine next Tuesday for a conference. I'd like to go."

"Hmmm."

They reached the top of the stairs.

"How would you get there? How long will it be? What would be involved?" he asked.

"It would only be for the day. We'll go by train, and I'll be home before dinner. Claudia will be here for the children." Sara was very convincing. "This would be my opportunity to express my feelings on education."

Henry put his hand on the small of her back as he led her to their bedroom. "I believe you will be an asset to the cause."

She wondered what he'd say if he knew the real cause she was fighting for. "Thank you for your support, Henry. I love you."

"You are my life." Henry closed the door.

Chapter Five

April ninth was a cloudy overcast day in Milwaukee. Sara fed the children and got them off to school, leaving Adam with Claudia. Henry dropped Sara at the railroad station on his way to work. "Don't come to get me," Sara said to Henry. "Catherine will bring me home."

"Where is Catherine now?"

"I wanted to get the children off to school, so I told her I would meet her here."

"Do you want me to wait?" he asked.

"No, she's probably in the depot." Sara leaned over and kissed her husband. "I'll be fine."

Henry rushed around the buggy and assisted his wife down.

Catherine was not there yet. Sara shivered as she stood on the platform, waiting to board the train. Where *was* Catherine?

The huge locomotive was being filled with water, and steam poured from the engine. Excited chatter filled the air as the ladies of the women's group greeted one another on the platform.

"Hello, Sara, I'm so glad you could make it," Ruby said. "Oh Margaret, do you have the pamphlets? Excuse me, Sara." She vanished.

"Mildred, have you seen Catherine?" Sara asked.

Mildred shrugged. "Catherine wouldn't miss this; I'm sure she is on her way. Did you check the depot?"

"Yes, I did. She's not there." Sara felt a nudge of panic. This was her first rally and she was counting on her friend's guidance and support.

Sara watched as the porter helped travelers with bags and trunks for their journeys to who knew where, but one car was being boarded by ladies without luggage. The only bags boarding that car were filled with flyers and banners.

She swallowed hard and was about to board alone when Catherine arrived. "Where have you been?" Sara was frantic. "I was beginning to wonder if you'd changed your mind."

"No chance," Catherine said. "This changeable weather has made the roads mucky. I got the carriage wheel caught in a rut. A neighbor helped me out. Come, let's board. We have so much to talk about on the ride. We don't want the train to leave us behind."

Catherine selected their seats and gathered her skirts to make room for her friend. "This is traveling in style, huh, Sara? This is one of the newer Chicago Northwestern trains. I hear it has a five-star dining car on board." Catherine gazed about, taking in the amenities and waving to familiar faces.

Sara ran her hand over the royal blue velvet tufted seats. "This *is* nice. I like the big windows, too. They provide so much light compared to the old, small windows."

"Enough small talk." Catherine settled in her seat. "Did you have any problem getting away?"

"Oh, no. Henry dropped me off at the station. The Women's Educational Research Fundraising Group is making it all quite easy. Although, I must admit, I still get very nervous deceiving Henry. He's been so supportive, but he's hoping the financial part of our group will swing some business to his bank."

"Is that going to be a problem?"

Sara shook her head. "Not for a while."

"What do you think he would do if he knew what this trip is really about?" Catherine asked, curious.

Sara shrugged a shoulder. "I don't know, but I do know he would forbid me to continue. He considers the suffragettes a threat to families, businesses, and even to our country."

"Sounds like he is threatened by women in power."

"You may be right." Sara lowered her gaze. "He feels women are simple-minded and should not be trusted with such matters as voting on the affairs of the country. When I protested, he qualified by saying it could be okay for me, but not for most women."

"We hear that all the time," Catherine said. "What rubbish. There are more *simple-minded* men, if you ask me."

"He said women would be ignorant to the issues and voice their opinions on things of no value, such as grooming habits or what the

First Lady wore to an afternoon tea. He thinks women would better serve their country by supporting their husbands and raising strong-willed sons."

Catherine laughed. "If only he knew how strong-willed his daughters are. Has Ella caused any more ruckus in school?"

"Not that I'm aware of, and I hope she never gives up that attitude." Sara gripped her dress tight. "I hope our work is not in vain. I'm doing this for my girls, for their future."

The loud woo-woo of the whistle sounded, and the locomotive chugged out great billows of smoke that wafted by the window as they pulled away from the station.

Before they knew it, two hours had passed, and the train pulled into the Racine station. The clouds had drifted away, and the sun shone bright.

Tillie made her way through the railroad car, distributing sashes. "Ladies, please wear these as we exit the train, then stand at the end of the platform until everyone is gathered there. We want to make an impression, and with a show of numbers this large, we should get some attention."

March leaders unfurled and held an enormous banner. It announced the group as the "Fighting Suffragettes of Wisconsin." Other members of the group waved posters high in the air stating, "We Want to Vote!"

The women began to chant in time to their footsteps as they left the station and headed downtown. "We want to vote! We want to vote!"

The farther they went, the more their volume increased.

The streets bustled with people going about their daily business. Many stopped to observe the commotion. Some cheered, others jeered. The young women lining the streets were not afraid to express their support. Among the older women, the degree of support was mixed. Most men were negative, but a few hooted their encouragement.

Some of the younger local women joined in the march, and by the time they reached the courthouse, their numbers had swelled to almost one hundred.

On the courthouse steps, onlookers greeted them, including reporters from the local newspapers who had gathered to listen to the speeches. A podium decorated with American flags had been set up on the landing.

Sara and Catherine found a place in front of the crowd just as Tillie took her place behind the podium. They were as exuberant as children on Christmas day. They felt safe, and confident they were winning the battle for the cause.

Sara couldn't help but grin. "Oh Catherine, this is so exciting. I'm so happy to be part of this."

"Me, too," Catherine replied. "Listen."

"Ladies and gentlemen," Tillie addressed the crowd, "citizens of these United States, it is my pleasure to address you today on a matter of utmost importance. One hundred and thirty-six years ago, our forefathers made a grave mistake when they drafted the Constitution of the United States of America. Whether it was an error of language or an error of judgment we do not know, but it needs to be rectified. Our Holy Bible has language in it that uses the term 'man' in a human context. We all know the words of the Bible are not limited to the male gender. Perhaps our forefathers also used the term men in a general context when they said, 'All men are created equal,' or perhaps not. This we do not know. In either event, they got it wrong and we must make it right."

The crowd applauded and cheered. Sara thought her heart would burst out of her bodice, she was so proud.

"We have many strong, intelligent women who could do a much better job of running the government than the men who have handled it, or should I say, bungled it," Tillie said.

More cheers and laughter erupted.

Tillie raised her hand for silence as she continued. "I shall not name names, but you know who they are. It may be some time before women will share in those roles to the extent they should, but at the very least, women should have a voice in the form of their vote."

Applause echoed throughout the streets, and women began to chant, "We want to vote. We want to vote. We want to vote."

Sara joined in, shouting so loud her throat ached. She ignored the pain and yelled louder.

Again, Tillie lifted her hands, indicating the crowd should quiet down.

Slowly the chanting died away, and then she continued. "The great citizens who are here to vote today are not voting on this important issue, but they are choosing a representative in Congress. Hopefully your representative will vote to pass an amendment to our great Constitution of the United States of America that will correct the founding fathers' error. This error has robbed this nation of an opportunity to hear the voice of one half of the population."

"Hear, hear!" came a voice in the crowd, and others repeated the cheer over the applause. It took Sara's breath away.

"Additionally," Tillie said, "voters here today will be selecting a candidate for President of the United States. It is our hope that candidate will be Woodrow Wilson, a great supporter of our cause."

Once again, the applause and cheers drowned out Tillie's words.

A man's voice rose above the rest. "Dammed be you all. Women should know their place, and it is *in* the kitchen, not in the voting booth!"

Sara turned to see the man a few feet behind her, shaking his fists.

A couple of his friends slapped him on the back, and then walked away. Tillie seemed unbothered by it. Her speech was followed by more speeches, each acknowledged with roaring cheers and the occasional heckles.

By the end, the atmosphere was electric. Sara's adrenaline surged. She and Catherine laughed and hugged each other, taking in the events of the day and the overwhelming support they'd received. Yes, there had been hecklers and naysayers, but they were the minority.

Sara and Catherine wandered to the courthouse lawn, where most of the women had gathered in anticipation of the oncoming parade, which would soon arrive at the grandstand area in front of the courthouse. The high school band could be heard in the distance.

Suddenly, Sara recalled the Danish pastry called kringles Catherine had told her about on the train.

"Catherine, I almost forgot. I need to get the kringles. I'm going to dash off to the bakery. I think I can be back before the parade gets here."

"Leave your things with me. You don't want to miss the parade."

Sara dropped her bag of leaflets and personal items she had gathered throughout the day, grabbed her tiny purse, and started on her way.

Catherine called out, "Bring a kringle back for me."

Chapter Six

Sara hurried through the crowd, across the street, and down the alley. The band was approaching. The music was so loud, she could barely hear her own footsteps on the cobblestone. She almost skipped with glee to the music.

About halfway down the alley and just a few feet in front of her, a man stepped out of a doorway.

Sara slowed her pace. Should she greet him and continue, or should she turn back?

The man had fire in his eyes. His face was grim. He faced her direction, and with a menacing look, stepped forward.

Sara pretended she had lost something. Looking down, she realized she was still wearing the suffragette sash. Her heart began to pound. She turned, expecting to hurry back out of the alley to safety. Then, she felt a strong hand on her shoulder.

Panic seized her.

She spun around and came face to face with the ogre.

Sara let out a scream, but by now the band had reached the Courthouse Square, and the cheers of the crowd drowned out her cry.

She spun around again, trying to run, but the man pulled her hair. Her hat flew off and her long auburn hair tumbled down to her shoulder. He grabbed her from the back with his arm around her neck and clasped his hand over her mouth.

Sara did the only thing she could do; she bit his hand. Hard.

"AGHH!" The man pulled away his bleeding hand. "You are a wild one, you suffragette!" He spat the words.

Sara stumbled backward, her eyes filled with fear.

The man flung out his hand and hit her on her cheek. He cursed her, and then backhanded her on the other cheek, catching her nose with his fist.

She screamed again as warm blood trickled down to her lip.

"Scream all ya' want, bitch," he said, grabbing and holding tight to her wrist. "No one can hear you."

He was right. If she was going to survive, she would have to free herself. "Leave me alone!"

He grabbed her by her skirt.

She pulled back and heard it rip. She had never been so frightened, but she couldn't let fear paralyze her.

She struck him as hard as she could, catching her assailant's ear.

The man sneered. "You think you can fight like a man! We'll see about that!" He punched her hard in the stomach.

It knocked the wind out of her. Sara struggled to breathe as she fell and hit her head hard on a cobblestone. The man was standing over her, but Sara could barely see him. Her head spun. Her vision was fuzzy.

He dropped to his knees and straddled her.

She struggled to get away, tried to push out from beneath him.

A switchblade snapped open. He pressed it against her throat, and she froze.

He held her down with one hand. The knife was cold against her skin as he sliced the bodice of her dress. She was afraid to move, afraid to breathe as the sharp edge skimmed over her heart.

One slip.

One slip with his knife, and her life would be over.

Visions of her husband and her children ran through her mind. *Would she ever see them again?*

She felt the cool April air on her partially naked body. Still, she didn't move. Silent tears flowed down her cheeks. She couldn't see clearly.

He unbuttoned his knickers. "I'll show you what it is to be a man."

No, no. She couldn't form the words, couldn't make her voice work. Henry. The children. *Please, dear God, let me survive this.*

Please.

She drifted into a semi-conscious state.

The man released his hard appendage from his trousers. He tore the rest of her dress away and took his knife to her bloomers.

Blood poured from Sara's body and ran in a puddle beneath her.

Suddenly he flung backward and jumped to his feet.

35

He must have thought she was menstruating, but she knew this was far too much blood for a cycle. Sara was expelling fetal tissue.

"Christ, woman!" He backed away further, buttoning his knickers as he ran down the alley.

***

A door creaked open. The butcher carried sacks with the remains of two pigs he had butchered. He could barely see past the large load, though he did spot a man fleeing down the alley.

"Thieves!" he mumbled. "What is this world coming to when thieves are out in broad daylight? Wonder what he is making off with."

He dropped his bundle into a large trash barrel and looked down for the cover when he spotted a woman's black high-button shoe protruding from behind a cluster of barrels. He bent to look closer and then he saw her...a beautiful wisp of a woman, nearly naked, bleeding and semi-conscious.

She moaned.

The butcher pulled her dress over her to cover her nakedness and saw the blood flowing from her body. His stomach lurched. This was very serious.

The door to the butcher shop was still open, and he called out, "Billy, Billy...come quick!"

Billy, his apprentice, appeared at the door. "Yeah, boss?"

"Go fetch Doc Andrews as fast as you can. We have a lady dying here." Billy sprinted down the alley.

The butcher stroked the woman's hair. "Lady, help is coming."
She blinked.

"Dear God, save this woman." The butcher continued to comfort her.

Billy was back with the doctor in a short while, but by then, the parade was over and the crowd had dispersed. Sensing a problem, people began to gather in the alley.

***

Catherine searched for Sara. Something was wrong. It shouldn't have taken her this long to get the pastries. She pushed her way through a crowd in the alley and spotted her friend's long auburn tresses. "No!" Catherine gasped, and rushed to Sara's side.

"Out of the way, people. Out of the way!" shouted a doctor. He knelt to examine Sara.

The butcher explained what he had seen and cussed at the long-gone attacker.

"We need to get her to my office." The doctor looked at the crowd. "Is there a cart we can use?"

"Never mind," said the butcher. "I'll carry her." He took off his large butcher's apron and wrapped it around her. He picked her up as though she were a small child and carried her the two blocks to the doctor's office.

Catherine followed at their heels. Tears stung her eyes as she prayed her friend would be okay.

A stranger in the crowd tried to comfort her. "Doctor Andrews is a fine doctor. He'll take good care of her."

Catherine called out to another suffragette in the crowd. "Get Tillie. Tell her to come to the doctor's office."

The butcher placed Sara on a cot in the corner of the room and stepped away.

Sara stirred.

"Lady, be strong. You're in good hands." The butcher slipped out the door.

The doctor placed a vial under Sara's nose, and she began to regain consciousness.

"Where? Where am I?" She tried to sit up, looking about, but he held her arm.

"Stay still," the doctor said.

Her eyes connected with Catherine.

"You had an accident, Sara. This is Dr. Andrews. Lie still, and he will take care of you." Catherine placed her hand on Sara's shoulder and gave her a weak, comforting smile.

Doctor Andrews put a mat under Sara and pressed her stomach to expel the remaining fetal tissue. "How far along were you?" the doctor asked.

Sara choked back tears. "Three, maybe four months."

He washed and dressed her wounds, gave her an elixir to help her relax, and said to Catherine, "Sara has a concussion. She will have to spend the night."

Sara struggled to keep awake. She spoke to Tillie, who had just arrived. "Don't tell my husband I was attacked."

"But Sara, what can I possibly say to him?" Tillie asked in dismay.

"Tell him I tripped and fell. I have a concussion, but I'll be home tomorrow." Then Sara slipped into quiet sleep.

The two women talked, trying to make sense of it all.

"What happened?" Tillie asked Catherine.

"We don't know the details. Sara managed to tell us very little, but..." Catherine choked back tears. "She was attacked in the alley on her way to the bakery. We think it was a march protester, but it could have been a rapist."

"She must have fought desperately," Tillie said.

Catherine shook her head in sadness. "Yes, and she lost her baby. I didn't know she was pregnant. She has a nasty bruise on her stomach."

"This isn't the first attack on one of our suffragettes. Oh!" Tillie shook her head. "When will it end? I don't want to go, but it is almost time to get to the train station."

"I'll stay," Catherine said. "You tell Henry. We will see you tomorrow."

"Oh dear Henry. This isn't going to be easy. Catherine take care of her." Tillie touched Sara's hair. "Be strong, be strong."

Tillie left to catch the train, and Catherine planned to spend the night with her friend.

Doctor Andrews instructed her, "Wake Sara every hour. If she is unresponsive, call me immediately."

Sara slept for the first hour peacefully, but after that her sleep was fitful. She often cried out, "No, No!"

***

Tillie returned with the group to Milwaukee, knowing she would have to give Henry the news. *What will he say? How will I deliver Sara's message?*

It was dusk when the train pulled into the station. Tillie's stable man waited with her carriage. "Take me to the Dewberry house," she instructed.

The carriage pulled up to the front door. The lights were on. Tillie tapped the door knocker. A moment later, she heard running and children calling, "Mother, Mother!"

The door flew open to reveal four children. Adam was in Ella's arms.

"Oh, Mrs. Morgenson. Do come in," Ella said.

"Good evening, Ella." Tillie forced a smile. "Is your father home?"

"I'll get him."

A moment later, Henry stepped into the parlor. "Good evening, Mrs. Morgenson."

"Mr. Dewberry, I wonder if I might have a word with you in private."

"Certainly. Mrs. Dewberry isn't home. She should be here momentarily. Do come into the library." Henry asked Claudia to bring tea.

"No, no, please," said Tillie. "I shan't be but a moment."

Henry shut the door to the library and offered Tillie a seat. He sat in a chair adjacent to her, his eyes worried. "I can see you're upset. Is there something I can do for you?"

"I'll get right to the point. There's been an accident. Sara was hurrying to purchase kringles from the bakery and caught her heel in the trolley track. She fell. She has a concussion and has to spend the night in Racine." Tillie leaned forward and touched Henry's arm. "Sara will be fine and should be home tomorrow, but I'm afraid she's lost the baby."

"Baby?" His eyes widened, and he sat back. "*What* baby?"

"Oh, dear." Tillie was shocked. "You didn't know? Sara was three months pregnant. I am afraid in the fall that she lost the baby."

Henry ran a trembling hand through his hair. "I didn't know. Why wouldn't she tell...?"

Tillie could understand his confusion. "I'm so sorry. I thought you knew. None of us knew until the accident."

"I must go to her." Henry rose and headed toward the door.

"Oh, no." Tillie stood. "You would never get there in time. She will be coming home tomorrow, if everything goes as expected tonight. Catherine stayed to watch over her through the night. There's nothing you can do. I'm sure she'll be fine."

Such bold words, but Tillie doubted after what had happened today, Sara would ever be fine again.

Henry fell back into his chair, propped his elbows on his desk and dropped his forehead into his hands.

"She's in the good hands of Dr. Andrews, a prominent physician," Tillie said. "Sara will be very tired when she arrives home. She'll need your attention then. A ride home on the train will be much more comfortable for her than a long, bumpy buggy ride."

Henry's shoulders slumped. "You're right. Of course, I'll wait. I'll meet the train in the afternoon."

***

Early the next morning, Dr. Andrews came in to check on Sara. "How are you feeling today?" he asked.

Sara wanted to roll over and go back to sleep.

Catherine answered for her. "She slept through most of the night, although not peacefully. Do you think she'll be able to travel?"

"Let's take a look." Dr. Andrews took Sara's hand and held it. "Can you sit up?"

Sara forced her eyes open and pulled herself into a sitting position, gathering the sheet around her to cover her naked body. As she sat, more blood expelled from her body. She silently mourned the loss of her baby, bowing her head.

Dr. Andrews reached for a towel and handed it to her. "Can you follow my finger with your eyes?" He moved his index finger back and forth, up and down, in front of her. "Do you have a headache?"

Everything ached. Her heart ached the most. She concentrated on his question. "I feel pain around my eyes, and I have a headache when I move. But if I lie still, I'm okay."

"Nausea? Pain in your abdomen?"

"No nausea, but my stomach is very tender," Sara confirmed.

"Lie back down," Dr. Andrews said.

Sara slowly leaned back and put her head on the pillow.

Dr. Andrews listened to her heart, took her temperature, and put light pressure on her stomach. She had a large bruise where the man had hit her stomach, and she winced again when Dr. Andrews pressed on it. "We need to check your bleeding and change some of the dressings on your cuts. You have severe bruising, but it will heal in time. You have no broken bones. Of course, you understand you have aborted a fetus, and we have expelled all the material we can without surgery. You'll need to watch for excessive blood flow and beware of infection. You must see your doctor when you return home. Do you understand?"

Sara nodded, though her heart still mourned.

"Then there's the matter of your clothing." He turned to Catherine. "Can you see to getting her proper attire for the return trip?"

"Of course." She focused on Sara. "You rest, and I'll find you the finest wardrobe I can in this city. It won't be from Gimbles, but I'm sure they have a good clothier here."

The doctor recommended a small ladies' clothing store on Main Street.

He turned to Sara. "I'll prepare a potion to help you endure the pain for the trip home. You must be sure to get plenty of rest for at least a week, and remember, see your physician as soon as possible. While you eat breakfast, I'll prepare something to place on your eyes to help with the swelling. You have quite the shiners."

Two hours later, Catherine returned with a simple black dress, new undergarments, a comb, and a smart black hat with a black veil. She would be stylish, but not so much as to draw attention. The veil would shield the bruises on her eyes from everyone except the close observer.

"Catherine, you think of everything. What would I do without you?" Sara asked.

Catherine shrugged, happy to help her friend.

That afternoon, Dr. Andrews dropped them off at the train station on his way to his daily house calls.

Sara slept most of the way home, exhausted from her ordeal.

Chapter Seven

The train pulled into the station. Out the window, Sara saw Tillie on the platform standing beside Henry. Her heart pounded. *Will he guess? Will he know?*

Sara's mind was so foggy, but a tear rolled down her cheek as she thought of her lost baby and what she had put Henry through. Was it all a mistake? It felt like a dream—no. A nightmare.

Catherine helped Sara step off the train. Henry reached for her, gathering her into his arms. Sara winced as his arms pressed against her bruises.

"Oh, my darling, are you okay?" Henry asked.

"Not really. But I should be better in no time." Sara drew back and gazed at Henry with tears in her eyes. She whispered, "I'm so sorry."

Henry took her hand and kissed it. "I'm just happy you are back home safe."

For a moment, Sara's throat tightened in panic. *Safe?* Did Henry know what had happened?

Tillie faced Sara and looked into her almost-hidden eyes. "Sara, my dear, I told Henry about your fall on the trolley track and about the baby. I'm sorry. I didn't know he didn't know about the baby, I…"

An overwhelming sadness engulfed Sara, and she could not help but let the tears fall. Her child. Her innocent child. "It's okay, Tillie. I was going to tell him when I returned from Racine."

She turned to Henry. "I wanted to be sure. I know how much you love children and…can we talk about this at home? I'm exhausted."

Tillie nodded and said to Sara, "Don't you try doing too much. I'll stop by tomorrow to check on you. Good-bye, dear." She touched Sara's cheek.

Turning to Catherine, Tillie sighed. "I have my carriage. Can I take you home?"

"That would be delightful," Catherine replied.

Henry took Sara's arm and led her to his carriage.

"How are the children?" Sara asked. She wanted to change the subject.

"I told them you had a terrible fall and a physician was taking care of you. Ella went into the nanny mode and was a dear in taking care of Adam and Elizabeth. She tucked them into bed last night. She was up early and got them off to school today. Claudia is watching Adam. They're all home now, awaiting your return. Let's get you home to rest."

Chapter Eight

The next morning, Tillie and Catherine arrived at the Dewberry home. Claudia showed them into the parlor, where Sara sat in her bentwood rocker wrapped in a blue afghan she had knitted.

Catherine said, "Good morning, Sara, how are you feeling today?"

Tillie added with a soft smile, "We are so happy to see you up."

After the customary small talk and making sure Claudia was out of earshot, they moved on to more serious matters.

"How is Henry handling this? Does he suspect anything more sinister than a fall?" Catherine asked.

"Surely, he must have noticed your bruises," Tillie added, frowning.

"He was quite alarmed by the bruises, but I told him the tracks and cobblestone were to blame. I explained to him I was rushing to get back in time to see the parade and didn't see a passing cart. The corner of the cart hit my stomach and I fell back. In doing so, I caught my shoe in the trolley rail. Then I fell and hit my head on the cobblestone."

"It's not right." Still standing, Catherine put her hands firmly on her hips. "The hoodlum who did this should be strung up and publicly castrated. You should have him hunted down and arrested."

"I couldn't," Sara said. "Exposing this kind of problem will only make people more infuriated against suffragettes. Henry, dear Henry, placed so much faith in me when I told him I was involved in improving the educational plight of children. It would have shattered him to know what I was really doing."

"But the man should be apprehended," Catherine protested. "He should pay for what he did."

Sara shook her head. "I want to put that evil man away more than anyone, but to do so I would not only have allowed him to destroy my body, but also my beliefs, my marriage...and my life. I would have to give up all I want to achieve. I can't let him shut me down. I must continue the fight."

"He is a monster and should go to jail," Catherine objected again, balling her hands into fists.

Tillie weighed in, "I agree, Catherine, but that is why we need to keep fighting. If he were caught, do you realize what would happen? He would have to go to trial. Sara would be made out as a liar and a harlot, a suffragette willing to deceive her husband and lurking in alleys where proper women have no business. The man could be set free, her cover would be exposed, her husband might leave her, her reputation would be tarnished, and she might even be fined or jailed for being a public nuisance."

"That is why we must keep fighting," Sara added. "Even if it means some will get away with dastardly deeds like this."

"You are right," Catherine conceded with a sigh, "but it just isn't fair."

"It's why we fight. We want an equal voice and equal justice," Tillie said, her chin lifted high. "Until we are able to have a voice and rights, we are considered disposable objects."

"What did Henry say when he saw your eyes?" Catherine moved over to examine Sara's face. "That *is* a nasty bruise."

Claudia entered the hallway outside of the parlor with her feather duster, close enough to overhear Tillie say, "You are a fighter, for sure. You'd make Susan Anthony proud."

Claudia gasped loudly.

As the ladies saw her, Catherine's hand rose, halting the speech. She placed her finger over her mouth, then forced a laugh and winked. "Tillie, you are so funny. Thanks for trying to cheer Sara up. Can you imagine Sara with her blackened eyes and bruises, hobbling along the march route with those crazy suffragettes?" They all broke out in gales of laughter.

Sara held her tummy and pleaded, "Ladies, please. It hurts to laugh."

"So sorry." Catherine chuckled. "But laughter is good medicine. We'll try to hold back on the medicine."

"I must have Claudia get us more of these delicious biscuits." Tillie smiled a little too wide as she dumped the biscuits from the tray into her large bag.

"I'll find her," Catherine offered.

Claudia ducked out of sight and then re-appeared, inquiring, "Did I hear my name? May I get you something?"

Catherine smiled at Tillie, betraying nothing. "Oh yes, could you please get us more biscuits? They are scrumptious. Claudia, you will never believe how silly Tillie is. She is trying to cheer up Sara and suggested she should get out of bed and participate in a suffragette march in New York, battered as she is. Isn't that the funniest thing you ever heard?"

Claudia laughed weakly, as if she didn't quite believe it. Then she disappeared into the kitchen for more biscuits. Catherine made herself comfortable next to Tillie on a loveseat.

Meanwhile, Tillie whispered to Sara, "We'll have time to discuss this later in private."

Claudia returned with biscuits and more hot tea. The ladies continued a lighthearted conversation for some time.

Then Catherine said, "We had better leave and let you get some sleep. Don't forget to see your doctor. We need you up and at 'em soon. We have lots of work to get done." She winked at Sara.

Tillie rose and put on her cloak. "Thank you for the biscuits. They were so good I'd like to take them with me." She smiled over her shoulder at Sara as she patted her bag.

"Don't get up," Catherine said, "we can see ourselves out."

"Come anytime," Sara called out with a smile. "Your visit was very therapeutic."

Chapter Nine

A few weeks later, Catherine and Sara walked to the meeting at church. The sweet fragrance of lilacs wafted through the air, a sure sign spring had finally arrived.

Along the way, they nodded to neighbors sitting on their front porches.

"Good afternoon, Mrs. Charles. Isn't it a lovely day?" asked Sara.

"Hello, ladies, a great day for a walk."

"Mrs. Harrison, your garden is so delightful; your tulips are out early this year," Catherine said.

"It looks like a good year for growing."

Sara was anxious, her heart beat rapidly. She couldn't wait to mingle once again with her comrades in the cause, but this was the first meeting she'd attended since her "dreadful accident" and she didn't want to talk about it.

"Sara, how nice to see you," one of the women said as they entered the church.

Ladies gathered around to give Sara a warm welcome back. "Oh Sara, I do hope you are feeling better."

No mention was made about her injuries. Sara was grateful not to have to go into details.

Tillie closed the door and called the meeting to order. She called Ruby to the podium. "Ladies, you all know Ruby. She has been one of our driving forces since we first gathered almost eight years ago. As the pastor's wife, she secured this private meeting place for us and has been a huge help in producing our flyers on the church duplicating machine. What a help the mimeograph has been."

The ladies expressed their gratitude and approval with applause. They knew Ruby made copies when no one else was in the church.

"Ladies, I have asked Ruby to step up and take over our meetings at the church since I will be doing a great deal of traveling. I have been invited across our great nation to allow others to hear our message. It is best that I'm not seen with this group. My presence could raise suspicions. I feel Ruby is the best person to take over my leadership. I hope you all feel the same."

Another huge round of applause erupted, accompanied by smiles and nods. Ruby took the podium with a grateful acknowledgement to the crowd.

"Thank you, ladies. Your support means a lot to me. As you know, I must keep my activities under wraps. The congregation at the First Presbyterian Church would take it out on my husband, Pastor Reinhart, if word got out. If you need to speak with me, you must always contact me on business of the Women's Educational Research Funding Group."

Murmurs of approval spread throughout the room.

Ruby continued the meeting, going through the agenda. "Now for upcoming business, we have two events planned for the summer. First is a rally in Chicago on Sunday, June 30th. It will kick off the city's long Independence holiday weekend. Of course, we all want to be home for our own Independence Day celebrations with our families, but some of us will have to spend one or more nights in Chicago. This could turn out to be quite a boisterous event, so be on guard."

"Chicago is an incredible city. They have some of the best artistry and culture in the nation," Catherine said. Her praise and beaming smile encouraged participation, as she noted its museums and concert halls.

"I heard they also have a high crime rate," came a voice in the back of the room. "Can you believe they had more than eighty murders and more than three hundred assaults last year?"

"A word of caution: stay away from the seedy side of town," Tillie said.

Keeping on track, Ruby asked, "Martha, will you please distribute the flyers?"

Martha obliged, and pulled a stack of flyers from her bag. There were more than enough to go around. She set the remainder on a nearby table.

"Look them over and we can discuss any questions you may have."

Ruby shuffled papers on the podium.

Almost immediately, questions began to fly regarding the Chicago Rally.

"Will we be traveling together, or should we book our own transport? If we stay overnight, where will we stay? Will there be danger?" one woman asked.

"What other events will be taking place? Should we take banners?"

"Will we have flyers to distribute?"

Ruby and Tillie answered the questions as best they could, keeping it calm and upbeat. They promised there would be a full agenda at the next meeting.

Gertrude arrived to the meeting late, coming into the room disheveled. "Ladies, there are people next door," she said with panic in her voice. "I think they are discussing the church picnic."

"Don't worry," Ruby assured everyone. "This room is sound-proofed. It is used for private matters. No one can hear us. We heard nothing from their room."

Sara thought she sounded confident, but Ruby's sideways glance betrayed her anxiety.

To allay their concerns, Ruby moved on. "The next event after Chicago will be the bicycle marathon through the downtown area of Milwaukee on Saturday, August 17th. Of course, I understand many of you, including myself, will not be able to participate for fear of retaliation from our community. For those who wish to remain incognito, there will be many ways we can support our sisters behind the scenes."

***

Hattie, who oversaw food preparation, was at the church picnic meeting. During it, she excused herself to check on a supply list in the kitchen. When she returned, she passed by the Women's Educational Research Funding Group room.

Hattie wasn't very educated, and she had no head for finance. The conversation from the room was intense, so Hattie crept closer to see if she could hear what all the excitement was about in the room.

Seemed to be a lot of political talk going on—another thing she knew little about. They were talking about the ratification of an amendment to the Constitution and lobbying the legislature.

This education stuff is very complicated. Sure am glad all I need to do is figure out how much potato salad to make.

Hattie shook her head and went back to her meeting. She gave it not another thought that night.

***

The suffragette conversation gravitated to how the cause was coming along in other parts of the nation, and what difficulties suffragettes in other states had faced.

Tillie reported, "The southern states are struggling, as is New England. New York is very mixed. It seems our friends out west are way ahead of us. Some have already granted women voting rights on non-federal matters.

"We must elect Woodrow Wilson. We need him to win our cause. We are hopeful in the president's next term that the issue of women's right to vote will be approved. Then it will go to the various states to be ratified. We are very confident Wisconsin will ratify this Nineteenth Amendment to the Constitution, but we must never put down our guard or take anything for granted."

When Ruby left the meeting that night, her mind was on a thousand things to be done. She forgot to check the meeting room before she left, as she usually did.

Chapter Ten

The next morning Hattie, a diligent volunteer at the church, was in the church kitchen making preparations for a funeral service the next day. Cora, her best friend and co-volunteer, had been tidying up some of the rooms.

Cora was breathless as she dashed into the kitchen. "Look, look at this!" she demanded. Wadded in her hand were six flyers.

"Them ain't edgycation people," Cora announced. "They are those suffragettes! See here." She jabbed at the words on the paper. "They have rallies and cause a lot of mischief. They're up to no good, lookin' for the right ta' vote. What fer? Most of them have good men folk who do the votin'. Next thing you know, they will be takin' men's jobs and wantin' to vote in the church."

"Would that be so awful?" Hattie asked.

"Why yes, it twould! Them suffragettes don't know their place. Instead of mindin' their childens, they're out on rallies and causin' decent folk problems."

Hattie frowned. "What kind of problems?"

Cora slammed a fist on the table. "Well, I don't rightly know, but I do know they are up to no good!"

"I heard them last night at the meeting. They seemed mighty excited about politics and stuff," Hattie said.

"You sawed them and you din't tell nobody?" Cora gasped.

"Twarant my business, and I didn't understand anyway," Hattie explained.

"Well I ain't gonna do nuthin. I am gonna take these to the elders." Cora held up the flyers and shook them in indignation. "They will know what to do."

***

Cora stuffed the flyers in her purse. After the funeral service preparations were done, she rushed home and dropped the heinous flyers on her husband's desk.

When Cora's husband, Alvin, came home, the railroad foreman went directly to the study and pulled out a big cigar. He bit off the tip, lit it, and plopped down on his huge leather chair. He looked down at the desk.

"Cora! Cora!" he bellowed. "What in God's name is this despicable material doing on my desk?"

Cora bustled down the hall, and with hands on hips, replied, "I found those at the church this mornin' when I was cleanin' up. Those edgycation finance women was meetin' there last night. I think they left them there. I think them women are really suffragettes!"

"Usin' the church for their dirty deeds?" Alvin's face went red with anger. "What gall! We will see about that," Alvin harrumphed. "I'll talk to the elders about this."

Cora hurried back to the kitchen and dinner preparation, smug in her exposé.

***

After work the next day, Alvin went with flyers in hand to see his friend, Martin, who was one of the elders of the church. Martin was a tall, thin man with a long nose that he liked to poke into everyone's business. Alvin knew not much slipped by Martin. He thoroughly enjoyed being in the know. He explained to Martin what his wife had told him.

Martin was very agitated. His face got red and he stiffened. "Who was at the meeting?" Martin demanded.

"Don't rightly know, but Hattie was there for the June picnic plannin' last night and she heard Ruby and Tillie's voices in that room," Alvin replied.

Martin's eyes went wide. "Ruby? Ruby, our pastor's wife?"

"Do you believe it? You never know what people are doing."

"Thank you, Alvin," Martin said. "We have a meeting of the elders tomorrow night at the church. I will bring this matter up for sure. We can't have these kinds of goings on right under our noses, in our very own church."

"I knew you would be the one to come to with this. I couldn't believe it myself." Alvin headed to the door with his hat in his hand. "You have a good day, Martin. I will be anxious to know how the elders will handle this matter."

"I can assure you there will be an investigation." Martin closed the door behind Alvin.

***

When he went to the meeting of the elders, Martin dressed in his most proper attire—his black gabardine suit and top hat. He carried a briefcase with the flyers inside and greeted the fellow elders with polite smiles.

The group of six men sat down at the table. Martin found a seat near the chief elder's chair, so when it was his turn to speak, he could easily rise to the occasion.

The meeting began with old business, dealing with the grounds keeping for summer and continued on to an informational report regarding the summer picnic. The chief elder made mention of some of the events of the past month: the funeral taking place the next day for poor old Mathew Parker and the baptism of the Whitney family's surviving twin. The elders gave praise to the ladies of the church for their support of the grieving families.

Then David Peterson, the chief elder, called for new business.

Martin stood, cleared his throat and began. "Gentlemen, I am sorry to report that not all of our kind womenfolk are taking care of our parishioners in need. Brother Alvin Larson has reported to me some very distressing news."

With a flourish, Martin whipped the flyers from his briefcase and waved them high in the air. "Alvin's wife, Cora, was cleaning in the meeting room on Wednesday when she came across these abominable flyers." Martin tossed the papers onto the table for all to see.

Each of the elders perused the flyers and gasped in turn.

"In our church meeting room?" one of the men inquired.

Martin took a flyer and read from it:

**SUFFRAGETTES UPCOMING
MEETINGS AND EVENTS
May 14 6 p.m.**

Meeting at the church – Discuss plans for the

June 30 Chicago trip
June 4   6 p.m.
Meeting at church
June 30-July 4
Rally in Chicago
July 9   6 p.m.
Meeting at the church – Discuss plans for the Bicycle rally
Aug 17
Bicycle Rally in Milwaukee – Wear bloomers

"Right under our noses! Such brazen insolence!" Martin went on, his voice growing loud with anger. "It gets worse. Hattie was at the church for the picnic committee meeting the night these women met and overheard some of their conversation…political stuff. Hattie, being the fine woman she is, dismissed it as talk beyond her comprehension and decided to tend to her own business. However, when questioned by Cora, she became alarmed."

"Who was at the meeting?" one of the elders questioned.

"I'm not sure who was all there. However, Hattie told Cora who told Alvin who in turn told me—the voices she heard were of Tillie Morgenson, whom we all suspected of having ties to the suffragettes movement, and no doubt was the instigator of this calamity, and also Ruby, our revered pastor's wife."

Now the room was electric with comments of excommunication.

"Order, order!" called the chief elder. "We must not jump to conclusions. We need to discuss how to approach this problem."

"Do you have anything more to add, Martin?" Mr. Peterson asked Martin.

"That would be all," Martin said as he sat down and smugly surveyed the chaos of the room.

"Does anyone have a suggestion on how we should handle this situation?" Mr. Peterson inquired, and once again, the chatter in the room reached fever pitch with all the men talking at once.

"Order, order!" Mr. Peterson called out again. "We will not solve anything by arguing. I suggest we move cautiously. We should schedule a special meeting and have Pastor Reinhart explain things from his perspective. We should find out who was in that room and then make some decisions regarding how to proceed."

Nods and murmurings went about the room. It was five to one in favor, while Martin on the other hand, wanted nothing more than to see heads roll. They scheduled a meeting for the following Thursday.

Chapter Eleven

At nine o'clock on Friday morning, Mr. Peterson knocked on the door of the parsonage. Ruby answered the door. Mr. Peterson stammered, "Ah, Mrs. Reinhart, ah…" Finally, he spat out, "Is Pastor Reinhart available? I have some rather urgent private business to discuss with him."

"Certainly," Ruby cheerfully responded, "the pastor is always available for you, Mr. Peterson. May I take your hat? He is in the study going over his sermon for Sunday."

Ruby took his hat and held it in her hands. "Come right this way."

She opened the door to the study and called, "You have a visitor."

Pastor stood and greeted Mr. Peterson with a warm handshake. "Do sit." He motioned to a chair at the corner of his desk. "Ruby, would you mind bringing some coffee for Mr. Peterson?"

Mr. Peterson declined the offer and looked toward Ruby. "I have some private matters I wish to speak to you about, Pastor." He turned back to the pastor as Ruby quietly closed the door to the study.

David Peterson made awkward small talk about the weather and how great it was not to have snow anymore. He stammered and looked at the floor frequently.

Pastor Reinhart let him ramble for a while and then said, "David, you have something on your mind besides the spring flowers. What can I help you with today?"

"This is very difficult," David began, then blurted it out. "We, the elders, have some concern that our church is being used to hold suffragette meetings."

Pastor Reinhart raised his eyebrows and tilted his head slightly. "And what makes you think that?"

"One of the parishioners found suffragette flyers in the meeting room."

"Well, well," began Pastor Reinhart. He hesitated, raising his hand to his chin with his index finger, cupping his mouth. With his elbow on his desk, he lifted his index finger away from his mouth and into the air. "You realize many people have access to the church. Anyone could have dropped the flyers there."

"That may be true, Pastor, but another parishioner overheard some conversation outside the meeting room while the Women's Educational Research Funding Group was meeting, and she said the bit of conversation she heard was political...about voting." David fidgeted in his chair.

"Well, David, I can't speak for the Women's Educational Group, but I would think they might have some interest in any legislative action dealing with education."

"This is true." David began to feel more confident. Perhaps this whole thing was a mistake.

"Pastor, we are having a meeting next Thursday evening to discuss this issue. Could you be there?"

Pastor Reinhart looked at his appointment book and made a note in it. "I shall be there," he stated firmly with a smile.

"Thank you, Pastor. I would hate to see this blow out of proportion, especially since it was Ruby who was talking." David stood and turned to leave.

Ruby produced David's hat. "You have a pleasant day."

***

Pastor Reinhart was no longer smiling. When the door shut, he called to his wife from his study, "Ruby...Ruby! Come in here."

Ruby hurried to the study. "Can I get you something?"

"No, sit down. We need to talk."

Pastor Reinhart explained to his wife what had just transpired. "I think maybe you got a little careless Tuesday evening. You need to be more careful. I must attend a meeting of the elders next Thursday and try to fix this situation. David was very open to my ideas on what might have happened, but I am not sure the rest of the committee will be so amenable."

Ruby frowned and wrung her hands. "I wonder how much of the conversation was overheard?"

"I don't know, but I do know your voice was one that was mentioned."

***

Thursday evening there was a chill in the air and a thunderstorm was brewing...both inside and out. The meeting was to begin at seven that evening, and Pastor Reinhart waited until the last possible moment to arrive. He didn't want to engage in small talk, and he was not going to lie to the elders. He would do what he could to protect Ruby and the Women's Group, but he would not compromise his integrity or offend his God by stooping to deceitful measures.

It was precisely seven p.m. when Pastor Reinhart opened the big wood doors to the church, shook out his umbrella, and placed it in the umbrella stand in the coat room. He took off his wet coat and hung it on the hook, pulled his sweater down and tightened his tie. He took a deep breath and headed down the corridor to the meeting room where the elders had gathered.

David Peterson greeted Pastor Reinhart with a firm handshake and motioned for him to take a chair. There were some nods as Pastor Reinhart recognized the elders by name while attempting to judge the temperature of the room. It was decidedly cool.

David Peterson cleared his throat and took a sip of water from the glass in front of him. "Reverend Reinhart, as you know, the elders are concerned about a revelation which has come to our attention. It concerns activities of a controversial nature that occurred on our premises. We are interested in knowing what knowledge you have concerning these activities." He looked directly at the pastor.

Pastor Reinhart glanced around and watched their faces carefully. "I will tell you anything I can, gentlemen," he said, shifting uneasy in his chair. "Please proceed."

Martin Maxwell was quick to seize the moment. "We have suffragettes meeting in our church. What do you know about it and what do you intend to do about it?" he blurted.

"Mr. Maxwell, can you please explain why you believe that?" Pastor Reinhart questioned, forcing his expression to remain calm.

Martin waved some flyers. "These!" he shouted. "Cora found *these* in the Women's Education Funding room after their meeting."

"May I see them?" Pastor Reinhart inquired. Martin all but threw them on the table in front of him.

Pastor Reinhart moved his glasses up on his nose as he perused the documents. He then lowered his head and peered over his glasses, addressing Mr. Maxwell. "Were these in the room before their meeting?"

Martin said, "Cora found them after the meeting."

"I understand," the pastor continued, "but were they there prior to the meeting?"

Another elder spoke up. "Hattie heard them talking about political matters, including the Nineteenth amendment. Sure sounds like suffragette talk to me."

"And what was the context of the conversation? Were they for it or against it?" Pastor inquired. He had learned long ago the best answer to a question or accusation in the hot seat was to ask another question.

David Peterson turned to Mr. Maxwell. "Did Cora say if Hattie heard why they were discussing this matter?"

Martin was a bit flustered as he replied, "She was confused and wasn't sure."

David Peterson began to look conflicted. "Gentlemen." He coughed. "It is clear this conversation is not productive. We do not have enough information to continue. It would be my suggestion we investigate further before acting on this matter."

The meeting was intended for information gathering so no vote was in order, but three of the elders had warmed in their ideas of what had transpired, two were very defiant, and David Peterson, typical of a chief elder erred on the side of caution.

"Thank you, Pastor Reinhart, that will be all we need from you at this time," the chief elder said. "Gentlemen, will you please stay while we discuss matters pending?"

Pastor Reinhart, feeling confident, stood to leave. "Thank you, gentlemen. I will cooperate in any manner you choose."

"There is one thing you can do, Pastor," one of the elders said. "Can you question Ruby regarding who attended the meeting of the Women's Educational Group?"

Pastor Reinhart was taken aback with the request. He didn't have a question in mind to respond. "I will see what I can do."

He exited the room, troubled, and walked quietly to the parsonage with a serious look on his face. How would he handle this? It weighed heavy on his mind.

Chapter Twelve

In the meeting room, the elders discussed what to do next. One of the men suggested, "Perhaps we could infiltrate the group with a spy."

Most of them laughed. However, after a while, the idea seemed to have merit.

Martin rubbed his beard. "Meetings at the church are open to all members. Maybe a spy is the best way to get to the bottom of this matter."

Another man asked, "Who can we get to be the mole?"

"We will have to be careful; whoever we choose will have to be believable. It will have to be someone who would be endorsed by someone in the group already."

After much discussion, it was decided if she was willing, Edith Warner, the librarian would be their best pick. She was a single woman, intelligent, and had access to information and people. She was committed to her job and avoided controversy but projected an adventurous spirit. Mr. Maxwell would contact Edith with the plan the next day.

***

The next day was Friday, and the library closed at six on Fridays. Edith Warner checked out books at the desk and noticed Mr. Maxwell arrive five minutes before close.

Mr. Maxwell hung around until the last person left, and then he approached Edith. "Miss Warner, I have a matter of utmost importance to discuss with you. I realize you are about to lock up, but I am wondering if you can spare a few minutes."

Edith knew Mr. Maxwell and his wife, so she responded with a smile. "Is this church business?" she asked.

"Sort of. We need your help in handling a sticky situation. It must be kept completely confidential."

Miss Warner was an avid reader and particularly liked mysteries. She was intrigued by the idea of becoming part of a real-life mystery. She leaned forward as if to share a secret, though no one was there to overhear them. "What will I need to do?"

"Please, Miss Warner, sit here and I will tell you all about it." Martin motioned to a nearby library table.

"One moment." She raised a finger of caution. "I'll lock the door." She scurried away, pulling the big key from her pocket. Then hurried back and took a seat. "Fill me in, Mr. Maxwell," she encouraged.

Mr. Maxwell told her a shocking story of a possible suffragette organization meeting within the church's walls. "Your role will be to find a way to endear yourself to either Tillie or Ruby, making suggestions that you are sympathetic to the suffragette cause. See if you can get an invitation to attend a meeting of the Women's Educational Research Funding Group. Then report back to me what you find."

"How exciting," Edith said. If truth be known this was not a difficult assignment—she secretly supported the activities of the suffragettes. But she wasn't about to reveal her feelings at this point, because the idea of participating in a real-life mystery was even closer to her heart.

She accepted the mission to become friends with Tillie or Ruby, the two suspects in this mystery. She barely knew Tillie, and Ruby she only knew through the pastor.

Perhaps I could volunteer for something else Ruby is involved in at the church...but what could that be?

***

The following week, Catherine, an avid reader and frequent visitor to the library, stopped by to peruse the latest periodicals. She sat at a table with *The Chicago Tribune*, the *New York Times* and several editions of *Life Magazine*.

As Edith walked by her chair while shelving returned items, she glanced over Catherine's shoulder and noted she was reading an article about the 1911 Census in London, which featured an article of the suffragette's protest of the census.

This was not the way Edith had planned to find her way into the suffragette movement, but she might never have a better opportunity.

Catherine's support was not a secret since she was a single woman without children and had no one to answer to for her convictions. She was not a militant participant, either, but simply followed what occurred in other hubs across the world, such as Europe. The suffragette movement was very active in Europe and in the larger United States cities. Catherine was, for all anyone knew, an interested observer.

Normally, Edith would not impose on anyone's choice of literature, but she took a chance. "Oh my," Edith said, "I haven't seen this article. I must read it. What magazine is it?"

Startled, Catherine turned the magazine to the cover so Edith could see it. "It's *Life Magazine.*"

"I have such admiration for those women," Edith went on. "Is it a good article?"

"It's amazing." Catherine smiled, as if recognizing the common bond they shared. "These women have more courage and fortitude than any man I have ever encountered. They are intelligent and driven. Look here." She pushed the article toward Edith.

Edith read, "Horse-drawn caravans drew up on Wimbledon Common carrying women who were to spend the night away from home to boycott the 1911 census. Carrying signs proclaiming, 'If women don't count, neither shall they be counted.' The suffragettes enjoyed a picnic of roast fowl, sweetmeats, and tea. Emily Wilding Davison was sustained by meat lozenges and lime juice as she hid in a broom cupboard in the Houses of Parliament."

"Look what the scientist, Hertha Ayrton wrote." Catherine gave the paper to Edith. "I will not supply these particulars until I have my rights as a citizen. Votes for women. In Birkenhead, Miss Davies wrote on her form the name of a male servant, adding 'no other persons, but many women.' Dorothy Bowker wrote: 'Dumb Politically, Blind to the Census, Deaf to the Enumerator.'"

Edith laughed out loud. "They certainly are rascals, aren't they?"

A voice on the other side of the shelving said, "Shush, this is a library."

Catherine giggled and gave Edith a knowing look. "Let's talk later," she whispered. "I had no idea we had so much in common. Come for tea on Saturday." She wrote her name and address on a scrap of paper and handed it to Edith. "Two in the afternoon?"

Edith took the paper, smiled, and nodded.

***

On Saturday, Edith dressed in her best purple dress and stylish bonnet, pulling up her brown hair in its usual bun. She was quite striking with her tall, trim frame. She arrived at Catherine's home promptly at two. After she knocked, Catherine opened the door.

"Do come in, Edith," Catherine said. "My, don't you look lovely. I'm so used to seeing you in your black skirt and white shirtwaist."

"I know," said Edith, with a confident smile. "It is the uniform of the librarian. It feels good to break out of the mold."

"Please sit. I have some delightful treats for us." Catherine disappeared into the kitchen, returning with a full tray of pastries. She placed the tray on the sideboard next to a fresh brewed pot of tea. "How do you like your tea?" she inquired.

"Just a bit of lemon and sugar. I simply can't resist," she said as she reached for a pastry.

"Oh, please help yourself," Catherine said. "I would be disappointed if you declined."

They shared the necessary pleasantries of the weather and how their respective gardens were growing, but the conversation soon gravitated to the subject for Edith's visit.

"Edith," Catherine began, barely containing her excitement, "how long have you been interested in the movement?"

"Oh, I don't know, I suspect most of my life. As you know, I'm a single woman who has a career. I have no husband to take care of me, but I consider myself an intelligent human being. So why shouldn't I have the right to vote?"

"Exactly. Have you thought about getting more involved?"

"Oh, I couldn't," Edith said, with feigned reluctance. "I am a public employee. The county would certainly object to any public defiance. I couldn't possibly do anything that would jeopardize my job... It is a job I love."

"Do you know you can be a suffragette incognito?" Catherine inquired.

"What do you mean? Isn't it risky?" Edith raised her hands, shaking them.

"You might be surprised to know there are a number of women you know who are active participants, but don't want to be revealed.

Women who either have positions in society or husbands who are averse to their views."

"No!" Edith exclaimed, surprised. "Who, for instance?"

"You must never reveal their names. Will you promise?" Catherine cautioned, her voice dropping low.

"Would I reveal such information when I am in the same situation?" Edith asked, using a ploy she had learned from listening to Pastor Reinhart at the church, answering a question with a question.

Catherine seemed to hesitate a moment. "Well, I am. I don't reveal much of my activism because I have close friends who might be found guilty by association. Most of my involvement is either out of the area or in private. There are few who are as blatant about it as our lady comrades in *Life Magazine*. Tillie Morgenson will soon begin traveling across the nation. Her late husband, Senator Morgenson, was an advocate, and Tillie is a very well-spoken ambassador. She is distancing herself from the group since she will be playing a much more active and public role."

"Group? You have a group?" Edith gasped.

"Yes." Catherine smiled. "We are the Women's Educational Research Fundraising Group at the Presbyterian Church, and Ruby Reinhart will be our new leader. Can you join us at our next meeting?"

Edith smiled to herself. "Yes, I would like that," she said with enthusiasm.

"Our next meeting is May fourteenth at the church. I will meet you there. We are very careful to screen our members. It's important you attend with me. And please, no mention of our true cause or any of our names. If you need to reveal your activity, state you will be attending a meeting of the Women's Educational Research Fundraising Group— or any of the shortened versions of the name. It's quite a mouthful."

"And what specifically is this supposed group's purpose, in case anyone should ask?"

"Why, we are soliciting funding to support education. No one can refute our intention, even those who are aware of who we really are," Catherine snickered.

"Very clever, Catherine, very clever!" Edith stood. "I really must go. Thank you so much for all you have shared. I will be seeing you in the days to come. I am so glad I spotted your reading material."

"We are always anxious to add new supporters to the cause. You will be a great asset to our group with your access to international information. We often use ideas from other areas in planning our events and in dispersing information." Catherine showed her new friend out, smiling.

Outside, Edith took in a deep breath and blew it out. She was torn. She had made a commitment to Mr. Maxwell in solving his mystery. But Edith also found herself intrigued by the suffragette cause and by her new friend, Catherine. Her choice was grim. Either she had to betray the trust of a cause she believed in or she had to renege on a promise she had made to expose this group.

Oh dear, what have I gotten myself into?

Chapter Thirteen

Martin Maxwell was almost salivating when he went to the library on Monday just before it closed. Once again, he waited until the last person had checked out at the desk. Edith locked the door, and they sat down at the table. "What do you have for me?" he inquired.

Edith wore a slight frown, but still provided him with the information. "Yes, the Women's Educational Finance Committee is a ruse and cover for the local suffragettes. Yes, Tillie and Ruby were involved. In fact, Ruby is about to become their new leader."

"How did you get the information so quickly?" Martin was curious. He needed something more than Edith's word.

Edith seemed to hesitate. "A good reporter never reveals her source."

"Go to a meeting," Martin prompted, leaning in. "Get any evidence you can."

Edith said, "I understand." Her eyes flicked away to the door. "I will go, but only if you promise not to be anywhere near the church that night."

"Why?" Martin was surprised at the request.

"Because your presence at church would make me nervous and would blow my cover."

"Very well," Martin conceded. He would go along with whatever she requested—after the meeting, he would have everything he needed to bring down this organization, and Pastor and Mrs. Reinhart along with it.

***

The next evening was May fourteenth. Catherine, impetuous with excitement, introduced her new friend to the group. "Ms. Warner, as you all know, is our librarian. She is very intelligent and has access to many resources. Her participation in our group will be most helpful."

Sara stood and voiced her approval. "Edith will make an excellent addition to our group. She is a good friend, a dedicated worker, and highly dependable. Unless anyone objects, please welcome our newest suffragette, Edith Warner." Everyone applauded.

Edith raised her hand for silence. "I have something to say, and I am afraid it is not good news." She hesitated. "I was approached by Mr. Maxwell and asked to infiltrate and expose this group as a suffragette organization. Apparently, some of your literature was discovered in this very room, and Mr. Maxwell is on a witch hunt. He's aware of this organization and two of its members, Tillie and Ruby." A buzz like a swarm of angry bees permeated the room.

Catherine stood aghast. *What evil did I bring here?*

Sara gasped.

Edith held up her hands and ameneded, "I am not going to report any confidential information to Mr. Maxwell. I only wish to inform you that your name and location have been compromised. They have a copy of your upcoming agenda, including a July rally in Chicago and a bicycle rally in Milwaukee in August. I would strongly suggest anyone who does not wish to be exposed should not attend either of those rallies and to change meeting locations. At this point, there is no reason for you to trust me, except by my word. I stand with you in secrecy to protect my job as a public employee. I have much to lose."

Edith bowed her head in shame. "I will understand if you ask me to leave. I am truly sorry."

The buzz turned from rage to empathy for all who realized the risk she was taking.

Questions came from around the room.

"You say you will not reveal the information you have to Mr. Maxwell? How can we trust you?" asked a woman in the back of the room.

"Why should we believe you?" another woman asked.

Edith said, "Quite frankly, I believe Mr. Maxwell is a donkey's behind and I am truly sorry for becoming involved in his scheme."

Ruby rose, visibly shaken. "Well, this is quite the revelation. However, part of this church is believing in the act of forgiveness, and I for one can see you are penitent. Your integrity is solid and your courage in bringing this to our attention is commendable. While we are about the business of confession, I, too, would like to confess. I was the negligent party who left the flyers in the room last meeting. I also must share in the blame."

Addressing the group, Ruby went on. "Can we have a motion to accept Edith Warner into our sisterhood?"

Martha raised her hand. "I so move."

Sara seconded the motion.

"All in favor?" Ruby asked.

There was a resounding, "Aye."

"Well, then," Ruby went on, "it appears we may have to change our agenda. First order of business is where we are to meet in the future."

Edith rose. "If I may suggest, I could form a book club. We can meet at the library after hours. You all would become the sole participants in the book club. The location is uncompromised by visitors after hours. I hope to make amends for agreeing to solve Mr. Maxwell's mystery. After talking with Catherine, I realized I wanted to become a part of this great cause."

The business meeting concluded with decisions made. All members would now be attending meetings of the library book club. The Chicago Rally was only encouraged for those who were openly active suffragettes, and the Milwaukee Bicycle Rally would go on as planned since it was a local event only for those willing to reveal their identities.

The meeting was adjourned. As the ladies left the building, there was no one in sight.

***

Ruby went home with a heavy heart. She knew the word was out about her participation in the suffragette movement and how it would have a great impact on the future for her and her husband.

When she reached the parsonage, she went to the study where Reverend Reinhart was working on Sunday's sermon.

"We have to talk," Ruby said.

When Ruby had finished explaining the situation, Reverend Reinhart held his head in his hands, looking down at the desk. "Ruby," he said quietly, "let's put this in the Lord's hands. If this is our station in life, He will provide a way. If we are asked to leave, the Lord will lead us where we must go."

He looked at her and moved from behind the desk, putting his arms around Ruby to comfort her. "This has been a long, difficult day. Let's go to bed."

They retired for the evening.

***

The following day, Martin couldn't wait to see Edith. He arrived at the library at his usual time and hurried to the desk. "Well, what did you find out? Who was there? Do you have any literature? What did they discuss?"

"My, Mr. Maxwell, aren't you the inquisitive one. There were no papers; they discussed women's education."

"Is that all? No discussion of the agenda? Who was there?"

"No one I know," Edith went on. "There was no agenda. The Women's Educational Finance Committee is terminating. There is nothing more to investigate. Mr. Maxwell, if you will excuse me, I have an urgent commitment and I need to leave now."

Martin fumed, completely taken aback. He picked up his briefcase and dashed out, slamming the door behind him. He would gather his supporters among the elders, and they would confront Pastor Reinhart tomorrow.

***

When Edith left the library, she went directly to see Pastor Reinhart, guilt in her heart. The least she could do was to warn Pastor Reinhart he would be confronted by the elders, and let God handle the rest for both of them.

She walked to the door of the parsonage and composed herself for a minute before taking a deep breath and knocking.

Pastor answered the door.

Edith cleared her throat. "Good…good evening, Pastor."

He smiled warmly. "Edith, do come in. It is a beautiful evening for a walk and so nice to see you. Please have a seat." He motioned to a nearby chair.

Edith took the seat and fidgeted, wondering why he wasn't yelling at her. Surely, Ruby had filled him in.

Edith looked down and twisted the handkerchief she held tight in her hand. "Thank you…um…well. I don't know what to say. I am so sorry," she blurted out. Tears formed at the corners of her eyes.

"Edith, Edith, it is okay," Pastor Reinhart comforted her. He placed his hand on her arm. "Ruby explained the situation to me. We are handling this matter in the best way possible. You know, Edith, we tend to worry and fret over everything when there is no need for it. I can't say I am pleased with the way things appear to be moving, but it is not my will. It is the will of our Lord and Savior that matters. He will lead us where we need to go."

"But Pastor, Mr. Maxwell and some of the elders plan to confront you very soon about Ruby's participation and your knowledge of the suffragette meetings. I feel so bad for my role in this mess." Edith was visibly shaking. "Can you ever forgive me?"

"Of course I can. The Lord works in mysterious ways. Sometimes, He uses us to move things in the direction He wants us to go. Perhaps, you were merely a vehicle in His plans. You did nothing wrong."

"Nothing wrong? Pastor, I have gravely sinned," Edith confessed.

"Did you lie? Did you steal? Did you take the name of the Lord in vain?" he inquired.

"Of course not," Edith wiped away a tear.

"Did you commit adultery? Did you covet your neighbor's property? Tell me, which of His commandments did you break?" Pastor asked.

Edith sniffed and blew her nose in a handkerchief. "I don't think I broke a commandment."

"Well, well then. I am afraid you are chastising yourself unnecessarily. You have not broken a commandment; you have not sinned. God's commandments don't cover mistakes or poor judgment. God knows we are mortal. We are not perfect. Come, have a cup of tea with Ruby and I. Everything will work out fine."

Edith went home feeling much better, but she still worried about what would happen when the elders came to call on Pastor and Ruby Reinhart.

Chapter Fourteen

The very next morning, Mr. Maxwell, Mr. Peterson, and two other elders called on Pastor Reinhart. Their greetings to him were very somber and curt. Still, Pastor invited them into his study and closed the door.

"We will get right to the point," David Peterson began. "We have had some additional information presented to us about the Women's Educational Finance Committee and we want to know precisely what you know about the group."

Mr. Maxwell said, "You were very cagey the other night and we are not going to stand for that today. We want direct answers and want them now!"

Pastor Reinhart rubbed his chin, then paced the floor with his hands behind his back. "Well gentlemen, it has come to my attention the Women's Educational Finance Group has disbanded, so it is no longer an issue. I can honestly say I don't know who all the members are. I was not part of the group, since it is the *Women's* Educational Research Funding Group."

"But," one of the elders broke in, "you authorized them the use of the church, and your wife was a member. You must know some of the women's name or have some information regarding their purpose."

"Certainly, he does," said Mr. Maxwell. "He knows about every organization that uses the church property. If he had no idea, he could be letting a *Devil* cult use the church for its meetings."

"Perhaps he has!" another elder chimed in. "Answer directly and honestly, Pastor, was our church the location for a suffragette group?"

Pastor Reinhart was quiet for a moment. There was no way of getting out of this other than outright lying, and he was not about to do that.

He took a deep breath. "Gentlemen, this was, in fact, a suffragette meeting place. Quite frankly, I support the movement. These are very intelligent women well positioned in our community, from good Christian families. Why should they not vote and why should I deny them a meeting place?"

Mr. Maxwell seemed taken aback by the directness and honesty of the statement.

"Devil's work!" he declared, his face going red. "Who are these women? Give us names."

Pastor shook his head. "I cannot reveal that. I am a pastor and I am bound by confidentiality in this case. I have been asked before God to keep their identities private."

David Peterson had remained quiet until now. "I respect your pastoral right of confidentiality, Pastor. I will not say you lied or deceived us in our previous questions, but you were not forthcoming with information until today. It is the duty of the elders to preserve the dignity and image of our church, and by allowing a controversial element to meet on our premises, you have crossed the line of what is proper. Your wife's involvement with the group is a clear indication you were very aware of what was going on within the walls of this church and therefore condoned it. As for the other members of the suffragette group, I respect your pastoral right of confidentiality, although that is reserved for the confessional. I am not sure of the validity of your claim but since the group has disbanded, if in fact they have, the names of participants at this point is irrelevant. Thank you for your time today, Pastor Reinhart. The elders and I will meet to discuss how we will proceed with this matter. I shall get back to you. Good day."

"Good day, gentlemen." Reverend Reinhart shut the door behind them. He leaned against the door and looked heavenward. "Dear God, this is in your hands. Please lead us in the direction you wish us to go."

***

A week later, after the elders meeting, David Peterson returned alone to the Parsonage.

"Reverend Reinhart, it is with great sadness I am here today to inform you that the elders have met, and with a unanimous vote, we are terminating your services. You will be allowed to stay until the end of the month of May. I would suggest you contact the Presbytery Council to find out where you will be reassigned. You will not have our good references, so I wish you luck. We have contacted the head of council to find us a replacement. I am sorry it has come to this. The decision was not because of the suffragettes, although I must admit it was an issue with some of the elders, but rather an issue of trust. It would be extremely difficult to move forward when we feel trust is no longer a cornerstone of our relationship. I am truly sorry."

David Peterson left with his hat in his hand and his head held low.

Pastor Reinhart went to his study to pray.

After only a moment of praying, Ruby poked her head through the doorway and interrupted him. "Can I get you something? You look depressed," she said.

"Ruby, my love, you need to pack our bags. We will be leaving this church at the end of the month."

Ruby gasped.

"I will contact the Presbytery Council to see if they have a new assignment for us. Be prepared. If there isn't an opening in this district, we may be exiled to mission work in Africa."

"Wherever the Lord calls us." Ruby smiled.

As she turned and walked away, her head dropped and Pastor knew tears flowed down her cheeks. This was home; this was where their friends were.

***

The summer began with a mixture of emotions. Reverend Reinhart and Ruby were assigned to mission work in East Africa. The farewell coffee reception after services on their last Sunday at the church was an upbeat event, with most of the congregation looking at the parting as a decision the pastor and his wife had made voluntarily. Their courage and commitment to the poor natives was applauded. The ladies of the congregation had prepared items for them to take to the starving children in Africa in the line of blankets and clothing items. Food items that could spoil were discouraged.

The mood of the day was a mixture of joy and sorrow. Most were sad to see their beloved pastor go, but there was joy knowing he was dedicating himself to God's work.

Of course, there were few who knew the real reason for the departure. The suffragettes wept with guilt for having put Pastor and Ruby in this position. Most affected was Edith, who wiped away tears throughout the morning.

The faction of elders who were privy to the facts of the matter were also mixed, some wishing things had turned out differently. Others who were internally gloating, but had the common sense and decency to be discreet.

And there were the gossips, like Cora, who gloated with her inside information, but most considered her tales for what they were...vicious gossip.

On Monday the twenty-seventh of May, the train pulled into the Milwaukee station and Reverend and Mrs. Reinhart went on their way to Chicago, then to New York, where they would catch a ship taking them to their new home in East Africa. Their large trunk filled with blankets and supplies was put into the baggage car, along with all the personal belongings they would take with them in one small trunk. They had a carpet bag with clothing and other items they would need on their journey.

Tillie, Catherine, and Edith were there to see them off. Sara had wanted to go but was afraid of the suspicion it might cast on her. Catherine relayed her best wishes to them for a safe journey. Tears were in their eyes as they departed.

***

Later in the week, it was Tillie who packed her bags and departed on the train for Washington DC. She was attending a hearing with suffragettes from across the nation and would be gone for several months. From Washington, she would travel to New York, where she would band with fellow suffragettes and attend rallies. Tillie had embarked on a mission to change the world.

From time to time, Sara and Catherine would hear news of their friend on the radio or in the local newspaper. Speeches and rallies were not always big news, but because of Tillie's connections to Milwaukee, the Milwaukee Journal followed her activities closely.

Meetings of the book club at the library seemed to be going smoothly. The only incident was when a woman who frequented the library had asked to join the book club. The lady was known for her anti-suffragette commentary.

With Ruby and Tillie gone, Edith took on an active role within the group. With a clever smile, Edith told her that she could become a member, but first the woman had to read Tolstoy's *War and Peace*, which would be discussed in the coming year. Since Tolstoy had published his massive work in 1869, it was common knowledge it was not casual reading.

As she told Sara and Catherine about the incident, Edith explained she was aware this woman was far more comfortable with Dickens or Mark Twain. The assignment was enough to discourage her.

So far, the ladies believed the library book club was the perfect ruse, but how long would it survive?

Chapter Fifteen

Sara once again was torn. Was it all worth it? She had almost lost her life. The poor Reinharts had been exiled to Africa. And she was getting tired of all the deceit.

She kept herself busy through the summer tending her gardens. By June, the tulips and daffodils were waning, the lilacs and apple blossoms finished for the year. Still, her gardens flourished. All the while she tended her roses, her mind was on the cause. It was ingrained in her, and although she knew she had to be careful, the drive to get involved again was overwhelming.

The children were off from school, so Sara taught Ella the joys of homemaking, including how to knit and embroider. She told Ella the rules about gardening, and even gave Ella a plot in the vegetable garden all her own. Claudia was a big help teaching Ella how to do things in the kitchen. Sara could find her way around the kitchen, but she'd never enjoyed it. Ella on the other hand, showed signs of becoming a gourmet cook.

Because the elders had in their possession a copy of the agenda for the suffragettes, the week of the Fourth of July in Chicago was no longer an option for most of the Milwaukee chapter's suffragettes. The few who were more militant in the organization went on as planned and joined forces with others around the state.

Sara did not join them. Instead, she spent the holiday weekend with her family. They attended the Independence Day parade in the morning. It was a grand parade, with marching bands and floats, clowns and horses. Sara enjoyed watching her children delight in the cacophony of sounds emitting from the bands and the crowd, but for her, it brought back the memory of the horrors of the Racine calamity. Sara shivered, but tried to put on a smile.

In the afternoon, they gathered around the gazebo in Lincoln Park. The park had a zoo, and the children couldn't wait to check it out. Little Adam squealed with delight at the antics of the monkeys while Sara was enthralled by the penguins. Liz (as Elizabeth preferred to be called) admired the tall giraffes with their elegant stride, and Thaddeus, of course, liked the snakes.

Sara and Henry enjoyed the afternoon concert at the gazebo while sipping ice cold lemonade from the street vendor. The children participated in games of tag and hide n' seek with their friends. That evening, after consuming a picnic lunch of cold chicken sandwiches, potato salad, baked beans, and apple pie, they spread blankets on the ground and took in the fireworks. The rockets whistled into the air. With a loud crash, streamers burst into red, blue, and white stars. "Oohs" and "Ahs" were heard everywhere. Adam clapped his hands with delight at the dazzling spectacle. After the display was finished, they gathered up the blankets they had been sitting on and headed for home. The family was exhausted but very happy.

"What a great nation," Sara said aloud. *It will be even better when they understand women should be partners in this nation's growth and development.*

***

The bicycle rally was scheduled for August sixteenth. Hundreds of women from across the state would be converging on Milwaukee to participate. Sara would've liked to be a part of it, but she thought better of it. She decided her commitment would be behind the scenes. Because she didn't often go to the book club meetings, Catherine kept her informed on their progress.

Since the July Chicago rally had fizzled, the suffragettes refocused on a Chicago rally on Election Day in November. Perhaps by then, Sara would be able to become more involved.

Life at the Dewberry house was quite pleasant, and the summer flew by. It would soon be time to think about school.

Ella had ambitions of becoming a school teacher one day, just like her mother had once been. Henry and Sara had many discussions about the future of their children, and Henry was still adamant about the children attending private school. He finally convinced Sara that Thaddeus should attend the Northwest Military Academy.

"At the age of twelve, young men should be more disciplined," Henry reasoned. "Here he is nearly twelve, still chasing snakes and riding his bicycle hither and yon with no purpose in life. Military school will provide him with some direction. It is high time he grows up."

"Have you talked to Thaddeus about it?" Sara asked.

"As a matter of fact I have, and he seemed quite intrigued by the idea."

Just then, Thaddeus clamored into the room, acting every bit like a five-year-old. As he ran into the house from outside, the door slammed behind him. He yelled, "Can't get me now!"

"Whoa, Thaddeus!" Henry commanded. "Young man, is that any way to act at your age?"

"I was playing...water balloons with Liz...in the back yard," he panted. "I was out of balloons, and she was about to clobber me."

"Well, never mind," Henry said. "Mother and I have been discussing school. Tell her what you think of the Academy. The one I told you about."

"Aaaw, jeepers, Mother. They have regular classes and they train military maneuvers, too, and do stuff with ships and airplanes... Airplanes, Mother, can you just imagine? One day, airplanes are going to be really important to the military. They have great uniforms and everything, in that school."

Sara was overwhelmed by Thaddeus' enthusiasm. "Well, well, gentlemen. It looks like you have done your homework. Military school it is. I will be sad to not have you bounding through the house after school each day, but I can see your point. Henry, go ahead and make the arrangements."

Thaddeus ran out of the house, yelling, "Wait til my friend Tom hears."

Henry sighed.

"What about our young lady Ella?" Henry went on, striking while the iron was hot. "Have you thought about Stevens Finishing School?"

"I'm trying not to think about it," Sara confessed.

"Sara, Ella will be thirteen before school starts. It is time she learns social graces and gets some exposure to the fine arts. I know you want the children to go to public school to learn diversity and commonality, but you also want her to be prepared to find a *proper* husband, don't you?"

"They grow up so fast," Sara lamented, her stomach twisting at the thought.

"Well, in my opinion, it's time for us to think about her future as well," Henry pleaded his case. "Stevens Finishing School is in town, so she can live at home. On a nice day, she can walk. Otherwise, she can take the trolley, or we can get out the carriage to take her."

"I will talk to her about it," Sara promised.

Sara was beginning to feel empty nest syndrome, even though her children were still at home. Henry was right. *It is our duty as parents to make sure they are on the right track in life. It won't hurt for her to learn social graces as long as her academics are good.*

The next day as they worked in the garden, Sara brought up the subject. "Ella, what do you think of enrolling in Stevens Finishing School this coming year?"

This was not a new subject, but it was the first time Sara had brought it up to her.

Ella's jaw dropped. "Mother, I like my school. I like my teachers and my friend, Rose, goes there. I would have to make all new friends at a new school."

"Think about it, please. You're becoming a young lady now. You must think of your future. In a couple of years, you will be a debutante and gentlemen will come to call. You will want to know how to find the richest and handsomest gentleman to call your husband," Sara teased. "This would be the best step to achieve that goal."

"Hmmph!" Ella rolled her eyes. "I think I would rather marry a strong, rugged cowboy! We won't need money. We will live on love and eat off the land." Ella flipped her hair as she turned her nose up to the sky in a haughty manner.

Sara laughed. "I think you have been reading too many of Laura Ingalls Wilder's books. Think about it. There may be some information at the library about the school. You can go see Edith tomorrow."

"Well, I suppose I could look," Ella said, likely just to appease her.

***

The next day after school, Ella made her way to the library with Rose. Her friend had not been pleased to hear of Ella going off to a different school, though she had expressed admiration for the opportunity.

"What can I do for you girls?" Edith asked as they approached the librarian's desk.

"My mother would like me to learn more information on Stevens Finishing School," Ella said, slumping onto the desk. "Do you have anything?" She rather hoped the library didn't.

"Oh yes," said Edith. "Come over here. Since the school is here in Milwaukee, they have provided me with several things. Of course, it would be best to visit the school in person, but perhaps this could get you started. Here is a photograph of theschool. It is a unique old building." Edith paged through a file. "Ah, here it is. They have prepared a brochure. It is a bit dog-eared and mimeographed, so it is not the best quality, but still quite readable."

Ella sighed, but took the brochure, pretending to be interested. Mimeograph material had a tendency to become lighter and blotchy after a long run. Here it was in blue and white, covering everything a fine lady needed to know in society:

English and literature – Broaden your intellect
Social Writing skills –Invitations, thank you cards, and general correspondence
Learning the Palmer Method of good penmanship
Taking Care of your Husband – Making life comfortable for the man in your life
Beauty & Health – Looking good at all times
Equestrian Skills – Riding skills
Food & Beverage – Know food preparation and presentation; understand protocol
Good Housekeeping – Keeping a home that is always welcome to visitors
Personality Development – Be a charming host and a guest who will always be asked to return
Hobbies & Appropriate Social Activities – Keeping busy and interesting
Social Graces – Proper etiquette for all occasions
French – Learn how to converse in French
Public Speaking – Preparation for being a social leader
Presentation Skills – Always be prepared and admired

Dining Etiquette – Be able to dine with the Queen

Ella wasn't impressed, but her friend Rose seemed to be.

"Ella, are you crazy? I would love to go to this school! You'll have to teach me everything you learn!" Her enthusiasm wore off on Ella.

Ella turned the brochure over. There she found listed the academic subjects, including literature, science, math, and several other electives. These of course were not considered necessary for women but were offered as an incentive for those who wanted them. The rest of the brochure described some of the "events," which were, in their words, "opportunities to use the skills they learned," and "opportunities to charm young gentlemen with your skills."

"Why don't they have men's finishing schools?" Ella observed. "It seems to me men folk need a lot more coaching than ladies."

The girls laughed together, then returned home.

***

Sara was pruning her yellow climbing rose by the front gate. "Hello, ladies," Sara greeted them. "Did you find anything interesting at the library?"

"Mrs. Dewberry!" Rose exclaimed, her eyes shining and hands clasped. "Ella must go to that school. It is fabulous."

"Well, Rose, I am going to leave the decision to Ella. Maybe we should make an appointment to look at the school," Sara suggested.

"Could I come with you?" Rose asked.

"We will see," Sara promised. "Right now, we must get cleaned up for dinner."

Over dinner, they discussed the school's attributes as well as their personal apprehensions, and Ella hesitantly agreed they should schedule an appointment with Stevens Finishing School.

Henry sent a courier to the school and was able to secure an appointment with the director of admissions. They would meet with him and the head master the following week on the last Wednesday in July.

Chapter Sixteen

Henry, Sara, and Ella, along with Ella's friend, Rose, dressed in their finest attire arrived ten minutes early for their designated appointment at Stevens Finishing School. They were impressed with the regal décor of the fine old building, with the heavy velvet drapes that framed ten-foot-high windows. A beautiful mahogany table and a set of Queen Anne wing chairs perched at one end of the room, while silk brocade sofas were situated on the opposite end.

They were directed by the secretary to have a seat on the sofas while they waited. An impressive cherub brass lamp—which they assumed to be from the French Renaissance period—sat on another massive mahogany table with cabriole legs. A matching coffee table had been placed in front of the sofas. A sparkling crystal chandelier hung from the ceiling between the designated areas. It was an elegant presentation for prospective students and their well-to-do families.

Rose looked around in awe.

Ella poked her friend. "Stop drooling," she teased.

Rose coughed daintily and placed her hands in her lap, trying her best to act sophisticated.

Ella snickered.

"Girls!" Sara warned. "Mind your manners."

Just then, the headmaster entered the room. He was a stout, proper man with gray hair and a receding hairline. His suit was of fine linen. He wore the latest style navy coat with striped trousers, a gold watch fob that hung from his pocket and sported a gold-rimmed monocle over his eye. He introduced himself as Headmaster Richard Goodfellow.

He greeted Henry with a vigorous handshake. Rose stifled a chuckle. Both girls stood and curtsied.

Mr. Goodfellow complimented Sara on her exquisite outfit, then turned to the girls and said, "So, young ladies, are you excited about the prospect of being students here at Stevens Finishing School?"

Henry stood next to Ella and proudly introduced his daughter, stating for her that she was indeed elated at the prospect. He nodded in Rose's direction. "Rose is accompanying us today. She is Ella's best friend."

"Oh, I see." The man looked Rose up and down, clearly taking in her attire. "Well, then, shall we take the tour?" He swept his hand in the direction of the classrooms.

The classrooms were not nearly as elegant as the waiting area, but many of the rooms were finely appointed with pleasing décor and the necessary desks and blackboards for a studious environment. They continued down the hall to a room with floor-to-ceiling mirrors.

"This," Mr. Goodfellow chirped, "is the room where we develop grace and posture. The young ladies take ballet classes, walk about with books on their heads, and learn how to properly bend in a ladylike manner."

Wouldn't it be better to read books? Sara was not impressed.

Once again, Rose stifled a snicker.

This time, Mr. Goodfellow caught it out of the corner of his eye and turned to give Rose a beady stare. "Shall we continue?"

"This," Mr. Goodfellow said after several minutes of walking, "is the cafeteria. We serve healthy lunches at noon. The girls learn proper nutrition and dining etiquette in this room."

***

Soon Ella was accepting of the idea of attending the school. *This place isn't too bad, but I wish Rose could be here with me.*

Mr. Goodfellow chirped himself in and out of several classrooms, much to Rose's delight, and by the time they reached the end of the corridor, Ella was also having trouble containing her laughter.

At the end of the hall, Mr. Goodfellow swung the door open to the outside, and with a grand gesture, in all the flowery elegance he could muster, he gushed, "This, my dear guests, is our courtyard. As you can see, our lawns are finely manicured. In the spring and fall, we have elegant garden parties out here. We open this area to various social groups during the summer months for teas and coming out parties. Isn't it lovely?"

It was impeccable and as manicured as any courtyard could be.

"Now ladies…and gentleman. I have a treat for you. Let us walk to the stables at the far end of the courtyard," Mr. Good fellow said. Once again, he made an elegant sweep with his hand, pointing the way.

Reaching the stable door, he opened it. They entered an almost pristine building, housing eight beautiful horses.

"This," Mr. Goodfellow chirped again, "is the finest stable in Milwaukee. Our stable hands keep it immaculate. We're able to get outdoors for the experienced equestrian, but we also have an indoor raceway for beginners where we train all of our students to ride side saddle and learn the etiquette of riding."

Rose poked her friend and tilted her head.

Ella looked in the direction Rose suggested. Across the riding trail was a young stable boy pitching hay, the sweat from his strong, muscular arms glistening in the sun.

Rose spoke up, "Mr. Goodfellow, I must say the view here is simply spectacular."

"I heartily agree," Ella chimed in.

"Wonderful, wonderful! Ladies, I am sure you will be spending many enjoyable hours out here."

Ella exclaimed, "I'm sure I will."

Her father seemed pleased Ella was finally coming around to appreciate the value of this institution.

"Well, then," said Mr. Goodfellow, "let us go in and find Mr. Pennywinkle and look at the paperwork."

Ella's friend couldn't hold it in any longer and broke out in laughter. Rose tried to cover it with a cough, but it came out strangely.

Mr. Goodfellow narrowed his eyes at her.

"Go ahead, I'll catch up," Ella said to her parents. "I'll help Rose. She seems to have something caught in her throat."

Ella handed her friend a handkerchief.

Rose looked at her friend and gasped, "Mr. Goodfellow and Mr. Pennywinkle!" She broke out into laughter all over again. This time Ella joined her, and they were both in tears.

"Breathe," Ella said to Rose. "We need to go inside. Control yourself."

They composed themselves and walked down the hall to the director of admissions' office.

Ella's parents were looking over the tuition papers. Mr. Pennywinkle handed Ella a sheet with the rules of the school on it. School would start at the end of August.

Her father seemed anxious to sign the contract. He picked up the pen and was about to sign when her mother touched his arm. "Wait a minute, Henry. Ella, is this what *you* want? You don't have to enroll."

Ella smiled as she thought about the stable boy. "Yes, mother dear. I want to go to this school," she said in her most proper manner.

Then, she shot a wink at her friend, Rose.

Chapter Seventeen

The week before the bicycle rally, Sara went to the book club. She wanted to find out what was scheduled for the event. The ladies gushed over her.

"Sara, it is so good to see you."

"Sara, we missed you."

"Sara, we hear Ella will be attending Stevens Finishing School. How exciting."

On and on came the warm greetings she received from her friends.

Edith was now in charge of the meeting. She called for order and began with suffragette news from around the world. Although news came through by radio, access was extremely limited. *The Milwaukee Journal* did a nice job of covering events, but sometimes the editor would relegate women's news to the back pages or not print it at all. However, there was a secret underground railroad of news from all the communities hailing their progress, bemoaning their failures, and notifying others of events to be held. Edith had this storehouse of information to share.

The rally in Chicago on Election Day in November was gearing up to be quite spectacular, with factions from around the whole country participating in the event. The driving force was the militant activists from Chicago, but even small rural communities had pledged their support.

Noteworthy quotations from speeches across the world were sent via Morse code and telegraphed to the leaders of area groups. Edith read some notable quotes from recent and relevant speeches at the meeting.

Since their own bicycle rally on August sixteenth was on everyone's mind, Edith shared a quote from Susan B. Anthony, who, when interviewed at the New York World Fair in 1886, declared, "Bicycling has done more to emancipate women than anything else in the world."

For the Milwaukee suffragettes, a bicycle rally would be the perfect statement. They had lined up a group of ladies who would begin the rally on horseback, riding side saddle in their finest garments and carrying the Wisconsin Suffragette flag.

In 1908, the popular style in jewelry featured gems in the colors purple, white, and green. Mappin & Webb, a London jeweler, issued a catalogue of jewelry in time for Christmas that featured precious stones such as amethysts and peridot. Although not connected to the suffragettes, the women had adopted the jewelry as a way to identify the sisterhood, using the same color scheme. Purple symbolized dignity, white for purity, and green for hope.

Sara had seen how the women had consistently used these colors in flags, banners, and badges. Some believed the colors were chosen as an acronym for "Give Women Votes" (green, white, and violet).

Although it was a myth, many suffragettes took advantage of the opportunity to make an anonymous statement. Sara, in fact, had such a broach, which she displayed proudly and without question since the fad existed long before the suffragettes adopted the colors as their own.

At this meeting, the group decided the bicyclists who followed the equestrians would display their colors. They would also wear the popular bloomers of the day, which were named after the American suffragette Amelia Bloomer, who had died in 1894. Inspired by fashionable women in Istanbul, Turkey, the bloomers had been invented for cycling, and had also been embraced by the suffragette movement.

To the disgust of some conservatives, ladies were giving up their large billowing skirts and corsets to don baggy trousers, a kind of divided skirt cinched at the knee. The battle of proper attire was fought largely on the huge popularity of cycling and the proper attire for that activity against the traditional propriety of female behavior and the unladylike appearance of "bloomers."Although not started by them or limited to them, the suffragettes embraced the fashion fad as their own.

"The cyclists in the rally will dress in their colors," Edith said, "carry banners, and decorate their bicycles with green, white, and purple crepe paper wound around their spokes. Those wearing green bloomers will go first, white second, and purple third. Following the cyclists will be several automobiles. We have a good showing of automobiles, including two Model T Fords, a touring car, as well as a Model T Torpedo Runabout. Ladies, we have quite a lineup of motor cars from across the country." Her enthusiasm was contagious.

Catherine said, "I think we can get a Case limousine from Racine, too. My cousin is an executive at the JI Case Threshing Machine Company there. I'll talk to him."

"Lovely." Edith smiled. "It looks like our little rally is turning into quite an event."

The meeting adjourned.

Catherine and Sara walked home together.

"This is so exciting," Sara said, finally voicing her thoughts. "I wish so much to be a part of it. I feel so useless in this cause I deeply care about. Oh, how I envy you for not having to hide your true feelings."

Catherine squeezed her hand, assuring Sara her efforts were appreciated all the same.

They reached Catherine's house.

"Would you care to sit on the porch for a bit? I can get us some cold lemonade."

Sara was somewhat parched, and gladly accepted the invitation. "Just for a while," she said. "Henry will be expecting me, and the children will stay up until I get home to tuck them in."

Sara and Catherine sat for another hour, catching up on the work of the suffragettes and all the other things happening in their lives. Sara shared her feeling of emptiness with her children growing up and going out on their own adventures.

"You will have company for a long time, Sara," said Catherine. "Liz is only seven and Adam will soon be three. And you will always have Henry. Don't envy my having no one. Not having anyone to share your feelings with can be very lonely." Her face became grim, though she held her smile.

"I guess I should count my blessings," Sara said, and realized the truth of her statement, turning her eyes to the setting sun. "Speaking of having someone to share feelings with, I must get home to my children. But remember, Catherine, if you ever need to talk to someone, I am always here for you."

"I know," said Catherine, her smile growing wide again. "You're a good friend." She rose and gave Sara a big hug.

Chapter Eighteen

The bicycle rally was in a few days and Sara wanted to see the festivities. She told her family August sixteenth would be a great day to go shopping for school attire and supplies. It was the perfect excuse to go downtown, which made her whole body tingle with excitement.

At dinner the night before the rally, Sara made the announcement. "We have had beautiful sunny days but now it is time we take care of getting ready for school. Ella should get some new dresses and we need galoshes for Liz. We won't need clothes for Thaddeus since he'll be wearing uniforms provided by his school, but we should pick up new underwear for him."

"Aw, Mother," Thaddeus protested, going red. "We don't need to talk about that at dinner."

"It is a perfectly acceptable subject." Sara smiled at her oldest son's sense of modesty. "And, oh yes, we will need shoes all around. Of course, we need school supplies, too. Children, perhaps you could each make up a list, so we are well prepared. Now mind you, just put the things you need on the list."

"Mother," protested Ella, "you might not consider some of the things for finishing school necessities, but barrettes and combs and such may be on my list."

"Understood," said Sara. "I will have the final say, so don't get too carried away."

Henry had been accustomed to the annual school shopping ritual and left it totally up to Sara. "I suppose you will need some money." He reached for his wallet. "How much will you need this year?"

"Hmm, I suspect thirty dollars will be sufficient," said Sara, standing up to clear the dishes.

"Thirty?" Henry asked, surprise on his face. "Wasn't it twenty last year?"

"The children are growing and finishing school isn't cheap. If you recall last year, we ran short and had to stop at the bank."

"You're right." Henry handed Sara forty dollars. "It will be hot tomorrow. Stop for ice cream at the soda shop after."

"Thank you, Henry." She bent down and kissed his forehead.

Someday, women will have their own money and not have to account for every penny. Henry is generous, but I hate having to justify every expenditure.

***

On the day of the rally, everyone was excited about shopping for new things. The children were up at the crack of dawn, putting on their good clothes for the trip downtown. The girls combed their hair into ringlets and splashed on a dab of toilet water. Lilac was their current favorite scent. They had a discussion on which bonnet and gloves they would wear, and decided their navy blue dresses with white gloves would be quite fashionable.

Sara chose her usual high button shoes and long black skirt with a white blouse. She donned her black fedora decorated with white gardenias and black gloves. She took her black, lacy parasol in case the sun was too hot on the parade route, although she didn't reveal her reason for needing shade.

Claudia prepared a hearty breakfast, complete with apple dumplings made from fresh apples in their orchard. Sara and the children were ready for their trek downtown.

It was a pleasant day, and the shoppes were less than two miles away, so they headed out on foot. When little Adam got tired, which he was most of the way, Thaddeus let him ride piggyback.

As they reached the downtown area, a crowd was gathering. Sara stretched for a look down the street. "Wonder what is going on?" she inquired, knowing full well the suffragettes were getting ready for their rally parade.

All the while they continued downtown, Sara contemplated where the best viewing area for the parade would be, and more importantly, how she would suggest they watch it.

As they walked along, Ella seemed more and more interested in the spectacle. By the time they reached Gimbles department store, the throng of onlookers had multiplied.

Ella spoke up, making Sara's plans much easier. "Can we watch, Mother? I know some of the people who may be in the parade and I think it will be fun."

"You know someone in the parade?" Sara asked, surprised.

"Why yes, Rose's Aunt Marie is a suffragette. She tells Rose about their work all the time and Rose tells me. I haven't mentioned it before because I know Father is opposed, but I think women should vote."

"I do believe my friend, Catherine, will be riding her bicycle in the parade, and I think Tillie may be in town in her new Model T automobile."

"Let's watch, let's watch," seven-year-old Liz said as she jumped up and down.

Adam was entranced with the horses, but Thaddeus only had his eye on the automobiles.

"Alright, children," Sara said. "We have the whole day, so let's stay here and watch." Sara let out a long breath of relief. She couldn't believe how easy it had been.

The parade began. The horses came first, looking beautiful with their high steps and elegant riders carrying the suffragette flags. The horse's tails and manes were braided with ribbons in green, white, and purple. Their hoofs clomped on the cobblestone in a steady beat. Sara felt her breath leave her chest, and she beamed with pride.

Adam clapped with glee as he watched them pass by. Clowns followed with their baggy costumes and big, round red noses. The clowns handled the pooper scoopers, so the bicycles wouldn't have to dodge the horses' deposits on their way down the street.

Thaddeus spotted the automobiles coming, and asked, "Mother, would it be alright if I go down there where the automobiles are?" He pointed to the next intersection.

"Me too, me too," cried Adam as he squealed with delight, waving his hands.

"Yes, Thaddeus, but keep an eye on Adam."

Adam and Thaddeus wasted no time. No sooner after they had permission, Thaddeus scooped up Adam and they were off.

"Come back here as soon as the parade finishes," Sara called after them.

Sara and the girls anxiously watched the parade as they searched for their friends on bicycles.

"Here they come," shouted Liz.

The bicycles approached—hundreds of them, riding six abreast. The first group was dressed in green bloomers and white shirtwaists with a sash crossing their chest that displayed the city or county they represented—Madison, Brown County, Washington County, Racine.

The second group was dressed all in white with colorful scarves of green and purple flying in the breeze. Their sashes announced Wisconsin Dells, La Crosse, and Wausau.

Sara took it all in.

Next came ladies in purple bloomers, sporting sashes from Florence County, Superior County, and Dodge County. Following close behind was a rainbow of colors. Those suffragettes hailed from Chicago, New York, St. Louis, and many other cities. All had colorful green, white, and purple crepe paperstreamers wound around their bicycle spokes, a carnival of spinning wheels.

Milwaukee suffragettes, the host city, brought up the rear. They carried banners with "WE ARE UNITED" and "GIVE US THE VOTE" written on them.

The crowd cheered loudly, blowing noisemakers and waving. The riders had practiced well and made figure eights and circles as they continued down the street, their wheels whirring on the roadway.

Sara spotted her friend, Catherine, and her heart soared at her friend's bravery. She cried out, "Catherine, Catherine."

Catherine waved and shouted back, "Sara, hop aboard!"

Sara waved her on her way, indicating her support but not a willingness to participate.

***

Clem Krueger, a local farmer, had come into town for supplies. He sat on his buckboard with his steed in hand, watching the festivities at the intersection, crossing the parade route.

His horse became fidgety with the unfamiliar snakelike hiss of the wheels on the cobblestone, and the loud noises emitting from the crowd. His horse jerked and bucked.

Clem tightened the reigns, and the bit cut into the horse's mouth.

"Thank God it is almost over," he muttered as he struggled to calm the horse.

The automobiles chugged along with their sputtering engines. The crowd cheered as the cars drove by in their magnificent splendor. As the last cars passed, their horns blaring, "OOGA, OOGA, OOGA," the crowd cheered and clapped wildly. The excitement in the air was palpable.

As soon as the last car passed, Clem saw a little boy dash out into the street to watch the parade disappear into the distance.

At the last *OOGA*, Clem no longer had control of his horse, and it surged forward.

His horse stampeded into the intersection to where the little boy still stood. Another older boy screamed out, but the small boy kept watching the distant cars, blind and deaf to anything else.

"Whoa, boy," Clem yelled and stood up on the buckboard, trying to regain control. He pulled back hard on the reigns with all his might, cutting deep into the horse's mouth.

The horse reared and came down with a crash, its hoof smashing into the unsuspecting little boy's head. Clem fell off the wagon, and the horse, now loose of Clem's hold on the reigns, went galloping down the street, buckboard and all.

***

Thaddeus was first to reach his brother. The sight made his stomach twist into knots, and Thaddeus dropped to his knees beside his battered body. "I am so sorry, Adam, I am so sorry," he cried. Tears streamed down his cheeks and he shook uncontrollably.

The crowd around Thaddeus made a mad dash to save the little boy, but to no avail. As they reached Adam, his tiny body already lay there crushed and bloody. The buckboard had run over his chest and the hitch on the back had dragged him a half a block before he broke loose. Adam lay on the cobblestones, dead, with one arm almost severed and his shin bone protruding through his leg.

One of the bystanders pulled Thaddeus up and led him away from the scene, back to the side of the road. He sat there with his head in his hands, guilt smashing through him just like the buckboard. He sobbed uncontrollably, wishing with all his heart he had watched Adam more closely.

***

Sara, Ella, and Liz had enjoyed the parade until the end. As the last automobile passed, they noticed a lot of commotion in the area where Adam and Thaddeus had gone to watch the automobiles.

Sara had expected them to be running back to their place in front of Gimbles, but she didn't see them.

Whatever was going on must have taken their attention. "Come on, girls, let's go find your brothers," Sara said. "Keep your eyes out."

As people passed by, they heard there had been a dreadful accident involving a horse and a boy. Sara began to panic, walking on her toes to try and see over the crowd. "Hurry, girls," she shouted.

They dashed to the site as quickly as they could. Sara hiked up her hemline, dropped her parasol, and ran as fast as she could.

One of Sara's neighbors was near the edge of the commotion and grabbed Sara. "Don't go," he said, his voice full of dread. "Don't go, Sara. It's Adam."

Terror jolted through her. Sara tried to pull herself away from his grasp, but others pushed her back, repeating the same words. She shouldn't go to Adam.

"But I must, I must. That's my baby," Sara cried, flailing against the arms that held her. "He needs me!"

A constable came by and took Sara by the elbow. "I am so sorry, madam. You can't go into the road. The boy was run over by a runaway buckboard."

"But he needs me!" Sara pleaded to the man through her sobs.

"I am sorry, but you can't," the officer gulped. "Your son is dead."

The world went black, and Sara fainted.

Chapter Nineteen

Ella and Liz stood in the crowd, shaking, their arms wrapped tightly around each other as people gathered around Sara to aid her.

"Girls, go get your pa," someone in the crowd yelled.

Ella didn't know what to do, because tears had welled in her eyes and everything had become blurry.

"We will tend to your ma," a woman said.

"Father!" Ella exclaimed, rubbing her eyes. "Come, Liz, we must get Father."

They ran the three blocks to the bank where their father was working.

***

Sara was aware of nothing until she opened her eyes and found herself in a hospital bed. Henry was at her side, holding her hand. Seeing their mother stir, the children leapt to her bedside.

"Mother, Mother, we thought you had died, too," Liz cried out, her face puffy from crying.

Sara remembered what had happened, and her blood went cold. She tried to hold back the tears for the children's sake, but her emotions swept over her and opened a floodgate. She cried inconsolably.

Henry, grief in his eyes, pulled her into his arms and held her tight as he stroked her long auburn hair. He kissed her forehead and said gently, "We will get through this."

A nurse stepped into the room with a glass of water and a pill. "Here, Mrs. Dewberry, drink this. It will help you relax."

At that moment Sara would've done anything to take away the pain that ripped through her heart. *Adam, her baby. Poor Adam.*

She was soon fast asleep.

Three days later, Sara left the hospital, but she was not the same woman who had gathered her children around her at the parade route.

The smile had slipped from her lips, the sparkle had faded from her eyes. Henry took her from the hospital in a wheelchair because she couldn't move her feet. She had been in a catatonic state for two days. Her body would not move, but her mind understood everything.

She knew, impossible as it was, that she had to prepare for a funeral. Henry took care of most of the arrangements, but Sara wondered how she would ever make it through the funeral itself without breaking down again.

The funeral was held at the Presbyterian Church on the following Saturday. Oh, how she wished Reverend Reinhart and Ruby were there. The new pastor was fresh out of seminary. Pastor Nelson was a pleasant person, as was his wife, but he was much too young to understand the grief of losing a child. His children were young and vibrant, brimming with life.

The day before the funeral, Pastor Nelson met with the Dewberrys in their home. "Let us begin with a prayer," he said, clasping Sara's hands in his.

Prayer! Sara silently scoffed. *What kind of god takes our children away?*

Pastor Nelson must have sensed Sara's pain and rejection. He squeezed her hand tighter and began, "Father in heaven, we thank you for the time you have given us with your dear child, Adam. We would have liked him to spend more time with us here on Earth, but the angels have carried him back to you, his sweetness and innocence preserved forever in your arms. We will one day see him again in heaven. Keep him safe; keep us all safe in your arms. Amen."

His words provided Sara with a small degree of comfort, but she still wondered, *Did God think I'm a bad parent? Did God punish me because I wasn't there to protect him?*

A wave of guilt spread over her. *If I had not been so involved with the suffragettes, would I still be holding Adam, and soon another babe who never had a chance at life at all?*

The questions made Sara shake, and she bit back tears.

Pastor Nelson went on, "Tomorrow, we will be celebrating Adam's life. We will speak of the joys he brought into our lives. Even in his short life, he taught us much. He taught us how to love unconditionally; he taught us how to appreciate little things like flowers and bugs. He taught us how to smile at adversity. He taught us perseverance in his first steps and his first words. He dreamed about fantasies while we were too involved with practical things to believe they could ever exist, but he taught us never to give up on our dreams. He taught us to take care of others. He even taught us that a little mischief isn't always a bad thing."

Sara was now listening intently. Then she remembered what Adam had said as he had watched the clowns in the parade.

"It's okay if the horses poop; God gave us funny clowns to pick it up."

With that thought still in her head, Sara spoke her first words in three days. "Horse poop."

"What?" Henry was shocked. "What did you say?"

Reverend Nelson seemed taken aback by her comment as well.

"It's...okay," she said. "God will make...a way...to...pick it up." A feeble smile crossed her lips.

Reverend Nelson smiled. "Yes, He will. Adam was here to fulfill a purpose. He most certainly has done that. Adam returned to God's arms because his work here was done. Our time is not. If we give up now, Adam's life would have been in vain. We all must go on."

***

People from far and wide came for the little boy's funeral, crowding the church.

In the last pew sat a man crouched into the seat, his tattered hat in his hand. His big, arthritis-riddled hands were rough with the labor of the land. His face was thin, his eyes red. His head bowed in prayer. "Father, forgive me. I can't live with this blood on my hands."

Clem Krueger went home that night and hung himself on the rafters in his hay loft.

***

Somehow, Sara made it through the funeral and was even able to comfort her other children through the ordeal, especially Thaddeus, who was overcome with grief. She knew she would struggle with the despair for a long time. Thoughts of Adam would stay with her throughout her life. He would never be forgotten.

***

Henry suffered the funeral in silence, struggling to deal with the thought that his son had died as a result of a suffragette parade. Anger filled his heart. "Damn those suffragettes!"

Chapter Twenty

The day after Labor Day, Thaddeus boarded the train for St. John's Military Academy in Delafield. School was in session the week before, but due to the death of his brother, Thaddeus was granted time off.

St. John's Military Academy had been founded in 1884 by Reverend Sidney T. Smythe as a private, all-male college preparatory and leadership development school. It was a highly regarded school where honesty, respect, and self-discipline were the cornerstones. His father had announced the acceptance of his son into the school in the *Milwaukee Journal*, beaming with pride at Thaddeus.

But Thaddeus had all the apprehensions of any youth venturing out on his own for the first time. He hated leaving his mother at a time when she needed him, but at the same time he looked forward to this new chapter in his life.

He struggled daily with the guilt he carried for his brother's death. He'd never forgotten he had been responsible for watching over Adam. He hoped this new school would help him cope and atone. He would endure whatever afflicted him without complaint and learn to be a good soldier.

***

Sara, Henry, and the girls stood on the platform and waved as the train chugged away with Thaddeus. They were now a family of four.

Ella started Stevens Finishing School and Liz was in second grade at Washington Elementary. Sara's nest grew more and more empty. Her heart ached.

Sara found she had a lot of time on her hands. Claudia did most of the cleaning and other household chores, but on days that Claudia had a full load of housework, Sara took over dinner preparations—unless company was expected. Sara had never considered herself a good cook.

She had knitting and other handiwork to keep her occupied, but she found that those activities gave her too much time to think about Adam. She missed seeing his smile.

Typhoid fever had been rampant in 1909, and Sara had contracted a mild case while she was pregnant with Adam. Claudia had been there for the other children. At the time, Sara had been anticipating the birth of her fourth child. She had worried all through the pregnancy that the typhoid may have affected the baby and was elated when Adam had been born perfectly healthy. Sara had pulled through and won the battle hundreds of others had lost. Adam had been her little miracle, always smiling, a perfect angel. Maybe that was what he really was, an angel.

After several weeks of mourning and pacing, Sara decided it was time to leave the house and get outside. It was a warm day in early October. The leaves had changed into a blaze of color and were falling to the ground in a deep blanket.

Sara went for a walk through Astor Park, the leaves rustling under her feet. Her thoughts traveled to the suffragettes, and after walking for a bit, she stopped at Catherine's house.

"Why, Sara, it is so good to see you up and about," Catherine remarked with a gentle smile. "Come in, come in." Catherine put a pot on the stove for tea.

They sat in the parlor, discussing the unseasonable warm weather and Wisconsin's anticipated long, cold winter. Their conversation was quite cordial and turned to the latest fashions of the day, an obvious attempt on Catherine's part to avoid discussing the trauma experienced two months earlier.

"Did you notice, Sara? A more risqué look is in *Vogue*, with hemlines revealing a lot more ankle." Catherine picked up the magazine from a nearby table. "The dresses this fall aren't accentuating the waistline. Look at this one, featuring an empire waistline," she pointed out. "Isn't it smart?"

Sara observed with a slight nod. "Of course, with ankles showing, shoes are becoming a much more prominent fashion statement."

Catherine picked up a millinery magazine from her side table. "And look at the hats; they are still our crowning glory and available in a wide array of styles. Look here, these wide-brimmed picture hats that frame your face. Aren't they beautiful?" She pointed to another page in the magazine.

Catherine turned the page. "Turbans are popular and worn with the casual bloomers."

Her friend kept the conversation light but had alluded to a topic much less superficial at the heart of Sara's visit. It made her heart skip.

"Ella keeps me informed on what is in and how I must look to achieve a sophisticated look." Sara laughed. "She is quite the fashion plate since attending Stevens Finishing School."

"How are the children doing at their new schools?" Catherine asked.

Sara smiled at the concern in her friend's tone. "Ella is thrilled with her new school, but she misses having Rose in her classes. They have remained fast friends and Ella passes on the couture information and the many proprieties of being an elegant lady. They spend hours on the weekend walking around my house with books on their heads." Sara laughed. "It is quite hilarious sometimes. Rose is much more of a tomboy and has a difficult time maintaining the proper lady look. But Ella is a patient teacher."

"What about academics? Is she getting an adequate education, and does she have plans for her future?"

"They feel young ladies should be quite educated." Sara hesitated. "That is, to converse properly with their spouse's associates and in school meetings with their children's teachers." Sara rolled her eyes.

"But is it preparing her for college?" Catherine asked, clearly curious.

"Actually, yes, it is. Their courses in history, science, and mathematics are quite good. Of course, they also emphasize the areas of language, arts, and social graces as well. Ella is starting her French lessons next semester."

Catherine put the magazine aside. "What about a career choice? Has she a goal in mind?"

"Hmm. I'm not for certain, but she has had an inclination to become a teacher."

"And what about Thaddeus? How is he doing at the academy?" Catherine refilled their teacups.

Sara appreciated her genuine interest. "I received a letter from him yesterday. He is struggling a bit with the regimen, but he believes in the program, and even said he might consider West Point after he graduates. But I know my son—he may change his mind twenty times before he reaches that decision."

"I really thought he might take up zoology or herpetology since he's so fond of reptiles." Catherine chuckled. "He is such a free spirit; I find it hard to picture him in military mode."

"I know. He wants so much to please his father, but he did seem interested in the curriculum, particularly in airplanes." Sara took a sip of tea and took a moment to think of her son. "If he finds his niche, I think he will do well."

"So, what does Liz think of all of this?" Catherine asked.

Sara laughed. "Liz turned eight last week, so she is happy playing jump rope and hopscotch. She does well in school, but she has this strange obsession of patching up her doll. I do hope this is not a subconscious need to fix because of Adam." Sara thought of the idea and nearly choked on her tea, her knuckles going white as she clenched them to regain her composure. "She misses him terribly, especially with her other siblings off on their own adventures."

"Well, keep an eye on her, but as long as she enjoys her playtime with her friends, I wouldn't be too concerned."

"You're probably right." Sara decided to accept that assessment for now.

"Speaking of friends, Sara, we miss you at our meetings. Do you think you might like to help us sometime?"

"Well, as a matter of fact, that's why I stopped by." Sara took a deep breath, happy to finally approach the subject on her mind. "I have had a lot of time to think, and I want to be involved in the Chicago Rally in November."

"Oh?" asked Catherine. "And what brought that on?"

"I've been thinking a lot about Reverend Nelson's words about Adam. We must be persistent; we must not give up on our dreams. That is what Adam taught us. He wanted horses to fly; he just knew they could…he had a book on unicorns, and he insisted that one day our horse, Nell, would grow wings. Nothing could dissuade him."

"And what do flying horses have to do with the movement?"

"Hmm, I presume, getting the vote for women has to be easier than making horses fly," Sara said.

Catherine tilted her head in puzzlement. "Is there more to this story?"

"Yes," Sara responded quickly. "Horse poop."

"What?" Catherine asked, giving Sara a look like she had gone totally daffy. "Can you explain?"

"We don't have to worry about horse poop, because God will send someone to clean it up."

Catherine stared blankly at her.

"Catherine! We have a dream. We can't give it up." Sara clenched her fists. "The arguments against it are a bunch of horse poop, and if we work together, we can clean it up."

Catherine laughed, lightening the mood. "Woman, you are talking in circles, but I get the message."

"We won't ever get this cleaned up unless we get started."

"What about Henry?"

"Someday he will know, but for now, I can't tell him...it would only make things much more difficult."

"Too much horse poop?"

"Exactly," said Sara, unable to keep from laughing. "Ella has friends connected to the cause, and she is a believer in the movement. I need to do it for her...and for Liz."

"Let's do it," exclaimed Catherine. "How will you manage to get to Chicago?"

"Early Christmas shopping with the book club, maybe?"

"You *have* given this some thought."

"I have had a lot of time on my hands and all I've had to do is think. I can't cry anymore; I can't change anything at home. Life is short, and we have much to accomplish," Sara said, smiling at her friend.

Chapter Twenty-one

The following Tuesday, Sara, armed with her bag full of books, headed for the library. Once again, she received a welcome from her comrades who had missed her. They all shared their condolences, but, respecting her privacy, did not dwell on it. Sara was grateful.

Sara spotted her old friend, Tillie Morgenson, and went to greet her. "Tillie, how wonderful to see you. When did you get into town?"

"Last week," Tillie said, giving Sara a brief hug. "I meant to stop by to see you, but I am afraid I must walk a narrow line. Everyone knows I am an active participant in the movement. I wasn't sure what your current status is with your husband and the movement. We wouldn't want Claudia's tongue wagging. I was hoping I would see you here this evening."

"Henry still doesn't know. Since the Bicycle Rally, he is even more adamant that the suffragettes are to blame for all the woes of the world. But, Tillie, this is something I need to do."

Tillie pursed her lips together. "I heard about the parade incident, Sara. I am so sorry."

"Thank you. It was very difficultfor me and my family, but it wouldn't have mattered if it was the fourth of July parade. It is tragic and difficult to talk about…" Sara wiped away a tear.

"I understand." Tillie patted her arm. "You know I am here for you if I can help in any way."

"I know. We will get together soon. Looks like we are ready to start the meeting."

Sara took a seat next to Tillie, then Edith called the meeting to order.

"Ladies, we have about five weeks to get our plans in order for the Chicago trip. We will be taking the train there. From the railroad station, we'll join our fellow suffragettes from around the state and march to the courthouse, much like we did in Racine. Does anyone have any suggestions as to what we want to do specifically for our group to shine?"

"We could wear our bloomer outfits from the bicycle rally," someone called out.

"No, no, it will be much too cold in November," said another woman from the back of the room.

Catherine said, "We should be distinguished and proper."

Comments were spoken throughout the room.

"Warm hats and muffs would be good."

"Yes, let's go to Chicago in style! Let's *wow* them."

The room erupted with sounds of approval.

"Get out your Sunday best; we are high stepping in Chicago." Catherine pranced about in gala movements, and her comrades chuckled and clapped in support.

Edith laughed. "Well, ladies, it appears we have made a decision. All in favor?"

A resounding approval rang out.

"Anyone opposed?" Edith asked.

No one responded.

Sara heard much chatter about the shopping trips many women were about to embark on to spruce up their wardrobes for the event. Sara's closet was filled with expensive outfits. She never wanted to be a socialite, but her husband's position required a certain degree of pomp and circumstance.

I think I will wear the black velvet skirt with matching short jacket. If it is cold, my fox jacket and matching hat would be quite elegant.

"Ladies, we know that wardrobe is important, but is there anything else we need to address?" Edith inquired.

"Banners. Mine is torn!"

"Sashes. Mine, too."

"Flags, do we have enough?"

"Speeches," Sara called out.

"I will get the flags," Catherine volunteered. "Wilson's Hardware Store just got a new supply."

"Thanks, Catherine. And what about the sashes? How many will we need?" Edith asked. "Can I have a show of hands for all who need a new one?"

There was some murmuring, and several hands went up. Sara remembered the last time she had her sash was in that alley in Racine. She shivered. Her hand went up.

Edith counted. "Looks like we need seven, and we should have a few extras. I think ten would be fine." She looked around. "Can any of you put them together?"

Sara and three other women volunteered.

"We have extra fabric in the storage room," Edith informed the group. "You can pick it up whenever you are ready to work on the sashes. You can discuss it on your own and decide if you will do it together or individually."

Sara and the other ladies nodded in agreement.

"Speeches!" Edith went on, clasping her hands together. "Tillie has agreed to speak on behalf of the Milwaukee group, and of course, many of the other locales have chosen speakers to represent them. Some are quite eloquent. We have an added treat, since our own Carrie Chapman will be speaking. She is getting on in years, but she has been our model for decades. We are honored that she will be coming from Iowa to join us in Chicago. For anyone who isn't aware, Carrie was born in Ripon."

"Looks like speeches are taken care of," said Catherine with a proud nod. "What about flyers? We have some, but we will have to create a lot more, and we don't have the church's equipment to use anymore."

"We can use the library mimeograph, but it would be best to make them when we are not so busy. After hours probably," Edith offered.

"I can do that," Sara said, volunteering, her hand eagerly raised.

All eyes in the room went to Sara.

She had been gone for several months, and now she was volunteering for almost every job. She wanted to prove she was still dedicated to this cause, no matter her personal affairs.

"That should be enough to keep us busy for some time," said Tillie. "This group is as active as any I have seen across the country. I am so proud to have been part of it."

Edith thanked Tillie for all she has done, and everyone applauded. Then, Edith wound things up.

"Now," Edith said, "it is nearing our time to leave. If anyone asks, our discussion today was on the poetry of Phillis Wheatly." It was the practice of the group to have a brief biography or sampling of works to keep up the ruse of the book club.

Tillie cleared her throat and read: "Phillis came to America from Africa as a small child. She was purchased and emancipated by John Wheatly, a Boston merchant. He raised her with his wife, who taught her how to read and write. His two children, Mary and Nathaniel, treated her with kindness and as a member of their family. Mary took note of Phillis's talent and reported to her mother that 'Phillis is a genius.' Initially, Mrs. Wheatly laughed, but at Mary's prodding, she read Phillis' poems. She was quite impressed, and showed them to her husband, who had some of them printed and distributed. People couldn't believe that a mere girl wrote them, particularly a black girl. Later, she was invited to England, where she was highly lauded.

"Phillis Wheatly wrote to General Washington, sending him some of her poems. He was impressed and invited her to visit him. After that, her life took a turn for the worst. She married a man who did not treat her well, became ill and died in 1784. She was only thirty-one years old. Her fame and poetry has lived on," Tillie concluded.

"Here is one of her poems that she wrote as a child.

> *On being brought from Africa to America*
> *Twas mercy brought me from my Pagan land,*
> *Taught my benighted soul to understand*
> *That there's a God, that there's a Saviour too:*
> *Once I redemption neither sought nor knew.*
> *Some view our sable race with scornful eye,*
> *"Their colour is a diabolic dye."*
> *Remember, Christians, Negroes, black as Cain,*
> *May be refin'd, and join th' angelic train.*

"Ladies have courage," Tillie said, and closed the book. "A child recognized her plight and spoke her mind. That was 150 years ago. Let her be an example to all of us. Never give up."

Immediately after the meeting, work began on their preparation for the Chicago rally.

Sara worked diligently and spent time both at the library printing flyers and at Martha's house sewing banners. They were prepared, and before they knew it, November had arrived.

Sara was excited but nervous. This would be her second out of town rally and recollections of the first weighed heavily on her mind. The work was a good distraction from her thoughts and her pain, and she hoped the rally would help heal her.

Chapter Twenty-two

The ladies dressed in their finery and had lunch in the dining car of the Chicago Northwestern passenger train en route. The train pulled into the Chicago station at twelve-thirty p.m. on November 5, 1912. It was a typical early winter day in Chicago. The wind was strong, but then Chicago was known as the "windy city."

Sara could hardly contain the excitement she felt inside as they departed the train.

Most of the women wore black dresses with hemlines down to their ankles, with various color coats that were either fingertip length or shorter. They carried fur muffs and had donned hats of fox and mink. Some wore felt hats adorned with feather plumes or artificial foliage or ribbons appropriate to the season. Many women had scarves around their necks to fend off the cold winds coming from Lake Michigan.

Sara was happy to be part of the group. *What a magnificent and elegant display. This ought to get respect.*

At the end of the platform, they put on their Wisconsin Suffragette sashes and unfurled their flags. According to plan, they'd sing suffragette songs as they marched the parade route.

They sang in perfect three-part harmony. Their practice sessions at every meeting for the past month had paid off. The women strode confidently forward and began with a plea of "Girls of To-Day" to the young women on the streets.

> *"Girls of today! Give ear!*
> *Never since time began*
> *Has come to the race of man*
> *A year, a day, an hour,*
> *So full of promise and power*

As the time that now is here!"

Their message heralded the strength and courage that was theirs. Sara sang proudly, her head held high.

Other songs spoke of women bringing men into the world, women guiding men through life: teaching, preaching, and being the power behind their men. The songs asked young women to heed their calling and stand up for their rights.

As the march continued, they told their story of strife and hope. They had come a long way and suffered much. They felt progress, but now, men and some women were trying to convince the government that women *didn't want* change. This was a notion demanding a response and the suffragettes were prepared with a rebuttal.

They marched on with voices clear and strong, singing the words to "Women Do Not Want It" by Charlotte Perkins Gilman.

> *"When the woman suffrage argument first stood upon its legs,*
> They answered it with cabbages, they answered it with eggs,
> *They answered it with ridicule, they answered it with scorn,*
> *They thought it a monstrosity that should not have been born."*

Sara was reminded of all the women who had come before her. They tried valiantly with reason and were met with ridicule. The song spoke of their growing power and the opposition grasping at straws, trying to refute their abilities, claiming women were inferior, naming disabilities, physical and emotional. The conclusion of the objections was that women "could not have the ballot because they were not fit."

Not fit, indeed! Thank God for the suffragettes who stood up to them and proved them wrong.

The claim by objectors was that women did not want it, so it shouldn't be.

Didn't want it, such rubbish!

Their song went on sarcastically noting:

> *"'Tis such a tender thoughtfulness! So exquisite a care!*
> *Not to pile on our frail shoulders what we do not wish to bear!*
> *Did we ask for the beating stick no thicker than your thumb?*

Did we want to be forbidden from trades that pay, lower wages?
How dare men demand that not a woman's child, nor her own body, is her own?"

Their voices got louder, and the women clearly took the words to heart.

A few men harrumphed at the thought, and one even spat on the ground to portray his disdain. The song obviously struck a chord with all who heard it.

It became a challenge to the male opposition, and the suffragettes responded in kind. From somewhere in the crowd, jeers erupted. The women marched on, paying little mind to the fools in the crowd who would never understand. Sara lifted a fist and sang louder, feeling her dress blow wildly around her in the wind.

Then from somewhere in the crowd came a shout. "Go home, suffragettes. You have no place in this town."

Another voice rang out, "Take this!"

From the crowd, eggs flew at the suffragettes. Then, rotten tomatoes. They splashed violently into the ladies marching, soiling their dresses, coating their hair.

The same voice snidely shouted, "Aren't you the fine ladies now!"

Sara placed her hand on her cheek, wiping at the egg that dripped down her face and onto her collar. Rotten tomato squished onto her finery, and Sara could not be kind and meek any longer.

She reached down onto the road, picked up a small rock, and hurled it at the smug man in the crowd.

Other women took her cue and responded in the same manner.

Soon the crowd was ablaze, accusations flung alongside stones and vegetables. A total melee erupted with shouts and fists flying when the vegetables ran out.

The confrontation lasted a short while, and for Sara, it was a release. The whole scene energized her.

The police came in with their nightsticks, attempting to break up the riot. Someone came up behind Sara. Feeling that person touching her and remembering Racine, she whirled and swung around, hurling a great punch into a man's chest.

Then recognizing it was an officer, Sara gasped. But it was too late.

He grabbed her arm just as it made contact and swung her around. He snapped handcuffs onto her wrists. She and several of her friends, including Catherine and Edith, were placed in a paddy wagon and taken off to jail.

It wasn't until she was contained that Sara realized what a mess she was in. Her hat was skewed, her hair tangled. She had dried egg yolk on her face and a bruise on her chin. Her dress was ripped and ruined by tomato stains. But that was the least of her problems. She realized then, not only would she miss the speeches at the Courthouse, but she'd also miss her train ride home.

As the officer booked her into jail, she realized they would call her husband. Her secret would be out.

The booking officer led her to a seat. "Name?" he asked mechanically.

For a second, she thought of giving an alias but figured that would only get her into more trouble. "Sara Dewberry," she said quietly.

"Address?"

Sara hesitated.

"What is your address?" he repeated.

She blew out a breath. "It's 3012 Astor Street."

"Milwaukee?"

"Yes," Sara murmured, looking down at her lap.

"Husband's name," he continued, "and speak up."

"Do you need to know?" Sara said louder, clutching her dress anxiously.

"So, your husband doesn't know what you are up to," the officer guessed. "Lady, he is going to know now, because he will have to come pick you up."

Sara shuddered. There was no other option. Shame coursed through her. "Henry... Henry Dewberry."

She was placed in a cell with several other suffragettes. Her heart pounded. She knew her husband was being called. The deceit was over. Was her marriage over? Sara wept silently.

***

Henry answered the new telephone that had been installed when the children had gone away to school. He wanted to reach them in case of an emergency.

"Mr. Dewberry? Mr. Henry Dewberry?"

"Yes," Henry said warily, hearing the strange man's voice speaking through the telephone.

"Mr. Dewberry, this is Officer O'Brien with the Chicago Police Department."

Henry panicked, thinking there must have been another terrible accident. "Yes, what is it?"

"Well, Mr. Dewberry, it seems your wife Sara has gotten herself arrested."

"What? Sara? Arrested?" Henry asked incredulously.

"Yes, we have one Sara Dewberry arrested for disorderly conduct on the streets of Chicago. She was arrested, along with several of her suffragette friends."

"Sara? Sara is not a suffragette." Henry wrinkled his brow and tried to make sense of it all.

"I understand Mr. Dewberry, but when she was arrested, she was marching with a group of suffragettes from Milwaukee. She is wearing their banner," Officer O'Brien explained. "You are not the first husband to find out in this manner what his wife is involved with."

Henry was speechless.

Officer O'Brien went on. "Can you pick up your wife? She can be released into your custody. If you don't come, she will be held for three days."

Henry was furious. "I will come tomorrow," he stated in a curt manner.

"Very well," said Officer O'Brien. "Have a good day."

Henry slammed down the receiver. *Who else heard the conversation? The operator for sure, and possibly some of my neighbors.* The house telephone was on a party line with four other families.

That evening, Henry stomped through the house. He poured himself a double bourbon. He snapped at the children when they inquired about their mother, leaving them and Claudia to speculate.

The next morning, Henry got into his new Model T Ford that he had purchased as a surprise for Sara. It was a bit early for Christmas, but he thought it would be a wonderful gift. He had picked it up the morning before, expecting to astonish Sara with it when she got home with her packages.

He knew she had dressed up that morning, and he had planned to take her for a long ride before dinner after picking her up from the train station. She would still have a long ride, but it'd be a far cry from the ride he had planned.

Chapter Twenty-three

In the morning, Henry called the bank to explain that Sara had missed the train and he was going to pick her up. He had spent a restless night lost in his own head, and now had a long drive with even more time to think.

The car chug chugged and then it stopped.

Henry slid out and cranked it up again. This time, the car started and ran without a problem. The longer he drove, the madder he became. *How dare she deceive me? How did she get mixed up in this?*

He remembered Sara's trip to Racine last April. His suspicions multiplied. *How long had she been involved with these suffragettes?*

When he arrived at the police station in Chicago, he was furious. He scrawled his name on the papers put before him. He glanced at the charges. There it was in black and white. Disorderly Conduct.

An officer brought Sara out. She was a mess. Henry grabbed her by the elbow and pulled her out the door. He didn't even say "hello."

"Thank you for coming for me," Sara said softly.

Henry whispered something under his breath and continued toward the automobile.

"What is this?" Sara asked when she saw the car.

"It was a surprise for you, but not nearly the surprise you sprang on me. Get In." Henry ripped open the door for her. He went to the front and cranked the engine. It started without hesitation, and they rode in silence on the trip home.

When they arrived back, the children were already in bed. Henry said bluntly, "Go to bed. We will talk in the morning. I'll sleep in Thaddeus' room."

***

Sara went quietly to her room. It was best to let Henry sleep on this.

She took a bath to rid herself of the jailhouse smell that permeated her clothing. She lay back in the claw foot tub and tried to relax, but her body was tense, her lip kept trembling. Henry was furious, more furious than she had ever seen him in her life. And she didn't blame him.

Now that the truth is out, I won't back down. He will just have to adjust.

She put her head on her fluffy down pillow, covered up with the warm comforter, and fell asleep. It was a restless sleep, but she managed to keep her eyes shut.

In the morning, Sara saw the children off to school and sat at the dining room table with a breakfast of oatmeal, fruit, and fresh steamy coffee. Henry entered the room and took a seat opposite her at the table. Sara sighed; her fingers clenched around her cup in anticipation.

Henry cleared his throat. "Sara, I don't know what has come over you, but I suspect this behavior has been going on for some time. You have lied, you have deceived me, and you have broken the trust between us. You have put our children in danger and have caused humiliation to me and to our family."

"Henry, I am sorry."

Henry interrupted her. "I don't need your apology. Just listen."

She ducked her head and let him speak.

Henry cleared his throat and continued. "Sara, I can see no way for us to go on. I will arrange for a room for you for the next two weeks at Williams boarding house. After those two weeks, you will have to find your accommodations elsewhere. I'd suggest you return to Wausau where your family lived."

"But Henry..." Sara's eyes welled with tears. "My family is gone. I have no one in Wausau. The girls will not want to adjust to a new community and schools."

"The girls will not be moving," Henry said firmly.

"You don't expect me to leave my children!" Sara blurted, getting to her feet. "You can't take them from me."

"Sara, be reasonable. You have no money, you have no skills, and you have no home. You can never be a proper mother to them. They will be staying with me. It will be easier on them, and you, if you just leave the area."

Panic coursed through her, and her hands shook in a frenzy. The room went blurry. It was true, women had no property; they *were* property. She had no skills to support her children. She had no place to go.

"Henry, please, don't do this. I will give up the suffragettes. I will be a dutiful wife. I will do anything you say—but please, don't take my children from me," Sara begged, her heart pounding.

"I'm sorry, Sara. The decision is made. I'll make arrangements for the room today, and I'll make the payment for two weeks. Pack your things. I'll be taking you there at noon. I will speak to my attorney and arrange for a small amount of money to tide you over, but you will have to arrange for employment. It would be best if you relocate as soon as possible so you can find work at your new location."

"I'll stay here. I'll find work here," Sara sobbed, her hands in fists.

His face was unreadable. "That is not be a good idea. When I speak to my attorney, he'll order no further contact with the children." Henry got up from the table, took his hat and umbrella, and went to work.

Sara couldn't think. She collapsed onto the table, breathing heavily. What would she do? How would she survive? Women didn't get money on their own. In fact, if a woman worked, her paycheck was delivered to her husband or father. Sara's parents had died years ago, but her inheritance had gone into the home she and Henry lived in, *her* home. The deed was in her husband's name. Even if it was not, she would not take her children's home away.

And Henry... Dear Henry. She had deceived him. He had every right to be angry. Despite everything, her heart broke for him. She loved Henry with all her heart. And now, she was losing him...

***

Henry went to see his attorney that very day. David Daniels had been a good friend and Henry's counselor for years. It was with a heavy heart Henry entered his office that day.

"What can I help you with today?" David greeted Henry. "You look a bit down at the mouth."

"David, I don't know how to say this gently," Henry began, "so I will just blurt it out. Sara and I have separated. I am securing a place for her at Mrs. Williams boarding house, and I wish to deny her access to the children." Grim-faced, he stared down at the floor.

"Whew!" David gasped. "You and Sara, umm, you and Sara…I don't know what to say. Are you seeking a divorce?"

"Oh, no!" Henry said. "Divorce has never entered my mind."

"Well, what is it you want? You and Sara have always seemed happy," David said. "Maybe we should just talk for a while. Tell me what happened."

"Sara is a suffragette," Henry blurted out, his hands shaking. "Yesterday, I drove to Chicago to get her out of jail. She has been lying to me for months."

"I see," said David. "I understand your anger and frustration. I'm trying to imagine how I would react if it were my wife, Ruth. Henry, is it unforgivable?"

"I don't know," he said honestly. "I just don't know."

"Isn't it a bit drastic to deny Sara access to her children?" David inquired.

"Yes, but Adam died while they were watching a suffragette parade." Henry choked back tears and lowered his gaze.

"Surely, you don't blame Sara for Adam's death."

"No, no, no." Henry shook his head. "Sara is a very headstrong woman, but she is a good person and a caring mother." He hesitated, drawing a breath.

"Then, what is the problem?" David asked, his eyebrows arched in confusion.

"Sara needs to learn her place!" Henry insisted, wiping the tears away. "Until she understands what she has lost and how easy her life has been, she will never give up this foolishness."

"But Henry, taking children away from a caring mother is very drastic."

"Precisely. I want her to feel the pain I've felt so that she begs to come home and will never stray again. The stronger the pain, the more quickly she will learn and will not fall back into her ways."

"Have you asked her to give up the suffragettes?"

"No, I didn't ask her. She begged to stay and promised to give up these shenanigans, but I can't trust her. She deceived me in her activities up until now. How can I believe her going forward? No, she must pay the price to learn."

"Very well then," said David with a grave expression. "You can provide for your children and you have the right to keep them, if you so desire. I'll draw up the papers and schedule a meeting before the judge. We will ask for a legal separation, giving you sole custody of the children without rights of visitation for Sara. From there on, it's in the judge's hands."

Henry stood. "Thank you, David."

Chapter Twenty-four

Sara packed the clothes she needed, some personal items, her books and knitting, and a few mementos of her children—photographs and pictures they had drawn. She managed to get everything in two bags and somehow managed to keep herself from crying further. She took a small bottle of her husband's cologne and tucked it into her bag. She wanted his scent near her, despite everything.

"I will see my children. I will fight for them," she vowed.

At noon, Henry arrived to take her to Williams boarding house. "Are you ready?" he asked with a blank stare.

"Yes," whispered Sara. "Henry, can't we talk, can't we work this out?"

"Maybe you should have thought of that before you went off making a fool of me behind my back," Henry shot back. "Let's go."

Henry grabbed her bags and hurried to the automobile. "I thought you might enjoy one last ride in the automobile I purchased so you could ride in comfort and style."

Without speaking a word, they continued to the boarding house.

Once there, they got out of the automobile and Henry took her bags up to the doorstep. His face revealed nothing. "Goodbye, Sara. You'll be hearing from Counselor Daniels sometime in the next few days." He turned and walked toward the vehicle.

"Henry!" Sara called out.

Henry turned.

Sara was silent for a moment as she stared at him. "Goodbye." She stumbled up the steps, her feet feeling as if they were held down by heavy weights. She knocked on the door.

Mrs. Williams, a short, chubby lady with a wide smile and rosy cheeks, swung open the door. Her white hair was tied back in a bun.

She wore a green frock covered by a ruffled white apron. "Sara, my dear, I have been expecting you. Come in, come in." She held the door while Sara struggled with her bags.

Once inside, Sara trembled. "Mrs. Dewberry, you must have gotten a chill. Come warm up by the fire." Mrs. Williams led her over to the fireplace.

Sara moved mechanically but managed to protest. "Mrs. Williams, I would like to go to my room and rest. I believe I have a bit of a cold." Sara sniffed.

"Fine, fine," said Mrs. Williams. "I had hoped we could get to know each other, but there will be plenty of time for that later. Follow me." Mrs. Williams led the way up the staircase.

Mrs. Williams gave a rundown of house rules. "Dinner is at five p.m. and I assume you will be joining us. No alcohol or smoking is allowed on the premises. Cooking is not allowed in the room, and I expect that all tenants will attend church services at their respective churches on Sunday. Housekeeping will be done on Wednesday mornings, so you might like to find some outside activity on that day." Mrs. Williams paused. "Do you have any questions?"

"May I have visitors?" Sara asked.

Mrs. Williams cleared her throat and answered firmly, "You may not have overnight visitors, and you must entertain any gentlemen callers in the parlor. I run a decent house."

"I'm sure you do, and I agree to your rules." Sara nodded, though she felt a little faint as the reality of living here settled in.

Mrs. Williams looked relieved.

"My, my, let's not stand here in the hall," Mrs. Williams said and placed a key in the lock to open the door to Sara's room.

It was a lovely room, with crisp, white Priscilla curtains on the windows, a brass bed with a beautiful homemade quilt, and a platform rocking chair by the window. Everything looked polished and homey. The windows were open, airing the room out.

"Let me close this. It is a bit chilly." Mrs. Williams closed the sash. "I hope this will do."

There was a dresser with a mirror against one wall and a wardrobe against the other. In the corner was a small washstand with a bowl and pitcher. The stand had a towel bar attached. A small table with a lamp stood next to the bed. The floors were well polished wood with a braided rug on it.

"This will be just fine, thank you." Sara held the door, silently dismissing Mrs. Williams.

"We'll see you at dinner?" Mrs. Williams inquired. "We're having baked chicken tonight."

"Yes, thank you." Sara closed the door.

She'd held her tears as long as she could. She pulled off her shoes and flopped onto the bed, embracing a fluffy pillow and sobbing herself to sleep.

She awoke at three p.m. and had thoughts of her children coming home from school to find her not there. She wondered what Claudia or Henry would tell them.

Sara rose and paced the room, before deciding she had better settle in. She took her things from her bags and placed them in the wardrobe and dresser, fixing the photographs on top of the dresser.

She glanced in the mirror and saw dark circles under her eyes. Her hair had loosened from its combs and lay in disheveled strands around her face.

She brushed her hair and re-pinned it. Then, splashed water on her face and straightened her frock. It was still an hour before dinner.

Sara sat on the rocking chair by the window, picked up the book she had been reading, and read mindlessly for a full chapter.

She shook her head, and took a deep breath, not recalling a word of text. Setting the book aside, she proceeded down the staircase for dinner.

"Ah, Mrs. Dewberry," Mrs. Williams greeted. "It is so nice to see you. Did you have a good nap?"

"Yes, thank you," Sara said softly.

"Come, come." Mrs. Williams ushered her into the parlor. "It will be just a short while before dinner. Come meet Mr. Carter."

They entered the parlor and Mr. Carter jumped to his feet. He was a short, weasel-faced man with balding hair and wire rim glasses.

"Mr. Carter, this is our new tenant, Mrs. Dewberry. Mrs. Dewberry, Mr. Carter has been with us for more than a year now. He is a traveling salesman for Watkins products. I am sure you are familiar with their line. They're building a new facility in Winona, Minnesota and Mr.

Carter has been offered a position in their main headquarters in six months. He handles our area and we would like to see him stay, but it would be difficult for him to pass up this opportunity."

"Pleased to make your acquaintance," Mr. Carter gushed. "Mrs. Williams runs a top-notch facility here. I am sure you'll enjoy your stay. Forgive me for being forward, Mrs. Dewberry, but I must say that you are a lovely addition to our family." He smiled fiendishly.

"Thank you," Sara said. "I am sure I will be very comfortable here." She turned to see another gentleman enter the room.

"Oh, Mr. Stewart, please come and meet our newest tenant, Mrs. Dewberry. This is Mr. Stewart. He works at the Goldman Shoe Store downtown," said Mrs. Williams.

Sara looked into the eyes of an older gentleman with grey hair, grey eyes, and a handlebar mustache. She guessed him to be about seventy years old. He was in remarkable shape for a gentleman of that age, dressed in a grey suit and held a bowler hat in his hand.

"How long have you lived here, Mr. Stewart?" Sara attempted to make small conversation.

"Just over a month," Mr. Stewart said. "My dear departed wife passed away last year. I found our home much too large for one old man, so I sold it. When the opportunity arises, perhaps I will find a small cottage to purchase."

"Tell us about yourself," Mr. Carter drooled to Sara.

"There isn't much to tell," Sara began, shifting a step away. She was delighted when they were interrupted by the call to dinner.

Sara picked at her food. Jolly Mrs. Williams kept everyone entertained about the happenings of the day. The woman had a delightful sense of humor, but Sara could not bring herself to engage in the conversation.

"You will never guess what I found in my garden this morning," Mrs. Williams began.

"Do tell," said Mr. Stewart. "I'd like to know what you grow in your garden in November." He chuckled.

"A cow!" she exclaimed. "Would you believe there was a *cow* in my garden? The nearest farm is at least a mile away, but there she was, chewing on the remains of my summer garden...a full-grown Holstein cow."

She had caught everyone's interest, except Sara's. She was lost in her own thoughts about Henry and the children and barely heard a word of the tale. She smiled and laughed when everyone else did, but if anyone asked later, she would not recall the story.

After dessert, which Sara refused, Mrs. Williams dismissed everyone. "Gentlemen, why don't you take your coffee into the parlor while Sara and I spend a few minutes together."

Reluctantly, the men left.

"Did you need help cleaning up?" Sara asked, meeting Mrs. Williams' eyes.

"No, dear, but I sense you need some help cleaning up."

Sara looked around, worry etched on her face. "I'm so sorry; did I do something wrong? Did I spill something?"

"No, dear, but I sense there's something spilled in your life. Running a boarding house, I have a second sense as to people's problems, and yours are weighing heavily. Tell me about yourself," Mrs. Williams counseled.

Sara's head dropped, and she wiped away a tear. "What did Henry tell you?"

"Mr. Dewberry was a bit confused," Mrs. Williams began. "First, he said he wanted to rent a room for a lady friend who was coming to town. I provided him with information on the room I had available. He agreed to pay the rent for two weeks and said you would be securing employment and would handle it thereafter. He said it was possible you would be returning to Wausau. When he gave me your name, Sara Dewberry, I questioned him."

Mrs. Williams smoothed the tablecloth in front of her, and continued. "'Mr. Dewberry,' I said, 'Sara has the same name as you do. Did you say she was a friend?'"

Sara listened intently.

"He went on to explain himself. He said, 'Did I say *friend*? She is my sister, but also my closest friend.' That was it, except…"

"Except what?" Sara wanted to know.

"Well, he said he has children and if they came around the boarding house, I should tell them to go home to their father. Then he said, 'They get a bit rowdy sometimes and have no business here.' I told him I understood, and he prompty left. Mrs. Dewberry, I love children, but they must behave so my other tenants are not disturbed. But if you wish to have children visit, it will be your responsibility to control them."

"Certainly," agreed Sara, her heart breaking at the thought of never seeing her children again. She swallowed hard, attempting to hold back the tears but one escaped down her cheek.

"So now," Mrs. Williams went on, "tell me the real story." Her kind, motherly face and warm smile melted Sara. More tears slid down her cheeks. Mrs. Williams shuffled her chair closer and put her arm around Sara. "There, there, take your time."

Sara took a big breath, then another, before she was able to compose herself. "Mrs. Williams, I don't know how you are going to feel about this, but I will be honest with you. I should have been honest with Henry all along. Henry is my husband and I am a suffragette." She waited for Mrs. Williams' disdain, but it didn't come. In fact, the woman smiled.

"Go on," Mrs. Williams urged.

Sara hesitated, but the woman's encouragement seemed genuine. "Henry is against the movement, so I didn't tell him I was involved with the local group. Earlier this week, I was in a march in Chicago. I told Henry I was Christmas shopping for the children, which wasn't totally a lie, because I intended to pick up a few items while I was there. But things got a bit out of hand and I ended up in jail."

Mrs. Williams broke out in gales of laughter. "My dear, we need more like you. Kind of makes my cow story sound silly."

Sara felt a warmth in her chest and smiled for the first time that night. At that moment, she and Mrs. Williams had found a common bond.

Mrs. Williams refilled their teacups, and they sat there at the table, sharing. They talked for hours about women's rights, the long road they had traveled, what was being done today and where they one day hoped to be. By the time they finished the conversation, both women were laughing.

"My, my, look at the time," Mrs. Williams exclaimed. "It's ten p.m., well past my bedtime. I must be up by five to fix breakfast for everyone. We can talk more tomorrow. Have a good sleep. If you ever need a shoulder, come see me."

Sara reached over and hugged Mrs. Williams. Her soft, warm body felt comforting and much like Sara remembered of her mother's. "Mrs. Williams, you are a lifesaver."

Chapter Twenty-five

The next day, Sara went to see Mrs. Williams. "I need to find a position, but I am not trained for anything. I have a good education, but as you know, all I have been trained for is to be a good wife." She thought about the teaching degree she had earned before she married Henry, but that was an impossibility, even now. Married women weren't allowed to be teachers. Running a boarding house, Sara suspected had introduced Mrs. Williams to people of various walks of life.

"Can you cook? Can you sew?" inquired Mrs. Williams.

Sara frowned. "I can cook...well, sort of. Claudia did most of our cooking, but I am a good seamstress. I have made most of my children's clothes."

"Hmm..." Mrs. Williams thought for a moment. "Marilyn Mason has a seamstress shop downtown and she may have need of help. She is very busy. Tell her I sent you."

"Thank you," Sara said gratefully, and listened as Mrs. Wiliams told her more about Mrs. Mason and her shop. "I'll go there today."

Sara picked out one of the finer frocks that she had made, then made her way to Marilyn Mason's shop. Mrs. Mason ran her business out of her home. Her husband had passed away some time ago, and she made her living by running a business that showcased her skills.

Sara thought about Mrs. Mason and Mrs. Williams' situations, and it became even clearer to her how unfair the laws of the land were regarding women. Here were two capable women who did what was expected of them, raising their families and caring for their husbands, only to find themselves on their own with limited resources, suddenly having to find their own way to make a living. They were the breadwinners of their families and took care of the household needs. Why should they not have a voice? Why should they not have a right to vote?

Sara entered Mrs. Mason's shop. A woman was busy at a sewing machine. A dressmaker's mannequin stood in the corner with a beautiful gown on it. In another corner was a play area with books and puzzles. From Mrs. Williams' description of her, Sara recognized Marilyn Mason. She was about Sara's age, a trim woman. She looked tired but still greeted Sara with a pleasant smile.

"Hello. What can I do for you?" the woman asked.

Sara glanced around the room and tried not to be nervous. "I am looking for employment and wonder if you might be in need of help. Mrs. Williams sent me."

"I'm Marilyn Mason," she said and looked about the room. "Help I need; equipment I am short on. Do you have a sewing machine, a mannequin, or a sewing basket? Things to keep children busy after school?" She pointed to the corner with books.

"Sara Dewberry," she said. "Umm, I don't have those things right now, but I may be able to get them." She wondered if Henry would let her get the sewing items she had left behind.

"Which do you have, the sewing things or the child restraints?" Marilyn chuckled.

Sara liked the woman right away, and grinned, her nervousness slipping away. "The sewing things, but maybe I can assist with the restraints, too. I can let you know in a day or two. Can I get back to you on Monday or Tuesday?" Sara was getting excited.

"Well, let's not get ahead of ourselves. I can only pay ten cents an hour. I know that isn't much, but it is all I can afford, and I can only pay you for twenty hours a week," Marilyn said somewhat apologetically.

Sara thought for a minute. Her room and board were two dollars a week. That would leave nothing for other expenses. "That would be fine," she said, hiding her frown. She would just have to figure out what to do beyond that.

Sara's next stop was the bank. She needed to find out if she could get her sewing machine and supplies from Henry. She walked into the bank and was greeted by Michael, the teller. "Hello, Mrs. Dewberry. What can I do for you today?"

"I need to speak to Henry, is he in?" she asked.

"Just one moment," said Michael. He knocked on Mr. Dewberry's door and announced Mrs. Dewberry.

Without a word, Henry arrived, took Sara by the arm, and ushered her into his office and closed the door.

"What are you doing here?" he demanded in a gruff voice. His eyes were cold, like those of a stranger's.

Sara bristled at his harsh manner towards her. "Well, Mr. Dewberry, since you have determined that I need to make it on my own, I would like to have the tools of my trade."

Henry laughed sarcastically. "And what might that be. Do you wish a loan?"

"No, Henry. I would like my sewing supplies, my Singer sewing machine, and my dress mannequin," Sara said haughtily.

He laughed again. "So, you think you can be a seamstress? You know nothing about running a business. Why don't you go back to Wausau?"

"Perhaps I will," bluffed Sara. "They sew in Wausau, too, you know." She had no intention of letting him know her precise plans.

"Well, then, they are yours," he replied, as though he was bestowing a gift on her that she should be grateful to receive.

"Very well, may I get them this weekend?" she inquired, hoping to see the children.

"I will have them delivered to you first thing on Monday," he snapped.

Sara left the bank quickly. She had hoped the conversation would be more civil, but she could see Henry was still upset with her.

That afternoon, a courier from Attorney David Daniels' office dropped off papers at the boarding house for Sara.

She trembled as she opened the envelope.

There it was in black and white—a legal separation from Henry. Sara was to have no contact with the children. She would get nothing beyond her two weeks of room and board. All her personal belongings were to be removed from the house before the court date, but only with Henry's permission. Everything else would be the property of one Henry Dewberry including house, furnishings, vehicles, livestock, and miscellaneous household goods. He would retain full custody of the children. The document argued that it was in the best interest of the children, since Sara had neither a place to live nor means of supporting them. The court date was set for November 29, 1912, the day after Thanksgiving.

Sara ran to her room, dropped the papers on the floor, and fell to her knees weeping.

***

On Monday, the courier delivered Sara's Singer sewing machine, her dressmaker's mannequin, and her sewing box filled with thread, needles, pins, and other notions. Another box contained knitting and crochet needles, yarn, embroidery hoops, and some unfinished, stamped pillowcases. There was also a box with dyed wool ready to be spun into yarn, along with Sara's spinning wheel. Sara wasn't sure where she would put all of this in her tiny room.

"Thank heavens he didn't send my quilting frame or loom," she murmured. As she sifted through the boxes, she found her tatting shuttle, along with a half-finished dresser scarf. "This will occupy some of my time."

While Sara stood in the entry among all her possessions, she looked about, trying to plan what she would do next when the courier returned.

"I am sorry, Madam. I forgot to drop off this." He handed her an envelope and was about to turn away when Sara had an idea.

"Would you mind taking the sewing machine, the mannequin, and this box of supplies to Marilyn Mason's shop on Water Street?" she asked.

"Certainly," the young man answered. "That will be an additional twenty-five cents. Shall I add it to Mr. Dewberry's bill?"

"No, no," she said, not wanting Henry to patronize her.

While the young man reloaded his cart, Sara opened the envelope. In it was fifteen dollars with a note scrawled in Henry's handwriting stating that it was a loan to get her started in her new business. At the bottom, she read, "Ten percent annual interest due upon repayment."

She resealed the envelope, marked REFUSED in large letters across the front, and handed it back to the courier. "Please return this to Mr. Dewberry, and on second thought, please add the twenty-five cents to Mr. Dewberry's bill." Sara closed the door.

Back in her room, Sara found space in one of the drawers at the bottom of her wardrobe to store her books, and she placed the spinning wheel next to the rocking chair. Mrs. Williams had provided her with a large wicker basket, which she put on the other side of the chair. It held all her yarn and needles.

She found room in one of her dresser drawers for the remainder of her embroidery and tatting supplies. In no time, she had restored order to her room. Now she had to try to figure out how to restore order to her life.

Marilyn Mason had been putting her space in order also. When Sara arrived on Tuesday for work, Marilyn had already divided her workspace into quarters. She had her sewing work in one corner and Sara's in another; the third quadrant was the play area, and the fourth, closest to the door, had a counter with shelves in the back for packaging materials and extra threads and notions. That area also housed a coat tree and two chairs for visitors. On the wall, she had photographs and sketches of some of the fashions.

Sara looked around in awe and declared, "Mrs. Mason, you are a true entrepreneur. This is simply delightful."

Sara dove into her work, and the two ladies got along famously. The time went by swiftly, and for those few hours, engrossed in her work, Sara almost forgot her problems.

However, when she returned to the boarding house, her thoughts went immediately to her children. She missed them terribly. At bedtime, when she crawled into bed, she missed her husband's strong arms around her. That night, she cried herself to sleep.

Sara made enough money to pay for her room and board, but it left nothing else. However, she still had most of the twenty dollars she had taken to Chicago for shopping and would manage it carefully. She needed another job if she had to fight Counselor Daniels in Court. Mrs. Williams had offered her a job helping with meals. That could be the answer.

After breakfast on Wednesday, Sara remained in the kitchen. "Mrs. Williams, do you have a moment to talk?"

"By all means," said Mrs. Williams with a rosy smile. "Do sit and have a cup of coffee with me." She pulled out a chair by the kitchen table and patted a seat. "What is on your mind, dear?" Mrs. Williams poured two cups of coffee and took a seat next to Sara.

Sara pulled the attorney's papers from her pocket and laid them on the table. "I need to retain an attorney and I don't have enough money. I thought maybe..." Sara hesitated, lacing her fingers together.

"You need to borrow money? Oh dear, I would like to help, but I..."

"No, no, Mrs. Williams. I thought maybe I would take you up on your offer to help with the cooking."

"Oh, I see." Mrs. Williams took off her spectacles and bit into the bow, looking pensively into space. "Well now, I believe I could use a bit of help in the morning. I get up at five and start coffee for the early risers. I make fresh biscuits, and then by six, I prepare the rest of the breakfast and set the table. It needs to be ready for six-thirty."

Sara nodded, and followed along while Mrs. Williams explained her routine.

"Do you think you can manage breakfast? It would just be Friday, Saturday, and Sunday. Breakfast is served between six-thirty and nine-thirty. Then, there is clean up."

"So, it would be about five hours, three days a week? I hate to ask, but how much do you pay?" Sara asked hopefully.

"I would take it off your rent," Mrs. Williams said. "Instead of two dollars per week, you would have to pay one dollar. Of course, if everyone is served early and you finish early, the pay remains the same. Likewise, if you are detained in the kitchen for any reason, you will not get extra."

Sara smiled, relief taking hold of her. "Mrs. Williams, you have just hired your new weekend breakfast cook." She knew this would barely get her by, but she hoped Mrs. Williams might be able to extend her job when her current weekday cook could not make it. Mrs. Williams filled in those times currently, but if Sara did a good job, maybe, just maybe, she would get more days.

Chapter Twenty-six

Retaining a lawyer proved to be more difficult than Sara expected. She visited three law firms and spoke with counsel, who promptly dismissed her when they discovered her circumstances. She had no means of supporting her children. How could she expect to gain custody? Even Sara wondered how she would manage. She had hoped that Henry might have to provide some support, but that just became a laughing matter. Finally, at her fourth stop at Milliken, Milliken, and Otter, she spoke with Jeremiah Milliken, who agreed to take her case.

Attorney Milliken was a young man of about thirty years with dark hair and brown eyes. He was clean shaven, had a friendly smile, and a warm handshake. He immediately put Sara at ease. He was realistic but he gave her hope.

"This is going to be a tough case, and I will need a ten-dollar retainer. I will caution you that your chances of winning custody are almost nil, but perhaps we can arrange for visitation rights."

"I am a good mother and I can see no reason why my children should be banned from seeing their mother," Sara pleaded.

"That's exactly the cornerstone of our case. I don't know which of our judges will be handling your case. If it is Judge McCarthy, we'll have a chance. Our outcome will be greatly hindered if Judge Hargrove is on the bench," Counselor Milliken explained with a frown.

"I understand," said Sara.

"I will draw up the appropriate response to Attorney Daniels' petition, and we will hope that Judge McCarthy is appointed to hear the case. Now, do you have the retainer?"

"Yes, I do." Sara reached into her purse.

"I have a standard contract. Apart from the retainer, we will need an additional ten dollars when it goes to court. The balance can be worked out in monthly payments of one dollar per month for one year. Your total bill will be thirty dollars, plus two dollars in processing fees." Counselor Milliken filled out the form as he explained the terms. He pushed the paper over his desk for Sara to read and sign.

Sara, head swaying at the idea of all that money, quickly signed the document, handed him the ten dollars, requested a receipt, and quietly rose to leave. "Good day, Mr. Milliken."

"Good day, Mrs. Dewberry." He showed her to the door.

Sara took a deep breath. Could she really win this case? Attorney Milliken seemed optimistic, but he did say it would be difficult.

She thought of her children's smiling faces and gripped her purse tight. *I will. I must.*

***

Thanksgiving arrived, and Sara was given an extra day of breakfast preparation. The cook would be preparing the Thanksgiving feast to be served at one p.m., so breakfast would be early and kept simple. The menu consisted of scrambled eggs with toast or oatmeal, and fresh fruit. It would be served from six-thirty to eight a.m. Sara would get an extra twenty-five cent allowance on her rent for the hours she worked.

She had a slice of cinnamon toast and a cup of coffee for breakfast. Her mind was far away in her home on Astor Street. It was a bit more than a mile in distance, but a world away in her mind. She thought of the children's reactions on Thanksgivings past, when seeing the turkey, the steamy mashed potatoes and dressing, and the homemade pumpkin pie piled high with fresh, rich, whipped cream. She thought of Ella and Liz gathering around Claudia to get a peek at the bird, golden-brown in the roaster. And she thought of Henry sitting in his study, a curled pipe in his mouth with apple-roasted tobacco filling the room with its rich aroma. He would be reading a book. Soon he would be saying grace and carving their juicy, scrumptious turkey. A lump grew in Sara's throat.

The same scenario played out at the boarding house, but with no children's laughter or rich smoke. The bird, the stuffing, the pie—it was all the same, but so different.

Guess it isn't the lovely meal but the love that makes Thanksgiving so wonderful.

At dinner, everyone was in a festive mood, but Sara went through the motions. She could have had gruel and enjoyed it just as much. Everything tasted like cardboard, though it had been prepared and seasoned to perfection. The people were friendly and the conversation was lively, but something important was missing. Family. It grew more and more difficult for Sara to swallow past the lump in her throat.

After dinner, her thoughts went to the court appearance scheduled for the next day. Beginning to feel sick, she excused herself and hurried off to her room.

Chapter Twenty-seven

Looking out her bedroom window, Sara could see it would be a blustery day. She dressed with great care, choosing her most conservative clothing and fixing her hair in attractive braids wrapped around her head. She wore a long, black dress that covered her ankles, softened with a white tatted collar, so she would not appear so austere.

She glanced out the window and shivered. On a nice day, she could walk to the courthouse. With this chilly weather, she decided to ask the lecherous Mr. Carter if he could drop her off. She didn't want to ask him, but at this point, she didn't see that she had a choice if she wanted to arrive dry.

She approached him over breakfast, standing a few paces away. "Mr. Carter, might I ask a favor of you?"

"Why, certainly, Mrs. Dewberry. It would be my pleasure. What can I do for you?" Mr. Carter gave a sleazy grin and stepped forward to put his arm around her shoulder.

Sara stepped aside with a shudder, releasing his arm from her. "I wonder if you would mind dropping me off at the courthouse on your way to your route this morning. I wouldn't impose, but the weather is dreadful and I need to be there by ten. I know you start your route at nine, but I don't mind arriving early."

"It will be my pleasure," Mr. Carter gushed, eyes all over her. "You look ravishing this morning and I might be tempted to steal you away." He winked at Sara.

"Mr. Carter, I am a married woman and have business to take care of. Please mind your manners or I will have to find another means to get there."

"I'm sorry, Mrs. Dewberry, please forgive me." He stepped away from her at once. "It is just that, well, you are a very attractive woman and I have not seen a gentleman by your side, so I assumed you are a widow…an available widow. I did not mean to offend you."

"My husband is away for some time, but I assure you that I am still very much married. I accept your apology. Now, may I count on you for that ride?"

"Of course." He nodded. "I will pull the truck around at quarter to nine." Mr. Carter seemed smart enough to know that he had been properly rebuked.

At precisely nine a.m., Sara saw Mr. Carter at the front of the boarding house in his Watkins delivery wagon. It was open, but it had a roof over the seat. Fortunately, the weather had calmed down. She descended the steps and Mr. Carter was at her side in seconds to see she had safe entry into his truck. She had put on her fox hat and muff for the extra warmth and wrapped her cloak tight around her, then pulled a scarf about her neck.

Mr. Carter watched her closely but said nothing as he held her arm to assist her aboard. He provided her a wool blanket to keep her warm. Then, he proceeded to the courthouse.

At the courthouse, Mr. Carter offered to come in with her, but she dismissed him immediately, thanking him for the ride.

"Would you like me to return to pick you up?" Mr. Carter offered. "I'd be honored to buy you lunch."

"Oh no, Mr. Carter, that won't be necessary. I have plans for the rest of the day and will manage fine, thank you." Sara was happy to have him go on his way.

"Lunch," she scoffed, shaking away the sickening feel of his eyes on her. "I think I was on his menu."

Sara went up the steps to the courthouse. She found a bench, took a book out of her bag, and passed the time pretending to read. The words became fragmented immediately after she read them. Her head was too full of other matters.

She looked up from her book to see Counselor Milliken standing in front of her.

"Good morning, Mrs. Dewberry," he greeted her. "I'm glad you came early. I need to go over a few things with you. But first, I have a bit of bad news. Judge Hargrove will be hearing the case. This will not be easy."

Sara's chest tightened. "Please have a seat, Mr. Milliken." Sara motioned for him to sit on the bench with her. "How bad is it?"

"Judge Hargrove came to Wisconsin from South Carolina several years ago. He is stuck in the traditions of the old south. His father, who was also a judge, was against the abolitionists' movement in the mid-1800s and passed many of his values on to his son. This case, of course, is not about suffragettes, so we can only hope that the issue will not come up. He has been a defender of motherhood, so hopefully that will be in our favor," Jeremiah Milliken explained.

"Don't expect custody," he continued. "I believe it is best not to contest the custody issue because, although you are employed, you do not have the means or a home to raise your children. I believe it is a foregone conclusion that Mr. Dewberry will be awarded custody. However, we will argue strongly on the issue of visitation. I think we have a good chance on that level."

"I understand," Sara said sadly, and looked down at her hands in her lap. "I need to see my children. I don't think I could go on without them."

They entered the courtroom and took their seats at the defendant's table. They had no sooner been seated when Henry came in with Counselor Daniels.

Sara's heart skipped a beat when she saw Henry looking quite handsome in a black jacket with gray pinstripe trousers and a gray ascot. He wore a top hat, which he removed and placed on the table. He sat, stone-faced, not looking her way.

Judge Hargrove came to the bench and the bailiff called out, "All rise, the Honorable Judge Harvey Hargrove presiding."

The judge instructed everyone to be seated. He announced the case of Henry Dewberry verses Sara Dewberry, then proceeded to read the petition that Henry's attorney had presented.

When Henry was asked if that was his position, Henry responded, "Yes, Your Honor."

Judge Hargrove spoke to Attorney Milliken. "It is my understanding you concur on most of these issues, but you have some counter proposals. Is that correct?"

Jeremiah Milliken rose and addressed the court, standing tall and proud. "We understand that Mr. Dewberry has deeded property and has other possessions, such as the automobile he recently purchased. Mrs. Dewberry contributed to the cost of their home when she provided money she had inherited from her parents upon their death. Mrs. Dewberry would like the children to enjoy the safety and comfort of that home, but she would like a stipend to assist her in moving forward. We ask that Mr. Dewberry provide ten dollars per month for Mrs. Dewberry's living costs for the next year."

Judge Hargrove and Attorney Daniels made notes with their quill pens on their legal pads.

"Further, Your Honor," he went on, "we request that the court award visitation rights to Mrs. Dewberry. There are three children. Firstly, a son, Thaddeus, who is away at military school. Mrs. Dewberry would like to be able to spend time with him during his upcoming holiday vacation and during the summer months while he is at home. Their daughter Ella, who is thirteen, is attending school in Milwaukee, as is their seven-year-old daughter, Elizabeth. Mrs. Dewberry would like to be able to see them once a week every week."

Henry bristled at the words, but still did not look at Sara.

Attorney Daniels rose to address the court. "Your Honor, we are willing to offer a one-time stipend of fifty dollars to Mrs. Dewberry, but we do not wish to concede on the issue of visitation. Mr. Dewberry wants a restraining order so that Mrs. Dewberry will never see her children again."

Sara gasped, her hands going to her mouth.

Attorney Milliken touched her arm, indicating she should sit quietly.

Judge Hargrove said, "Counselor Daniels, this is very harsh. Does your client have a reason to suggest such drastic measures?"

Sara had told Attorney Milliken she was an impeccable mother, and he smiled smugly as they awaited the plaintiff's response.

"Your Honor, Mrs. Dewberry is a suffragette," Counselor Daniels said.

"Objection!" shouted Counselor Milliken. "This is an issue of visitation. Being a suffragette is not an illegal activity, nor is it grounds for denying visitation. The issue is whether she is a fit mother, and it is, in our opinion, in the best interests of the children for her to be able to see and spend time with them."

Before Judge Hargrove had a chance to respond, Counselor Daniels spoke up. "Your Honor, Mrs. Dewberry has participated in suffragette activities which could endanger and did, in fact, endanger her children."

"Please explain," Judge Hargrove said, looking directly at Daniels. "This better be good, or I will have to sustain the objection."

"Your Honor, Mrs. Dewberry took her children to a suffragette parade this past summer and at that event, her youngest son was crushed by a runaway buckboard. It is our contention that Mrs. Dewberry was more interested in the parade than in keeping her three-year-old son safe."

Sara gasped. She couldn't believe Henry would bring Adam into this.

Counselor Daniels continued, "There was another incident last spring when Mrs. Dewberry likely attended a rally of the suffragettes in Racine. She was injured, causing the death of her unborn child. We do not know the particulars of that incident, but had she not attended that rally, that child would be alive today."

Sara jumped from her seat. "Henry," she screamed, trembling from head to toe. "Henry, you know neither of those incidents were my fault. You know how much I love our children. You know I would never expose them to danger. Henry, please!"

Henry winced but remained silent.

"Mrs. Dewberry, please sit down," Counselor Milliken tried to calm her.

"Henry, don't do this. Henry, please," she pleaded.

Judge Hargrove declared a thirty-minute recess for Counselor Milliken to compose his client.

Jeremiah Milliken ushered Sara from the room.

Tears streaming down her face, Sara cupped her hands tightly over her mouth to stifle the screams of agony that shuddered from deep in her being. She shook violently as waves of nausea overtook her.

"Mrs. Dewberry." Jeremiah Milliken tried to still her, his hands placed gently on her shoulders. "I will argue against this, but it is bleak. Take some deep breaths. We will have to go back in, and I will do whatever I can."

Soon, the thirty minutes were up, and they returned to the courtroom. Sara's eyes were red and swollen.

Counselor Milliken argued valiantly that the incidents that took place would have happened, even if they were not connected with the suffragettes.

In the end, Judge Hargrove awarded full custody to Henry and left Sara with a fifty dollar stipend, but no visitation of her children until they reached the age of sixteen, and then, only if it was the children's wish to be reunited.

Sara was heartbroken.

***

Sara never left her room for the duration of the weekend. She didn't eat, she didn't drink. She sat staring blindly out of her window.

On Sunday evening, a knock sounded on her door. "It is Mrs. Williams, may I come in?"

Sara didn't answer. She couldn't speak, she was so weak.

Mrs. Williams opened the door and peeked in. "Mrs. Dewberry... Sara?"

She bustled in with a roast beef sandwich and a glass of milk, putting the food on the dresser, she went to Sara's side.

Sara knew her face must look miserable. A single tear rolled down her cheek as she clung to the quilt.

Mrs. Williams gathered Sara into her arms and cradled her like a child. She stroked Sara's hair and murmured, "It will be okay, child. It will be okay."

It seemed like hours passed while Sara cried, holding nothing back.

Momentarily, Sara's tears ceased, and Mrs. Williams stood to straighten her back. Then, settling in, she sat on the edge of the bed across from Sara. "Tell me about it," she prompted softly, taking her hand.

Sara let it all out—her pain, her fears, her pain, her guilt, her pain, her anger.

Mrs. Williams listened.

When Sara had spilled out everything, her tears dried up and she felt strangely cleansed. She still felt the pain and guilt and fear, but it was no longer tied up inside of her. She was no longer angry.

Mrs. Williams patted her hand. "Sara, what didn't happen?"

Sara looked at her, puzzled by the question. "What do you mean?"

"You have been through a lot this year. You have lost a battle; you haven't lost the war! You are a strong woman. You have lived through the death of your son, lived through the loss of your unborn child, watched your older son go away to school, suffered through an attack where you might have died, and you have been rejected by your true love. Nothing as terrible as that happened in the court room. *You* are a mother, and nothing can ever take your children from you, outside of death. You don't have to seek your children, they will find you. It is nature. You have a purpose on this earth, and perhaps God is providing the means for you to carry it out. I am not saying that what has happened is a good thing. I am telling you that you must go on... that you *can* and *should* go on."

Mrs. Williams got up to leave, setting the plate on the bed. "Make sure you eat the sandwich and drink your milk. You need your nourishment. Get a good night's sleep and I will see you in the morning for breakfast." She slipped out the door, leaving Sara to her thoughts.

Sara took a deep breath, realizing that the savory smells of roast beef filled the room. Her stomach growled, and she knew she was hungry. She nibbled at the sandwich, thinking of all that had happened.

Mrs. Williams is right. This isn't the worst thing that has ever happened to me, and it isn't the end. How can I do right by my children if I give up? I need to fight for myself and for them.

What was it that Tillie said long ago?

"'Nothing worthwhile is ever achieved without sacrifice?'" Sara said aloud to the empty room. "But," she anguished, "how *much* must I sacrifice?"

Chapter Twenty-eight

The streets were beginning to glow with the signs of Christmas. Fresh snow covered the ground, and the store windows were decorated with candles and snowflakes, intermingled with holiday merchandise. Santa and his elves rung bells summoning little children to tell their wishes. Carolers were out singing on the street corners as the church bells pealed, beckoning people in and reminding everyone there was something special about this holiday beyond the trappings of the local merchants.

People bustled through the street, trying to get all their preparations done early. The shop where Sara worked was extra busy getting out all of the specially-ordered holiday dresses. Sara worked longer hours, so her pay was more than usual. She saved those extra pennies to purchase gifts for her children. But what could she buy, and how would they get them?

Sara purchased a beautiful bone mirror with roses hand-painted on the back and a matching brush for Ella. Sara thought about Ella's beautiful long locks of hair and how it shined when it was brushed and styled.

She found a porcelain doll for Elizabeth. The doll had dark tresses that matched Liz's and wore a purple dress and bonnet. Purple was Liz's favorite color, and Sara knew she would enjoy playing with the doll.

Thaddeus was a bit more difficult, but Sara decided on a Swiss Army knife she thought he would like. All its utensils would come in handy, and it wouldn't take up a lot of space in his room at the Academy.

Sara wrapped the gifts in plain brown paper and tied them with a red and green plaid ribbon. Each package had a tag attached to it on which she had written their names and a message.

Merry Christmas. I miss you.
All my love, Mother

The week before Christmas, Sara summoned a courier and had the packages delivered to the house on Astor Street.

***

Henry stepped through the front door of his home on Astor Street, and set his hat on the rack.

"Mr. Dewberry," Claudia said, meeting him in the hall. "I accepted a delivery and placed the packages on your desk in the study."

"Thank you, Claudia." Henry went into his study, removed the tags from the packages, and placed the gifts with the rest of the presents that would be found under the tree on Christmas morning.

***

On Christmas Eve, Sara walked to the cathedral two blocks from Williams boarding house. It was a cold, crisp evening and huge, white snowflakes fell from the sky. She remembered her children and stuck out her tongue to catch a big flake. Adam had so loved to do that. She thought of making snow angels in the fresh snow, building a huge snowman in the front yard, gathering together to decorate the tree, and celebrating its beauty over a cup of hot chocolate. She wondered if that was what her family was doing this very minute.

Aching at the thought, she picked up a fistful of snow, packed it into a snowball, and threw it as hard as she could at a hitching post. She bit her lip to stop the tears from escaping her eyes and turning to mini icicles on her cheeks.

She entered the cathedral and took a seat in a pew near the back. She didn't even know what kind of church it was, but when she looked at the bulletin, she read the name: St. Nicholas Episcopal Church.

St. Nicholas. How interesting that this church bears the name of the patron saint of children? Sara was aware that because of the many miracles attributed to his intercession, St. Nicholas was also known as Nikolaos the Wonderworker. *I could use a few miracles.*

The church was filled, and there was joy all around—except in Sara's heart, which was as heavy as a rock. The usual Christmas carols rang throughout the cathedral as the giant pipe organ led the choir. A kind looking, white-haired priest delivered the Christmas message.

Anticipating the usual passages from Luke, Sara barely heard what he had to say. But then, almost as though he was speaking directly to her, Sara listened and heard new words.

"Just as Jesus Christ our Lord and Savior was born upon this earth to fulfill a purpose, so each and every one of us is here for a purpose as well. Jesus was born in a lowly manger; he was not born of royalty or nobility. His parents fled for fear of his death under the hands of Caesar. They could not return to their family, their home, or their life. They were exiled to Egypt for their own preservation.

"Christmas is a difficult time for many. There are more accidents and more people who give up and die. Those people have lost sight of their purpose, or perhaps they never knew what it was. If only we could implore those souls to look into the face of this tiny baby and see the reflection of their life...a life with purpose.

"Christmas is a joyful event. It is a time of rejoicing in the birth of the Christ child. Because this child was born, we live. Because this child was born, he will show us the way. All we must do is follow Him. It may not be easy. The journey may be filled with sorrow and tribulation, but if you stop trying to run your life and that of others and place your life in His hands, you will find peace; you will find joy."

Sara tried hard to find meaning in his words. In her heart, she had always believed that each person had a purpose, even if there were trials along the way, God would lead everyone to a better place. She wasn't sure she could believe it now when it wasn't just a teaching, but reality. How could so much pain be on purpose? She had believed that God didn't give more than she could endure. She wasn't so sure about that either at this moment. She longed to speak to Pastor Reinhart. He always knew the right answers to all her questions.

"You will find peace; you will find joy," she repeated. She wondered if she were a fool to believe that such a thing could exist. Peace and joy. How foreign those words sounded!

She trudged back to the boarding house with a huge lump in her throat. She thought of her children nestled in their warm beds, anticipating the joy of Christmas morning. All around her were people full of joy and laughter.

She forced herself up the steps to the front door of the boarding house, stomping her feet before entering and went directly to her room.

There was a note slipped under the door. She flopped down on the bed and opened it.

The note was from her good friend.

> *Sara dear,*
> *You mustn't spend Christmas with strangers. Please join me for Christmas dinner tomorrow at one p.m. I have a capon with all the trimmings. I don't want to eat alone. I will be by to pick you up in my carriage at eleven a.m.*
> *Catherine*

At first, Sara thought she couldn't spend Christmas with anyone in her distraught state. Then she thought of Catherine spending Christmas alone, and she knew she needed to be there for her friend. They had always invited Catherine to join them for Christmas dinner at their house—but my, how everything had changed. It had affected Catherine, too.

Catherine had lost her parents when she had been just a child. Like Sara, she was raised by an elderly aunt who had passed away at least ten years ago. She had never married, although she had come close about five years ago. She had been engaged to be married to a mariner in July of 1906, but her betrothed had disappeared at sea that June. His ship was never recovered, his body never found. Catherine understood pain and hardship. Catherine understood loss and loneliness.

***

On Christmas morning, Sara heard the church bells peal. She bathed and dressed in her holiday red velvet dress she had purchased last Christmas. She wrapped the new barberry candle that was sitting on her dresser. Why she had taken it from her home on Astor Street she didn't know, but it would make a wonderful holiday gift for Catherine.

Sara went down to get coffee and a muffin for breakfast early that morning and wished Mrs. Williams a Merry Christmas. Mrs. Williams seemed happy that Sara had plans for the day. She told her to have a wonderful time and promised her a hot toddy when she returned that evening.

Catherine arrived at the boarding house with her carriage at eleven a.m. and Sara was ready and waiting for her arrival. She donned her cloak, wrapped her scarf around her neck, grabbed her muff and Catherine's present, and called out another Merry Christmas to Mrs. Williams, who was setting the table for dinner.

Sara hurried to the carriage and greeted her friend with a hug, which Catherine returned tightly. She covered herself with the mohair blanket, and they were on their way to Catherine's home. They had to pass the Dewberry house on the way and Sara strained to catch a glimpse of her children, but not one was to be seen.

Catherine led the filly to the stable where Ned, her stable boy, took care of the horses. Then, Sara and Catherine hurried into the house.

Catherine took Sara's cloak and hung it on a clothes tree. "Come sit by the fire," she said gently.

Sara was very comfortable in Catherine's home. She pulled off her boots and curled her legs under her on an overstuffed chair near the fireplace.

Meanwhile, Catherine went into the hallway and opened a small cabinet. She took out two wine glasses and filled them with sherry. She came back and handed Sara the stemware and took her place in an identical chair on the other side of the fireplace.

"Holiday cheers!" Catherine said, lifting her glass. "I think you can use an aperitif." She smiled.

"How are you doing?" she asked more somberly.

Catherine had reached out to Sara during the past month but Catherine's anger at Henry only intensified Sara's pain. Sara had longed for the comfort of her friend, but she distanced herself because in her mind, she was the guilty one, the one who deceived, the one who had lied. As difficult as Henry had made her life, she did not blame him. She went through the stages of grief: shock and denial, pain and guilt, anger and bargaining. Now it was time to move forward and Catherine was just who she needed.

"How am I doing...?" Sara started tentatively, then poured out her heart to her friend.

Catherine listened attentively, saying little. Occasionally, she reached out to pat her hand or rub her shoulders. She opened the decanter and refilled Sara's glass.

At one p.m., they went to the dining room for dinner. Their dinner conversation was reminiscent of their good times and the close bond of sisterhood they shared. By the end of dinner, they were giggling like schoolgirls, and Sara was grateful for the light-hearted mood. The sherry they consumed during dinner didn't hurt, either.

After dinner, their conversation gravitated to the suffragette movement and what was happening across the nation. Catherine filled Sara in on Tillie's activities in Washington, D.C. and in New York City. Tillie had been traveling with Carrie Chapman Catt. She spoke before the Senate, and individually, with various representatives. Her late husband's contacts gave her unlimited access to the lawmakers of the nation, and Tillie was attempting to win them over one by one.

For those she couldn't speak with directly, she arranged to meet and have tea with their spouses, who sometimes proved to be more effective than battling the aides and hectic schedules of the congressmen themselves.

Catherine spoke of the local grassroots outreach and how Edith had proved to be a driving force in the local movement in spite of operating under the veil of secrecy. She had been able to recruit many new members. Those who remained incognito were still an asset to the cause, but there were more and more members coming to the forefront of the movement, making great strides on the local scene.

Sara was pensive, her hands kneading in her lap.

"*Mrs. Dewberry*, whatever are you thinking?" Catherine grinned at Sara.

"Well, I see no reason for secrecy anymore. What more can I lose?"

"What about your children?" Catherine inquired. "Aren't you afraid of losing your children forever?"

"I am forbidden to contact my children now. That will not change. Ella is an advocate of the cause and Liz is too young to care. Right now, they have no idea where I am. They have no way to contact me. If I should become openly active, at least they will know where I am. The court order prevents me from contacting them, but they are not restrained from contacting me."

Catherine reached a hand over to squeeze hers. "Sara, think about it. Are you sure?"

Sara sat up straighter in her chair and lifted her chin. "I am sure. I need to do this for my children." It was because of women's lack of rights that she was in the position she was now. "I have no rights, no money, no children. I don't want my girls to suffer that same fate. It is about the vote, but it is much more than that. It is about the freedom and rights of all women."

She remembered the priest's words and closed her eyes. "Each of us has a purpose; it is our right and our duty to listen to Christ's calling and live a purposeful life."

Sara opened her eyes. "I must speak to Edith tomorrow. Do you think Tillie is in town for the holidays? I need to speak to Tillie, also." A sparkle glinted in Sara's eyes. Her face glowed. If she couldn't be with her children, she could at least fight for them.

They had a few more sherries and Sara fell asleep on Catherine's sofa. For the first time in a long while, Sara slept peacefully and spent the night at Catherine's house.

When Sara returned to the boarding house, she was already making plans for the next chapter in her life.

Chapter Twenty-nine

Sara went to Marilyn Mason's house the following day. They were still incredibly busy sewing the holiday apparel for the New Year's celebrations. She had a skip in her step as she entered the shop. "Good morning, Mrs. Mason. Did you have a nice Christmas?" she asked cheerfully.

"How can you not have a good Christmas with a houseful of children?" Marilyn asked, then seemed to remember Sara was without her children this holiday. "You appear in good spirits. How was your holiday?"

"I don't think it was as good as yours." Sara recalled the slight headache she had woken up with that morning. "But, Mrs. Mason, I have seen things in a different light. I guess I had an epiphany of sorts. I have great hopes for my future."

"I am so glad to hear that, Sara. And by the way, when it is just the two of us, please call me Marilyn." Marilyn, who was already at work hemming a holiday gown, peered over her glasses at Sara. "So, what great revelations have you discovered?"

Sara continued to smile. "Not any that I wish to talk about at the moment, but soon my direction will be clear. I think you will see a *new* Mrs. Dewberry."

"Well, I hope that 1913 will be a wonderful year for you." Changing the subject, Marilyn explained about all the dresses they needed to get done that week.

"Looks like we have a lot of work to do before the New Year." Sara decided the formulation of her plans could wait another week.

The New Year came without so much as a toot, and Sara was ready to begin her new life. First, she needed to talk to Edith. At three p.m. on Tuesday, she visited the library, getting an update on the latest suffragette activities. Catherine had been right; the new focus was on areas outside the state. Wisconsin seemed to be on board for the reformation.

"Of course," Edith reminded Sara, "we must be vigilant. We must always keep the movement on the front burner with the state legislature and in the minds of the voters. This is not a done deal yet."

Their conversation drifted more to personal matters and Edith inquired, "Did you have any opportunity to see your children over the holiday?"

"Unfortunately, no. I did send presents by courier, and hoped they will know their mother still cares for them," Sara confided sadly.

"I don't know if you are aware, but Ella has been frequenting the library on a weekly basis," Edith revealed. "She has inquired on occasion if you have come by. She tries to make it seem like casual conversation, but if you ask me, she wishes to contact you. Since you have not been around, I have not been able to give her a clue. However, unless she changes her pattern after the new semester starts, you may be interested to know she comes by at about four p.m. every Wednesday after her classes. Occasionally, she comes on Monday as well. Since school is back in session, I will expect her tomorrow at four."

Sara gasped. "Of course, why didn't I think of that? Edith, I shall be back tomorrow after work." She hurried out of the library, almost forgetting the book she had selected. Tomorrow could not come soon enough.

***

At three-thirty on Wednesday, Sara put away her sewing.

Marilyn said, "Sara, we have so much to do. If you would like to work a bit later, it will help us catch up."

"Oh, Marilyn, I would love so much to stay, but I can't today. I have an engagement. I can be here as long as you need me tomorrow," Sara promised.

"That will be fine," said Marilyn. "We need to finish everything by close of day on Friday."

"I will stay until midnight if need be," Sara offered. "I need to rush now." She was already opening the door and putting the wool scarf around her neck on the way out. "Goodbye, Marilyn."

Sara hurried to the library and found a place by the reference books where she could watch the door. She thought she had read every title in the aisle as she glanced back and forth from the books to the clock on the wall. Four o'clock came and went. Sara's elation turned to nervous fidgeting as the clock ticked away the minutes that felt like hours.

At four-fifteen, her nervousness became despair. She glanced toward Edith, who shrugged her shoulders. The hands of the clock reached four-thirty, and Sara was about to give up. The library would close at five and chances of Ella showing up at this late time were slim.

At four thirty-five, the door opened and a young lady in a green cloak came in and moved toward the desk. Sara didn't see her face and didn't recognize the garment. She continued to peruse the books.

The young lady returned a book and inquired about material for a thesis she was composing on the writing of the Constitution.

Edith smiled and said, "I think you might find something you like in the aisle over there." She pointed in the direction of the aisle.

The young lady turned, looking in Sara's direction. She let out a shriek. "Mother!" She ran into Sara's arms.

They clung to each other, not wanting to let go. "Ella, Ella, I've missed you so," Sara cooed into Ella's neck as she stroked her daughter's hair.

"Mother, we didn't know where to find you. Father said you had left and didn't leave an address. Where have you been? Why didn't you say good-bye or come see us?" Tears rolled down Ella's cheek, and Sara knew they were a mixture of sadness and joy.

Sara gripped her daughter tight. "Ella, it is complicated. Your father is very disappointed in me. I have been a suffragette for almost a year, and I kept it a secret from him. He has banished me from our home and received full custody of you and Liz from the court. I have no money or means of taking care of you. I live in a single room at Williams boarding house, but I am forbidden by law to have contact with you or Liz or Thaddeus."

"But why, Mother? You have always been there for us. Why would the judge deny you?" Ella's eyes were huge and confused.

Sara looked down at the floor, not meeting Ella's eyes. "The judge felt I was unfit because I was watching the parade when Adam died." Sara choked back tears. "I will always regret that day."

Ella scowled in indignation. "But Mother, that was a horrible accident. You are no more guilty than I. How can a judge be so misguided?"

"Your father has very good lawyers," Sara said sadly. "My lawyer was no match, given the laws of the land. I had no rights as a woman, and that is why I must continue the fight. I must try to fix this atrocity, not just for me but for you and Liz, and all the other women in the world."

Ella seethed with anger. "I will speak to Father. I will tell him."

"No, no Ella," Sara interrupted. "You must not. I have finally been able to put my arms around you again. Father must never know. He has the court on his side and measures would be taken to keep us apart. We must not let that happen ever again. Promise me you won't speak of our meeting. Promise that you will continue to come to the library every Wednesday after school. If you need to meet me at any other time, leave a note with Edith. We must be careful, so others don't see us together. I will see if Edith can provide us a quiet room."

"Yes, yes. I promise, Mother," Ella vowed.

They hugged again and Sara ended their visit with a kiss on her daughter's cheek. "I will see you next Wednesday. I don't know how I can wait that long, but I will count the days."

Ella slipped out the door, blowing a kiss back to her mother on the way out.

Sara took a deep breath, closed her eyes, and thanked God and Edith.

***

Sara and Ella continued to meet on a weekly basis. Sara wanted to see Liz, but she couldn't ask a mere child to keep a secret. It was too risky. She told Ella to make sure Liz knew that her mother loved her and one day, they would meet again. Sara found joy in getting news from Ella on how her younger daughter was doing in school, fun things they did at home, and stories full of laughter. It wasn't enough to fill the hole in Sara's heart, but it was the second-best thing to it. She continued her activities with the suffragettes. There were rallies in various parts of the state and Sara attended them all, however she would not go if they interfered with her weekly meeting with Ella.

Months flew by and Easter was near. Sara went to the milliner and purchased a charming spring bonnet for Ella. She also bought a pretty string of silk spring flowers for Ella to braid into Liz's hair.

***

When Easter arrived, Ella braided Liz's hair and placed the fashionable hat on her own head as they headed off for Easter services. Mr. Dewberry greeted his girls and smiled. "My, how lovely you young ladies are today."

He twirled Liz around and examined her hair. "Your sister should be a hairdresser. She did a very professional job on your braid. You look like a breath of spring."

Then he turned to Ella. He looked at her quizzically and inquired, "Where did you get the beautiful bonnet?"

"Oh, this old thing?" Ella responded with a deflective laugh. "Just add a few flowers and you can fool a man any day," she teased.

Mr. Dewberry shrugged. "You are very talented." He held out his hands. Each girl took one as they scurried to the automobile and went off to church.

As they left church, Suzanne from the millinery shop stopped to say hello to everyone. "My Ella, you look fetching in that bonnet. It is one of my favorites. Your mother made the right choice for you. She couldn't decide between the one with roses or gardenias, and when she decided on the gardenias, we knew it would complete any outfit. I didn't realize she was selecting it for you, but I can see why she did."

Ella gulped. There was no way of talking her way out of this one.

Mr. Dewberry drove home in silence. When they got inside the door, he snapped the bonnet from Ella's head and crushed it. "When did your mother give this to you?" he demanded.

"That is between me and Mother," Ella snapped back.

"To your room, young lady. This instant!"

Ella ran to her room in tears. She slammed the door and flung herself unto the bed. Thoughts of never being able to see her mother again swirled in her head, and she sobbed harder.

Chapter Thirty

On Monday, Sara was off from work. All the Easter garments had been made and picked up before the holiday. Now they were entering a slow period.

That day, Henry arrived at the boarding house looking upset. "We need to talk."

Sara heard the anger in his voice. "Whatever is the matter with you? You look like you swallowed sour grapes."

"Whatever is the *matter* with you?" he snapped back. "You know full well you are not to have contact with the children."

Sara was about to speak, but he held up his hand to silence her. "Don't tell me more lies, Sara. I saw the hat you bought for Ella. Suzanne from the millinery store confirmed that you purchased it. It is clear you don't understand what a court order is, so perhaps I can put it into terms you will understand." He glared at her. "If you continue to see Ella or any of the children, I will have you committed to an insane asylum. I am still your husband and I have the power to do so. You have acted erratically and dangerously. You have disobeyed court orders and you are not seeing clearly."

Sara stiffened. "Mr. Dewberry, it seems to me if anyone is not seeing clearly and acting insane, it would be you." She turned and stormed out of the room.

This was not a threat Sara took lightly. Her second cousin Mary Jane had been placed in an insane asylum by her husband John, claiming she had threatened him with a butcher knife. Mary Jane had spent three years in the asylum because she had continued her rampage there. She had found John in bed with the maid and had went into the kitchen, throwing all the maid's things out onto the back porch. When John entered the kitchen in a tirade, she had grabbed a butcher knife and ordered him out of the house as well.

John had her committed and the maid became his concubine, still sleeping in Mary Jane's bed. This had not been a case of insanity. Mary Jane had been angry, and rightfully so. Her husband had suffered no consequences for his actions, and she had been helpless to defend herself. Sara needed to be careful not to find herself in a similar situation.

Henry would not carry out this threat...or would he? A year ago, she would not have dreamed such a thing could happen, but Henry had changed...and so had she. This was the first time the word divorce had entered Sara's mind. She soon dismissed the idea. Divorce was opposed on almost all grounds. In any event, she had no means for legal resources to fight it.

Sara had heard of a case in North Carolina where a woman had been horsewhipped and beaten by her husband. Her plea for divorce had made its way to the North Carolina Supreme court in 1862. The chief justice had denied her, stating, "The law gives the husband power to use such a degree of force necessary to make the wife behave and know her place." Nothing had changed.

Sara had some decisions to make. Would she continue to see her daughter and risk being placed in an insane asylum? Would she *not* see her daughters for the rest of their childhood?

After Henry left, Sara went to see Catherine. They discussed the matter of Henry's threat.

Catherine clenched her fists in anger but kept her voice calm. "Sara, what are you going to do?"

"I have no choice," Sara said. "I need to go away. If I stay, Ella will come to me. She knows where I am staying; she knows where I am working. I don't want her to be punished because of my actions. I can't go to an asylum."

Catherine shuddered. "Oh my Lord, Sara. They do atrocious things to people in asylums. It would be better to be in a prison. Where will you go?"

"I need to talk with Tillie. She is traveling with the movement. Perhaps she can take me with her. I only have twenty dollars, but some funding is available for those who travel for the cause. Tillie will know if there is something I can do."

Catherine nodded, and squeezed Sara's hand. "Tillie is in town for the holiday. I believe she will be leaving Wednesday or Thursday. Go see her tomorrow. She will be delighted to see you."

***

On Tuesday, Sara came calling at Tillie's home.

Tillie answered the knock. "Sara, my dear," Tillie said, seeming surprised by Sara's visit, "it is so good to see you. Do come in."

"Thank you, Tillie." Sara smiled, happy to see her old friend. "It has been some time. You have been traveling and I hear wonderful reports on your progress."

"Oh my, yes, I have been so busy. I need to hire a secretary. I am not so young anymore, you know." Tillie laughed, leading Sara to the study. "I will be back on the road tomorrow. We can't let up on the cause. Tell me, dear, what have you been doing?"

Sara sat on a chair across from Tillie and shut her eyes a moment to compose herself. She must not cry. "That is why I am here." She filled Tillie in on all the events that had taken place in the past year, about Henry's actions and threats, and about her recent meetings with Ella.

Tillie poured tea for them and listened with a grave face. "What can I do to help?"

"I need to leave," Sara blurted. "I was hoping I might be able to travel with you and help with the cause. I have no money, but there is a lot I can do. I can organize and write and clean and cook."

"As a matter of fact, I wasn't joking when I said I need a secretary. There are pamphlets to distribute, correspondence to send, and speeches to write and research. There won't be much cooking and cleaning except brewing a pot of tea on occasion, but there will be materials to keep track of at various events and a lot of lugging about of boxes of materials and arranging for accommodations at boarding houses and inns. Do you think you could handle that?"

"Tillie, it sounds like a dream job." Sara sighed with relief.

"Do you drive?" Tillie asked.

"No. I'm sorry, I don't." Sara frowned, worried that might change things.

"No problem, you can learn." Tillie patted her hand. "Can you be ready by Wednesday about noon?"

"I will be," Sara said enthusiastically. "Oh, by the way, where are we going?"

"New York City. The annual convention of the National Women's Suffrage Association will be meeting in June, but it is a long journey with several stops along the way. Carrie Chapman is the president and keynote speaker, and I am looking forward to it."

Sara hurried to the boarding house to let Mrs. Williams know she would be leaving. "Mrs. Williams, may I ask a favor of you? I don't have a lot of things, but I do have some special mementos from my deceased parents and of my children that will be difficult to take with me. Could I possibly store them with you?"

Mrs. Williams gave Sara a big hug. "Of course, Sara. I will consider it my small contribution to the movement. Tillie is often quoted in the newspaper, and her whereabouts and activities are often published. I will think of you every time I see an article. Be safe and change the world."

Sara wrote a note to Ella and went to the library to drop it off. She told Edith of her plans and left the library in silence with a lump in her throat. She then went to say her good-byes to Catherine.

Later that day, she went by Washington Elementary School and waited for the children to get out of school. She watched from a distance as Liz clamored down the walk with her friends. She was laughing, and although Sara wanted to say good-bye, she didn't want to sadden her daughter in any way.

Instead, heart racing at the journey ahead, Sara left and went to the boarding house to pack.

Chapter Thirty-one

Ella arrived at the library at her usual time on Wednesday and looked around. Mother was nowhere to be seen. *Where was she?*

Edith beckoned her to the desk. "Your mother left a note," she whispered, and took an envelope from a drawer behind the counter.

"Thank you," Ella said and quickly ripped it open.

> *My dearest Ella,*
>
> *It is with a heavy heart that I write this note. When you read this, I will be on my way to New York City. It will be a long time before I return. Just remember that I will always love you and miss you terribly. One day, women will have rights so they will never be separated from their children again, so they can own property, and have a voice and be heard. I must do my part to secure that right for you and your children so you will never have to suffer the pain and loss that I have endured.*
>
> *Take care of Liz and let her know my love for her will remain strong for as long as I live. Ella, I know you want to be a teacher or a writer, and you have the advantage of your education. Follow your dreams. My arms ache to hold you and to be with you on your journey.*
>
> *Should you need any motherly advice or someone to talk to, go see Catherine. She will greet you with open arms. Keep focused on the day that we will once again be together. If there is an opportunity that we can meet again, I will make every arrangement to do so.*
>
> *All my love,*
> *Mother*

Ella held the letter close to her heart and left the library quickly.

Chapter Thirty-two

Henry had to take care of some banking business for his friend, Attorney David Daniels. After the appropriate gentleman's handshake and small talk about the weather, Attorney Daniels turned to the matter of Henry's separation. "Henry, my friend, how are you doing as a single man?"

Henry slumped, rubbing his head with one hand. "Sara is one headstrong woman! She has been seeing Ella behind my back and in violation of court orders."

"I see," said David. "So, what do you propose to do about it?"

"I have taken care of that," he said emphatically, handing David a cup of coffee and pouring himself a cup. "I threatened to have her committed to an insane asylum if she continues."

David choked on the coffee he had just sipped. "What? How did that go over?"

"Not well. She said I was the one who belonged in an insane asylum. But I think she will think twice before seeing Ella again."

"Henry, this is none of my business, but what do you hope to accomplish with this exile and these punishment threats? It doesn't appear to me that any good can come of it."

"Sara needs to know her place. When you have a young stallion, you need to break it. You need to let it know who is in control. The horse needs to realize that compliance makes things easier. Once the horse understands this, he will become your best friend. Once Sara understands that her place is in the home as a dutiful wife and mother, she will be rewarded, and our lives will be rejoined."

David sat in silence for a moment, his hand in a fist over his mouth. "That would be fine if Sara was a horse, but she is not. She is an educated, beautiful woman who has needs as well."

"Every need she has would be fulfilled in our home. Only by making her realize the price she has paid will she understand her place."

"Henry, you know Sara. Why did you fall in love with her, why did you marry her?"

Henry thought for a moment. "We were young. I was still in college. We were poor. Sara had a small inheritance, but she didn't want to spend it on foolishness. She wanted to save it for a house. I admired her practicality. She could have had anyone; she was that beautiful. The day I proposed, we were on a picnic. Her long, auburn hair flew in the breeze as she ran down the hill in the meadow. I picked some wildflowers and presented them to her, and then I gave her an engagement ring. I would have asked for her hand from her father, but her parents had passed away and she was on her own. She was the sweetest girl I had ever met, but she had a feisty side, too. She had compassion for the poor and lonely, she had a sense of justice for anyone in trouble, and she wanted her children to know the real world. We could send our children to the finest schools available, but she insisted they attend public school to mingle and know all kinds of people."

"And what did you think about that?" David asked.

"I loved that about her. It made me respect her." Henry gave a wistful smile, then just as quickly, wiped it off his face.

"It doesn't seem to me that Sara has changed. When did *you* change? When you became wealthy? When you entered the proprieties of society? When your profession made you a stuffed shirt?" David reprimanded, meeting Henry's gaze with a challenge.

Henry was taken aback by his friend's frankness.

"However," David went on, "if you still want to stay with the crazy horse analogy, whoever tried breaking a horse by setting it loose? It seems to me that you have driven her away."

Henry wanted to respond, but he had no words. David was right. He had changed. *What have I done?*

"Go home and think about it," David urged.

Henry finished the meeting and left in a daze. He still felt this suffragette thing was wrong, but he also wondered about other things. *What have I done to our marriage? What have I done to Sara? How can I fix this?*

He went to the boarding house.

Mrs. Williams answered the door.

"I need to speak with Mrs. Dewberry," Henry announced breathlessly.

"I'm sorry," said Mrs. Williams tersely. "Mrs. Dewberry doesn't live here anymore."

"What? Do you know where she is?" Henry asked, desperate.

"No forwarding address. Good-bye." Mrs. Williams shut the door.

Henry raced to see Catherine, his heart pounding in his chest. He knocked several times on her door before she opened it. "Catherine, I have made a huge mistake. I need to talk to Sara; do you know where she is?" He panicked.

"Yes, Henry, you have made a huge mistake. Sara is gone. I have no address; she has left the area," Catherine said dryly, no sympathy showing on her face.

Henry rubbed his face with the back of his hand. He got into his automobile and laid his head on the steering wheel and let the tears flow. His shoulders shook, and he felt total despair. "What have I done, what have I done?" he said aloud to the emptiness of the automobile.

He couldn't tell the children their mother had left. He had already told them that. Now he realized the pain he had inflicted on them.

That night, when the children were getting ready for bed, he gathered them into his arms and said, "Pray for your mother. She loves you. Pray that she will come home soon."

Chapter Thirty-three

Sara and Tillie packed up the Model T Ford for their journey to New York City, and went on their way. It was about a thousand miles to New York City, and at forty miles an hour, it would take several days to get there on less than perfect roads. It was a pleasant spring day in early May. The Model T was an open-bodied touring car built in 1910. It was rich forest green and had a brass radiator and headlights. The trim, including the horn and other small parts, were also brass. The motor car was one of the first to feature electric lights as opposed to the gas lights on the original Model Ts.

It was a beautiful automobile and drew a lot of attention as it chugged its way down the dirt roads, especially from young boys. Traffic only became a problem when a horse and buggy were in the way. Tillie had to slow down so as not to spook the horses.

Tillie drove the first day, and shortly after crossing the Illinois border, she decided that was enough driving for one day. She had friends in Illinois who put them up for the evening. It seemed to Sara that Tillie had friends everywhere.

Frank and Martha Mueller were German immigrants who had settled in the area around the middle of the last century. They were dairy farmers, and were just about to sit down to dinner, so they graciously invited Sara and Tillie to join them for wurst and kraut, which they washed down with mugs of German beer.

They spoke little English, but Tillie was well-versed in the German language. They spoke with enthusiasm throughout the evening, and at about nine p.m., a few hours after dark, Martha showed Tillie and Sara to a room with twin beds covered with feather beds and fluffy goose down pillows. Since it was early spring, the nighttime cooled down fast, so the warmth of the patchwork quilts was a much-appreciated comfort.

Sara had never slept in a feather bed this plump before. She pulled on her flannel nightgown and blew out the candle. She pulled back the comforter and rolled into the bed, which enveloped her in a cloud of fluff.

"Oh my!" exclaimed Sara.

Tillie giggled.

"I have never been hugged by a bed before." Sara joined in the laughter.

"Glorious rest," Tillie murmured. "Look out the window, Sara. The stars are so bright in the country."

It was the prettiest sight. An almost full moon hung over the barn, filtering light through the lace curtains on the window. Sara thought of Ella and Liz and wondered if they were admiring the same celestial view she was.

***

Morning on the farm came at the crack of dawn. Sara heard the rooster crowing just as the sun came up in the east. At this time of the year, the weather was unpredictable, but it looked like it was going to be another glorious day.

Sara went to the window and saw Frank Mueller headed to the barn with a bucket in his hand and his dog at his side. The cows were waiting by the barn, ready for their morning milking. The chickens milled around the yard, scratching up scraps from yesterday's feeding. She heard some clanging in the kitchen and dressed quickly to see if she could be of assistance. Tillie was already up.

Sara yawned as she entered the kitchen.

"Good morning!" both Tillie and Martha called out at once.

"Coffee?" Mrs. Mueller held a mug in her hand.

"Yes, please." Sara had smelled the coffee from the bedroom, and it was that sweet aroma that pulled her out of bed.

Mrs. Mueller filled the mug and offered her the cream pitcher.

"Thank you so much." Sara wrapped her hands around the cup to take a bit of the morning chill away. She could smell biscuits baking in the old cook stove. She hadn't realized until then how hungry she was.

When Mr. Mueller came in from the barn, they sat down to a breakfast of sausage, eggs, and hot biscuits. Martha asked them to stay another day and she would fix her favorite meal—wiener schnitzel. Martha was an excellent cook, and her plump frame indicated that she loved to eat as well.

Tillie thanked her kindly, but said they had to be on their way, or they would not be able to make the necessary stops they had on their itinerary. By ten a.m., the temperature had warmed up and it was time to get back on the road.

"You drive," stated Tillie as though it was an everyday occurrence.

"What? Me?" Sara replied, her eyes widening. "Tillie, I don't know *how* to drive."

Tillie gave her a wink. "Well, it is high time for you to learn."

They stood in front of the car and Tillie proceeded to give Sara a lesson. "This is a three-speed car...drive, get out of the ditch, and reverse. There is a throttle—this thing here." She pointed to a lever on the steering wheel. "That gives you power. It has something to do with air and gas, but all you need to know is it will control how fast you go."

Tillie pointed to three pedals on the floor. "Look down there. The left pedal will engage the gears. If you depress it fully and hold it, it will be in low gear...the 'get out of ditch' gear. If you depress it slightly, to the mid-range, it will do nothing. That is called neutral. If you don't depress it at all, it will go forward. Do you understand?"

"I think so," said Sara doubtfully, the mechanics of it all spinning through her head.

"Well, you need to have it in neutral when you start the auto, or you will be run over," Tillie warned.

"That, I will remember." In her head, Sara pictured a runaway vehicle dragging her down the road and shuddered. She listened intently to the rest of Tillie's instructions, but still felt nervous.

Still processing it all, Sara asked, "And what is the right pedal for?"

"That is the brake. Try not to depend on it too much because it doesn't always work well. You should get used to using the lever beside the seat. That is the parking brake. You should always use it when you get out of the vehicle. Try pulling it all the way back." Tillie looked at Sara.

"Like this?" Sara grabbed the lever.

"Yes, that's right. You've got it."

"Tillie, are you sure you trust me to drive your motorcar?" Sara asked, still hesitant.

"Of course! Now get inside and try the gears." Tillie climbed in the vehicle and had Sara review all the operations. "Now, do you have it in neutral?"

"I think so," said Sara, her hands feeling unnatural on the steering wheel.

"Then, set the throttle, get out, and start it. Go to the front and crank it," Tillie commanded.

Sara stepped to the front of the car and looked it over. After a deep breath, she grabbed hold of the handle and gave it a swift turn. There was a slight grunt from the engine, but nothing happened.

"Try again," urged Tillie. "This time, pretend that you are making ice cream. It will require some steady muscle power."

Sara thought of the ice cream bucket with the crank on the top. She pushed her way through the heavy cream and continued until the engine sputtered and chugged, then began purring. She ended up pushing too much, and the automobile sputtered and stopped.

With a look to Tillie, she tried again, taking a good hold of the crank and giving it a swift turn. Before she knew what had happened, she was flat on her derriere on the ground.

"What happened?" Sara laughed in surprise.

Tillie laughed with her. "I know *horsepower* isn't quite the same as horses, but sometimes they have the same temperament. They balk, they lurch, they sputter, they kick—but once they are moving along, they purr. Well, most of the time, at least."

Sara got up, brushed herself off, and made one final attempt. The vehicle started, and they were on their way. Sara got used to steering it in short order, but down the road, she spotted a buckboard with a horse.

"Slow down a bit," cautioned Tillie.

"I don't know how," panicked Sara, thinking of the horse and buckboard that had killed Adam. "I've forgotten."

"Use the throttle," directed Tillie. They were coming up fast on the horse.

Sara, shaking and praying, pulled up on the throttle, and the little car lurched ahead, speeding past the buckboard. She glanced back and saw the driver shake his fist in the air as he attempted to calm his horse.

Tillie leaned over and pushed the throttle, slowly bringing them back to a steady pace as Sara zigzagged across the road in her attempt to control her runaway horsepower.

Once they were back to the open road, Sara regained her composure after the close call. "Are you sure you want me to drive?" Sara smiled weakly at Tillie.

"You will be just fine. You need practice, that's all. You can drive to Chicago, but I will take it into the city." Tillie laughed. "We wouldn't want you to start another Chicago Fire or anything by running over Mrs. O'Leary's lantern."

Chapter Thirty-four

Tillie took over driving several miles outside of the city of Chicago. As they neared, the skyscrapers loomed over the horizon. Sara was in awe. She had never seen such an amazing sight. Sara had been to Chicago twice before, but the last time she had been arrested before she had even seen the city, and the time before that was during the devastation from the Chicago Fire. This was a whole new spectacle.

Tillie gave Sara some background on what she was seeing. "Chicago led the way in skyscraper design. The Chicago School of Architecture is responsible for this flourishing sky rise."

"You mean to say students designed all of this?" Sara swept her arms out at the panorama before her eyes.

"Yes. This was an era that produced some very prominent architects. There was a need, and they filled it beautifully. Originally, skyscrapers were built for space conservation and with little architectural aesthetics. But by the late 1800s, buildings became not only practical, but attractive."

Tillie went on. "In 1892, Chicago banned the construction of new skyscrapers taller than one hundred fifty feet. There was fear for the potential for fire hazards after the Chicago Fire of 1870."

"They must be frightfully expensive." Sara wondered how anyone could afford to build such magnificent structures.

"The economy was such then that the buildings were not out of reach for the investors," Tillie assured her. "The Astors, the Rockerfellers, the Woolworths were major money contributors, and they had money to burn, no pun intended."

And here they were in their magnificent glory, unbelievable with their towers and spires reaching to the heavens. Sara could scarcely believe her eyes.

They drove down Lakeshore Drive and through the city, and Sara could not stop gazing up in amazement. She made Tillie stop to see the Home Insurance Building, the first-ever skyscraper built in the United States of fireproofed metal frame. It was a whopping ten stories high.

"It was built in the typical historical style, but in 1895," Tillie pointed out.

"My, Tillie, how did you ever learn so much about these buildings?"

"My husband was a senator, but he was also very involved in building and rebuilding in this great land. He often told me stories of the magnificent growth in our large cities. He could keep me mesmerized for hours. Wait until you see our nation's capital. You will be awestruck."

"I am awestruck already."

Tillie began to give Sara a tourist view account of the surrounding buildings. "See the Second Leiter Building? The walls are becoming more glass than stone. Over there is the luminous Reliance Building. It was built with continuous horizontal bands of windows that appear not to have supporting walls at all. That one intrigues me."

Sara's eyes glowed with anticipation of something new and exciting around every corner. As Sara gazed up, she saw an unbelievable crystal city that took her breath away. "I'm astonished."

They went to the Palmer House, where they would stay for two days. "One more day to sightsee," said Tillie, "then we will be attending a program sponsored by the Chicago Area Suffragettes. Carrie Chapman Catt is the primary guest speaker." Tillie would speak as well.

The Palmer House was elegant. It had been built a few years earlier in 1906 and was home to the elite visitors who came to the city. Being in the heart of downtown Chicago, it gave its patrons access to all the downtown amenities. Sara had stayed at hotels in the past, but none so elegant as this.

Sara and Tillie had dinner at the hotel's restaurant, ordering pheasant under glass served with rice pilaf and fresh asparagus. Their first course was a garden salad with bleu cheese dressing, and they each had a glass of white house wine with the meal. The food was delicious. Sara had difficulty finishing her portion but was too astounded at its succulence to stop eating.

She went to bed that night like a child who had just experienced her first Christmas. She could not believe the wonder of it all. She was sure it was a dream.

***

They woke to another stunning spring day. The lilacs and tulips were ablaze at the botanical garden not far from the hotel. The apple and cherry trees lining the lakefront were all decked in their spring blossoms of pink, purple, and white. It seemed to Sara that she had dropped into a fairyland. It wasn't a dream after all.

Sara was not able to eat that day. The adrenaline of this adventure and the fascination of all that she was taking in was overwhelming. That evening, she sat down to a Caesar salad and a cup of tea.

"Tillie, I can't tell you how grateful I am to be traveling with you. I am so excited about the suffragette movement and so proud to be a part of it. I never would've dreamed I would drive a car and see such wonders. Thank you."

Tillie leaned over and squeezed her hands with a soft smile. "We have just begun our journey, and you will see many more sights and have many more experiences before we are done. I can't think of a better traveling companion. Thank *you*, my dear."

"I am so happy to be here with you."

"You never inquired about your wages. You might not be so thrilled when you find out what they are."

Sara looked questioningly at Tillie. "I didn't expect to be paid. I had hoped that you would cover my food and travel costs. I just had to leave before things got worse."

Tillie was thoughtful for a moment. "You told me everything that has happened, but I don't understand why you had to leave. Your children are there. Are you in physical danger? Are you afraid of Mr. Dewberry?"

"No, I am not afraid of him, but I am afraid of what he can do legally."

"Does Henry want a divorce?" Tillie hesitated. "Do *you* want a divorce?"

"Neither of us has grounds for divorce. We have a difference of opinion, and he is of the mind that I need to *know my place*." Sara sighed. "Don't get me wrong. I love my place in the home and with my children, but I need to be a *person*, not just property. I believe Henry thinks having nothing of my own will send me back home begging for forgiveness, but instead, I have found that I am stronger with nothing. I started out wanting the right to vote, but now I want much, much more. I want equality. I need to be worthy in my own right."

Tillie nodded. "I understand, dear. Do you think you and Mr. Dewberry will ever reconcile?"

"Hmm," Sara pondered. "That is difficult to answer. I still love him, but he needs to learn to compromise and to respect my beliefs. To treat me as an equal. I am not sure that will happen. I don't want to be anyone's property."

"Will you compromise?"

"If we win this fight...if the movement is successful, and this country recognizes that women are intelligent, equal partners in life with the same rights as men..." Sara paused. "Yes, I will know my place, and I will be happy to be a wife and mother and nothing more... Well, nothing outrageous, anyway. I don't think I will ever be without a voice."

Tillie grinned, and said, "I think the genie is out of the bottle and it is very difficult to put her back in."

"We could use a little genie to grant us a few wishes." Sara laughed.

"And by the way, you will be paid one dollar a day for the days we work, and for days like today when we get to take a break, you will get fifty cents as my companion...along with all of your travel expenses and meals, of course," Tillie revealed.

Sara's mouth dropped open, and then she sighed. "I am in a fairyland."

Chapter Thirty-five

Sara and Tillie met with the other suffragettes for dinner. Many suffragettes were also involved in the prohibition movement, so no alcohol was served at dinner or throughout the evening. Dinner was baked chicken with all the fixings. After a dessert of lemon meringue pie, the president of the Chicago chapter introduced the keynote speaker.

"Ladies, we are pleased to have with us tonight several people who have worked very hard for the cause. Please help me welcome Tillie Morgenson from Milwaukee. She is the widow of the late Senator Morgenson. Later, we will be hearing from our beloved Carrie Chapman Catt, who has been a tireless advocate for the cause. We are pleased to have both women with us this evening.

"First, I wish to introduce Tillie Morgenson. Tillie has been fighting for the cause for nearly a half century. When her late husband Stanley Morgenson was with the United States Senate, Mrs. Morgenson was there as well, encouraging her husband to pass legislation giving women the right to vote, and in fact, Senator Morgenson did introduce many such bills.

"Unfortunately, though her husband supported the bills, they fell on deaf ears. Still, Tillie would speak to the senator's colleagues and try to encourage them to support women's rights issues. Senator Morgenson served in the senate for thirty-six years, and all those years Tillie was there behind the scenes pleading for the cause with his colleagues and the wives of senators. She made herself available for all the social events sponsored by the wives of senators and congressmen so she could influence the wives of those lawmakers, believing that behind every successful man is an intelligent woman. She hoped that if minds were changed it would not necessarily be in the halls of justice, but in the dining rooms and boudoirs of influential people.

"After her dear husband suffered and died from a stroke, Tillie Morgenson continued her mission. She started the grassroots organization of housewives and mothers who perhaps couldn't act in the same way that Washington, D.C. operated, but they could collectively have a voice. She has been responsible in establishing suffragette organizations in seven states. Meanwhile, she kept her contacts and periodically lobbied for women's rights in Washington. She was influenced by Elizabeth Cady Stanton and Susan B. Anthony and spread the message of hope. We are so pleased to have with us this evening, Mrs. Tillie Morgenson."

The applause shook the room.

Sara stood by, proud she was able to be a part of this wonderful woman's life. She watched as Tillie stepped to the podium, and the roar of enthusiasm for her presence became even louder and longer.

Finally, Tillie raised her hand for silence and began her speech. "My dear friends Elizabeth Cady Stanton and Susan B. Anthony were pioneers in this great cause. In 1848, Elizabeth Cady Stanton attended the first meeting of the Women's Rights Convention in Seneca Falls, New York, later recognized as the Seneca Falls Convention. She was the principle author of the Declaration of Rights and Sentiments which she patterned after the Declaration of Independence."

Tillie adjusted her glasses and picked up the document. "This is how she began; let me read it to you: 'When, in the course of human events...'"

The audience was enthralled.

"'We hold these truths to be self-evident: that all men *and women* are created equal; that they are endowed by their Creator with certain inalienable rights; that among these are life, liberty, and the pursuit of happiness; that to secure these rights governments are instituted, deriving their just powers from the consent of the governed.'"

Tillie went on amidst shining eyes, elaborating on the effect of Mrs. Stanton's speech with a warm but powerful voice. Sara watched and listened in awe.

"These words were very controversial," Tillie said, "causing quite an uproar amongst not just men, but women, and even suffragettes as well. Some felt she had crossed the line and even undermined suffragette progress. Many people respected the abilities and courage of the document but considered it shocking and radical. There was a fear that it would cause the women's rights movement to lose the much needed public support. The document outlined the many opinions of the women, and like so many new ideas, they were summarily questioned and rejected. However, when dissected they are approved. Let me go through some of them with you." Tillie cleared her throat, looking regal and purposeful at the podium.

"'He has never permitted her to exercise her inalienable right to the elective franchise.' Primary to our cause is the right to vote. Correct?"

There was a resounding cheer from the audience.

"'He has compelled her to submit to laws, in the formation of which she had no voice.' Is this correct?"

Once again, the crowd cheered.

"'He has withheld from her rights which are given to the most ignorant and degraded men—both natives and foreigners.'"

Each item was met with applause and cheers, which Sara joined in on as Tillie's voice grew louder.

"'Having deprived her of this first right as a citizen, the elective franchise, thereby leaving her without representation in the halls of legislation, he has oppressed her on all sides. He has made her, if married, in the eye of the law, civilly dead.'"

Tillie paused for a moment and looked thoughtful at the crowd, then said, "My dear secretary and assistant, though she had been a partner in a marriage, contributing financially with a substantial inheritance, raising several children admirably and providing the comforts and duties of a wife, found herself alone and penniless. Why? Just look to the next item. 'He has taken from her all right in property, even to the wages she earns.'"

The audience gave out sharp gasps of disapproval.

Sara began to shake, both honored to be mentioned and furious at her situation. She met Tillie's eyes across the room and gave her a sharp nod.

"So, my friends," Tillie continued, "suppose she has had enough and chooses to leave... 'He has so framed the laws of divorce, as to what shall be the proper causes of divorce, in case of separation, to whom the guardianship of the children shall be given; regardless of the happiness of the woman—the law, in all cases, going upon a false supposition of the supremacy of a man, and giving all power into his hands.'" Tillie paused. "What that means, ladies, is he has the right to take the children you bore. The children you nurtured. So, ladies, are you outraged now?"

Tillie hesitated, though her gaze did not waver. "There is more. Suppose she is on her own, either by leaving a marriage or never marrying to begin with. This is her plight: 'He has monopolized the profitable employments, and from those she is permitted to follow, she receives but a scanty remuneration. He closes against her all the avenues to wealth and distinction, which he considers most honorable to himself. As a teacher of theology, medicine, or law, she is not known. He has denied her the facilities for obtaining a thorough education—all colleges being closed against her.' Ladies, has Elizabeth Cady Stanton gone too far?"

The audience began to chant. "Equality for all, Equality for all, Equality for all!"

Sara chanted alongside them, unafraid to raise her voice louder.

Tillie held up her hand for silence. "Wait ladies, there is still more. 'He has created a false public sentiment by giving to the world a different code of morals for men and women, by which moral delinquencies which exclude women from society are not only tolerated but deemed of little account in man. He has usurped the prerogative of Jehovah himself, claiming it as his right to assign for her a sphere of action, when in fact that right belongs to her conscience and her God.'

"Finally, and in summary, 'He has endeavored in every way that he could destroy her confidence in her own peers, to lessen her self-respect, and to make her willing to lead a dependent and abject life.'

"Now ladies, if you think any of these sentiments go too far, now is your time to stand up and speak."

The ladies murmured among themselves.

Sara shook her head, quiet with her thoughts. Watching the room, no one moved from their seats, and after a short pause, the room once again erupted in applause and cheers.

Tillie once again raised her hand for silence. "The conclusion of this bill of rights should be the mission statement for each and every one of us. Here is Elizabeth's conclusion."

Tillie adjusted her glasses as she read from her notes. "'Now, in view of this entire disfranchisement of one-half the people of this country, their social and religious degradation—in view of the unjust laws above mentioned, and because women do feel themselves aggrieved, oppressed, and fraudulently deprived of their most sacred rights, we insist that they have immediate admission to all the rights and privileges which belong to them as citizens of these United States. In entering upon the great work before us, we anticipate no small amount of misconception, misrepresentation, and ridicule; but we shall use every instrument within our power to affect our object. We shall employ agents, circulate tracts, petition the state and national legislatures, and endeavor to enlist the pulpit and the press in our behalf. We hope this convention will be followed by a series of conventions, embracing every part of the country.' The words of Elizabeth Stanton, the sentiments of us all. Let us move forward for this great cause. Thank you." Tillie waved to the crowd.

The applause was deafening.

As she departed the stage, Tillie hugged Sara fiercely.

Chapter Thirty-six

After a brief break, the meeting continued with the introduction of Carrie Chapman Catt. Sara was eager to meet the woman who had been such an influence on the movement and sat high in her seat to see her over the rest of the crowd.

The chapter president began, "Carrie Chapman Catt has carried the torch of women's independence. She was not one of the earliest pioneers for the cause, but she is no less instrumental in seeing the cause through. Ever since she was a young girl and discovered that her intelligent, politically-informed mother did not have the right to vote, she vowed to do something to change that. Carrie became an activist, arguing with anyone who opposed her, starting with her father who was a defender of the status quo. She once had a heated debate with a boy from school, and her father worried that she would never find a husband with her attitude.

"She became a high school principal and met and married Leo Chapman. She gave up her ambitions for a while and concentrated on her role as a wife. Unfortunately, her husband died of typhoid, and a devastated Mrs. Chapman was forced to take a job as a secretary. One day, while delivering business papers, she came into a situation that reminded her of her cause. A businessman tried to make advances at her, and when he was rebuked, he exclaimed, 'Why do you come into a man's world if you don't want a little friendly attention?'"

The audience gasped.

Sara thought of Mr. Carter's advances and clenched her fists. How many other women had been in that same situation?

The moderator went on. "This ignorant action was enough to thrust Mrs. Chapman back into the mindset of her youth. Why does it have to be a man's world? Why shouldn't women have dignity and respect in the workplace?

"Carrie Chapman decided then and there that she wanted to help women attain rights as individuals, starting with the right to vote. She joined the Woman's Suffrage Association in Iowa and working for their cause became her life. She was admired and respected by both men and women alike, even those opposing her views. She gave lectures and was an excellent speaker. She helped with campaigns for supporters of the cause.

"She married one of her supporters, George Catt, and became known as Carrie Chapman Catt. With her husband's support, she has continued her mission, lecturing, writing, and traveling, meeting people, and bit by bit moving the cause forward. We are pleased that she has chosen this stop in Chicago to share with us her insight. Please help me in welcoming Mrs. Carrie Chapman Catt to our city."

Mrs. Catt took her place at the podium.

Great applause welcomed her—an iconic symbol of women's progress—and Sara clapped hard enough to make her hands ache.

"Thank you for that introduction," Mrs. Catt nodded to the chapter president. She explained that she was born not far from Chicago in the little town of Ripon, Wisconsin.

The Wisconsin contingent applauded.

"Since then, I have had the privilege of meeting with women such as yourselves all over this great nation of ours, and abroad as well." Mrs. Catt spoke of the many places she had visited throughout the world, how it had encouraged her that progress had been made, and that great success was imminent.

"I once heard a university professor say, 'The women's suffrage movement has reached and passed its climax, the suffrage wave is now receding.' Although he delivered the message with conviction, I recall a quote from Julius Caesar. 'Men believe for the most part, that which they wish.'"

The audience laughed heartily and broke into applause.

Mrs. Catt observed with a wry smile, "Thus, another fly resting upon the proverbial wheel of progress has commanded it to turn no more. This man engages our attention because he is representative of a type to be found in all our lands: wise men on the wrong side of a great question—modern Joshuas who command the sun to stand still and believe that it will obey."

She went on to outline the progress of the movement in the United States, Great Britain, Australia, Norway, and the Netherlands. Other more recent participation came from Canada, Germany, Denmark, and Sweden. She spoke of the atrocities women have endured and progress they had made.

"It is not the growing strength of our campaign forces alone which has filled us with this splendid optimism," Mrs. Catt said, "there are actual gains which in themselves should tell the world that the goal of this movement is near. Of the nine associations uniting to form this alliance in 1904, eight have secured a permanent change in the law, which is a step nearer the political suffrage. Of the twenty-four nations represented in this congress, the women of fifteen have won more political rights than they had seven years ago." She went on to list those achievements, which ranged from repeals of laws to gaining suffrage, and generated much optimism among the audience for the future.

"We have come upon a new time," she concluded. "It has brought new and complex problems. Our old problems have assumed new significance. We will join together, and we will strive to accomplish what we have so long worked to achieve. To the wrong that needs resistance, to the right that needs assistance, to the future in the distance, we give ourselves."

Tillie had told Sara that Carrie Chapman Catt had delivered much of this address in Stockholm, Sweden two years earlier and its power and enthusiasm had not changed. It was a message of hope and progress, and it left the auditorium in a frenzy of confidence and invigoration Sara could tangibly feel. It infected her, too. They would succeed. They could feel it in the air.

As with every rally they attended, Tillie and Sara were fueled with the energy of each encounter and excited to go forward to spread the news and bring people into the cause.

That night, Sara was beaming with excitement. "Tillie, that was the most amazing day I have ever had. The enthusiasm is contagious, the commitment astounding. I don't know when I have been so energized. I doubt I can even sleep."

"I understand," said Tillie. "I recall my first rally I attended in Washington. I thought my feet would never touch the ground. You should try to sleep because tomorrow we will be on the road to Ohio."

Chapter Thirty-seven

As Sara and Tilllie neared Dayton, Ohio, they encountered a horrific sight. There had been a great flood in March just a few months before their arrival. The banks of the Miami River had overflowed; hundreds of lives had been lost. Buildings were destroyed, and Ohio was in a state of despair. Devastation was everywhere. Tillie and Sara gazed about with their hearts in their throats, not able to believe their eyes.

The Ohioans were not interested in the political concerns of the day; they were only interested in survival.

All the same, Tillie looked forward to meeting with her old friend, Maude Comstock Waitt, and tried to keep Sara positive. Maude was a strong believer in the cause. She had come to Ohio after her marriage to Walter Waitt in 1901.

"Sara, you will like Maude. She is a real go-getter. She believes that if there is a way to succeed in this fight, it will be done from the inside out. She's often told me, 'It doesn't matter what party you affiliate yourself with, but it does matter that you can change things if you have a voice in the legislative process.'"

Sara knew Tillie understood this position, and the two women had forged a friendship.

Tillie went on, "Maude loves quotes, and she often quotes Carrie Chapman Catt who said, 'Get into the boat. It's vain to try to get hold of the steering wheel until you do.'"

Tillie chuckled, and Sara could not help but join in.

"How long has Maude been involved in the cause?" Sara asked.

"My, my." Tillie contemplated the question. "If I were to guess, I would say Maude is in her fifties. But you would never guess it. She has the energy of a thirty-year-old and has been involved since at least the McKinley administration. On March 3, 1897, President McKinley's inauguration day, she attended a parade there. As I recall, the parade included ten bands, five mounted brigades, twenty-six floats, and around eight thousand marchers, including many notables such as Helen Keller."

"You are quite amazing yourself, my friend," Sara complimented. "You are as sharp as a tack. How do you remember all that information?"

"Well, dear, I was there with Maude. That is where we first met."

"Tell me more," Sara encouraged.

"The parade got off to a good start, but soon turned ugly. The marchers were jeered and harassed while attempting to squeeze by the scoffing crowds. The police were of little help; some even participated in the harassment. Over two hundred people were treated for injuries at local hospitals that day. Despite this, most of the marchers finished the parade."

Sara was wide-eyed with concern. "Were you and Maude okay?"

"Just a little scuffed up, but we were younger then. As I recall, the commotion energized us." Tillie smiled, seeming to recall more memories from her younger days. "Maude still believes in peaceful means as the answer."

Despite the optimistic talk, Tillie and Sara became more concerned as they neared the city. The devastation of the flood was far greater than they anticipated. Tillie hoped to find her friend safe from the flood and still committed to the cause. She hadn't had word of Maude for some time, and she hoped that her health was good.

"I need to find her and know that she is okay," Tillie said, clenching her hands in worry.

After almost getting stuck in the muddy streets, they realized their map was useless. Maps utilized landmark directions since most streets were not named. Many streets were little more than cow paths.

The map suggested, "Follow the main road to the Methodist church, turn left, and continue down the road until you reach the white picket fence on the right. Turn right at that corner and proceed four streets to the fueling station."

If only they could find the picket fence. It was hopeless. They stopped a man at the corner and inquired if he knew where the fueling station was located, and from there, found the general store to inquire about

Maude.

The general store attendant knew where they could find Mrs. Waitt and pointed the way with great enthusiasm. They hadn't had lunch, so Tillie purchased sausage and bread.

Sara held up her jug and addressed the gentleman behind the counter. "Might we get our jug filled with some cold water?"

"Water? We have too much of it, but none you can drink unless it is boiled," he explained.

What would they do? Sara was already parched from the trip and the thought of going on without water was shocking.

The clerk took compassion, understanding their situation. They were grateful when he offered to fill their jug from the supply he had boiled that morning. The water wasn't cold, but at least they didn't have to worry about typhoid.

Eventually, they found Maude's home and Tillie knocked on her door.

Maude's hired girl answered, and Tillie provided her calling card.

The girl had no sooner disappeared than they heard a shriek from the other room.

"Tillie. Tillie Morgenson?" Maude cried out as she rushed to hug her old friend.

Maude was a well dressed, intelligent woman who stood tall in her 5' 6" frame and had a commanding presence. She was trim, well spoken, and a great conversationalist.

Maude was well but was deeply worried about the people in her town. "So many people died when buildings collapsed or when floodwaters trapped them. Now there is a continuing danger of contracting diseases from the contaminated water," she explained, deep concern evident in her eyes as she wrung her hands in despair.

Sara and Tillie commiserated with Maude on the plight of the people but knew there was little they could do to alleviate the situation. Conversation became more upbeat as they gravitated to other subjects.

They reminisced about the Washington, D.C. parade.

Maude was still outraged that such a well-planned peaceful demonstration had turned into a melee. She had heard that one person was seriously hurt. "It was fortunate no one died there," Maude said.

Maude invited them to spend the night, which they appreciated. Tillie and Sara needed to get cleaned up and changed. It was impossible to ride in an open automobile without getting a coat of dust upon yourself.

"There is clean water in the pitcher, but please use it sparingly," Maude directed. "We have a tremendous shortage, so we need to conserve."

They continued their pleasant chat and later had dinner together. It had been an exhausting day with their long drive, but the exhilarating conversation kept the adrenaline flowing.

Their bodies soon felt the exhaustion of a long day, and Sara could hardly keep her eyes open at the end. They turned in early and slept soundly.

The next day, Sara awoke to the smell of coffee brewing.

Maude served a hearty breakfast of pancakes and sausages, and they were soon in their vehicle and on their way to New York City.

Chapter Thirty-eight

They spent one night in Philadelphia, where they visited Independence Hall and saw the Liberty Bell.

"The Liberty Bell," Tillie told Sara, "is an iconic symbol of American Independence. At first, it was in the steeple of the Pennsylvania State House, which is now called Independence Hall. Look, Sara." Tillie pointed to the inscription cast in it.

Sara leaned forward to read it. "Proclaim Liberty throughout all the land unto all the inhabitants, thereof."

"It doesn't say all men. It reads, 'all the inhabitants,'" Tillie repeated.

"True. Why is it cracked?" asked Sara.

"It originally cracked when it was first rung. It was used to summon lawmakers to legislative sessions. But it is believed that it cracked the rest of the way while ringing after the death of Chief Justice John Marshall in 1835."

"It must have pealed loudly on July 4, in 1776," Sara assumed with a smile.

"Actually not," Tillie explained. "At least not that day. The Second Continental Congress voted for independence, but an announcement was not made on that date. It wasn't until the reading of the Declaration of Independence on July 8 that the bell tolled."

Sara looked at the bell again and had an idea. "Tillie, we should adopt it as a symbol for our cause," she said, showing her excitement. "Just look at the inscription. It should be our mantra. Liberty for all! Do you think we could get them to ring the bell for us? When we get the vote?"

Tillie beamed. "Wouldn't that be something? Unfortunately, I think this bell is retired."

"Oh. Will it ever be rung again?" Sara inquired.

"The City of Philadelphia owns the bell. It went to a series of exhibitions after 1885, but as I recall, more cracking occurred and small pieces chipped away. They are still loaning it out for political events, but there is opposition to continuing the practice. It draws huge crowds, but takes a toll on the bell, excuse the pun." Tillie smiled.

"Maybe it should be fixed."

"When the 1876 Centennial took place, that very idea came up. After a lot of discussion, the idea was dismissed; the custodians of the bell concluded that the crack had become part of the bell's character. So instead, a replica was made."

Sara thought on that. "Do you think we could get the replica?"

"I'm afraid not. See the bell in the steeple of Independence Hall? That is the replica. They made it thirteen thousand pounds, one thousand pounds for each of the original states. I believe they melted it from cannons, two from each side of the Revolutionary War and two from each side of the Civil War. The bell sounded on July 4, 1876 at the Exposition grounds. Then it was sent back to be recast to improve the sound. This bell," Tillie said, motioning toward the original bell encased in glass, "has been traveling to various exhibitions and celebrations, but it appears that may soon come to an end."

"Why is that?" Sara was mesmerized by the whole story.

"Well, it seems that vandalism is a problem. Also, the crack appears to be getting larger. Furthermore, as I mentioned there are chips out of it. In 1893, it returned from Chicago bearing a new crack. The private watchman who was to guard the bell had been cutting off small pieces for souvenirs. Opposition to further exhibitions is becoming very strong. Just last year there was a request to display the bell at the 1915 World Fair in San Francisco. There was a lot of debate, and they finally decided to allow this trip, but it's looking like that may become its last journey."

They left the bell, and Sara, still thinking about the bell's message, followed Tillie to an inn near Independence Square. They appreciated the good night's sleep before starting the final leg of the journey.

Once they reached New York City, they would stay at Tillie's New York apartment on Park Avenue. It had been a long journey, and Sara would be happy to settle in for a time.

Chapter Thirty-nine

Back in Milwaukee, Henry was at his wit's end. The girls were upset with him and made his days miserable. That didn't take much effort, because Henry was already miserable.

Ella would chide him, "If Mother were here, we would go shopping together for my party dress. If Mother were here, she would fix my hair, so it didn't look like a squirrel's nest. If Mother were here, we would be invited to the mother-daughter banquet."

Liz would chime in, "Mother would make it interesting when she read to me. Mother would have tea parties with me. Mother would let me bake cookies with her."

It got much worse when they accused him. "Mother would be here if you hadn't chased her away!"

Even Thaddeus wrote to him and made him feel foolish and selfish.

Father,
Ella has written me. You need to move into the twentieth
century. Mother is a brave woman to do the things she has
done. You should be proud.

No one berated him more than he did himself. When everyone retired for the night, he would sit silently in his bedroom, staring out the window and praying. "Lord, forgive me. May Sara forgive me. I have been a foolish man. Keep her safe and lead her back to us."

His every waking thought was of Sara. If only he knew where to find her. He'd learned she was headed for New York, or at least, that was the best information he had. He worried about her journey. How would she survive without money? Who would she encounter along the way? Was she safe?

It was rare that he slept, and when he did, he had nightmares. He dreamed of Sara being abducted by hooligans. He'd try so hard to save her, but he couldn't reach her. Other times he woke in a cold sweat, swatting the air about him and calling out her name.

In the daytime, he went to work at the bank, but he had difficulty concentrating. The Board of Directors approached him and told him bluntly that he needed to take a week off and get his life on track, or he would possibly lose his job. This jarred Henry. He knew he had to learn to focus again for his children. They needed his income to survive.

He took the week off and went to see Reverend Nelson.

Reverend Nelson greeted Henry with a handshake. With his other hand on Henry's back, he led him into his office. "Have a seat, Henry, and tell me what's on your mind."

Henry sighed and refrained from putting his head in his hands. "I don't know where to begin."

Reverend Nelson waited patiently. "I am going to assume this has to do with Sara. Perhaps you can begin with the day she left. Maybe you can tell me why. Was it because of Adam's death?"

"Oh, no," Henry replied. "Actually, Reverend...it is my fault that she's gone. I made her leave."

Reverend Nelson's eyebrows rose. "Why? Why would you do that?"

Henry lowered his head. "I am a very foolish man," he began. He told the pastor the whole story, even about what happened in court. By the end, he was weeping and crying out, "God forgive me."

Reverend Nelson went to the corner of the room where a washstand sat with a pitcher and bowl. He took a clean cloth from the shelf below and poured a bit of water onto it, handing it to Henry.

Henry wiped his face as he attempted to compose himself.

"Well, my son, you have gotten yourself into quite a pickle." Reverend Nelson took the cloth from Henry.

"Let me start at the end. You *are* a foolish man." He minced no words. "Your last plea, we can take care of this instant. You asked God to forgive you. Let me assure you with that plea, your heavenly Father has forgiven you. As for Sara, we will have to see if she has forgiveness in her heart for you."

Henry sniffled and wiped his nose with his handkerchief. "What can I do? How can I fix this?"

"That is a bit more difficult but let me tell you this—if it is God's will, He will show you the way. We try to take things into our own hands. We fret and worry and bungle things up, because we are human."

"Are you telling me to do nothing?" Henry said, aghast, wondering if the visit was yet another mistake.

"Oh, certainly not," Reverend Nelson said. "But, before you can act rationally and before you can see clearly, you need to get it off your shoulders. Let the Lord carry the burden. He wants to, you know."

"How can I do that?" Henry asked, a bit defiant.

The pastor steepled his fingers together. "I can see this is going to be difficult for you. Let me tell you an old adage. A wise man once said, 'if you have a bird and you let it loose, and it returns, it is yours; if it does not return, it was never yours to begin with.' If you truly love Sara and if she truly loves you, she will return. You need to allow her to be free. You have kept her in a cage for a long time. She needs time to decide if she will be free, or if she will return."

"But Reverend Nelson, I *pushed* her out of the cage. I told her to go away. Why would she return?" Henry was beginning to feel sick.

"First of all, her children are here. Do you believe she will stay away from her children forever?"

"No, no, of course not," Henry agreed. "But I did threaten to put her in an insane asylum if she returned to see her children."

The pastor gasped. "You did *what*?"

Henry withered in shame. "I know, I know. I wish I could take those words back. I was angry, and I wanted her to change her mind, to come back home and know her place."

"Well, Henry, I must say you have a strange way of putting out an invitation." Reverend Nelson shook his head. "Now, let me understand this. You pushed her out of the house without any means of support, you took her children away, you threatened her with an insane asylum, and you expect her to beg to come home? Can you explain to me how that works?"

"Sara had a good life," he explained. "We were well off financially. She had a nice house, a new automobile. She could decorate and shop and spend all her time with the children because she also had a maid to take care of the housework. I thought...if her life were miserable, she would realize she had a good life and would *want* to return. I know

now that I was wrong."

The pastor took a deep breath and blew it out. "When you said your wedding vows, you did the part with love, honor, and obey. I find so many times that men accept the honor and obey part for their wife, but forget about their own commitment—the love and honor thy wife part. Henry, Sara is not a naughty child; she is a woman with a mind and convictions of her own. She is your partner in life. She needs to be honored in that way. She needs to believe that even if her convictions differ from yours, she is still loved. Love is a very strong bond, but it *can be* destroyed. You have come very close, if not beyond repair."

"Are you saying that there is no hope?" Henry interrupted.

"There is always hope," Reverend Nelson said, though he sounded doubtful. "Maybe we should pray for a miracle."

Both men were silent for a moment.

Then, Reverend Nelson took a deep breath. "Next, you need to forgive yourself. You are human, and humans make mistakes. Forgiving yourself will be much more difficult than allowing God to forgive you."

"How can I do that?" Henry asked.

"You will have to figure that out for yourself. If God can forgive you, you can forgive yourself. Ask for His help. Recognize what you did, and believe you will never make that mistake again. Then maybe, you can find a way to forgive yourself."

Henry sat back in his chair, trying to figure out how that was possible.

"Once you have forgiven yourself, your sins will be lifted from your shoulders and you will be able to see more clearly and to function without the burden you carry now. You will be a happier, more positive person. Believe in the future and let the Lord show you the way."

Henry wasn't sure if this was a bunch of religious mumbo jumbo or if it had some validity. It kind of made sense, but he wasn't sure it was possible.

"Reverend," Henry questioned. "Shouldn't I be in control? Shouldn't I be making the decisions on what to do and how to solve this problem?"

"Well, you haven't exactly done a very good job so far, now have you?" the pastor responded, his eyebrows raised. "You should think about putting someone else in the driver's seat. I can't think of a better choice than God."

"I'll try."

But Henry was still skeptical as he left the pastor's house.

Henry had a few more days off and a lot of time to think. He berated himself over and over again. Then one evening, while he was saying the Lord's Prayer, it hit him. *Forgiveness. Was it possible? God help me.*

And slowly, Henry began to forgive.

He forgave his boss for taking away one of his accounts. He forgave the neighbor for getting too close to his vehicle and getting a scratch on it. He forgave Claudia for ruining his best shirt in the wash. He forgave Ella for being angry and belligerent.

Why shouldn't she be?

That night, he went to bed feeling a little bit better, a little less weighted.

The next morning, Henry greeted his family with a smile and plans for a picnic. He asked Claudia to fix a picnic basket, and at ten a.m., he enticed both girls to get into the automobile for a ride out to the country. On the way, they sang songs. During the picnic, he told them funny stories that made them laugh.

When they arrived back home that day, Ella kissed him on the cheek. "I'm sorry I have been so difficult lately, Father."

He tweaked her nose. "That's okay, Angel. I already forgave you." He hesitated a moment. "I understand, and I am sorry, too...for everything." He couldn't quite get out exactly what he was sorry for, but hoped she understood.

That evening at the dinner table, Henry delivered the meal prayer. Usually, everyone bowed their heads in their own silent prayer, but he asked the girls to hold hands as he prayed.

"Heavenly Father, thank you for the food we are about to receive. Thank you for the beautiful day we shared together in the country. Thank you for all the blessings you have bestowed upon us." He hesitated a moment and continued, "And please Lord, bring our mother Sara back home to us. We love her and need her. Amen."

Ella squeezed her father's hand and mouthed, "Thank you."

That evening, as Henry spoke the Lord's Prayer again, he prayed, "Lord, I have forgiven everyone I can think of that has transgressed against me, except one. But now, I forgive myself." He said the words softly, head bowed, still unsure if he truly meant them.

Later that night, he repeated those same words over and over again. Each time, he told himself why it was right to forgive. "Because I didn't know what I was doing... Because I am a foolish man... Because it is right to forgive. Because I need to move ahead... Because, because, because..."

Little by little, Henry began to feel alive again. Little by little, he began to function, both in the home and at his place of work. Little by little, he was getting better, but he still carried a cloud of guilt and sorrow over his head. That would never be gone until Sara could forgive him.

When he went to see Reverend Nelson again, the pastor inquired, "Well, Henry, how have you been?"

Henry sat down and took a deep breath. "I have prayed every evening; I have forgiven everyone I can think of, including myself. I have been able to function at work and I have had some delightful times with my daughters."

"Wonderful," said the pastor. "Do you think you can move on now?"

"I'm not sure," Henry pondered, his hands shaking. "I can't forget what I did. I can't remove the guilt. I can't forget how much I hurt my dear Sara."

"Of course you can't," Reverend Nelson replied, his eyes gentle. "Forgiving does not mean forgetting. God lets us hold that guilt until we can reconcile it. It is so we don't repeat the same error of our ways. It is so we will become a better person. A person who acts as God would want us to act. Through forgiveness, He has taken the burden and carried it for you."

Henry nodded, still not sure he understood, but feeling some relief.

"However, you must remember not to force your way into Sara's life or demand that your needs be met," Reverend Nelson stated firmly.

"But Reverend, I don't even know where she is. I don't know how to reach her." Henry was frustrated. "My only need is Sara. She is my life. Since she has been gone, my children and I have been miserable. How can I find her?"

"Hmm...I suggest you try New York City. Contact the National Association or the local chapters of suffragettes. Perhaps the library, or the Milwaukee Journal can help," the pastor suggested.

"Thank you, thank you," Henry said as he pumped the pastor's hand.

"I am so grateful."

"There is nothing to be grateful for yet. You have a lot of work to do and you may not find her. Those organizations are very protective of their members' identities. We have no way to know if she will be willing to speak with you after you do find her."

Henry knew that, but it would not stop him from trying. For Sara. For the children.

***

The following day, Henry visited the library. He went to the desk where the librarian, Edith Warner, greeted him politely but coldly. "Mr. Dewberry, what may I do for you today?"

"I need to find my wife," Henry blurted.

Edith stiffened.

"I mean…I need an address for the suffragettes in New York City. Can you help me?" he asked.

"I don't believe I can, Mr. Dewberry," Edith replied, her voice even colder now. "The only thing I can do is provide you with the correct name of the organization. It is The National Woman's Suffrage Association."

Henry jotted the name on a scrap of paper, thanked her profusely, and exited the library. His next stop was the Milwaukee Journal. Once there, he asked to speak to the editor.

"In what regard?" the secretary inquired.

"I need to know the address of the National Woman's Suffrage Association in New York City." He hesitated. "If there is more than one organization, I need addresses for all."

"May I take your name and get back to you? No one is available to provide that information at the moment," the secretary stated dryly, handing him paper.

"Of course." Henry took out a pen and wrote his name and address, both at home and at the bank.

The secretary looked over the information on the paper and seemed a bit more interested. "Is this a business inquiry?"

"No, it is a personal matter. I would appreciate a quick response," Henry stated as he anxiously tapped his fingers on the counter.

"We should be able to have that information for you tomorrow morning."

"Good day then," Henry said, and left the building.

As promised, a courier delivered a letter to the bank the following morning. On it were three addresses, along with a handwritten note stating that there could be more of which they were not aware. The letter was signed by one Franklin Thomas.

Henry had seen Franklin Thomas' byline on many articles and knew him to be a determined reporter. He made a mental note. Perhaps Franklin Thomas could be of assistance if these leads didn't pan out.

Henry sent telegrams to all the addresses.

HENRY DEWBERRY SEEKING TO FIND SARA DEWBERRY STOP
URGENT STOP
CONTACT MISTER DEWBERRY AT 3012 ASTOR PLACE MILWAUKEE, WISCONSIN STOP

He had thought of providing more information, but he knew Sara would be more likely to contact him if she had no idea of the nature of the emergency.

Within two days, he received replies from each of the addresses stating they were not aware of a Sara Dewberry. All contacts had been made with the New York organizations in the name of Tillie Morgenson. Sara had not registered herself independently at any of the organizations.

Henry was dejected. *What can I do now?*

Then he had an idea. Perhaps Franklin Thomas would be able to provide more leads. He made a mental note to contact the man.

Chapter Forty

Tillie and Sara chugged into New York City. The poor, old Model T had undertaken a rigorous journey and would have to be taken to a garage for maintenance. This would be the number one priority tomorrow.

They found their way to Tillie's apartment and immediately opened the windows to let out the musty air from the winter shut-in. The apartment overlooked Park Avenue and had a fabulous view of the city from the fifth-floor dwelling. They removed the dust covers from the furniture and found the apartment surprisingly clean.

The sounds and smells of New York wafted into the open windows, and Sara couldn't stop looking out the window. She was as giddy as a teen on her first date.

Chicago's skyscrapers were amazing, but they didn't compare to what she had seen so far in New York. She couldn't wait to step out onto the streets and take it all in.

The ladies freshened up and went to dinner since there was no food in the apartment. Tillie called the doorman to get laundry service for their entire luggage. Travel had taken quite a toll on their wardrobes.

They stepped into the New York streets to the sweet and spicy smells of delis and street vendors. Added to this was the smell of exhaust from all the automobiles, more vehicles than Sara could've ever imagined. Those smells mingled with the sweat and droppings of horses.

Skyscrapers were everywhere, and Sara nearly hurt her neck trying to stare up at all of them. Its recent and most impressive skyscraper being the Woolworth building. It was a grandiose monument named for its founder F.W. Woolworth of the five and ten cent store fame. It was the largest building in the world, with forty-six stories plus an additional tower, making it fifty-five stories in all. It was located at the corner of Barclay Street and Park Place, taking up most of the block.

"Can you imagine how much a building like that costs?" Sara asked in awe.

Tillie responded, "It was reported that the building cost seventeen million dollars and was paid for in cash."

"Cash? Really?" Sara had a hard time understanding how one man could have so much money by selling things for nickels and dimes. She was mesmerized…and determined to see them all—the Singer building, the Flatiron building, and the Metropolitan Life Building.

"It seems to me that a big wind would blow them all down." Sara wondered at their stability as she gazed at the structures that appeared to reach into the clouds.

Tillie continued to enlighten Sara, pointing to the landmarks. "Just a little over a year ago, a major cyclone passed through New York City. Many were sure that its winds at over one hundred miles per hour would take down these looming structures. The Woolworth Building sustained quite a bit of damage since it was still under construction. The giant sign from the Knickerbocker Hotel plunged to the road in front of the building. Automobiles and even people, were hurled about, but for the most part, the skyscrapers made it through unscathed."

"That's amazing!"

Sara soon learned she could travel throughout the city with the New York subway company, which had been in operation since 1904. Commuter railways operating out of Grand Central Terminal and Pennsylvania Station could take her almost anywhere.

Tillie announced that they were going to have a special treat to celebrate their successful journey. "We're going to have lunch at the Waldorf Astoria."

Sara gasped at the thought. At one time, the Waldorf Astoria was a facility for transients, but it had developed into the social center of the city. It was now considered prestigious and most influential in advancing the status of women, who were welcomed singly without escorts. This grand urban hotel had evolved as a women's choice venue for social events.

An elegantly-clad doorman held the door for them as they arrived. The magnificent lobby was decorated with crystal chandeliers, fine Persian carpeting, and beautiful upholstered furnishings. The woodwork glistened. It was enough to take Sara's breath away.

They were ushered into the elegant dining room. Although Sara wore one of her nicer ensembles, she began to feel a bit underdressed. Despite that, the inviting staff made her feel like royalty. They dined on a baked chicken cacciatore and their famous Waldorf salad.

After eating, Sara and Tillie were almost too stuffed to do anything but decided to take a walk about the area. They spotted art museums, stores, office buildings, and parks. New York was a potpourri of things to see and do. There were plays and musical productions; there were new moving picture establishments.

"Can you believe they are saying one day they will have talking features?" Tillie asked as she took Sara's arm to stabilize herself as they walked the streets, taking in all the sights and sounds along the way. It was all so new to Sara.

At this point, Sara would've believed almost anything. She was amazed by all the things she had seen and experienced in just two months. She was in a headspin of magical experiences, but when evening came, she felt an overwhelming sadness envelop her. She missed her children and her heart ached.

After such a glorious lunch, neither lady was hungry for dinner. They stopped by the market to pick up a few items and munched on juicy, fresh melon slices instead of having a large dinner.

As they sat gazing at the skyscrapers from their window that evening, Tillie asked Sara, "Well my dear, how are you enjoying this adventure so far?"

Sara beamed. "The trip has been amazing. I am overwhelmed by it all. But..." Sara hesitated, not meeting Tillie's eyes. "I feel guilty and sad, too."

"How so?" Tillie asked.

Sara confided in her friend. "I miss my children terribly. When I am with you and we are having a wonderful time and experiencing such remarkable things, I am delighted. But then I feel guilty because I am enjoying myself. Do you understand?"

"Of course, I do," Tillie acknowledged. "When Stanley was alive, we spent a great deal of time either working for various causes or charities or socializing with the Washington insiders. My son James was a young boy, and we had to leave him with a nanny a great deal of the time. I believe it is a mother's curse that we cannot find true joy when we are separated from our children…and any joy we do feel is turned to guilt."

"Precisely! You do understand," Sara exclaimed. "The joy you feel is turned to guilt and the guilt is turned to sorrow. It is as though you don't *deserve* to be happy."

"It is a punishment we inflict upon ourselves. What man do you know who throws himself into his work or his hobbies, then feels this kind of remorse and pain?" Tillie asked.

"None!" said Sara in awe. "We women make excuses when we cannot fulfill our promises or when we miss our child's events. We make it up to the children however we can. But you're right; men feel no guilt or shame. I guess because they look at it as our responsibility…our duty… our place."

"Exactly," Tillie confirmed. "I would like to tell you that Henry took that responsibility on himself when he denied you the children, but I know that will not relieve you in what you perceive is your job."

"How did you cope?" Sara asked, her eyes watery.

"We find ways to make it up to them…or so, we appease ourselves with that explanation." Tillie sighed, and suddenly looked very tired. "Why don't you write to your children? Every night when you feel sad, write them letters. Tell them of the joys and the sights you have seen and felt. They will look forward to your letters and will feel closer to you."

"But Tillie," Sara reasoned, "Henry would never let them get the letters. He would intercept them. It would only make him angry and the children more isolated."

"Send them to Edith," Tillie suggested. "Ella goes to the library quite regularly, doesn't she?"

Sara thought for a moment. "I'm going to start this instant." Brimming with excitement, Sara got up from her chair and gathered a pen and paper and began to write.

Chapter Forty-one

Sara and Tillie went to the closest chapter of the NYC Suffragettes and registered. Their meeting room was at the Astor Hotel. There, Sara ran into a delightful lady from Ireland. Her name was Kathleen McGuire.

Kathleen was about Sara's age, a buxom redhead with a hearty laugh that could be heard above the din of the crowd. Sara was drawn to her laugh from across the room. "I need to meet that lady." Tillie stayed to talk with old friends and Sara smiled as she crossed the room to find the face that belonged to that happy laugh.

Sara approached and introduced herself.

"Sara, Sara Dewberry!" Kathleen repeated. She was sharp-witted and looked like she was mentally placing Sara's name in her irrefutable memory. "Sara, love. Ya're but a sprite but ya look like ya got some spunk, girl."

Kathleen was not shy about sharing her story with Sara. She had only been in this country a couple of weeks. She and her sister had learned English when they were children, although in Ireland, their first language was Gaelic.

"Tell me about the movement in Ireland?" Sara inquired.

"Like here, we don't all think alike," Kathleen began, leaning against a table. "Me be'en strong-willed all me life. Most are peaceful like, but I don't see progress. Genteel manners and polite whimprin' gits no attention. There be a group of womin folk from Dublin that teamed up with the Brits. They called us militants, and I spose we war, but we jist needed to find ways to be heard."

"Why did you come here?" Sara was curious and wanted to know.

"The war over thar is fierce. It is takin' a toll on Britain and has taken all the attention. Me sister has been here ten yars. She got married to a bloke from New York. She said thar was work to be done here and sent word fer me ta come here ta live."

She went on to tell Sara that the movement had slowed considerably in Europe, since all focus had been placed on the aggressive activities of Japan and Germany, so Kathleen had decided America was the place she needed to be.

Kathleen was a bit on the tawdry side, but when she spoke of women's rights, she was very passionate. And for the most part, she wasn't vulgar, but it was clear she was not a genteel lady who would avoid conflict.

Sara smiled, fully embracing her personality. "Tell me, Kathleen, how did you fight for the cause in Ireland?"

"Katy, call me Katy. All me friends do. Come, let's sit." Kathleen proceeded to tell how it was in her homeland. She mentioned how militant Irish suffragists were imprisoned in England and Ireland. Some of the women went on hunger strikes while jailed. Suffragettes were active in cities throughout the United Kingdom. Their activities ranged from chaining themselves to railings, setting fire to the contents of letterboxes, and smashing windows.

"About three yars ago, I larned of something Emily Davison wrote about in the paper. It twar her favourite quotation. Here." Katy reached into the pocket of her dress and pulled out a tattered press article and handed it to Sara.

Intrigued, Sara read the article about one of Katy's country women.

'REBELLION AGAINST TYRANTS IS OBEDIENCE TO GOD' WAS WRITTEN ON PIECES OF PAPER, WHICH SHE TIED TO ROCKS AND THREW AT THE CARRIAGE OF CHANCELLOR OF THE EXCHEQUER DAVID LLOYD GEORGE AS IT DROVE BY. SHE WAS SENTENCED TO DO HARD LABOUR AND WAS LATER FORCE FED WHEN SHE REFUSED TO EAT.

BY 1911, SHE BEGAN TO BELIEVE THAT THE SUFFRAGETTE CAUSE NEEDED AN ACTUAL MARTYR TO BRING IT THE PUBLICITY IT NEEDED. HER FINAL ACT WAS TO RUN OUT ONTO THE RACETRACK AT THE EPSOM DERBY AND GRAB THE REIGNS OF THE KING'S HORSE. SHE DIED A FEW DAYS LATER FROM HER INJURIES.

AT THE TIME, HER ACTIONS WERE DISMISSED AS THE ACT OF A CRAZED WOMAN. SHE IS NOW SEEN AS A MARTYR TO THE SUFFRAGETTE CAUSE. THE

SO-CALLED CAT AND MOUSE ACT WAS PASSED BY THE BRITISH GOVERNMENT IN 1913. IT PROVIDED FOR THE RELEASE OF SICK FEMALE HUNGER STRIKERS, AS WELL AS THEIR RE-IMPRISONMENT ONCE THEY HAD REGAINED THEIR HEALTH. THE AIM WAS TO PREVENT FEMALE PRISONERS GETTING ANY PUBLIC SYMPATHY.

"Ya see, Sara, we gotta fight. We can't sit by ladylike. We need to get attention."

Sara was not convinced fighting was necessary, so Katy suggested she visit her sister's house the next Thursday.

They seemed to be making progress on the streets, but their voices went unheeded in Congress. Now, Sara wondered if maybe Katy was right as she walked to her sister's house.

"Sara darlin', do come in." Katy welcomed her new friend at the door, appearing breathless.

"Guess I be gittin a wee bit outta shape," Katy explained. "So, Sara, do tell me how the suffragettes are fairin' here."

Sara described the rallys and how the cause was going well with women across the country, but many still needed convincing. She pursed her lips together. "I am concerned about our progress in the government. When it comes to voting, they find something else to vote on or they table it for the moment. My friend, Tillie, has friends in Washington, D.C. and she has spoken before various committees, but I'm afraid that although they seem to listen, they don't act."

Katy nodded in understanding. "Tis why we became militant, we needed to get thar attention."

"But what good is destruction?" Sara asked. "I can't see how we can gather sympathy for our cause when we are acting like hooligans."

"For one thing," Katy replied, "we git press. We get back page news if it is a rally, but we get front page headlines when we git thar attention. In thar minds, we are only women, less than dogs. They let us bark and pat our heads, but we get nothing but table scraps. When we bite, they pay attention. What man will hold onto his steak when a mad dog is at his heels?"

Sara tried to take it all in. It made sense, but she still wasn't convinced.

"Sara love, next week Father McLaughlin at St. Francis Cathedral is deliverin' a sermon on the evils of givin' women authority, particularly in the church. This is my parish. I am ashamed. We are going to mass on Sunday. Will you come?" Katy pleaded, her eyes honest and determined. "The church has been one of ahre biggest adversaries."

Sara thought for a moment and considered her plans with Tillie. "Yes, I will, what time should I be there?" Sara in her naivety wondered, *how bad could it be? We are going to church!*

"Mass is at ten. Be there by nine-forty-five," Katy directed.

Sara nodded, a mixture of nervousness and excitement clouding her mind, and got up to leave. As she went out the door, Katy called after her, "Sara, don't forget to wear your bloomers."

Chapter Forty-two

"Sara," Tillie said one day, "This will be our home for several weeks, so make yourself comfortable. I have many friends here that I wish to catch up with and we will have no more meetings until the annual convention next week. You are certainly welcome to join me, but I have a feeling you would like to explore the city. Next week, we can get back to business, but for now, I want you to enjoy yourself."

"Thank you, Tillie. Do you remember Katy McGuire? I met her on registration day. She is from Ireland."

"Yes, the boisterous redhead. How could I forget?" Tillie laughed.

"She has invited me to her church on Sunday at St. Francis Cathedral. I told her I would go with her."

"That is lovely, but you are not Catholic," Tillie questioned.

"I know, but Katy told me several of the suffragettes will be gathering there that day and I don't mind visiting."

"I see no harm in that. As you know I am Episcopalian, but I have friends from all religions and walks of life. Enjoy your time there. I'm glad to see you're making friends so quickly."

Sara smiled, thinking of Katy's comment to wear her bloomers. "I think I will spend time this week exploring New York. There is so much to see. I am so eager to see everything here. I'll be ready for the real work that starts next week."

On Sunday morning, Sara got up and struggled with her wardrobe. She put the bloomers on but decided to wear a more conservative and proper church attire.

Sara arrived at the church early. She wanted to get there before her friend, so they could enter the church together. At nine-forty-five, Katy, along with a stream of churchgoers converged on the cathedral. Some wore bloomers and some did not. They nodded to each other and entered the church amass. Katy, Sara, and the other suffragettes took their place in the last four pews. The congregation stirred.

Father McLaughlin entered the sanctuary and took his place on a stiff chair at the side of the altar. This was the first time Sara had been in a Catholic church. She took her cues from the fellow congregants on when to stand, when to kneel, and when to bow her head in silence. Most of the mass was in Latin, which Sara didn't understand, and she watched the room nervously.

"Now comes the homily," Katy whispered.

"What is a homily?" Sara whispered back.

"Tis a sermon on a moral theme," Katy responded.

Father McLaughlin went to his place in the pulpit. He had a large Bible in his hands and slammed it on the lectern. "Who among us believes they know more than God?"

The church was silent.

"Who among us questions the Bible?" he asked.

Silence still prevailed.

"There are not one, not two, not even three verses in the Bible which state women's role in the church and in society."

The people stirred.

"There are fifty-nine verses!" he boomed. "First Timothy, chapter two, verse twelve: 'But I suffer not a woman to teach, nor to usurp authority over a man; but to be in silence."

A suffragette rose and shouted back, "The words of Timothy, not of God!"

The priest, undaunted, went on to read First Peter 3:1. "'Likewise, ye wives, be in subjection to your own husbands, that if any obey not the word, they also may without the word be won by the conversation of the wives...'"

Another suffragette rose and interrupted, shouting, "Only words of Peter, not of God!"

The next several passages—1 Peter 3:1, Ephesians 5, 22-23, 1 Peter 3:5, Titus 2: 3-5—were all met with the same response.

Then Katy rose from her seat next to Sara. "Galatians 3:28," she shouted. Katy raised a fist for emphasis. "'There is neither Jew nor Greek, there is neither bond nor free, there is neither man nor female, for ye are all one in Christ Jesus.'"

The priest rebutted, "Genesis 3:16. Unto the woman he said, 'I will greatly multiply thy sorrow and thy conception, in sorrow thou shalt bring forth children, and thy desire shall be to thy husband and he shall rule over thee!'" The priest's face reddened with anger as he clenched his fists and hurled them in the air at the congregation.

Katy again repeated Galatians 3:18, and a melee broke out in the back of the room.

Sara gasped at the sudden commotion but could not deny how her heart had stirred at Katy's words.

The priest's facial muscles tightened as he gritted his teeth and spat out the words of 1 Corinthians 14:34: "'Let your women keep silence in the churches, for it is not permitted unto them to speak; but they are commanded to be under obedience as also saith the law.'"

Another suffragette shouted out, "Read your Bible, Father; it says *Jewish* law, not God's law. Not the law of our Lord and Savior Jesus Christ. It is the law as written in the first century. It is now the twentieth century. Wake up and know there is a difference. Even Jesus said, 'Give unto Caesar what is Caesar's,' and held many women in high esteem."

There was a crash, and a big stained-glass window went shattering to the ground.

Sara and Katy both gasped, flinching backward. Someone had hurled a rock through it.

Some men of the church attempted to remove the suffragettes from the premises, but they were not about to leave.

Another window shattered.

Many of the congregants got up and exited the premises through the side door. There was a riotous confrontation and a fever pitch of verbal exchanges, some not fit for a church. The adrenaline soared, and Sara could feel the intensity. She got caught up in the excited exchange, screaming words, and raising her hands in the air.

Soon constables were on the scene, and many of the women, including Sara and Katy, were taken off to jail and booked for disturbing the peace and for assault. Other charges ensued, as some women spit on the police officers and resisted arrest.

Sara once again found herself in a jail cell, though this time, she was not ashamed.

This time, when asked about her husband, she said, "He is dead."

Since she was in a different state, no one checked, and she was put into a cell that was dingy and crowded.

Sara noticed Katy was once again having difficulty breathing. She had dismissed it initially as the heat of the moment. Katy managed to find a place to sit in the cell and Sara noticed she was pale and sweating profusely.

"Are you okay?" Sara went to her friend's side.

"Me ticker's not too good," Katy confided, wincing in pain, "so I will rest a moment."

"Katy, talk to me," Sara pleaded. "What is wrong?"

"I think I strained me back; I have a very bad pain in me back between me shoulders," she admitted.

Sara reached out to rub her shoulders to ease the pain.

But Katy slumped forward into a state of unconsciousness, and Sara began to tremble. She needed to wake her.

"Katy, Katy," Sara whispered.

No response.

"Guard, guard!" Sara called out.

Others joined in her plea, but no one responded.

Down the hall, Sara could see two guards having a conversation about the suffragettes, laughing and making fun of their plight. They were clearly not about to give them the satisfaction of responding to their calls for help.

"It is just a trick to get attention," Sara heard one say to the other.

Enraged, Sara continued yelling until one guard finally came.

She went to the back of the cell and cradled a lifeless Katy in her arms.

Seeing truth in her statement, the guard returned with another man. Picking her up by her arms and legs, they removed Katy from the cell. "This one won't be causing us any more grief," the guard said to the other guard, while Sara strained to look on. "She's a goner."

Katy had suffered a massive heart attack, and Sara weeped for her friend.

Chapter Forty-three

Two days later, Sara returned to the apartment and a worried-sick Tillie. The usual jail time for her offense was three days but considering the traumatic effects of a death in the jail, the authorities had decided they had been duly punished and released them early.

Tillie had been out shopping for dinner. When she returned to the apartment, Sara was there, attempting to wash off the stench of the jail.

"So, you are now part of the militant faction of the organization?" Tillie inquired with deep concern. She had long since learned from other suffragettes where Sara was, and Sara could only imagine her unease the last few days. Would Tillie forgive her? Sara was truly remorseful.

"Tillie, a woman died. It was Katy McGuire."

"Yes, I heard," Tillie replied. "It can be very dangerous out there."

"I thought that the militant faction might be the answer. It seems like when we struggle peacefully, we get nowhere. Will we ever win our rights?" Tears started to glisten in Sara's eyes.

"No doubt about it," Tillie assured her.

"But women have been fighting this cause for over forty years," Sara lamented.

"And we *are* making progress. Some states have already given women the right to vote. Wyoming Governor John Campbell granted women the right to vote in December of 1869 when Wyoming was still a territory. They still enjoy that privilege. Utah had it for a time, but it was disenfranchised in 1887 because their Mormon populous thought the women would dispose of polygamy. By the end of the nineteenth century, Idaho, Colorado, Utah, and Wyoming all had enfranchised women. That was accomplished by the effort of the State Suffrage Associations." Tillie went on, her eyes determined. "We have hopes that the Wilson Administration will be our salvation. We plan to focus more on Washington until we prevail."

"So, you believe there is hope?" Sara asked, wiping her eyes.

"Absolutely, dear, but I believe we need to do it sensibly."

Sara sighed, guilt stabbing under her ribs. She thought of Katy, and her sacrifice. "Oh, me too. I am done with the militants. They are sure that their way will accomplish the task, and maybe it can, but it is not for me."

"I'm glad you feel that way. I would hate to lose my faithful assistant." There was a note of relief in Tillie's voice. "After all, I'm going on seventy-seven years of age. I hope one day we will see this fight to the end together."

Tillie and Sara had a dinner of ham, beans, and cornbread. Dinner had never tasted so good. She hadn't been able to eat the swill served in jail. Sara was exhausted, so she put on her nightgown and crawled into bed early. But before she turned in, she sat at the desk in her room and wrote a letter to Ella.

Sara wrote one of her children every night, but she mailed them all once a week. Mail service was sporadic and sometimes took up to two weeks to arrive. Postage was two cents per letter and ten cents a week was about all Sara could afford.

Dear Ella,

I hope you are in good health and liking your studies. You will soon be fourteen and I wish I could be there to share your birthday. I picture you as I last saw you, and it is hard for me to imagine you are a young lady now. I guess you will always be my little girl.

New York is a fabulous city filled with skyscrapers and amazing sights and sounds. I learned how to ride the subway. You can get almost any place on the subway. Can you believe it? Subway trains can go very fast. If you watch for the moving picture shows, you might be able to see one of New York City. There are several. Look for somebody in the picture show; a face in the crowd. Pretend it is me. I think of you every single day.

On the way to New York, I learned how to drive an

automobile. I hope one day you will be able to see and enjoy all the wonderful things I have seen. But my dear Ella, I would trade them all to see you growing up into a fine young lady.

Take care of your little sister, and if you ever need any advice or woman to woman talk, remember to see Catherine. She promised me that she will be there anytime you need her. I send you my warmest hugs and best wishes for a happy birthday.

All my love,
Mother

She folded the letter, a tear streaming down her cheek, and put it next to the letter for Thaddeus.

Chapter Forty-four

Within a few weeks, Sara and Tillie were back on the road on a journey that would take them across the United States and would last more than three years. Sara's chest hurt at the thought of all that time away from her children, but she wouldn't think of turning back now. She was doing this for her girls' future. She had to remember that.

They left New York and proceeded through the Appalachian Mountains. It was midsummer, and the trusty Model T occasionally overheated. They carried a big jug of water for such occasions. When the hills were steep and the gas level on half full or less, they had to back up the hill to let gravity take care of the fuel reaching their engine.

Outside of Virginia, on a country road, their trusty Model T sputtered to a halt.

"Oh no," said Tillie with her hands on her hips, looking down the lonely road. "What will we do now?" Attempts to restart the automobile were futile.

"Let me take a look," Sara said as she lifted the hood.

Tillie looked at Sara as if she were mad. After all, she had learned to drive only months ago.

But Sara was confident. She checked the hoses and caps to make sure everything was tight. Then, she went to the back of the car and pulled out a small satchel with an assortment of tools. She worked at it diligently for about an hour, after which she put down her satchel and wiped her hands on a rag tucked into the case. "Try it now," she suggested.

Tillie didn't seem to expect much, but humored Sara for her efforts. She opened the throttle and cranked up the engine. There was a sputter, then another sputter and a chuga, chuga—and soon the engine was puffing smoke out the exhaust and ready to go.

"Whatever did you do?" Tillie asked in amazement.

"I changed the spark plugs." Sara smiled. "I did okay, huh?" She beamed.

They got into the vehicle and continued with their journey. "How did you learn to do that?" Tillie asked, still gaping at Sara.

Sara hid her embarrassed grin. "Sometimes, when you are napping or giving a speech, I have a lot of time on my hands. I love to read, and the only thing available except our brochures is the automobile manual. There is a whole section on trouble shooting so you can figure out the problem."

"Well, I declare, I am impressed." Tillie laughed out loud. "I wondered what you did to fill those hours. I know sometimes you take walks or write letters to your children, but I never dreamed you were becoming a technician."

Sara tingled with pride. "I also had a little help from Samuel at the garage in New York. When I took it in for an oil change, he showed me what all the parts are and explained how it worked. The book was helpful, but seeing how it is done was important to understanding it all."

"Well, I can't tell you how glad I am that you did. This is going to be a long journey, and already, I am realizing how valuable you are to me." Tillie reached over and patted Sara's arm. "We make quite a team."

***

They were soon in Washington, D.C., where Tillie was again speaking before a committee in Congress. Whenever they could, they spent time with some of Tillie's friends and acquaintances and with the local chapters of suffragettes.

Through the winter months, the ladies traveled to the southern states. Come summer, they traveled further north and west. Since Arizona had become the forty-eighth state of the Union in 1912, there were no longer any territories. Many of the western states were still unpopulated and somewhat removed from the news links of the eastern states, but women had a right to vote in local and state elections. Once a constitutional amendment was passed, it was necessary for the states to ratify it, so keeping the movement in the forefront and encouraging the vote was still important. In many ways, despite their limited access to news, the states in the west had surpassed the east in providing women with the right to vote. In some states, the right was limited to school boards or certain issues, but at least progress was being made.

Wherever they traveled, Sara and Tillie found discussions on various issues and recent amendments passed in Congress. There were an unprecedented number of amendments on the table at this time.

In May of 1913, the Seventeenth Amendment to the Constitution was passed. It established the direct election of United States senators by popular vote of the people. Prior to this, the senators had been elected by state legislatures.

"It's high time to let the people pick their senators," Tillie stated. "Stanley was put into office by the legislature. He did a great job for the people he represented, but if the other party was in power, they could have ousted him in favor of their good ole boys. He worked for the people, not the party, and that is the way it should be."

"I agree," said Sara, "but what do you think of the Eighteenth Amendment?"

"It established prohibition in the United States by making it illegal to produce, transport, or sell alcoholic beverages. That one has brought controversy for the suffragettes. It is one amendment that is splitting us. I am mixed on the issue."

"Although I am against the amendment, I can see some need for liquor control. Public drunkenness is out of control."

"It is the one issue that men fear women want most in their quest for the vote. Some think it is the only reason. They fear if women get the right to vote, prohibition would become a reality."

Wherever Sara and Tillie went, there was a lot of conversation about the pending amendments. But none was as dividing as the Fifteenth Amendment, which prohibited the federal government and the states from using a citizen's race, color, or previous status as a slave for voting qualifications.

Tillie said, "Elizabeth Cady Stanton was quite vocal on this subject, and in fact, it had divided the suffragette movement into two camps—those who had opposed the amendment because it didn't go far enough, and those who felt it was a step in the right direction. Stanton had been adamant that it should also include the right to vote for women, but the final version adopted by Congress had not included that provision.

"This amendment had made it clear that all free native-born inhabitants of the United States, though descended from slaves could vote. Despite objections by several key states, enough support from states had been generated to enact the amendment, but that didn't stop the heated discussion.

"Some had mistakenly believed that they could still discriminate against Chinese or Irish people, but the law of the land was clear. All were now exempt from discrimination. It had become a law in January of 1867. The amendment had been ratified, but the battle continues even today with the formation of the Ku Klux Klan and discriminatory voting regulations."

As Sara learned about the amendments from Tillie, she wondered if the Nineteenth Amendment would ever pass. The Fifteenth Amendment was made law in 1867 and it was still being debated. That had been 46 years ago.

Chapter Forty-five

During their travels in the south, Sara and Tillie spoke directly to black women. They met in small, secret places under the guise of some harmless cause or activity, which reminded Sara of her first introduction to the suffragette movement. The women supported the movement, but rarely participated or spoke their inner thoughts for fear of retaliation. Danger was always present. The Klan was also an ever-present fear for them, and Sara's heart ached alongside them as she heard their stories. Opposition would have no qualms in squashing their belligerence with little or no consequences, since they were just "coloreds." The thought enraged Sara. But there were still a few who felt their plight was unbearable and worth any price for change.

While in a small town in Alabama, Tillie and Sara were thrilled to find a larger than usual crowd of black women gathered at one of the outbuildings of a large plantation for a quilting bee. Close to twenty women were there. The plantation owner had supported freedom from slavery and had hired black families as indentured servants, paying them a small wage and providing living quarters. The building was at the edge of a field away from people, a place where quilting bees had taken place before on a regular basis. This gathering would not be looked on with suspicion.

Sadie, the hostess for the gathering, was a large woman with a raucous laugh and a welcoming attitude. She gathered her friends and acquaintances around a large quilt frame and said to each new arrival, "Ya'll knowed we here fer quiltin'. Take a place and thread up yer needles."

On such occasions, Tillie enlisted the help of one of the women in making their presentation. It added a great deal of credibility, since white folk were always under suspicion, and the ladies worked with diligence. They listened to Tillie speak, while their fingers were busy tying a large quilt.

"Ladies, I could speak to you all day and you would leave here saying, "That fine white lady from up north knows nuthin'. She comes here tellin' us what we should be doin'." Tillie dropped her g's to speak in their vernacular in hopes of gathering confidence, but not so much as to appear haughty or disrespectful.

The object was not to gain support for herself, but to enlighten the women to open their eyes to their own plight. A message delivered from one of their own seemed the best way to go about it. "I have asked Sadie to read for you the words of one of your sisters. But first, allow me to tell you about the author of this speech, Isabella. She was born in 1797 in Hurley, New York. Her parents were slaves. Many of her twelve siblings were sold into slavery, some at very early ages."

The ladies moaned at the loss of a sister's children.

Sara understood, at least to a degree, the pain of loss they felt, and mourned with them.

"Belle, as she was called," Tillie explained, "was sold into slavery at the age of nine for one hundred dollars. A few sheep were added to the deal to make it more profitable for her new owner, John Nealy. She was mistreated, and then sold again to a man named Scriver. A year and half later, she was sold yet again to John J Dumont, who was a good man and treated her well.

"In 1828, Isabella was emancipated. For a while, she lived with Isaac and Martha Van Wagener, whose surname she adopted. Since she was emancipated, she petitioned the court to get her son Peter emancipated also. He was in bondage at an Alabama plantation. She was successful in her appeal and was the first Negro to do so. She was a true pioneer for women's rights."

Tillie waited as a few cheers erupted, and Sara shared a smile with her friend. They felt a connection.

Eventually, Tillie continued. "She and Peter journeyed to New York, where she worked as a domestic servant for the Folger family. She met and was taken in by a self-proclaimed Messiah named Matthias. He dealt in illegal activities. Although she was uneducated, Isabella was very intelligent and had great courage. She petitioned the court once again after a highly-publicized scandal involving this man. She again, won the case and became the first person of color to file and win a lawsuit against prestigious whites. She was awarded one hundred twenty-five dollars."

Sara marveled that this uneducated woman of color was so successful in the courts.

"After that, she left New York, where she met a Quaker woman who asked her name. 'Sojourner,' she replied. 'The Lord gave it to me cause I'm to travel up and down the land.' The woman, so impressed with her, inquired as to her surname. I suppose because her mother taught her to always tell the truth, she declared that to be her name, and thereafter, she became known as Sojourner Truth. She felt a deep calling to lecture on the hope and enlightenment within her. She soon became the first Negro woman anti-slavery speaker. It was in1843 that she boldly spoke of freedom for slaves, temperance, and prison reform, but also for women's rights."

By now, the entire room of women was grinning, and Sara knew Tillie had been successful in her cause today.

Tillie finished, "Her six-foot frame was a commanding presence. Her strong, deep voice, humor and wit, indisputable logic, and charismatic nature soon made her a much sought-after speaker. In 1851 in Akron, Ohio, she delivered her most compelling speech, 'Ain't I a Woman.' This speech delivered to a small audience in a small church would become her most famous speech of all time. I would like you to welcome Sadie to my small podium, and she will read to you Sojourner Truth's speech."

Sadie, one of the few women who could read, got up from her seat by the quilt with an enormous smile and lumbered to the podium, which was a barrel from the barn where they worked. She picked up the papers and began to read aloud the words of Sojourner Truth.

Sadie cleared her throat and began to read.

"Aint I a Woman"

"'Wall, chilern, what dar is so much racket dat must be somethin' out o' kilter. I tink dat twixt de niggers of de Souuf and de woman at de Norf, all talkin' bout rights, de white men will be in a fix pretty soon. But what's all dis here talkin'

'bout? Sojourner say, 'Dat man ober dar say dat woman needs to be helped into carriages, and lifted ober ditches, and to hav de best place everywhat. Nobody eber helps me into carriages, or over mud-puddles, or gibs me any best place! And ain't I a woman? Look at me! Look at my arm!'"

Sadie bared her own arm to the shoulder, showing her tremendous muscular power.

"'I have ploughed, and planted, and gathered in barns, and no man could head me! And ain't I a woman? I could work as much and eat as much as a man—when I could get it— and bear the lash as well. And ain't I a woman? I have borne thirteen chilern and seen all sold off to slavery, and when I cried out with my mother's grief, none but Jesus heard me! And ain't I a woman?'"

Sadie cleared her throat and went on with Sojourner's speech, as Sara followed along and felt the words course through her, hearing the centuries-long struggle within them.

"'Den dey talks 'bout dis ting in de head; what dis dey call it?'" Sadie said.

"Intellect," someone nearby whispered.

"Dat's it, honey. What dats got to do wid woman's rights or negros' rights? If my cup won't hold but a pint and yourn holds a quart, wouldn't ya' be mean not to let me have my little half measure full?"

The women all nodded, Tillie and Sara included, and Sadie continued with Sojourner's words.

"'Den dat little man in black dar, he say 'women can't have as much rights as men 'cause Christ wasn't a woman!' Whar did Christ come from?'"

Applause rang out, just as it had in that long ago time in Akron. Raising her voice, Sadie went on.

"'Whar did your Christ come from? From God and a

woman! Man had nothin' to do with Him.'"

"Amen!" shouted a woman near the back.

This was followed by the thunder of applause, laughter, and great shouts of approval, which echoed beyond that little shed.

"If de fust woman God ever made was strong enough to turn de world upside down all alone, dese women togedder," Sadie said, spanning her hand across the crowd, "ought to be able to turn it back, and get it right side up again! And now dey is asking to do it, de men better let em."

Sadie hesitated a moment and then finished.

"'Bleeged to ye fer hearin' on me, and now old Sojourner han't got nuthin' more to say.'"

Sadie took her seat at the quilt, looking rather proud.

Tillie went back to the barrel podium as the women still applauded and stood, believing that they as black women could fight the fight. Sara believed in them, too, and felt a warm bond with them. One of their own had fought the battle. She had died more than thirty years earlier in 1883, but her words echoed on and her spirit moved the women in this room.

Tillie and Sara led the women in a song. It was typical of Sojourner to incorporate music into her lectures and into her everyday life.

Sara distributed leaflets with the words for those who could read. The others clapped in rhythm to the music.

"Song for Equal Suffrage"

Day of hope and day of glory! After slavery and woe,
Comes the dawn of woman's freedom, and the light shall grow and grow
Until every man and woman equal liberty shall know,
In Freedom marching on!
Woman's right is woman's duty! For our share in life we call!
Our will it is not weakened and our power it is not small.
We are half of every nation! We are mothers of them all!
In Wisdom marching on!

We will help to make a pruning hook of every outgrown
sword,
We will help to knit the nations in continuing accord,
In humanity made perfect is the glory of the Lord,
As His world goes marching on!

Sara felt for these women of color. They had suffered so much. Sojourner Truth, one of their own had spoken to them from the grave. Her words from more than a half century earlier rang true today and energized the women.

***

Joseph and Jacob Johnson had been working in the nearby fields and were curious as to the goings-on in that small building. They were white brothers from a neighboring farm—ten boys in the family, so their pa was more than happy to have two of them hire on as helping hands for other plantations.

"Never hurt to bring in a few extra dollars in these hard times," he would say.

Joseph crept up behind the shed and peeked through the cracks into the room where the women were gathered. He waved his arm, motioning to Jacob to come look.

Both boys watched in astonishment as a negro woman read from a book.

They ran across the field to tell their pa what they had just seen. Negro women who were riled. Women who wanted to put men down. Women who did not understand their place in life. They all needed to be taught a lesson.

Chapter Forty-six

The Negro women were all from various parts of the community and had traveled on foot to Sadie's place. It was a hot, sticky day in August, but the women were used to hard labor in the fields, so they paid no mind to it. A few of the women had stayed back at Sadie's to chat with the white women who had spent the day with them and delivered such an inspiring message of hope.

The women who left split up at the end of the trail. Seven headed north, and ten went south. Mildred, the oldest member of the quilting group, lived just a short way up the road. She waved good-bye to her friends and hurried into her house to make bread for supper, humming the tune they had sung at Sadie's as she went.

The remaining six ladies continued their long route home. Some had to walk as much as three miles.

As they turned the bend, they headed west past the Johnson home. The Johnson barn was at the edge of the road. They had finished talking about the day's activities and turned their attention to the fruit, which would soon be harvested and put up into canned peaches, apple butter, and blackberry jam. Their mouths salivated at the thought.

They didn't notice any activity until they passed the barn and came face to face with a group of men with white cone shaped hats that hid their faces. They instantly recognized them as members of the Ku Klux Klan, and the women froze in fear. Under normal circumstances, a group of women returning from a quilting bee would have little to worry about, but this situation struck sudden panic in all of them.

A gruff voice demanded, "Where ya' been?"

The men surrounded them.

In an unwavering voice, Olivia, the self-appointed spokesperson for the group stated, "We been quiltin'. Yo'all let us pass. We ain't botherin' nobody."

"Quiltin', huh?" the gruff voice challenged. "Ya'll been doin' more than quiltin'. You been listenin' to those high falootin' white women from up nort. They been afillin' yer heads wit trash."

"We been quiltin!" Olivia insisted.

"Hear that, fellas? They been quiltin'. Seems they don't know the difference tween quiltin' and trash talkin'. Maybe they needs to be taught a lesson."

The crowd closed in, and the ladies huddled together, trembling and staring wide-eyed at each other. There were six women and ten men. The women attempted to run, but they were quickly caught.

One young woman almost escaped. She managed to slip between two men and started running as fast as she could. Her long skirt almost tripped her, but she held her balance and ran.

Two men grabbed hold of her skirt from behind and pulled her backward, ripping it. Each man grabbed a section of her skirt while taunting her as she shrieked.

They began a game of tug-of-war with her skirt, tearing it completely off.

Once again, she attempted to run away, beginning to sob, but was tackled from behind. She landed on the ground facedown with her assailant on top of her.

He grabbed the back of her pantaloons and stripped them from her. She struggled to get up, tears streaming, but the other man held her down with his knees on her shoulders. They raped her as she begged for mercy.

Breathless, he pushed himself up with his hands on the small of her back and then rolled aside.

"You want some of this bitch?" he asked the other man.

"Naw, I think ya tore her up too bad. Leave her here."

They walked away.

The woman's body ached. Her torn body burned like fire. She wept on the ground, unable to stand. She was seventeen. She had been born a free woman and was a virgin. She was to be married the next week. Her name was Maggie.

Four of the other women lay at the side of the road in various stages of assault. Most had been beaten with clubs, their bodies bruised and bleeding. One had a broken arm. Lord only knew what the other injuries may have been internally. Another had been clubbed beside the head and was in a semi-conscious state. They were all left bruised and broken, and most cried or whimpered in pain.

Not long after, two women who had lingered behind at the shed came upon the scene. They were horrified.

They ran back for help.

Sadie enlisted the help of several of the farmhands and the plantation owner, who all arrived. None could believe the sight before their eyes.

One woman, gathering her wits about her, asked, "Where is Maggie? Where is Suzanne?"

A search began.

A short way up the road they found Maggie, crumpled over in a fetal position, weeping and grasping her torn skirt in her hands. She had tried to cover herself, but her trembling hands were of little use.

They pulled her to a sitting position, and she sat staring blankly into the sky, huge tears rolling down her dirt-smeared cheeks.

They gathered all the women into a cart, and one of the landowners drove them to their respective homes. Meanwhile, the search continued for Suzanne. Suzanne was twenty-eight and the mother of three children, a girl and two boys. She attended services regularly at the local Baptist church and sang in the choir. Her husband picked cotton at one of the nearby plantations. She was nowhere to be found.

It was dusk, and the search team discussed giving up the search for the night. They had searched all along the roadway and up to the woods. They hoped, perhaps, she had escaped and would show up at her house. Darkness began to settle in; they would have to wait until morning to continue.

The next day, they brought out bloodhounds to aid in the search for Suzanne. The hounds led them into the woods, where they found Suzanne's body. The police looked over the crime scene. Her naked body was covered with dry semen. It appeared she had been raped by two or more people. A Klan mask lay on the ground next to her. It was possible that she may have pulled it off her assailant. Her throat was slit. It was assumed that since she had been able to identify one of her assailants, she had to die.

***

Cries for justice for these women went unheeded. After all, they were only women of color. Sara heard one officer say, "They were just a bunch of *nigger* women; don't waste too much time on this case." She cringed at his use of such an ugly word.

Sara found herself crying often after learning of what had happened, and even more so after hearing the officer's words. It was beyond not fair—it was getting away with murder and worse.

Tillie and Sara were to leave the next day, but they delayed their journey to go with Sadie to the sheriff's office. Sadie was aching with grief, and Sara's heart hurt to see it.

When Tillie brought up going to the sheriff to seek justice, Sadie shook her head and replied, "Ain't no use. We can't fight the Klan. No sheriff gonna pay no mind to some black folk. Women besides."

"It isn't right!" Tillie exclaimed, trembling. "I will talk to the sheriff."

"Suit yersef," Sadie sighed. "Twont do no good."

Tillie, Sara, and Sadie got into Tillie's Model T and went to see the sheriff.

Tillie introduced herself as Tillie Morgenson, wife of the late Senator Morgenson from Wisconsin. "I would like to speak to the investigating officer regarding yesterday's attack on six women by the Ku Klux Klan"

The sheriff smiled. "Investigation? What investigation?"

"Surely there is an investigation to bring those hooligans to justice!" Tillie was dismayed.

"Ma'am, we know who done it. It was the Klan. We don't have any other information to investigate. When those Klan people let us know who they are, we will bring them to justice." The sheriff continued to show his contemptible smile.

"Sheriff, are you serious? One poor woman lost her life. Her children are left without a mother. Five other women were brutally attacked with serious injuries, and you don't think it is worth an investigation?" Tillie's hands clenched, and Sara watched as her face got redder with anger.

"Ma'am, ya'all aren't from these parts. If we were to be investigatin' all the mischief those Klan folks get inta, we'd have to hire five more people. In case ya'all din't notice, those were all nigger women. Next thing you know, we would be investigatin' dog fights and lost cats. We cain't be wastin' ar time with this kinda shenanigans."

"Shenanigans? Shenanigans?" Tillie shouted. "They are *women*, American citizens who have been violated by lawbreakers. It is your job to find and incarcerate the perpetrators."

The sheriff smirked. "Them are some mighty fancy words, but you best just go back up north to your justice system, and if ya'all want, ya'all can take a bunch of them *niggers* with ya' since yar so all fired anxious for them to have justice. Now, I have important things to do, so if ya'all will excuse me, I need ta get back to work on important things." The sheriff turned to walk away and then looked back over his shoulder.

"Tell you what, Madam Senator's wife, just for you, I'll have Ben over there look into it. Hear that, Ben?" he glanced toward a deputy standing at the doorway.

"Got it, Sheriff. I'll get right on it soons I get some time," Ben replied, equally disinterested.

"Good day, Ma'am." The sheriff disappeared into another room.

"Outrageous! Simply outrageous!" Tillie stammered. "The governor will hear about this."

"Told ya', ma'am." Sadie shook her head. "Nothin's gonna' change."

"It will, Sadie, it will," Tillie promised. "This is another reason we need to get rights for women. Black women need it even more than white women. If you aren't owned by the slave master, you are owned by your husband or father or brother. Things *have* to change, they just have to."

As they left the building, she looked at her new friend. "I am so sorry, Sadie, I am so sorry."

Chapter Forty-seven

S ara and Tillie continued their journey, spanning thousands of miles throughout the country over the next two years. They traveled back to the east coast, the southern states, the Great Plains, and the Pacific coast. Their message resonated with every woman in every part of the nation. Men far outnumbered women in the western states, and they took their message to them as well.

Men in the far west seemed much more open to women having equal rights than in the more sophisticated eastern states. Women had a much harder life out west, and were working as hard, if not harder, than men on ranches and in wilderness areas. They plowed fields, they tended to the crops, and they milked cows, as well as took care of the children and made meals. Sara couldn't believe the lives these women led and told them how strong they were whenever she met them.

There also seemed to be a shortage of women in the gold mining states and the rough countryside. Men would be happy to have women think of themselves as equal if they would just come and join them. Life was lonely out there.

Just like the fight for abolition of slavery, women of means in the south seemed more content with the status quo. They lived lives of luxury on their plantations and had little to worry about, except raising the children and socializing. They seemed to enjoy being taken care of by the men folk and didn't want to bother thinking about voting. Many of the plantation owners had mistresses, and their wives turned their head and pretended to be ignorant. After all, what could they do, anyway?

Not all women lived lives of luxury. Sara and Tillie saw many women struggling in the south, and they were more open to the message of hope. Some had been dismissed by husbands who chose their mistresses.

Those who had not found the wedded bliss of a wealthy suitor were dubbed old maids. They became teachers of small children, librarians, nannies, and cooks; although many of those jobs were covered by black women who would work for a much lower wage. The single, poor, and disadvantaged were the women who were more interested in the words Tillie and Sara spoke.

After hearing stories of women who lost property, children, and homes to men, it wasn't difficult for Sara and Tillie to convince them to form suffragette organizations of their own. Sara often thought of her own family at home and all that had been taken from her, and it kept her both soft and strong as she traveled and heard these women's stories.

Eastern women seemed the most militant and educated about the political issues of the suffragettes. They were the most vocal, and received the most press, which was then distributed to all corners of the country. It took a long time for news to travel to the far western reaches of the country, but in time, their message would show up in local newspapers. Congress was finding it harder to sweep these issues under the table.

Tillie tried at least once a year to address a committee in Washington, D.C. in person. Her contacts were not as plentiful as they had once been, but knowing the system and a few influential people, she was still able to make her point. Progress was being made albeit very slowly.

A proposed amendment to the Constitution granting women's suffrage had been defeated by a vote of two hundred-four to one hundred seventy-four in 1915. Another battle lost, but the war went on.

Sara and Tillie were once again on the road and headed for the Great Plains. They had passed near this area in the past, but often returned to places they had been before, driving home the message they had introduced on an earlier visit. They had come across the purple Rocky Mountains and now headed to the heartland with its "amber waves of grain."

Their previous experiences here had been eye-opening. The pioneer women welcomed them, and often invited them to stay in their homes. Mr. and Mrs. Baker in particular, were enthusiastic about having Sara and Tillie stay with them, and gave them a delicious hot meal of stew and biscuits. Mrs. Baker fed them and insisted that they take the one bed in their modest cabin. She said she would sleep in the living room and Mr. Baker would sleep in the bunkhouse. Mr. Baker was equally insistent.

Sara protested, "We appreciate all that you are doing for us, but we are used to modest accommodations. We don't want to inconvenience you and your husband. Please sleep in your bed; we will be quite comfortable here." Sara pointed to a sofa. "It is quite long, and we are short. It will accommodate us just fine."

Mrs. Baker wouldn't hear of it. After a few more protests, Tillie said to Sara, "It looks like the Bakers are generous people, and we don't want to offend by refusing their kind offers." She looked at Mrs. Baker with a gentle smile. "We will accept your generous offer with great gratitude. If there is anything we can do for you, please let us know."

That evening, Sara and Tillie readied for bed and slipped between the covers. They were exhausted from their travels and were soon fast asleep. When the morning dawned, sun streamed through the dusty window.

Sara jumped out of bed, feeling a strong itching sensation on her legs.

"Tillie, Tillie, look at me." She shook her friend in a panic.

"Oh, my gosh," she gasped, as she saw Tillie's arm and neck covered with a line of multiple small welts. She had clusters of the same welts on her legs.

Sara felt an itch on her face and didn't know if she had the same welts, or if seeing them on Tillie had given her the idea to scratch. The mirror revealed that it was not a psychotic episode. She also had a welt-like rash on her cheek and the back of her neck. Some of the welts had started to blister where Sara had scratched them in her sleep.

By now, Tillie was awake and had begun to itch, too. "Bed bugs!" she exclaimed. "I am afraid we had added guests in our bed last night."

"Whatever will we do about it? The itch is dreadful!" Sara complained. She had never encountered bed bugs before.

"Don't panic." Tillie suggested they ask Mrs. Baker for some warm water to wash the infected areas. "Perhaps Mrs. Baker has some ointment we can use."

When faced with this dilemma, Mrs. Baker was not at all surprised. She looked over the rashes and provided some warm water for washing.

"Don't concern yourself; it will be gone in three or four days," she said. "This is a normal thing out in these parts. Those little bugs are everywhere. I wash everything down with lye soap. It helps for a couple of days, and then the critters are back."

They left that day, not wanting to stay another night.

From that time on, Sara and Tillie checked every bed they slept in to make sure they had no unwanted visitors.

Chapter Forty-eight

"Next stop, Cimarron County in Oklahoma," Tillie said one hot, dry summer day in 1916.

Most of the population were ranchers, who had come as homesteaders. There were a lot of wide-open spaces and not many places to stay the night.

Tillie had not been feeling well. They blamed it on the scorching heat.

Sara drove into Boise City, where they would meet with Mayor Samuel Hayes. He had been elected mayor in June after a recall election of his predecessor J.W. Robinson.

Tillie had connections. Samuel Hayes had been born in Wisconsin of course. Sara used to be surprised, but with Tillie, nothing was a stretch.

They checked into a local inn, and Tillie went directly to her bed to lie down. She was to address a group of women in the town hall that evening.

"I don't think I feel up to it," Tillie said. "Sara, you will have to take my place."

"Tillie, how can I do that? I am not prepared." Sara panicked.

"Of course, you are, dear," Tillie encouraged her. "You have assisted me in all of our rallies and lectures. You know everything as well as I do. In fact, Sara, you have written most of the recent material."

"Maybe, but I am not a speaker," Sara reasoned with a frown. "You *are* the speaker."

"I have heard you talking with the women at every function we have attended. You can do it," Tillie rebutted.

Sara shook her head in protest. "That is different. I talk to the women one on one. Getting up in front of everyone is different. I will probably wet my pants."

"Use the material you wrote, and if that doesn't sound right to you, talk from your heart. You have several hours to prepare," Tillie said. "You will be fine. You will be a star."

"Oh Tillie, you make it all sound so easy." Sara hesitated, fixing her hair in nervousness. "I am being so selfish. Here you are, ill, and I am fretting about speaking in front of a group of women. Are you okay, Tillie? Is there anything I can do for you?"

Tillie managed a weak smile. "I am sure I will be fine. I just need rest. And yes, there is something you can do for me. Can you find me a nice cup of hot tea?"

"Of course." Sara hugged her friend. "I'm going to the general store to get some salve for these awful bug bites, and I will pick up a container of tea. I am sure the innkeeper can fix us a pot of hot water. You rest. I will be back, and we can have a cup of tea together."

Sara left Tillie sleep. She proceeded down the boardwalk toward the General Store. While there, she picked up a few items they needed. Her mind, however, was on the lecture that evening, and how she would manage to get through it. It scattered her thoughts and made focusing difficult. She asked the storekeeper for herbal tea and for his recommendation on a salve for bed bug bites. She also inquired if he had an elixir to soothe Tillie's ailments.

While she was at the counter, she heard a voice behind her.

"Mrs. Dewberry? Is that you, Mrs. Dewberry?"

Sara turned to find a pretty, young woman—a very pregnant young woman. And she was familiar. "Rose? Rose Meyer? I can't believe it! What are you doing here?" Sara clasped her hands to her mouth in utter surprise.

"I might ask you the same." Rose smiled, her eyes bright and cheeks rosy. "I live here. What brings you to our fair city?"

Sara paid for her purchases and then grabbed Rose's hand. "Where can we go to talk? I can't believe it. I can't believe it." Sara was giddy, unable to process the sight of a piece of the world she had left behind.

"We can go to the hotel. They have a place to eat. We can order lemonade," Rose suggested. "And by the way, it is Rose Corrigan now."

"Come." Sara couldn't contain her excitement. She couldn't let go of Rose's hand, either. Rose had been Ella's lifelong friend, and grasping her hand was almost like having Ella here.

At the hotel, Sara ordered lemonade and couldn't stop looking at Rose. "Tell me. How did you come to live here? Do you keep in touch with Ella? When is your baby due? Tell me everything." Sara was elated.

"Cody and I got married last year. You remember Cody, the stable boy from Ella's school?"

"Of course, of course. Go on."

Rose beamed, her hands at her stomach with pride. "My baby is due in two weeks, but let me skip all of the stuff about me. Ella is coming here next week to be with me when I have my baby. She's going to be the godmother. She will stay until she must go back to school in September. How long will you be here, Mrs. Dewberry? And you never answered me, why are you here anyway?"

"I am here with Tillie Morgenson. We have been traveling and speaking to suffragettes all over the country. We are speaking at the town hall tonight. But that can wait. Ella is coming? Ella is coming here?" Sara couldn't help but change the subject, leaning forward in eagerness.

"Yes, she is coming by train to be with me when the baby is born. She should arrive on Monday and will be staying for about six weeks. She has been trying to reach you. Sometimes, she gets word that you will be in a certain town, but when she tries to write you there, you have already left. She always reads your letters from Edith," Rose said.

Sara's heart skipped a beat and her lip trembled. "Oh Rose, I miss her so. I miss all of my children, but Ella and I had a special bond. Our plan was only to be here for two days, but I can't leave now. Not if Ella is coming. Tillie is ill and needs her rest. We can delay. We will delay. Oh Rose, I am so happy we ran into each other!"

"Ella would be so disappointed if she missed you again. Do you need a place to stay? Our cabin is small, but I am sure we can make room if you would like to stay with us."

"Thank you so much, but I need to stay with Tillie at the inn. If Tillie needs to go on without me, I will reconsider, but for now, you can reach me here."

Sara took a breath and finished her lemonade before changing the subject. "Rose, would you be free to come to the lecture tonight? It would mean so much to me. This will be my first lecture alone, and if you were there in the audience, I could speak directly to you and maybe I wouldn't be so nervous."

Rose grinned. "I wouldn't miss it. Ever since my aunt was involved with the suffragettes in Milwaukee, I have supported the movement. Of course, I am limited in what I can do way out here, but I have got in some heated debates among friends." Rose laughed. "Ella is also involved now, you know."

"Really? I hope Mr. Dewberry doesn't find out." Sara's heart leapt at the thought of Ella following in her footsteps, despite the worry.

"Mr. Dewberry has been trying to reach you as well," Rose revealed. "According to Ella, he is heartbroken and remorseful. Apparently, someone was able to get through to him, and he is a different person. Of course, he is still a stuffy banker, but he has had a change of heart when it comes to women's rights."

"Rose, are you sure? I would never believe it could happen." Sara was in awe.

"Ella says that Mr. Dewberry would love to turn the clock back if he could. He keeps hoping you will return to Milwaukee so he can talk to you. He wants your forgiveness."

Sara scowled, ignoring the effect the words had on her. "I am afraid I am not the person I was back in Milwaukee. I have seen and experienced so many things. I don't know if I could ever return to that life again. I guess I still love the Mr. Dewberry I met when we were younger, but we have both changed."

Rose stood to go, leaving Sara with her thoughts. "I need to get back home and prepare dinner. Cody has been busy on the range, and he will be home soon, dusty and hungry and tired. I will see you this evening. It won't be too late, will it?"

"Oh no." Sara beckoned the waiter. "It shouldn't be more than about an hour long. We will meet at six-thirty, and you should be home well before eight. It should still be light out."

"I will see you then." Rose headed for the door.

"Rose," Sara called out. "Sit in the front seat where I can see you."

"I will!" Rose waved good-bye and slipped out the door.

Sara paid for the lemonade and requested a pot of hot water to be delivered to her room, unable to stop thinking about her family. It made her chest tighten, both in frustration and tentative hope. She hurried to their room to check on Tillie.

Tillie had just awoken and was feeling refreshed. She was still pale and not her old self, but the rest had helped.

The water for the tea arrived. Sara put the tea into cups, and while it steeped, Sara told Tillie about all that had happened that afternoon.

Then, Sara looked through the notes for the meeting. Forget the couple of hours to prepare. She would just have to wing it.

***

The town hall was filling up rapidly when Sara arrived. Butterflies leapt in her tummy, but she felt confident. Rose was right there in the front row, smiling when she saw her.

Sara went to her and gave her a big hug. "You are my good luck charm tonight," Sara whispered in her ear.

Sara went to the podium, organized her notes, looked out at the crowd, and took a deep breath. "Good evening, ladies and..." She stopped and gazed about the room. "Ladies. Had to make sure there are just ladies here."

She greeted the assembly with a nervous smile. "Not that we don't welcome gentlemen, we certainly do, but since there are none to be found, let me look out at all of you amazing friends and neighbors, and let's chat...a little woman to woman talk." Already, she began to feel the butterflies leave.

"In fact, ladies..." Sara waved her sheaves of notes in the air. "I am going to address you with my first paragraph of notes, and then I am going to put these away and we will have a conversation."

She took out the first page and put on her wire-rim glasses. She had never worn glasses before, but for the past year, she had grown to depend on them.

Sara cleared her throat. "I am here tonight to talk to you about pioneers. Women pioneers, to be specific. That would be every one of you here today. Whether you were born here or if you traveled from faraway places, you are pioneers. It takes special qualities to be a pioneer—it takes pride, it takes determination, it takes strength and fortitude, and it takes vision. It takes self-worth and self-reliance. It takes confidence, it takes faith, and it takes hard work.

"This is not unlike the journey suffragettes are taking today to seek their just reward for the efforts and hard work they do, for the vision they have of a life where women can reap the rewards for their determination and fortitude. Rewards that men have always enjoyed. You are worth it, and you have earned it." Sara put her paper down and began her own story.

"Ladies, I had an easy life. I was married and had most of the comforts of an upper-class woman. I had a nice home and three children. If there was anything I wanted, it was available to me. That is the bright side." Sara thought about her old life briefly, then put herself back on track.

"I lost my parents when I was very young. The inheritance I got from them was a good down payment for my home...my home that was in my husband's name. When my husband decided that he didn't like my point of view regarding women's rights, he ejected me from my own home and forbade me to ever see my children again. The home I paid for was not mine; the children I bore and cared for were not mine. If I defied his order and spoke to my children, he would have had me committed to an insane asylum...and he could. I had no money to fight him. As a woman, I had no rights. I had no right to vote, so I had no recourse to legally fight the system of male domination."

This time, Sara could not avoid remembering the sting of Henry's words, and she let it fuel her fire.

The women whispered to each other in a low buzz around the room.

"Ladies, you may not have had the monetary status I did, but you have worked as hard as your husbands, brothers, and fathers, with your own blood and sweat. You have children and you have everything you worked to achieve. But do you realize that if your husband decides he doesn't like your attitude or if he likes his mistress better, he has the right to take it all away from you? And ladies, doesn't that make you fighting mad?"

The room erupted, and Sara gripped the podium tight to steady herself.

"Now, ladies, let's talk woman to woman." Sara sat at the edge of the platform and spent the next hour talking about stories others had to share, answering questions about what they could do and seeing their indignation when they realized they were so vulnerable. The women left at eight that evening wanting more. They were prepared to fight the fight. Their pioneer spirit was alive and well.

Feeling successful and unable to stop smiling, Sara announced that she had had a change of plans and would be staying for a few weeks, so if any of the women wanted to meet again, she would be available.

Before they adjourned, they made plans for a meeting the following week and would be recruiting even more women to the cause.

Before Rose left, she went to Sara, her eyes glistening with tears. "I was so proud listening to you. You have been like a mom to me, Mrs. Dewberry, and you were great. I can't tell you how happy I was to listen to your words tonight."

"So, I did alright?" Sara asked.

"You were fantastic!" Rose exclaimed. She handed Sara a note with directions to her house. "Can you come for dinner tomorrow? Bring Tillie, if she's up to it. We have so much to talk about."

Sara grinned. "Tillie was doing much better this afternoon. We would be delighted to come to your home for dinner. If Tillie can't come, I will still be there, but I do need to make sure she is okay before I venture out."

"Good. Come tomorrow at three. That will give us plenty of time to talk before dinner." Rose seemed excited, which made Sara smile wider. "I am so happy you are here." She gave Sara a hug and a peck on the cheek. "See you tomorrow." She waved good-bye.

"Tomorrow," Sara called after her. She then turned her attention to the ladies who had lingered behind to ask questions and share their thoughts.

It was after nine when Sara returned to the inn. Tillie was fast asleep. Sara got into bed and turned off the gas lamp beside it.

The next day, Tillie seemed to improve even more. Her eyes looked brighter and she had the energy to sit up.

"How are you feeling?" Sara inquired.

"I am feeling much better, my dear. How did it go last night?"

"Oh Tillie, it was so exciting! I did as you said and talked of my own experiences from my heart. It was fun after I got rid of the butterflies in my stomach. We have a new group of suffragettes forming out of that talk last night."

Sara told her all the details of the meeting and the responses she received. "We will be meeting again next Tuesday, and everyone thinks there will be even more women in attendance."

"It does sound like you had a successful evening," Tillie said with approval. "I knew you could do it. It looks like my work will be a lot easier for a while. My dear, please tell me again about yesterday. I am afraid my mind is a bit foggy. I am not sure if I heard you correctly or if I was dreaming…"

"Oh, it was so exciting. Rose, Ella's childhood friend is here." Sara told Tillie again what Rose had said about Ella being godmother to Rose's baby, and that Ella was coming to Oklahoma on Monday. "I hope you don't mind staying a bit longer. If you can't, I understand, but I must stay. I must see Ella."

"Well, I think a bit more rest will do me good. I don't know how I could continue without you, and I would be disappointed if you didn't see your daughter. Leaving would be unthinkable." Tillie expressed exactly what Sara hoped to hear in a warm voice, and her hand patted Sara's.

"Oh, thank you for understanding. We are invited to Rose and Cody's home for dinner tonight. She asked us to come early so we have time to talk. Do you feel up to it?"

"I think I can manage just fine. But right now, I need a bit of nourishment. Do you think you could go down to the restaurant and fetch a biscuit and honey for me? A cup of coffee would be most appreciated. I need a jolt to start the day." Tillie seemed in good spirits.

Sara grinned. "You get dressed and I'll be back before you know it." Sara left, humming a bit of "She'll be Comin Round the Mountain When She Comes."

"Ella's coming, Ella's coming. Around the mountain or through the valley makes no mind. I can't wait to see her."

Chapter Forty-nine

That afternoon and every afternoon after, Sara visited Rose's home. They had three years to catch up on. Ella had shared some of Sara's letters with Rose, so she knew some of Sara's experiences, and she was mesmerized to hear even more.

Sara, meanwhile, wanted to know everything about her family, since she had heard nothing. They reminisced, and the days sped away in joy and tears as they shared so many hopes and memories.

Since Rose was expecting her first baby and had no mother or mother figure there to answer all her questions about delivery and caring for a small baby, Sara became the comforting voice of experience she needed.

They readied the baby's cradle, which Cody had woven months ago from a nearby harvest of dogwood twigs. They went through clothing from neighbors whose infants had outgrown them. They stitched diapers, and after years away from knitting needles, Sara picked them up and began to knit a warm sweater for the baby's first winter. She relished tending to Rose as though it were her own child who was about to become a mother. All the maternal instincts and experiences Sara had missed came pouring out, and she cherished every moment.

On Thursday, Tillie who was feeling much better, decided she would explore the city on foot.

Sara took the automobile to Rose's house alone. She found Rose huddled in a chair in obvious pain. "Rose, child, what is the matter?" Sara rushed to her side.

Rose moaned, a sheen of sweat across her skin. "It hurts, and I am afraid there is something the matter with the baby!" Rose sobbed. "Please don't let my baby die."

"Rose, you are due in less than two weeks. Maybe the baby is early.

Tell me what you feel." Sara pressed a comforting hand to her forehead and urged her to sit back. "Try to relax and take some deep breaths."

"The pain comes softly and then gets more and more." She took a deep breath. "Then it stops, but only for a while, and then it comes again."

"How far apart are the pains?" Sara asked, rubbing Rose's back.

"It started at four o'clock this morning, and they were about an hour apart, but now it is only about fifteen minutes." Rose grimaced.

"Those are contractions, my dear. You are going to have a baby today, and probably very soon." Sara smiled. "Where is Cody? We must get him; he will want to be here for the birth of his child."

"Oh, no!" Rose gasped. "Cody can't come. They drove some cattle to Texas, and he isn't expected back for two days."

"Well, I am afraid this baby isn't going to wait two days. It may not wait two hours." Sara wrung her hands. "Your midwife, Rose, where is your midwife? We need to fetch her."

Rose was between contractions. "She is not here. My midwife is delivering a baby on the other side of the state. She won't be here until tomorrow. What will we do?"

"Let me think," Sara said, placing her knuckles to her mouth and looking toward the ceiling, contemplating the situation. After a moment, she dropped her hand and immediately took charge.

"First, we need to get you into your nightgown and into bed. Where do you have extra blankets? We need to make a pad for the bed. Do you have a fresh muslin sheet?"

Rose told Sara where to gather the items.

Sara made up the bed while Rose got changed. She had barely gotten under the cover when another pain struck. "Oh dear, Mrs. Dewberry. I think I wet the bed. Oh, dear."

Sara laughed, pulling out the wet pad beneath her and inserting another dry one. "Your water broke. It is normal. I was going to suggest I go into town to get the doctor, but I can't leave you. We are going to have to do this alone."

"Can you do this?" Rose winced, trembling hard.

"Well, I have never been a midwife, but after giving birth to four children of my own, I think I know a thing or two," Sara comforted.

Inside, butterflies bounced in her tummy even more so than they had at her first speech, but she did not want to worry Rose.

"I'm so glad you're here." Rose managed a weak smile. "What would I have done if you didn't come by?"

"I am glad I'm here, too. We will manage." Sara needed to convince herself as much as she needed to convince Rose. "I am going to boil a pot of water."

Sara rose to go to the kitchen.

"Why are you boiling water?"

"Babies need to be cleaned after they are born," Sara said seriously.

Rose looked alarmed. "Mrs. Dewberry, you aren't going to wash my baby in boiling water, are you?"

"No, sweetie, it was a joke. I am going to fix a cup of tea for both of us while we wait," Sara laughed. "We do need some warm water for bathing the baby though, so we do have to have it available. Sometimes, midwives need boiling water to sanitize their instruments, but we don't need those. However, we will need some string to tie the cord. I found a piece in your cupboard that I can use. I am not sure if it needs sterilization, but it is better to be safe, so I will. When it comes time, I will wash my hands thoroughly, and I'll need some pretty warm water for that as well."

Rose breathed a sigh of relief.

Sara returned minutes later with two steaming cups of tea, a big scissors, and a wooden spoon. She laid the scissors on a clean towel on the table next to the lamp. She laid the spoon on the bed next to Rose.

Rose looked nervous again, worry etched in her brow. She took the cup of tea and looked at the scissors on the nightstand. "What is that for?" She pointed to the scissors.

Sara cocked her head and looked directly at Rose. "Sweetie, you really know nothing about babies, do you?"

Rose looked down. "Mama never wanted to talk about such things. When I got married, we came home that night and Cody wanted to, well, you know. I had no idea what he was doing. He pulled me into his arms, kissed me, and I felt him next to me. I jumped back and squealed, 'What is that? What are you doing?' I was lucky that Cody was a kind and gentle man. Right then and there, he had to explain to me about the birds and the bees. I was so embarrassed. He told me not to be embarrassed, and that it was natural. Well, Mrs. Dewberry, it took me more than a month before we actually, well you know, did it again."

"You are lucky to have such a considerate husband," Sara said.

"Are you going to tell me about the scissors and the spoon?" Rose asked again.

"Relax, my child. The scissors are to cut the umbilical cord that attaches mother to child. We will tie it with the string and then it needs to be cut free from the placenta."

"Will it hurt?"

"No, of course not. The placenta is formed with the baby and allows you to feed the baby when it is developing. It will be free from you, but it needs to be free from the baby. It is just another one of those natural things. God doesn't make childbirth easy, but it isn't cruel. There is a wonderful reward at the end." Sara comforted Rose as she brushed hair from her forehead.

Rose winced. The contractions were less than a minute apart now.

"Well, Rose, you don't have a month to get ready for this, so maybe it will help if you drop the Mrs. Dewberry thing and just call me Mama Sara. Okay? I need you to let me pull your covers back and examine you. I need to see if there is any sign of your opening enlarging."

Rose nodded.

Sara looked, let out a soft whistle, and said, "Rose, this is it. I see the baby's head. That is good; it's coming the right way. Are you ready? The next time you get a large pain, I want you to push. You asked what the spoon was for?" Sara handed it to her. "When you get the next big pain, put the handle in your mouth and bite down hard."

Just then, the big one came. The spoon went immediately to Rose's mouth, and she bore down. "Eeeewh, eeewh. Puff, puff, eewh, eeewh."

One deep breath and Rose stopped as the contraction did, sweating and out of breath.

It started again almost immediately.

"Push, push, push!" Sara prompted loudly.

Rose bore down with all she had in her. She took a deep breath and pushed again.

Sara coached, "That's my girl, push, push, push."

Rose let out a scream, which she stifled by biting down again on the spoon handle.

Sara thought she might bite the spoon in half, but in a minute, it was over.

Then, Sara lifted the tiny baby girl by its ankles and gave it a sound slap on the behind. Almost immediately, the baby let out a cry. Sara and Rose smiled, as overwhelming joy filled the room.

Sara laid the baby on the clean muslin sheet and began to check it over, cleaning its mouth and checking its ears. She tied the cord. After a quick snip of the scissors, Sara laid the baby in Rose's arms.

Sara turned around to get a warm bowl of water to wash the baby when Rose let out a muffled scream. "Oh, oh, oh!" She was bearing down again.

Sara swung back to see what had happened, and momentarily she wondered if something had gone terribly wrong. Would she lose Rose to childbirth?

She quickly realized that Rose was having another contraction. She grabbed the baby and placed it in a safe corner of the bed, moving to Rose's side.

"Oh, my," Sara exclaimed. "Push, push, push!"

Within a matter of minutes, a second baby girl arrived.

Sara lifted it by the ankles and spanked its bottom. There was no response.

Sara tried again, and again received no response.

She laid the baby on the bed and swabbed its mouth with a dry cloth. There was a bit of a sputter and then a loud cry. "Little girl, you scared me half to death!" Sara cried.

She checked over both babies thoroughly. "Five fingers, five fingers, five fingers, five fingers, five toes, five toes, five toes, five toes." Sara breathed a sigh of relief.

"Are we done now?" she asked Rose with a broad smile. "It appears you have two very healthy baby girls. Rose, you are amazing. Have you picked out names yet?"

Rose was taken aback. "We have one name; the first baby is Ella Sue Corrigan. I am not sure what we will name the second. How do you like Emma Sara Corrigan?"

Sara smiled and busied herself with bathing Ella. "There you are, Miss Ella Sue Corrigan." She placed Ella into her mother's arm and took Emma.

"Hmm, Emma Sara Corrigan…I think it suits you just fine." Her heart was about to burst with joy.

"I think you are going to need a bit of help for a few days since Cody won't be here until Sunday and Ella won't arrive until Monday. Looks like I am going to be your house guest."

Sara got word to Tillie through a neighbor who stopped by to check on Rose that afternoon. The neighbors, Mr. and Mrs. Parker, took a buckboard into town and summoned the doctor and Tillie. Tillie rode back to the ranch with the Parkers.

Everyone was so excited, and poor Rose was exhausted. Exhausted, but happy and content, knowing her babies were safe in the hands of Mama Sara and Aunt Tillie.

"I wish Cody were here," Rose whispered as she dropped off into a deep sleep.

Chapter Fifty

On Monday at precisely eleven twenty-five in the morning, the locomotive chugged into the Boise City station. Billows of smoke poured from its stack. As it chugged to a halt, Sara saw passengers in the window gathering their things to exit the passenger cars. She searched for a familiar face, standing on her toes, but she would have to wait. The engine released a huge charge of steam as the conductor put down the stool to assist the passengers from the train.

Sara stood on the platform in her usual garb, a white starched high-collar shirt and black skirt that cut off just above the ankle, exposing high-button black shoes. On her head, she had a large brim hat adorned with artificial flowers. The hat shielded her face from the late-July hot sun. The temperature outside was pushing ninety-five degrees Fahrenheit. Sara was so nervous; she barely noticed the heat. Her mind was on seeing her daughter for the first time in close to four years.

Ella was thirteen when Sara had left Milwaukee. She would soon be a young woman of seventeen. Sara watched as one by one, passengers exited the train.

She spotted a young woman with reddish hair and her heart skipped a beat.

No, it wasn't her.

She waited several minutes more, hoping Ella hadn't missed the train or if somehow the arrival information was incorrect. She looked at a sheet of paper in her purse. No, this was Engine 323. Ella should be aboard.

Then her eyes focused on a lovely lady with auburn hair in a beautiful navy eyelet dress with light blue underlay. She wore white shoes and had white stockings, with a small stylish hat with blue flowers. She carried a parasol that was also white. The conductor took her hand to assist her from the train. She was looking down to watch her step, but as she raised her head and looked about the dwindling crowd of people, Sara knew this was Ella. Ella all grown up.

Sara ran to her side, shouting, "Ella, Ella!"

Ella's eyes looked in the direction of the voice and she immediately ran to meet Sara with arms opened wide. "Mother, Mother. How did you know I was coming...here of all places?" Emma embraced her.

Sara took both of Ella's hands and flung them outward. "Let me look at you. Oh my, you have grown. You are a beautiful young woman." Sara had to fight back tears of joy.

"I ran into Rose when we arrived here two weeks ago. She told me that you were coming for a visit, so we cancelled the rest of the tour. I couldn't be so close to seeing you and continue our journey. I would never be able to live with myself. I have missed you so."

"I have missed you, too, Mother. Where is Rose?" Ella inquired, her eyes becoming watery.

"She is at the ranch. She was as big as a house when I first laid eyes on her. I barely recognized her. There is so much to tell you, Ella dear. Let's gather your things and we will be at Rose's house in no time," Sara directed.

"I would imagine she is feeling rather uncomfortable traveling. I understand why she couldn't come to meet me herself. But this...seeing you, oh my gosh, it is so fabulous. It feels like a hundred Christmases," Ella gushed as they picked up her trunk and carpet bag.

They went outside the depot where Tillie's car was parked. "Here is your magic carriage, my princess." Sara smiled, recalling the games they had played when Ella was but a tiny tot.

All the way to Rose's house, they couldn't stop talking in animated tones, catching up little by little on their three plus years of separation.

Sara wanted to know about Elizabeth and Thaddeus.

Elizabeth was eleven now, and quite a tomboy. She played with dolls, but she didn't play house. Her focus was on bandaging their injured limbs and treating them for god-awful illnesses. Liz wanted to be a doctor. Father hoped such nonsense would pass but encouraged her to enter the nursing field. Thaddeus was now enrolled in West Point, and would one day become a soldier in the United States Army Corp.

"What about you, Ella? What are your ambitions?" Sara asked.

"I am enrolled to start at Downer College for Women in September," she announced with a smile. "I wanted to be close to home, so I could look after Liz. It is important that she have a woman around at this stage of her life."

"I am so sorry." Sara reached out and squeezed her daughter's hand, guilt eating through her. "I wasn't there for you. I hope you understand I had no choice, but it tore me apart. I wanted to be there for you. I wanted to be a part of your growing up. Every day, I go to sleep thinking about my children, praying that they are safe and happy."

Ella's voice was soft as she made a small smile. "Mother, I understand. I know that Father drove you away. But Father has changed. He misses you terribly. He has tried to contact you, but by the time he knew where you were, you had left for a new destination. He sent letters and telegrams, but most were returned unclaimed. A few were responded to by someone in the organization who informed Father that you had left and where you were headed, but by the time he received the reply, you had already moved on."

"You received my messages? At the library?" Sara needed to know that her daughter knew how much she had missed her.

"Oh yes, and I looked forward to each letter. I kept them all. They are at home in my dresser," Ella confided. "Liz asks to read them sometimes, especially hers. She misses you, too. That is why I want to be there for her. Thankfully, Catherine was always there when we needed to know some womanly information, like you said. She is very funny, and we have had some wonderful times with her. Claudia took care of most of the home chores, and we could go to her when we needed something, but we've grown to dislike her immensely. She always blamed you for the situation, and she would frequently tell us what a bad mother you were. One day, Father overheard her ranting and quickly dismissed her. Liz still has Catherine to go to, but she has depended on me for so long that I know it would be more difficult for her, should she be left on her own."

Sara took in all the information and let herself tentatively smile at the thought of Catherine's humor and Henry's defense of her. She did not know quite what to think, but she was grateful everyone missed her.

Eventually, they arrived, and the old Model T sputtered up the drive to the front porch. "Rose is so excited to see you," said Sara. "She would be waiting on the porch if she could."

Sara pushed open the door, holding it so Ella would be the first to enter. There, on a rocking chair in the corner of the room, was Rose, with tiny Ella in her arms. Her foot rocked the cradle that sat on the floor beside her, with Emma quietly asleep inside.

Ella dropped her bags and gasped. "Rose, you didn't wait for me!"

She ran to Rose's side, knelt, and stroked the baby in her arms. "And what is your name, little girl?" Ella cooed as she stroked the baby's downy hair.

"This is Ella Sue Corrigan. Would you like to hold her?" Rose handed the baby to Ella.

"She is so tiny and so beautiful." Ella beamed at her namesake. "And whose child is this?" she inquired as she nodded to the baby in the cradle and looked about the room for another mother.

"This is Emma Sara Corrigan, Ella's twin sister," Rose said with a grin. "And would you believe, Mama Sara delivered them both." Rose's face filled with pride.

"Seriously?" Ella asked in disbelief. "Two babies? And Mother delivered them?"

"Seriously," Rose said, still beaming. "She is quite the woman! Cody was on a cattle drive in Texas and my midwife was across the state, delivering another baby. Your mother took over. Little Emma gave us a bit of a scare, but Dr. Dewberry here knew exactly what to do. She has been watching over me ever since. I don't know what I would've done without her."

The ladies spent the rest of the day catching up on old times, cuddling babies and taking turns rocking them. They had so many questions about Sara's travels and Rose's life on the ranch. They talked of Ella's future and her college education. Time flew. Cody was helping a rancher across the plain with some branding and birthing tasks, so he was not there in time for supper.

Sara fixed a light meal of fresh greens with vinegar and oil dressing, along with cheese and cold meat, and then announced she would be going back to the inn. When she had left Tillie earlier in the day, Tillie had not been feeling very good and Sara wanted to check on her friend.

With reluctance, she hugged her daughter and left her with Rose. She promised to be back in the morning.

***

When Sara arrived at the inn, she inquired of the innkeeper if Tillie had been out. He hadn't seen her all day. Sara climbed the stairs to their room and opened the door. Tillie was on a chair by the window with her head slumped down.

Sara rushed to her side. "Tillie, Tillie, are you all right?" she demanded.

Tillie nodded weakly. She opened her eyes, briefly acknowledging her friend, but then fell into a sleep. Her breathing grew shallow.

Sara ran downstairs to the innkeeper, her heart pounding hard in her chest. "Please, fetch the doctor. Something is wrong with Tillie. She needs help."

The innkeeper sent his wife down the street to summon the doctor. She returned momentarily with him in tow.

"Her heart is very weak," he diagnosed with a somber frown. "She has heart disease and hasn't more than a few months to live. She needs bedrest. When she is strong enough to travel in a week or so, she can go home. But I don't think it is a good idea to go by automobile. She is much too weak for that kind of journey."

The doctor left medication and advised her to eat healthy food, but in small quantities, and to let her rest whenever she felt the need. He turned to Sara and the innkeeper's wife. "You ladies get her into her nightgown, and I will help you get her into bed."

Tillie helped a little, and they managed to accomplish the task and prepare her for a good night of rest.

Sara sat awake next to Tillie for a long time that night, watching her breath. Her heart clenched at the thought of only a few more months at her side—it wasn't enough. What would she do without Tillie's guiding light?

She let a few tears fall, then climbed into bed.

The next morning, Tillie seemed a bit more alert. She was still having difficulty breathing and refused most of the food offered to her.

"You must eat to regain your strength," Sara encouraged, hiding her sorrow.

That afternoon, Tillie slept. Sara summoned the innkeeper's wife to check in on her while Sara was away.

Sara went to the ranch to explain why she had not returned earlier.

They discussed Tillie's situation and how she would travel home. They determined that Tillie would use Ella's train ticket for the return home. Sara and Ella would return to Milwaukee by automobile. They could spend another month—the month of August—tending to Rose and the babies. Tillie would need a good deal of Sara's time for the coming week, but they would arrange for a nurse to stay with her once she reached her home in Milwaukee. At least, until Sara returned.

It was painful for both Ella and Sara not to be able to see much of each other that first week, knowing they were so close. Thankfully, Tillie recovered more rapidly than expected, and they shared their plan with her. She agreed that it was the best for everyone.

Typical of Tillie, she took the news of her mortality with grace and understanding. "I so wish I could see this fight to the end, but I know my time is near. Sara, you will continue the fight. We are winning. I can feel it. We are winning…"

"Of course I will fight the fight for you, Tillie. You are my rock."

"No child, not for me. For yourself, your daughters, your granddaughters, and all the women in this Nation."

Then, Tillie fell asleep once again.

Tillie improved remarkably with bedrest and with Sara's constant care. The weeks sped by, and finally the doctor gave the okay for Tillie to travel.

Exactly three weeks from the day that Ella arrived, they went to the train station with Tillie. The conductor helped Tillie aboard and they waved good-bye to her. Sara and Ella stood on the platform until the train pulled out of the station.

"God be with her," Sara said softly, her heart aching.

They watched the train disappear down the track with its black smoke waving good-bye, and then they returned to Rose's house.

Rose asked Sara to get all her things from the inn and stay with them for the duration of her time there. Cody was there, and wholeheartedly agreed. He offered to fetch her things from the inn, but Sara insisted on going along.

Cody took the buckboard that could hold more than the Model T, and they went into town to the inn. He and Sara had time to talk as the horses trotted into town. Cody told Sara how grateful he was that she had been there for Rose when his little girls were born. Sara saw the kindness in him she had heard about from Rose.

The next few weeks went by fast. The baby girls were doing great. Eventually, Rose felt she could handle them by herself, with help from Cody and Mrs. Parker next door.

Soon it was time for Sara and Ella to leave. They climbed aboard the Model T, which was loaded with all their luggage and other paraphernalia. They hugged Rose and Cody and picked up the babies to cuddle them one last time. Those little girls would probably be five years old before Sara and Ella would get another chance to travel west. Ella had to finish school, and Sara had more work to do with the suffragettes. She would not give up until the task was accomplished.

They waved back as they headed out the driveway and onto the road home.

"Want to learn how to drive?" Sara asked Ella with a smile.

"What? Seriously?" Ella asked.

"Why not? This is how I learned," Sara said, pulling to the side of the road. "Get out and I'll tell you how it works."

Sara showed Ella all she knew about driving. Ella turned the crank and promptly ended on her behind. They laughed, climbed aboard, and Sara wondered what Tillie would be thinking now if she knew. Then, Ella zigzagged down the road. They were hooting and laughing as she pulled off the side of the road and barely missed a tree.

They chugged down the road to home. Together! It felt good. It felt right. It was as though mother and daughter had never been apart.

Chapter Fifty-one

It was the beginning of September when Sara and Ella arrived in Milwaukee in Tillie's Model T. There was a briskness in the air that always occurred this time of year in Wisconsin. The trees had not yet turned colors but there was a definite feel of autumn in the air.

They arrived at the Dewberry house on a weekday morning. Sara looked at the old house with great nostalgia and a feeling of loss. It stood strong and proud among the tall oak trees. The mums Sara had planted long ago at the side of the front porch were in full bloom, gold and burgundy. The house was painted teal with burgundy shutters and burgundy gingerbread trim. The porch was gray. It was a welcoming house, but not for Sara any longer.

"Mother, would you like to come in?" Ella asked. "I am sure Father is at work."

"No, dear. Not today," Sara replied sadly. "I really need to check on Tillie. Can you meet me for coffee tomorrow at the Knickerbocker?"

"Absolutely! What time?" Ella asked eagerly.

"How about ten o'clock? Your father should be at work by then. I am sure he'll want to spend a little time with you in the morning before he goes to the bank."

"Ten it is." Ella began to drag her trunk up the walkway to the porch.

"Let me help you," Sara called out as she jumped from the automobile.

Together they carried it by the handles on either side, then stood silently for a moment at the top of the steps. Sara grabbed Ella and gave her a big hug. "I'm never going to let you out of my sight for very long again."

Ella smiled at her.

Sara got back in the vehicle, and within a few minutes, was at Tillie's doorstep. A maid answered the door. Someone Sara didn't know. "I am

Sara Dewberry," she announced. "Mrs. Morgenson is expecting me."

"Oh yes, Mrs. Dewberry. Mrs. Morgenson is taking a nap right now, but she left word to show you to your room when you arrived. I am sure you know where it is. May I help you with your bags?"

"Thank you," said Sara. "Is Tillie, um, Mrs. Morgenson all right? I mean, how is her health?" Sara stammered. She took off her cloak and the maid placed it on the hall coat rack.

"Mrs. Morgenson has good days and bad. Today she is very tired, but otherwise in good spirits. She didn't eat breakfast, but took an early lunch before she retired," the maid informed her.

They ascended the staircase. "I am a bit tired myself." Sara yawned. "Perhaps I will lie down for a short nap. If I am asleep when Tillie—Mrs. Morgenson—awakes, please wake me."

"Certainly, Mum." The maid closed the door, leaving Sara alone.

She lay on the bed, contemplating where life would take her next. It was impossible to imagine Tillie not there beside her.

It seemed certain that she would be caring for Tillie for some time. What did the doctor in Oklahoma say? She will probably only live a few more months. Sara shuddered again at the thought.

Tillie awoke about three in the afternoon. Upon learning Sara had arrived, Tillie asked for her to come to her room.

Sara got up from the bed, straightened her dress, primped her hair, adjusted one of the hair pins, and headed immediately to Tillie's room.

"Margarette," Tillie addressed the maid, "would you please bring Mrs. Dewberry and I a pot of tea and some biscuits?"

"Certainly, Mum." Margarette disappeared and returned shortly with a steamy pot of tea on a silver tray and a dish of fresh baked cookies. She poured the tea. "Will there be anything else?" she inquired.

"No, Margarette. Thank you," Tillie answered.

Sara gave her old friend a peck on the cheek and squeezed her frail hand. "You are looking much better than you did in Oklahoma."

"Oh, I am a tough old bird. I will be fine for a long time." Tillie quickly changed the subject. "Tell me, Sara, how was your trip home? Did our old Bessie hold up?"

"Oh, Tillie, we had a wonderful time. We had a nasty rainstorm in Iowa and took shelter at a rather expensive hotel there. It was one of the Astor hotels, and they charged ten dollars for the night, but it was worth every penny. I don't know when I last experienced such luxury. It was good to soak in their huge clawfoot tub. They had a flush toilet and wonderful rose-scented soap. I felt like a queen. Ella was quite impressed."

"I am afraid when I left Oklahoma, I wasn't thinking clearly. Did you have enough money to buy your food and lodging for the trip home? I do hope you didn't have to sleep in old Bessie."

"Oh no, you have paid me well and I have spent almost nothing in the past years we have been together. I have a nice sum left."

"Good. I would hate to think you had to find refuge with bedbugs again." Even in her condition, Tillie kept her chin up and enjoyed a bit of humor.

Sara laughed, which made Tillie smile. "We were quite comfortable, thank you. No bedbugs. Sore bottoms from the journey, but other than that we traveled well, with only minor repairs. Tillie, I can't tell you how wonderful it was to spend the past six weeks with Ella. On the ride home, we talked incessantly. I think we have caught up on almost everything that has happened these past years. It is as though we had never parted."

Sara reached for her third cookie. She didn't realize how hungry she was. She hadn't eaten since the previous evening. They had planned on stopping for breakfast, but she and Ella had grown so engrossed in conversation, they had forgotten about it.

That evening, the maid served a meal of stew and biscuits. Sara filled her tummy but still found room for the fresh apple pie Margarette had baked that afternoon.

Sara went to bed that evening feeling very satisfied both in body and soul. That night she prayed.

"Dear God, you have blessed me. My life may have been hard, but it has been purposeful and fulfilled. I lost my children, but you are reuniting me with them. I have lost my home, but you have given me the world, the home you created for me. You have showed me the beauty of birth, the strength that is born out of perseverance, and the undying love of being a mother with her child. I have been penniless, but you have provided security. You have allowed me to experience life as so few have, and I pray that you will be with me on my journey forward. My children have always lived in my heart; please help me to bring them safely back into my arms. Be with Tillie in her final hours, keep her free from pain, and allow her a peaceful passing. Amen."

Henry crossed her mind just before she closed her eyes. Sara added an addendum to her prayer. "Thank you for allowing Henry to see more clearly the plight of women. Thank you for letting him be there to raise our children. I loved the man you brought into my life nearly twenty years ago. If it be your will, let me see that man again. Amen."

Sara fell into a deep sleep, at peace with the world, dreaming about what tomorrow would bring.

Chapter Fifty-two

Sara arrived at the Knickerbocker at nine-thirty the following morning. Ella was due at ten. Sara picked up a newspaper while she waited. It was September 1, 1916. Headlines centered on the Great War in Europe, which had been escalating since 1914. President Wilson was trying to keep the United States out of the conflicts, but it was becoming increasingly more difficult.

The newspaper announced Bethlehem Steel, one of the world's largest arms merchants, was the recipient of a contract from the British government for millions of artillery shells and ten fifty-ton submarines. This was an illegal transaction, but the Wilson administration turned its back, letting America profit from the war.

This is a war of money, there seems to be no interest in human rights or even law.

The German sinking of the British ocean liner Lusitania in May of 1915 brought some outcry in America for its lost American passengers, but overall Americans were still reluctant to go to war. Wilson reacted with restraint, but eventually was forced to retaliate against German intrusion.

Still, few Americans were willing to declare all-out war. The American passengers who had boarded the Lusitania in New York were warned by the Germans via full page ads in the New York Times that heading into the war zone would place them at risk. However, no one warned them that they were essentially in a floating munitions dump.

First Lord of the Admiralty Winston Churchill in fact drew Americans into the conflict to preserve British victory. He wrote, "The more neutral 'traffic' the better. If some of it gets into trouble, better still."

Sara had lost herself in the news, so Ella startled her when she slipped into the chair across from her. "What is the special today? I'm starved," Ella asked.

Sara put the newspaper down and grinned. "And a wonderful good morning to you, too."

"Good morning, Mother. I hope you slept well."

"I slept very well, thank you. It was so nice to be in a decent bed. It has been years since I have been home, and although Tillie's house is not 'home,' I felt very comfortable there last night."

"And how is Tillie?" Ella barely took a breath before asking, "Mother, I know you could come home. Won't you please talk to Father?"

Sara stiffened, and chose the topic she wanted to address. "Tillie slept well, though she continues to deteriorate. I am afraid she hasn't long in this world. Her heart is getting weaker. She barely has the strength to eat.

For now, Ella let her ignore the second question. "Tillie is such a dear. Does she have children?"

"Yes, she has a son—James—in Washington, D.C. We always stopped by to see him when we were in the area. He has a job with the United States Department of Interior," Sara said proudly.

"What does the Department of Interior do?"

"It protects our nation's natural and cultural heritage. They honor our trust responsibilities to tribes and our commitment to our communities. They manage public lands, minerals, national parks, and our national wildlife refuges. James is a geologist and an expert on such things," Sara explained.

Ella looked at her mother in awe. "Mother, you have changed. I know I am older now and you speak to me as you would to an adult, but you are so intelligent. You are so brave. The mother I recall was content to darn socks, knit mufflers, and plan meals. You had an interest in education and in the plight of women, but your world was limited. I am so proud of you. I hope that one day I will be as charming and intelligent as you are."

Sara's heart swelled at the praise, and she took Ella's hands. "I know one day you will experience life in a whole new way, as will all women. Men are fools. They don't recognize what they have. Instead of embracing and valuing their women and cherishing wives as partners, they choose to keep women down and won't listen when they speak. They are losing out on a good thing. One day, they will recognize this. I hope it will be sooner rather than later, for your and your sister's sakes."

"I don't believe all men are fools. I have run into one or two who have some sense." Ella giggled.

"Of course, my dear. I was referring to the populace of men who want to have women under their thumb. Those who don't appreciate the value of women. We hope to change that."

"Well, Father has changed," Ella said, returning to her original subject. "I really wish you would talk to him."

Sara frowned. "I suppose I will, but not just yet. I want to see Liz. I was going to ask you to bring her with you today, but I thought it best that you prepare her a bit. After all, she was only seven when I left. She probably doesn't remember me, though I have never forgotten her."

"Can we meet at the library tomorrow?" Ella asked. "I have an appointment at Downer College tomorrow morning. I can bring Liz to the library at two."

"Of course! That is a wonderful idea. I can't wait."

Sara and Ella continued their conversation through breakfast and the rest of the morning as they strolled through the city. So many of the places now seemed so familiar yet so remote from Sara's life.

They ended their walk at Catherine's house, where they parted. Sara hugged Ella and went up the steps to Catherine's front door. Then, turned and watched Ella disappear around the corner before she knocked.

Catherine let out a hoot. "Sara, Sara, Sara," Catherine repeated as she grabbed her old friend and swung her around. "When did you arrive? I thought you would never return. Come in, come in."

They went inside, and Sara sat on the rocker by the window while Catherine poured a glass of ice-cold lemonade.

"Things are so familiar and so different," Sara commented, looking around the room. "I feel like a stranger, yet I recognize things. But they seem so far in the past."

"You have been gone a long time. I received your letters, and my, how I have wanted to talk to you. You have been so many places and learned so many things. I am envious. Start at the beginning and tell me everything you have done for the last five years and don't leave out a single detail," Catherine coaxed. She could barely contain her excitement.

"Well, that is a bit much for one sitting, but let me start now and work backwards. I want to know about you as well," Sara began. "The last thing I learned was how to birth a baby. Two, in fact!"

"What?" Catherine almost choked on her lemonade. "This ought to be good!"

"It is wonderful." Sara told of her meeting with Ella and stories of Rose's twins.

Catherine listened in amazement.

They talked well into the evening, stopping only for a bite to eat and nature's call.

Finally, Sara said, "Oh Catherine, we could go on all night, but I must get back to check on Tillie. Her maid Margarette is with her, but Tillie is not doing well. I really need to see her before she retires for the evening."

"I'd heard Tillie was not doing well." Catherine gave Sara a hug good-bye, and Sara walked to Tillie's house, arriving at dusk.

Tillie was hanging on, but her breathing was laborious. She was propped up with several pillows and was awaiting Sara's return.

"So, my dear, did you have a good day?" Tillie inquired.

"Fabulous, simply fabulous!" Sara tried to keep in good spirits for her friend's sake.

She shared all about her activities of the day. Sara tried to cheer Tillie with some of the funny anecdotes Catherine had told her that afternoon.

"Catherine shared with me her attempts at meeting suitors," Sara began with a giggle. "It seems her friends, the Millers, have been very concerned about her being an old maid and have attempted to marry her off at any cost. She said they introduced her to a 'nice gentleman,' who it turns out is a hog farmer. Catherine said he grunted like a hog, too. Then, there was another very tall and skinny gentleman who had a nervous twitch, who continuously cleared his throat much too loud. Catherine said, 'he made one long attempt at clearing his throat that sounded like he was about to start a car engine.' When she asked, 'Having trouble starting your engine?' he nearly choked and, in the process, noisily passed gas.

"Catherine then said, 'Whoops, your engine backfired.' He was so embarrassed, he grabbed his bowler and headed for the door as quickly as he could, mumbling something about a previous engagement." Sara laughed heartily, recalling the conversation.

Tillie attempted a laugh, but didn't seem to have the strength, making Sara's smile start to slip.

Sara propped up Tillie's pillow and continued to entertain her. After about fifteen minutes, Tillie drifted off to a sound sleep.

Sara covered her and opened her window to let in some of the fresh evening breeze. She turned off the lamp and quietly slipped out of the room and retired herself.

***

The next morning, Tillie asked Sara to summon her son. "I know I haven't long to live, and I do so want to say good-bye to James."

Sara sent a telegram that morning. When she left the house, she asked Margarette to send for her at the library if there was any problem.

Sara went to the library early. She was there by mid-morning, whereas anticipated, she was welcomed with open arms by Edith.

Once again, she had to recount her adventures, and got updated on the activities of the local suffragette movement.

"The war is causing great difficulties for us," Edith lamented. "Many are afraid of the consequences of being too vocal and others are joining the war effort. Women are rallying the workforce since there is a shortage of men to get out the orders for military supplies." They discussed the war at length.

Edith was upset with Wilson, who stood his ground, and she felt he would eventually give into the imperialist opposition. Edith observed, "Some consider it a disgrace for America to not throw its weight into the fracas of the Great War, and I fear Wilson is listening to them."

Edith went on, "I will vote for Wilson in the coming election, though, because I feel of the two candidates, Wilson will be less of a risk than Hughes."

"Ah, the vote for the lesser of two evils?" Sara pinched her lips and shook her head pensively. Someday things needed to change.

Edith talked about Sara's children and how mature and polite they were. "They were so excited on the days that your letters arrived."

Just as with Catherine, the time passed swiftly, and it soon neared two o'clock.

Sara felt both anxious and nervous. Anxious with the anticipation of meeting Liz, but nervous that her youngest child may have lost the connection she hoped to reestablish.

She sat at the same library table where she had long ago waited for Ella to appear. Sara straightened her skirt with her hands, then primped her auburn hair, which was in a bun at the top of her head but now showed streaks of gray.

The door opened, and a beautiful twelve-year-old girl walked through it with Ella close behind, her hand on Liz's shoulder. She had long, shiny dark brown hair, those same mischievous green eyes, and a smile that lit up the room.

Liz gazed in Sara's direction.

Sara stood, and this amazing young lady ran across the room and into Sara's arms.

"Mother, Mother, I missed you so. Please don't go away again." Tears streamed down Liz's cheeks.

Sara rocked Liz in her arms, her cheek resting on her daughter's head, relief coursing through her.

After some time, Sara pushed her away. "Let me look at you, young lady. You are beautiful." Sara remembered this was the age Ella was when she had first left. Oh, how she regretted the time she had lost in both girls' lives.

They went out onto the library lawn and sat on a bench, spending the rest of the afternoon together.

"Mother, can you come back home? Please?" Liz pleaded.

Sara shivered with guilt. "No, dear, I am sorry, I can't. But I won't be far away, and I will see you every day."

"Promise?" Liz asked with an imploring look in her eyes.

"Promise!" Sara confirmed.

After a long conversation, the girls got up to go home. "We need to talk about Father," Ella commanded.

Sara nodded, unable to avoid it any longer. "Soon."

Ella gave her mother a hug and Liz did the same. They waved good-bye and started for home.

Sara looked up. "Thank you, God. I have waited so long for this reunion." She gathered her things and went home to Tillie.

***

James received the telegram and left for Milwaukee immediately. He sent them a message stating he would be there in two days.

Tillie seemed to pick up a bit of energy in anticipation of his arrival.

On the day he arrived, James stayed by Tillie's bedside the entire day. That evening, Sara came in to say goodnight.

Tillie said, "Sara, stay awhile."

Sara sat at the end of Tillie's bed.

"It is good that an old lady like me has people to love and who love her back. Sara, I have so enjoyed our time together. Keep up the fight."

"I will, Tillie. I've learned so much from you," Sara said, tears in her eyes.

"Now, I just want to fall asleep seeing the two of you here at my side." Tillie closed her eyes and never opened them again. The great lioness who had fought the fight so hard and for so long was gone.

Sara cried herself to sleep that night.

Chapter Fifty-three

James went to see Tillie's lawyer the next day, and then began the arrangements for his mother's funeral service. Sara had not given much thought to what she would do after Tillie's passing. With a heavy heart, she knew she'd need to find a new place to live. Perhaps James would allow her to stay at Tillie's home until the estate was settled and the house was sold. After that, she would have to find work.

Thankfully, with the war underway, work should not be a problem. Many women were filling jobs vacated by men who were serving in the military. There was so much to consider.

James came home later that day and discussed funeral arrangements with Sara over dinner. Neither was very hungry. Tillie would be laid out in the parlor for visitation.

James asked that Sara be there to greet guests. He said the Last Will and Testament would be read the next day, and the lawyer had requested her presence there also. Sara was puzzled by that but agreed to be there at the designated time.

Sara spent a few days with James, reminiscing about Tillie's unending energy and devotion to the cause. James was very proud of his mother and her accomplishments. He had a great deal of love and admiration for his mother, and it made Sara's grief easier to bear.

Catherine was one of the first to stop by to give her respects and condolences. Sara introduced her to James, and they spoke for a long time. When Catherine made her way to the door to leave, James took her hands in his and thanked her for coming by.

Sara couldn't help but wonder if he was this gracious to all guests he had never met before.

Many suffragettes stopped by to give their respects, and Sara saw many faces she hadn't seen in years. Edith was one of the last ones to visit.

The next day, James and Sara took the Model T to the attorney's office. It was a cold, rainy day and the canopy provided at least some degree of comfort. The attorney asked them to take a seat, and he proceeded to open the Last Will and Testament of Otillia Martha Morgenson. Funny, Sara hadn't known Tillie's full name was Otillia. It made her smile.

James explained, "Mother never used that name. She hated it."

"It is a lovely name. Otillia." It rolled off Sara's tongue with royal fervor.

The attorney read the usual details regarding the paying of the debts and funeral arrangements. Tillie had requested that two thousand dollars be left to the local orphanage and two thousand dollars to the poor house.

He then read, "To my dear friend, Sara Dewberry, I leave the sum of ten thousand dollars and request that she take the Model T and trade it in for a new vehicle of her choice, one that will keep her warm and dry in her travels. I also direct that Mrs. Dewberry be allowed to live in my home in Milwaukee without rent for as long as she so chooses. I direct that my son James pay all the taxes and utilities for that property during her stay. I further direct James to provide Sara Dewberry with a weekly stipend of one hundred dollars so that she can continue the work we started. At such time that she decides to leave the property on State Street, it will be sold, and ten percent of the proceeds should be given to Mrs. Dewberry. Further, any items such as artwork and furnishings that are in the house may be taken by Mrs. Dewberry after James has made his selections and before the remainder is sold on public auction."

The attorney continued to read the Will, and went on to direct the balance of Tillie's assets to be given to her only son and heir, James Grover Morgenson.

Sara was speechless, and tears streamed down her face. Even in death, Tillie had chosen to take care of her.

James was more than happy with the arrangements. He was pleased that his mother had such a true and loyal friend to accompany her on her travels. He had worried less about her safety and well-being with Sara by her side.

Over the next three days, they welcomed a stream of guests into the house. Many of them, Sara knew. A few were friends and associates of Senator Morgenson, and James knew most of them. A few more came and introduced themselves as old friends and associates. All were welcomed.

One guest who returned several times over those days received special treatment and attention. Catherine and James seemed to be enthralled with each other.

James had decided to stay in town for a month. Sara grinned. Perhaps Catherine would not stay an old maid after all.

***

After the funeral, things were quiet in the house on State Street. Sara tried to keep busy to distract herself from her grief, and often found herself at the library catching up on the latest news and talking with her friend Edith, who was a storehouse of information regarding the progress suffragettes were making at home and abroad.

Edith lamented over the inconsistencies of the president—the president they had voted for and counted on for support.

"President Wilson campaigned on the slogan, 'He kept us out of war'. However, less than ninety days into his second term, he called on Congress for a declaration of war against Germany to 'make the world safe for democracy,'" Edith complained. "Very few citizens support the war, and few have volunteered for service in the army."

Sara agreed. "The problems are escalating all over the world. Free market is temporarily shelved. Governments are involved in price, wage, and rent controls. They're rationing food supplies and materials, regulation of imports and exports, and nationalization of transportation systems and industries. Some governments have taken control of compulsory employment and mobilized all resources for the war effort." Sara shook her head. "It is a sad state of affairs everywhere around the world."

"I am most concerned about what is happening with our own president, who has become a tyrant to other nations despite campaigning as a peaceful soul, to the point that he is leading imperialistic invasions and expanded government control over the people in several critical areas during his term," Edith observed. "The women's issues have been put on the back burner. In fact, things are getting much worse." She pursed

263

her lips and shook her head in disappointment.

"There have been atrocities," Edith continued with a frown. "Did you know that Historian Walter Karp told of a woman who wrote to a newspaper during the war, stating, 'I am for the people and the government is for the profiteers.' Can you believe she received a ten-year prison sentence for speaking out? Where is our right to free speech? It's happened to others, too." Edith's face went red as she fumed.

Sara, having seen the unfairness in race and ethnic discrimination, was appalled, but not surprised. "German Americans and Irish Americans, especially Irish Catholics, receive harsh treatment by many government agencies. They are suspect because both Germany and Ireland are at odds with England. Elected government officials are under pressure if they dissent against Wilson's politics. Even our Wisconsin Congressman Robert D. Lafollette credited Wilson's expansion of military expenditures to the influence of 'the glorious group of millionaires who are making such enormous profits out of the European war.' I heard that a congressional committee investigated LaFollette, and for months, he was in jeopardy of prison although, thank the Lord, after the investigation, no charges were ever filed. At least there are bits of sanity," Sara observed.

"It is a shame," Edith said, "but there is probably more freedom of speech in the German Reichstag than there is in the 'land of the free'. Because of official repression, many independent-minded Americans have disappeared into political solitude and kept their bitterness and contempt to themselves. I see much of this fear occurring among suffragettes who have families and are growing weary of the struggles. Our numbers are dwindling."

During this tumultuous time, Sara stayed close to home and became a key player in her daughter's lives. She attended their school functions and spent days with them cooking, shopping, doing homework, or just lulling about in girl talk. Both girls supported the suffragette movement and were proud of the work their mother pursued. But could she continue in today's political climate? Would the whole cause fail?

***

Sara was so proud of her children. Ella was engrossed in her studies at Downer College and aspired to become an elementary teacher. Liz wasn't sure where her calling was yet but knew it would be something in the medical field. The world wasn't ready for Doctor Elizabeth Dewberry quite yet, but she could be a nurse and that was just fine with her.

Thaddeus had entered West Point and was looking forward to a career in the military. This worried Sara because of the wars going on across the world. Especially since the United States was now involved in it and lives were lost every day.

Sara spent most of her time in Milwaukee, but did travel to Washington, D.C. in the spring and fall of that year. She loved the cherry blossoms in the spring in Washington. She had gotten to know many of the people in Congress and had enough support that she didn't feel her life endangered by the government. However, she quickly learned her limits.

She also had an added reason for traveling to Washington these days: Catherine, in the spring of 1918, had become Catherine Morgenson, the wife of James Morgenson, now a government official in the Department of the Interior.

Tillie would have been so proud of her son and thrilled to have Catherine as her daughter-in-law.

Sara had promised Tillie she would see the movement through to the end and she vowed she would do just that. But now, she embraced the cause as her own fight. No matter what she had to sacrifice for the girls that were once again her life, she would see this fight through.

Chapter Fifty-four

Another proposal to pass the Nineteenth Amendment was brought before the House on January 16, 1918, and with the support of President Woodrow Wilson, had passed with a two-thirds majority vote. Hopes ran high, but the bill had been defeated in the senate by only two votes. There had been an outcry among the suffragettes. It had been so close and disappointing and yet, in some ways, energizing. This was the closest they had come to passage in the past forty-one years since the movement had taken shape.

Sara visited her friend Catherine again in the fall of 1918. Word was that treaty negotiations were taking place, and the war would finally end. Catherine was always curious about Sara's view of the world as a Washington outsider.

They were sitting in the parlor, drinking tea, when Catherine asked, "What do you know about the war, Sara?"

"I hear there is widespread starvation…especially in Germany and Russia. It seems to me that the war is winding down, thank the Lord," Sara replied.

"Word is that it is over," Catherine stated knowingly.

"Over?" Sara didn't understand and frowned. Where was the hoopla, the dancing in the streets, the men coming home?"

"Until the treaty is drafted and signed, the blockades will continue until it becomes official. It could take as long as a year. In the meantime, the suffering will continue. Herbert Hoover from the Department of U.S. Food Administration is quite the humanitarian, and he has vowed, with much resistance from allies, to provide aid to the hungry worldwide." Catherine scratched her head. "Don't exactly know how he can manage that volume of aid, but I have worked with poor people, and my heart goes out to them."

"I know what you mean," said Sara. "I read that eight hundred adults die of starvation every day in Germany, and the death toll is in the hundreds of thousands. One journalist found a hospital full of starving, feverish babies with hands like slender wands."

Catherine looked pained. "Germany has been barbaric to the world, and even to their own people, but it is not the fault of those who are suffering most. What could those children have done to endure such atrocities? Britain, France, and Italy claim that the motives of the United States are selfish, but if we believe in God and what He teaches, how can we turn our back on such suffering?"

"The wounds are too deep. One day, they will understand. Politics and religion often collide. Maybe if we took the Christian approach to politics, we could end wars and suffering. I doubt such a calamity will ever happen again. This Great War is the war to end all wars. I believe that." Sara wondered if things would be different if women were in charge.

"The war took its toll on the President as well," Catherine observed. "Wilson campaigned hard to generate support for the formation of the League of Nations. He was exhausted. His speeches became confused and hecklers pushed him to the brink. He suffered a critical cerebral thrombosis, you know."

"Yes, I heard about that," Sara recalled. "There is gossip that his wife Edith orchestrated a scheme to keep the president's medical condition from the American people. There is a rumor he is not the man he once was, that he has little knowledge of the issues and events outside of his protected world. If that were the case, who would be in charge?"

Catherine responded, smiling, "Mrs. Wilson is a clever woman and very intelligent."

"Do you really think she is in charge?" Sara inquired with awe.

"It is all rumors, but what I know of Mrs. Wilson, she is quite capable of pulling off something like this. I guess for now, we watch and see. In any event, if she is, she will do a good job," Catherine surmised. "I wish she would be on board for the suffragette cause, but in truth she has been resistant."

After some more talk, Catherine changed the subject. "On to more concrete information: how are things faring in Wisconsin?"

"It is a tumultuous time. Nothing is certain but uncertainty itself,"

Sara said with a sigh. "Wisconsin has felt its own turmoil. The women's suffrage movement had its ups and downs. After Governor LaFollette left to hold office in the U.S. Senate, there has been a succession of governors. None of them have given us the support that LaFollette did. The latest is Governor Philipps, who is very conservative and tied to the old traditions. He's bad news for the suffragettes."

"I remember. He took office in 1915. He was more concerned with business and farming than coming to women's aid," Catherine recalled. "Does the movement have a strong leader there?"

Sara smiled. "Yes, indeed! While Tillie and I had been crossing the country, a new advocate came to the forefront in Wisconsin.Theodora Youmans is her name. She was a journalist and editor. Edith filled me in on her background. Theodora worked her way up from a freelance writer with the Waukesha Freeman, where she started out primarily on women's issues. Reader response convinced the paper to give her a byline, the only byline in that paper. She married the Freeman's editor and publisher, Henry Mott Youmans, and became the associate editor the following year."

"Way to work your way to the top!" Catherine grinned.

"True, but Theodora is a real go-getter. She has been a great asset to the movement. She is very connected, and her name is recognized in all aspects of community foundations and events." Sara praised her work.

"Sara, I'm impressed. You have done your homework. Theodora seems like a qualified leader. Funny, I don't know more about her."

"I can tell you a bit more," offered Sara. "She's an interesting lady. Theodora became the president of the Wisconsin Suffragettes in 1913, the year that I began my tour with Tillie. She went to New York in 1915 to work with their national leader, and former Wisconsinite, Carrie Chapman Catt. Catt felt that gaining support on the local level would eventually force the federal government to act. We were part of that plan but traveled in different circles. Our travels were designed to raise support in the grassroots level of all states. Theodora was more intent on reaching the media."

"I see," said Catherine. "We hear about Elizabeth Catt a lot, so I suspect Theodora didn't get that degree of publicity nationally. The name is somewhat familiar, but I guess I just didn't focus on it."

"Well, do so now, because Theodora is making herself very well known, and I had the opportunity to compare notes with her in 1917." Sara smiled. "I will forgive you for not knowing in the past year because I know where your focus was. Catherine is in love," Sara teased.

"Oh, pshaw." Catherine blushed. She immediately changed the subject. "What is going on now for the cause in Wisconsin?"

"You aren't off the hook that easy." Sara recognized the conversation switch. "Tell me about you and James. How has your life changed, and are you still honeymooning?"

Catherine conceded with a sigh and couldn't help but grin. "Sara, I am so glad I waited til later in life to marry. James is wonderful. He is kind and generous and intelligent. He is my knight in shining armor. And this city is amazing! I was totally awestruck when I arrived, and I am still in awe whenever I look out and see the Washington Monument and the majesty of the city. They are building the Lincoln Memorial now. You must see it. It won't be completed for about five more years, but even now, it is amazing."

Catherine was a private person. Dragging details of her personal life to the forefront was a daunting task, but Sara could tell that she was happier now than she had ever been. It warmed Sara's heart to see her friend so content.

***

Visiting Catherine was great, but Sara didn't rest long. There was still so much work to be done. Opponents to convince.

Sara went to speak to a congressional delegation from Wisconsin that was supportive of the cause. Through them, she was able to gain an audience with some of the major opponents across the country.

Her message to the politicians was clear. She addressed the delegation. "Women have worked side by side with men in this Great War and were instrumental in keeping up with the supply demands while men fought the battles. Nurses healed and comforted the wounded.

"Consider life in general, women have raised their sons and taught them. Think of your own mother and the sacrifices and gifts she has given you to make you the men you are.

"Women are intelligent. Women understand the issues. Women have a right to a voice, and property, and the vote. Is there any amongst you who know of any reason why this right should not be granted?"

A voice from the group feebly protested, "Women are meant to bear children, and they are too emotional to handle the business of life *and* government."

Sara did not back down, lifting her hands in determination. "The men in government show a great deal of emotion as well. Emotion on issues that they oppose and passion for those they support. All we need is a chance, and our record will show our abilities. All we need is our unalienable right to life, liberty, and the pursuit of happiness. All we need is, like all men, to be created equal. Please consider a nineteenth amendment to our great Constitution to grant that right."

Afterwards, the men spoke in hushed whispers, but none approached Sara as she gathered her notes. Had she made progress? She didn't know. She only knew she had scattered the seeds and hoped that some would take root.

Sara returned home to Milwaukee and continued a letter-writing campaign to every senator and representative in the United States government, as well as every state official and governor. Sara was a busy woman, but she wouldn't have it any other way.

Chapter Fifty-five

Sara met with her children regularly but had no contact with Henry, although both girls encouraged a meeting. She met with Liz at the library on Tuesdays and Thursdays after school. She wrote to Thaddeus on a regular basis and looked forward to seeing him during the Christmas break.

Ella's visits were sporadic, but they managed to get together whenever they could. Most weekdays she was deep in her studies and it seemed that a young man at the Wisconsin State Normal School in Milwaukee had piqued her interest. John Ellington was pursuing his undergraduate studies there, but his plan was to transfer at the end of the year to Madison to enroll in their medical program. One day, he would be Doctor John Ellington.

Ella tried the name out often. "Mrs. John Ellington. Ella Ellington… Ella Ellington."

Ella would often talk to Sara about John. "Oh Mother, I love him so. His name fits me, don't you think? Mrs. Ella Ellington."

Sara liked the ring to it.

"John is just beginning his studies, so it will be quite some time before we can entertain thoughts of marriage, but he is intrigued with the idea. He mentions our future together often. Mother, I am so happy. We don't have much time together, but we spend weekends together whenever we can. I can't wait for you to meet him."

"And I can't wait to meet the love of your life, Ella," Sara said, patting Ella's hand.

***

It was a blustery Tuesday in November 1918 when Sara hurried from her automobile to the library, gathering her scarf tight about her neck and trudging through the early snow.

This is going to be a long, cold winter.

She rushed up the steps to the library entrance. Once inside, she stomped her feet on the mat and shook out her coat, hanging it on the rack in the corner. She took out a book and proceeded toward the table where she normally sat to wait for her children.

Someone was already there: a gentleman with gray hair and a handlebar moustache. He seemed deeply engrossed in a newspaper laid out on the table.

She slipped into a chair at the opposite end of the table.

The gentleman raised his head and the unmistakable blue-gray eyes of the gentleman met hers.

"Henry!" Sara exclaimed, her heart catching in her chest.

"Sara," Henry said softly, "it is so good to see you." His smile was warm and apologetic.

Too shocked to say anything, Sara looked about and stood to leave.

Henry half-rose and grabbed her hand. "Sara, please," he implored. "Please sit here a moment with me."

Sara reluctantly sat back down, though her heart had not stopped thudding.

"I know you have been seeing the girls. They are quite beautiful, aren't they?"

"Yes, they are." Sara kept her voice emotionless. "You have done a fine job of raising them. They are quite gifted and well-mannered."

"They remind me very much of their mother."

Sara looked away, embarrassed. She couldn't speak. She felt a tightness in her throat and tears welling in her eyes. She blinked and kept her eyes away from his.

Henry reached over to touch her hand.

She quickly pulled it away as if lightning had struck it. She placed her hands in her lap.

"I am so sorry, Sara. Can you ever forgive me?" Henry beseeched her.

Sara sat silently.

Henry shook his head in regret. "I have been such a fool. There is no reason you should forgive me. I looked at you as only a wife and a mother but failed to see you as an intelligent and practical woman. I failed to recognize your needs and your aspirations. As a wife and mother, I loved you dearly. As an activist...well quite frankly, you frightened me. I feared losing the wife I knew. I couldn't see that you could be both. It took my attorney and my pastor to make me see the light. But by then, it was too late. You were already gone."

Sara glared at him, finding her voice. "Henry, you *are* a fool. Don't you understand that a whole woman is much more of an asset to you than a bearer of your children? Don't you understand that women are bright and capable of much more?"

The warmth never left Henry's eyes, despite Sara's anger. "I do now. I've changed. I wish we could start over. I want us to be a family again. I would support you in every way. I would love you even more than I could ever have loved you before. I have never stopped loving you."

"I have changed also. I am not the meek, timid woman who left here five years ago. I've learned and experienced so much. I have seen life at its best and I have seen life at its ugliest. It is impossible for us to forget those years and go on." Sara clenched her hands in her lap to keep her voice steady.

Henry frowned. "I suppose you are right. We are both different people. But we are people who have shared our lives in the past, and in time, we could learn to love again. Sara, would you at least allow us to be friends? Will you come for Thanksgiving dinner? Please?" Henry gave her the puppy dog look that had melted her heart in days gone by.

Sara sighed. His warmth had finally got to her. "Let me think about it."

"The girls would love for you to be there. Ella will be bringing her young man for dinner, so we can meet him. Both girls have gotten to be very good cooks. Liz is the baker, but Ella is quite the gourmet cook. I'm afraid I have never mastered the kitchen, but they do allow me to set the table." Henry continued to plead his case.

"I'll *think* about it," Sara reiterated as she stood to leave.

"Promise?" Henry stood and retrieved her cloak for her.

"Promise," she said as she took it and skipped down the steps of the library.

"May I give you a ride home?" Henry was right at her heels.

"No thank you. My vehicle is right down the street."

Henry followed. "Nice chariot." He whistled as his eyes spanned the length of the automobile. He closed the car door for her and said, "Til

Thanksgiving."

Sara sat in the car and finally let herself fully react. Why was her heart pattering like the first time she had met him? He had been horrible to her.

Has he really changed, or is this just another ploy to get me back into my role as housekeeper?

A myriad of questions rolled about her brain. She thought of almost nothing else for the rest of the evening.

During the next week, Sara found her thoughts drifting to Henry throughout the day, and at night, he crept into her dreams. In one dream, she was being served up as the turkey on the platter, but in most of her dreams, she and Henry found comfort and solace in each other's arms.

In one particularly sensual dream, she awoke with her arms about her pillow and her face buried deep into it, almost cutting off her ability to breathe. Her body longed for him. Her lips ached to be kissed by him. She yearned to feel his body entwined in hers and the culmination of her desire satisfied within her. But she was left wanting.

The Thursday before Thanksgiving, she met both Ella and Liz at the library. Ella had come to do some research, and Liz tagged along. Henry had told them of his conversation with Sara.

"What is your answer, Mother?" Liz asked. They were both anxious to hear her reply.

"Yes," Sara responded, "I will be there."

***

Sara was up early on Thanksgiving Day. She had been instructed to arrive by two in the afternoon, so they would have plenty of time to chat while they prepared dinner. Liz had baked fresh apple and pumpkin pies the day before and whipped up some fresh cream that morning. Ella had their enormous turkey stuffed and in the oven long before Sara arrived. She had made fresh cranberry orange sauce earlier, and was now busy peeling potatoes when Sara joined her in the kitchen.

It felt strange being in her own kitchen, but it felt good, too, and, in some ways, it felt as if time had melted away.

"Let me help you with that," Sara offered as she sat on a stool by the kitchen counter.

Instead, Ella gave her a bowl of snap beans to prepare.

Sara picked up the paring knife and worked beside Ella. "Since we are going to meet, tell me again about your young man," Sara said.

Brightening instantly, Ella went on about his charms, his good looks, his intelligence, and his aspirations. Sara barely had to say a word. Ella was obviously mesmerized by John Ellington and very much in love.

"When will he arrive?" Sara asked.

Ella looked up at the clock on the wall. "In about an hour." She grabbed a towel and dried her hands. "Oh my, I need to get ready yet. Can you excuse me, Mother?" Ella hurried from the room.

The house was quiet without Ella's chatter. Liz was gone for most of the day. She was a volunteer at the local hospital and had agreed to work until four that afternoon.

Everything was ready except for the table. Sara took out the clean white tablecloth and had just finished spreading it over the dining room table when Henry entered the room.

"Sara, I am so glad you are here." He gave her a brief hug.

It felt so good, but Sara quickly stepped back and picked up the pile of plates she had taken from the hutch.

"Thank you for inviting me," Sara said politely, though she felt her face heat.

"Let me help." Henry took the stack of plates from her hands and Sara reached for the silverware.

Sara looked at the gleaming silverware and stated, "Looks like someone has been busy polishing."

"Liz is forever cleaning and polishing; she is really quite a fanatic in that area." Henry chuckled. "We joke that if a mouse dared to come into the house, she would never be able to kill it, but it would leave cleaned and polished and wondering what just happened."

They both laughed.

They continued the small talk while they prepared the table. Sara moved the large cornucopia from the buffet to the center of the table. They looked over the table and admired their work.

"Come to the parlor and have a glass of sherry with me." Henry was as awkward as a schoolboy on his first date.

Sara had put on a lovely royal blue skirt that exposed her ankles and then some. She had a matching peplum belted jacket and a white ruffled blouse. Her strapped shoes accented her thin ankles. Her stylish beauty was clearly not lost on Henry, who followed close behind.

They went to the parlor and Sara took her place in her old bentwood rocker next to the fireplace. She was almost tempted to reach for her knitting, but obviously, it was no longer there. Henry poured the sherry and handed her the glass, brushing her hand with his. Sara sensed his longing and had to steel herself against it.

They continued their conversation. Henry asked about all her adventures over the past five years, and Sara obliged him.

"You learned how to drive and repair your vehicle?" Henry said, astounded and proud.

"Yes." She went on to tell him of the black women in Alabama, and how unfair it was that black women had no recourse for such blatant atrocities.

Henry listened, providing sympathy and praise in the appropriate places.

Sara noticed he was not patronizing her; he truly understood the enormity of the problems women faced.

A little flustered, Sara inquired about his position at the bank. He had moved up to vice president in charge of loans and explained how much the bank had grown.

They discussed the war and how it had affected the economy. Their conversation was at times serious and at times humorous as they told of incidents that happened in both of their lives. The tension lifted, and Sara began to enjoy their conversation.

They talked about the children, particularly Thaddeus, who seemed very dedicated to a military career. Henry was obviously proud of all his children...their children.

Before long, John Ellington arrived. This tall, thin young man with black hair, dark skin and eyes, impeccably dressed, was quite impressive.

Ella quickly entered the room and embraced him. She was dressed in a very fashionable burgundy linen dress with white eyelet underlay and matching eyelet collar. She had her auburn hair tied up in a burgundy grosgrain ribbon.

John turned out to be as charming as he was attractive, and everyone could plainly see why Ella was so taken by him. Sara was delighted Ella had found him.

Liz bounced in eventually, excited about her day at the hospital. She also was enamored with John, but for a totally different reason. They shared their aspirations in the healthcare field, and they openly discussed gory details of cases they had encountered. John had worked as an assistant to a local doctor, so he was not immune to the suffering of so many human beings.

Dinner was fabulous. Typical of Thanksgiving feasts, everyone was stuffed. Henry and John retired to the library while the women cleaned up the kitchen and put the leftover food away.

Things had gone well, and Sara didn't want to stay to a point that might become awkward, so she made a feeble excuse to leave... something about a mysterious friend who might possibly be stopping by that evening.

"It was very nice to meet you, John," she said. She hugged her girls, and thanked Henry for his hospitality. Then went to her automobile.

Henry walked her out and held the door for her. "Sara, thank you for coming; it means a lot to the girls...and me, too. I hope you enjoyed yourself."

"It was delightful," Sara replied, trying not to stare at him too long.

"Will you come again?" Henry asked. "Sunday for dinner?"

"Ah, not Sunday, I have another engagement," Sara lied.

"Perhaps, the next Sunday?" Henry pressed.

"Perhaps. I will let you know." She'd had a marvelous time and did want to return, but she didn't want to appear too anxious, either.

She returned for dinner the following week and made an excuse for the week after that. Christmas would be next in line, and with the prodding of her daughters and the fact that Thaddeus would be there, she agreed to spend Christmas with them. She could not deny her nervous excitement at the thought. Her family would be together for Christmas.

Chapter Fifty-six

Ella instructed Sara to come early on Christmas Eve Day so she could be there for the annual decorating of the tree. Thaddeus would arrive in the morning. He and Henry would trudge into the woods to pick out the best tree they could find. No one particularly cared what kind of tree it was. Henry had always preferred a balsam, while Sara would lean toward a spruce.

There was a sufficient blanket of snow on the ground to harness up the horses and take a sled out into the woods. Elizabeth had finished her chores; the house was spic and span. She begged, "Can I go along to pick out the tree? Please can I? Please?"

"You can't go trampling out in the woods dressed like that!" Thaddeus pulled at the string on the back of Liz's apron. "You'd better get your red riding hood," Thaddeus teased, referring to Liz's favorite red coat. "There are big bad wolves out there and you could get eaten alive." He tousled her hair.

"Wait just a minute," Liz called as she raced up the staircase.

A few minutes later, she returned, dressed in knickers, a heavy jacket, and boots. She had on a hunter's cap with flaps over her ears and a scarf tied tight about her neck. "Ready!" she announced.

Thaddeus laughed. "Where did you get those clothes?" he asked with glee. "My little sister has turned into a brother."

Liz rolled her eyes. "They are yours, Thaddeus. When you went away to school, they were in your room. No one has ever taken them out. They are really warm, and they fit me." Liz twirled around to model her attire.

Henry came into the house from harnessing up Nell to the sled. "What the?" He stared at Liz, his mouth dropped open.

"I'm going with you to pick out the tree. It is very cold out there, near zero, and I plan to stay warm," she announced.

Henry shook his head and laughed. "Come on boys, time is wastin'."

A light snowfall had started. They took all the time and patience they needed to select just the right tree, deciding on an eight-foot tall Norway pine.

Liz thought it was the best selection because the sturdy branches would hold the candles secure. The distance between the branches would make it safer when the candles were lit. She had thought this out carefully.

The tree fit perfectly in the parlor. Once it was in its stand, there would still be room for the star on the top. Liz didn't know how tall the ceilings were, but she knew they were at least half again as tall as Father. Yes, this tree would be perfect.

When they returned to the house, Sara had already arrived. Her automobile was parked in the circular drive in front of the house, a feature Henry had added to the house a few years earlier. There was a beautiful wreath adorning the front door, complete with a large, red velvet ribbon. Liz immediately recognized it as the handiwork of her mother. Although there was a hook on the door, it had been a long time since anyone had prepared a wreath for it.

They placed the tree on the stand outside, so it was ready to be raised to the ceiling. Then, came into the house dragging the enormous tree with them.

Liz grinned, because she had been right—the tree was perfect. It stood straight and tall, almost reaching the ceiling, but with enough room to top it with the traditional star.

***

While Henry, Liz, and Thaddeus were away getting the tree, Ella and Sara went to the attic to retrieve the Christmas ornaments. It was nostalgic and a bit scary for Sara to be poking into the objects of her past. They walked by Sara's old trunk that held her honeymoon trousseau. She passed the old dresser she had gotten from her aunt, running her fingers across its inlaid top wistfully. There were old pictures and a lamp or two, as well as boxes of canning jars and barrels filled with hickory nuts.

In the back corner was the stash of Christmas ornaments. There were boxes of hand-blown, hand-painted Santas and reindeer, candy canes, and snowmen. There were Mercury glass balls and tinsel twisted stars and other magical treasures. Many of the pieces were imported from Germany.

There was a bag filled with yards and yards of garland, green with red holly berries. Sara preferred real boughs, but these would do on such short planning. Among the treasures was also a box of ribbon of various sizes and textures.

Sara and Ella managed to carry it all downstairs to be sorted and selected for the traditional Christmas decorating of the tree before the evening church service. This was something the whole family had looked forward to since the children were toddlers. Ella told Sara it had become not a tradition, but a dreaded chore through the recent years without her presence.

The "boys" came into the kitchen, where Ella and Sara were busy stringing popcorn and cranberries for the tree. The house smelled of fresh popped corn and apple cider.

Sara jumped from her chair and flew across the room to her son. Five years had changed him dramatically. Long gone were the gangly arms and legs of a scrawny teenager. His red hair was all but shaved from his head. He was at least a foot taller than she remembered. But the mischievous glint in his eyes was still there.

He picked her up in his arms and swung her around. She felt the ripple in his muscles as he lifted her.

"Thaddeus, Thaddeus," she wept as she encircled his taut waist in her arms. Looking up into those deep blue eyes, she choked, "I have missed you so."

Tears welled in his eyes as he pushed her at arm's length. "I have missed you, too, Mother. Let me look at you."

He looked her up and down. "Perfect in every way," he proclaimed. "Dad said you are a sight for sore eyes, and he was right. You are as beautiful as ever."

Sara blushed.

She looked over to the stove, where Liz ladled hot cider into mugs. Spotting her youngest daughter dressed like a boy, Sara gasped. "Liz, what are you wearing?"

Liz curtsied.

"Looks like you lost a daughter and gained a son," Thaddeus teased.

"I think he is going to be a lumberjack. We should give him a different name, though. How about Elias, or...I've got it. How about Eggbert?"

Liz chased him around the table, walloping him with a towel.

Henry looked at Sara. "I thought joining the military would take the prankster out of him. I guess if that didn't work, nothing will."

"I wouldn't want him any other way." Sara chuckled, letting the warmth of family fill her.

Liz ran up the stairs to change into her own clothes, and the family gathered around the table for a noon dinner of apple cider and meat pies.

After dinner, the decorating of the tree commenced. They put the garland of popcorn on the tree, with Thaddeus taking the upper part of the tree, and the others, according to size, working their way down.

Henry placed the candles in their holders on the appropriate branches while everyone else supervised.

"A branch higher, Father...a little further left."

Per tradition, the youngest child selected the first ornament, and so they continued.

Several hours later, the tree was decorated, and they stood back to admire their handiwork. There was just one more thing—the star at the top. That was always held until they got back from church on Christmas Eve. The star of Bethlehem was a special symbol of the holiday and the one ornament that made the tree complete.

Ella had hoped that John could make it before the decorating of the tree, but he arrived shortly after and apologized for the delay. He had returned from Madison that afternoon. The roads had gotten a bit treacherous in that part of the state. He had heard that the storms were headed east and gaining in intensity. That meant they were headed right for Milwaukee, which made the children cheer in antitipation.

The afternoon had started with a light snowfall, which by now had advanced to huge flakes. The family looked forward to snow for Christmas, and snow on Christmas Eve was especially welcome.

They had always walked together the few blocks to the Presbyterian Church, and that was the plan for this night. They dressed in their holiday outfits and cloaks and stepped into the brisk winter night. The snow crunched under their feet. The white blanket of snow lit up the night as though it were day. Liz stuck out her tongue to catch flakes as they fell. Soon, they were all in the playful mood of catching snowflakes on their tongues, even Henry.

Reverend Nelson welcomed the entire Dewberry family with the warmest Christmas greeting. They all entered and took their place in the pew the family normally occupied, only this time, they took up the whole row. Sara detected a few raised eyebrows and murmurings, but she didn't know if it was real or imagined.

She looked around to see familiar faces. There was Martha and Emma, who were at her very first suffragette meeting. Edith was there, too. She nodded greetings to all.

Sara recognized the people from the council who had exiled Pastor Reinhardt. Friends or foes—it didn't matter. It was Christmas Eve, and there was peace on earth and good will toward men and women alike. She knew once the holiday was over and the meetings of the Ladies' Aid commenced, there would be a good share of tongue wagging, but Sara didn't care. Nothing could spoil this moment she shared with her family. They were not together, but they were probably as close as they would ever be again, and she let herself enjoy it.

The services began with the little children singing "Away in a Manger," and Sara thought of the children she had met in the South with no cribs for their beds, either. She thought of the women, the mothers in Alabama who suffered because of their skin color and because they were women, but even more so because they were negro women. She thought of Rose out in the prairie, giving birth to twins. She thought of Adam...poor Adam who never got to share but three Christmases with them. It all made tears prick the corners of her eyes.

Children in various age groups recited their passages and sang the traditional Christmas hymns. "Hark the Herald Angels Sing" and "Joy to the World" and Sara felt joy and at peace.

Pastor Nelson delivered the Christmas message. Had he changed it just for them, or had he planned it all along?

"Dear members and friends of the congregation. Peace on Earth, and good will to men. We are gathered here tonight to celebrate the birth of our Lord and Savior, Jesus Christ. Just like the Wise Men, many of us have traveled far and from various places. We have soldiers who have fought in the Great War who were fortunate enough to return to their families, and we have those who are serving the military today." He looked directly at Thaddeus, who sat tall in the pew in his West Point dress uniform.

"We have students who are home from school. We have many who have served in various capacities and for numerous causes who have returned to share this special day with their families. God has called on each and every one of us to serve in various ways, but in the end, he welcomes us home to his arms. So, it is with families who are separated for different reasons who return to the arms of their family and gather here that we give thanks for their many blessings this evening."

Reverend Nelson continued with the Christmas message, but Sara heard little more. She felt the warm glow of family on this holiday season, and it filled her entire being.

When they left the church, many well-wishers shared their joy.

"Good evening, Dewberries, and a Merry Christmas to you all."

"Happy holidays to your lovely family."

"Enjoy your Christmas together."

They returned the greetings and left the church with the holiday spirit they always experienced after services.

The wind had picked up considerably while they had been in church, and the snow pelted down upon them. The cutting wind made the cold air seem colder. They hurried along the path home, two by two. Ella and John led the group, hand in hand. Sara thought about the many years ago when that would've been she and Henry. The young couple was clearly in love, and it was bittersweet to watch.

Sara and Liz followed, Liz talking nonstop about the Christmas tree and the presents she hoped to receive. "I know that presents are not the object of Christmas, but I am still excited," she confessed. "I do hope I get the new board game called Monopoly. I asked Father for it, but he just said, 'We will see.'"

Sara inquired what the game was about and how it was played.

Liz said, "Dad would love it. It has to do with buying and selling property, mortgages, and stuff like that, and you can play it with several people."

Sara thought for a moment. "Banking is a very dull occupation in my mind. Why would they make a game out of it, and why would anyone buy it?"

"Maybe that's the point." Liz pulled her scarf up around her face to keep the wind from her cheeks. "Maybe this is an opportunity to learn how exciting banking really is. Father enjoys it, so it must have some appeal."

"True," Sara agreed, thinking of the effort Henry had made to understand her vocation. "I will have to play the game."

Henry and Thaddeus brought up the rear and were engrossed in a conversation about the Great War and its economic impact. Henry inquired about West Point and how Thaddeus was faring at the school.

The conversations were short since they arrived home—and none too soon. The weather was deteriorating rapidly.

***

Inside, Ella and John went to the kitchen to warm up some hot chocolate.

John brushed a snowflake from Ella's hair and cupped her cold rosy cheeks in his warm hands. "Merry Christmas, my lady," he murmured.

Blushing, Ella put her arms around his neck and murmured back, "Merry Christmas, my knight in shining armor."

"Close your eyes," he whispered in her ear.

She expected him to kiss her, and she turned her face up to his in anticipation. She waited, wondering what was taking so long.

John rustled into his pocket, took her hand in his, and slipped something on her finger.

Her eyes popped open to see a beautiful marquise diamond ring.

"Will you marry me?" John asked with a bright smile.

Ella let out a squeal, which caused Liz to run into the kitchen.

"What's going on?" she asked.

"Will you?" repeated John.

"Yes, yes, yes!" Ella jumped into his arms and planted a kiss on his lips. He embraced her passionately.

"Yes what?" Liz asked, her face wrinkled in confusion.

Ella raised her left hand, showing off the beautiful ring. "We're getting married," she squealed.

"Mother, Father!" Liz called out.

Both had just entered the room.

"Mother, look." Ella waved her hand in the air, displaying the ring.

Sara took Ella's hand and her eyes widened at the sparkling ring. "Simply stunning. Ella, oh how wonderful!" She hugged her.

Thaddeus offered his congratulations.

Henry shook John's hand. "I was wondering what took you so long. We talked at Thanksgiving, and then I never heard another word. I thought maybe you changed your mind."

Ella turned to her father, shocked. "You knew? You didn't even give me a hint?"

"Well, John tells me he wants to finish school before he ties the knot, so I figured there was no rush. That would be in three more years, right, John?"

Sara turned to John. "You're a lucky man." She hugged him. "Three years is a long time. Are you sure you want to wait that long?"

"No, ma'am, I don't but it seems like the practical thing to do. Ella has four more years at Downer, and I will be very busy in medical school and then with residency. The hours are grueling. I'm afraid neither of us will have enough time to devote to each other. It wouldn't be fair to Ella," John said, putting his arm around Ella.

"What do you think about that?" Sara asked Ella.

"John and I discussed our lives after our education. He totally surprised me with a ring. I didn't expect this until much later. He is right. It will be a long engagement."

Ella saw her mother detect the sadness in her voice. They would discuss it later in private. Now was the time to celebrate, and Ella would not let thoughts of waiting bring her down.

They went into the parlor and toasted the young couple. John had brought a bottle of champagne. In the corner, Ella watched Liz sip at hot chocolate, her face in a frown. Ella realized then how much her sister would miss her as she moved on to a life of her own. She'd have to make sure to spend as much time with her while she could.

Chapter Fifty-seven

After the celebration had died down, Henry reached into a box and pulled out the traditional star. He stood on a chair to place it at the top of the tree. They lit the candles and sang "Oh Little Town of Bethlehem," looking at the tree with wonder in their eyes.

The Dewberry tradition was to open gifts and eat from a buffet of smoked salmon, venison sausage, and headcheese served with small crispy biscuits. Fresh oranges and apples and small tarts completed the buffet.

John sat on an overstuffed chair with Ella perched on the arm. Henry sat on the other overstuffed chair in the room, his favorite chair, facing the fireplace. Sara took her traditional spot on the bentwood rocker, and Liz found a spot with Thaddeus on the rug in front of the tree. She tried not to look too long at Ella and John for fear her sadness would show on her face—she was so happy for them, but Ella had been almost a mother to her these past five years, and it would hurt when she left to pursue her own life.

The tree was piled high with presents. Liz spotted something that could be the Monopoly game she wanted but decided to keep it until last. She slipped it under the library table, and then began to distribute the presents one by one, beginning with her gifts to everyone.

Liz had worked diligently in the kitchen all week, baking and preparing for the holiday. She had secretly prepared small boxes of confections for everyone. They were all delighted with their treats.

Thaddeus hadn't had the time to shop for everyone individually, but he had purchased a crate of fresh assorted nuts. They distributed the nuts, along with a nutcracker, and the rest of the evening was spent cracking and picking the meats. Sara set out a box to take all the shells.

Sara's gift for each of the men was a hand knitted muffler. Thaddeus commented that they should have opened that gift before their walk to church, which made everyone chuckle.

She had selected a pair of Kidd gloves for Ella. "You will need those for driving in the winter," Sara suggested.

Liz opened her gift and found a beautiful cameo locket. She got up and hugged her mother. "Thank you so much. I love it."

Ella's gifts were next. Sara opened the package carefully to find a beautiful sampler, which Ella had been working on since Sara had left. She had finished it in the summer before she left for Oklahoma. "Ella, it is beautiful," exclaimed Sara. "I will treasure it always."

When the men opened their gifts, they laughed heartily. Ella had knitted each of them a muffler as well. She slipped John a special gift. He opened it to find a gold watch fob.

Liz looked about, and not shyly, asked, "Hey, where is mine?"

"It's there," Ella said, pointing under the tree.

Liz's lip curled up in a pout. "I thought you forgot."

"You, my dear are unforgettable." Ella laughed.

Liz opened the package and found a beautiful pearl comb for her hair. Tears welled in her eyes, and she wrapped her arms around Ella in a hug.

Ella kissed her hair. "Even when I am gone and can no longer brush it for you, you will still have the most beautiful hair." Then, she lightly punched Liz's shoulder, lightening the mood. "But that won't be for a very long time."

Liz couldn't help but smile. "Thank you," she whispered, and then shook herself in embarrassment.

Liz then distributed boxes, all similar in shape and size to everyone. "These are from Dad," she said. "He even got one for himself." She shook the box, trying to guess its contents. She couldn't tell.

"Okay, all together," Liz announced, and paper flew in every direction.

Everyone seemed genuinely thrilled with the contents. There they were—six gleaming pairs of new ice skates.

"I thought we might all go ice skating tomorrow afternoon," Henry said. "Mother and I used to be quite good at this. Of course, it has been a few years since we took to the ice, but we sure had a lot of fun in the day."

Everyone thought it was a great idea.

That was the end of the pile. John had not brought gifts. Being a struggling student and their guest, they thought nothing of it, and were about to devour what was left on the buffet table.

"Wait," said John. "There is one more present." He pointed under the table, where Liz had stashed the box she had thought was Father's gift to her. "I'm afraid I have only one gift for everyone. I hope that is okay."

"Of course," everyone chorused their approval.

"Liz, you do the honors," John said to her.

Liz picked up the box and shook it. It rattled. She quickly tore away the wrappings. It was a brand-new Monopoly game. They were hard to come by, but John managed to find it for them.

They all chattered at once, voicing their approval.

"I hope you all enjoy it," said John.

"We will," they all chorused again. It was a wonderful gift.

***

It was getting close to eleven p.m., and Sara decided it was time for her to leave. John had planned to stay in the guest room, but Sara wasn't quite ready to get too comfortable in her old home.

Ella peered out the window and said, "Mother, have you looked out? Are you sure you want to leave? We can make room on the sofa for one of the fellas and you can sleep in the guest room."

"No, no. I've driven in many conditions. I am sure I'll be fine," Sara said, somewhat unsure of herself. She put on her coat and opened the door.

A roaring blast of snow hit her directly, and there was a two-foot drift in front of the door.

She shut the door and pulled her scarf tighter around her neck, bracing herself for the outdoors. She took a deep breath and headed into the blizzard, lowering her head so her face was shielded.

She stepped into the drifts, which went all the way up to her knees. She had difficulty putting one foot ahead of the other to get to her vehicle. Since she had parked in the circular driveway, she only had a few feet to get to her automobile.

She pulled open the door and somehow managed to get it started. It groaned a few times, but then it sputtered, and the engine turned over. She put it in drive and was about to leave, but she couldn't go anywhere. The wheels spun, and the engine died. She tried again and again.

By now, the men had come to her rescue.

"Sara, you can't go anywhere tonight," Henry said. "You will need to stay here. You can sleep in our bed and I will sleep on the sofa in the library."

Sara didn't know what to do, but she instantly felt helpless and nervous.

They began suggesting various sleeping arrangements when Thaddeus said, "Can we please get in out of this blizzard and discuss it?"

They agreed and helped Sara toward the house.

The debate continued inside the house.

Sara suggested she sleep on the sofa, but no one would hear of it.

Finally, they drew straws, and Thaddeus got the sofa. Henry said he would sleep in Thaddeus' bed, and Sara would sleep in the master suite. After much ado, they agreed that would be the arrangement.

Soon, everyone retired to their assigned bedroom, but Sara and Henry lingered in the parlor. Sara hesitated because she felt a bit uncomfortable sleeping in Henry's bed, and Henry didn't seem to want to say good night.

They talked way past midnight. They covered various subjects, from the weather to world news, from automobiles to the events of the day. Just like last time, Sara found it strangely natural to talk with him.

They settled on the discussion of Ella's engagement.

Sara asked, "Henry, do you think it is wise for this young couple to wait three years for marriage?"

"It is a practical decision, but I am not sure it is a good emotional decision."

"I think long-distance romances are more difficult. If my husband were in medical school, I would want to be there to support him."

"But what about her education, her career?" Henry asked. "Is it fair that she has to give up her ambitions for his career pursuits?"

Sara chuckled.

"What's so funny?"

"Listen to us," said Sara, still smiling. "You're defending women's rights, and I am defending her support of his career. Isn't that a bit ironic?"

Henry laughed. "It certainly is."

"Henry, can we help them to figure this out? I know Ella chose Downer so she could be here for Liz. Both girls had Catherine when I was gone, but I am back now. Ella can go to school wherever she chooses. Perhaps she can attend college in Madison as well. I am sure they have other programs that aren't medical. Madison is a state college and would be less expensive than Downer. Maybe we could assist them with living expenses, too."

Henry looked pensive. "I believe John had intended to live in a dormitory. That would not be possible if Ella were with him. Madison has a lot of housing options. Perhaps they could find a boarding house, or an efficiency apartment with a Murphy bed."

"We can discuss it with them. I know what emotional separation can do to a person. I don't want Ella to be hurt," Sara stated, perhaps a little coldly.

Henry winced, obviously picking up on the hint. He recovered and cleared his throat. "There is another kind of separation that concerns me in such a long-term engagement. Sara, I think I can be candid with you. Men cannot have an emotional attachment without eventually giving in to the physical aspect of it. I would like to see my daughter go to her marriage bed a virgin, and I most certainly don't want to have her go to it pregnant."

Sara felt emboldened. "So, in my absence, did you find an outlet for your physical needs?"

Henry startled backward. "No, I did not. There were times I ravished you in my dreams, but no, I had no desire to replace you. I love you, Sara."

He hesitated. "What about you? Did you find companionship? A lovely woman like yourself would certainly be a temptation."

Sara flushed, but kept her voice flat. "No, Henry, that never entered my mind. It is a dangerous world out there, with women often raped and tormented. I was fortunate to have Tillie as my rock to keep me safe. I had no desire to seek the companionship of a man. I spent most of my time as their adversary. Quite frankly, I met none that measured up to you—which is alarming, since I often considered you a stupid fool."

Henry looked taken aback. "Rightfully so. I hope you will learn that I have changed."

"I hope you can see that I, too, have changed. The question is, have we changed apart or together?" Sara shivered, and found both her body and mind suddenly tired. "I think I need to retire."

"Yes, my dear, that is the question. If you need anything at all, please knock on my door. I will accommodate you in any way I can." Henry winked.

Sara rolled her eyes. "Ella has provided me with the items I need for overnight. Good night, Henry."

"Good night, my dear."

Sara went to the room she had once shared with Henry.

She walked to the window and looked out at the blizzard. Her car was nearly buried in the snow.

Sara turned back to the bed, let down her hair, undressed, and put on the nightgown Ella had provided for her. She slipped between the covers, shut out the light on the bedside table, and lay there in the dark in the four-poster bed. She rolled to her side and smelled the spicy odor of her husband on the pillow. Then, she hugged the pillow tight, drifting into a deep sleep.

Chapter Fifty-eight

Typical of winters in Wisconsin, the weather changed dramatically from the blizzard of the previous evening. Christmas Day was calm, sunny, and twenty degrees warmer, but the prospect of digging Sara's car out from under fourteen inches of snow still remained.

Sara yawned and stretched. The morning sun peeked through the lace-covered window. She looked around the room. Henry hadn't changed a thing. Everything was the same as the day she had left.

Sara hugged herself and shivered in the morning's chill air. She went to the closet and found her quilted housecoat still there, hanging up. She pulled it over her nightgown and went back to peek out the window.

She heard some activity below. Thaddeus was already up and outside shoveling the driveway. It looked as if he had cleaned off the front porch and released her vehicle from the grasp of the drifted snow. John was helping him, wiping the snow from the top of her motor car. It looked like she was no longer hostage to the weather and could leave whenever she wanted.

But, Sara realized, she didn't want to leave. She thought of the cold and lonely atmosphere of Tillie's house and wished the storm would have lasted for days. She was grateful for Tillie's graciousness in taking care of her even beyond death, but this was her home, and it felt good to be here. She knew she would return to Tillie's house eventually, but she wanted to drink in all the joys of this holiday for as long as she could.

She went back to the closet, and as she suspected, all her clothes were still on their hangers. She flipped through them and found the dress she had worn on Christmas six years earlier. It was an ensemble of a dark green skirt with a matching short jacket. She found the white ruffled blouse she had worn with it.

Sara got dressed and sat at the dressing table to fix her auburn hair, piling it high on her head and fastening it with the comb from the small jewelry box still on the corner of the dresser. She found a gold angel brooch that looked elegant against the dark green, as well as some emerald earrings. She stood and walked to the full-length mirror and admired the transformation. She was pleased with what she saw.

She made the bed, took a deep breath, and started down the staircase. They had decorated the banister with holly garland and big red bows the day before, and her descent felt picture-perfect.

Henry stood when he heard her steps on the stairs, and gasped. "Sara, darling, you are an angel. You are absolutely beautiful!" He reached out to take her hand.

He was quite handsome himself, in his gray three-piece suit with a red kerchief in his pocket and a red and gray ascot.

"You are just in time for breakfast," he announced and escorted her to the dining room.

His hand felt warm in hers, and Sara could not ignore the electric feeling. "I saw the fellows out shoveling snow. Where are our girls?" she asked. "It smells delightful in here."

She looked around and discovered the dining table had been set.

Just then, Ella emerged from the kitchen with hot coffee and a tray of hot cross buns fresh from the oven. Liz was behind her with a pan of scrambled eggs and a huge bowl of grapefruit, oranges, pineapple, and cherries. The smell of freshly brewed coffee and bakery made Sara realize she was hungry.

Henry held her chair for her.

"Thank you, Henry," she said.

Just then, the boys clomped in from outside, rowdy laughter filling the house. They shook the snow off from their clothes and removed their galoshes before entering the dining room.

"We just had a snowball fight and I won," Thaddeus said.

"Did not," John argued. "You didn't warn me that we were embarking on a battle and you had more firepower."

"John, you can't compete with the military. We are always prepared for battle. You are such a city softy. I think I need to teach you a thing or two," Thaddeus teased. "I am hungry as a horse. Shoveling snow can build an appetite."

"It smells and looks fantastic," John agreed as he took Ella by the

293

waist and pulled out a chair for her next to him.

Sara chuckled at it all, not wanting to let the moment go.

Henry sat at the head of the table. "I feel so blessed today. Please bow your heads."

The girls looked at each other and shared a smile with Sara.

Sara winked, and wondered if it was the first time Henry had offered a verbal prayer since she had left.

He bowed his head and prayed, "Dear Lord, thank you for your many blessings. Thank you for bringing our family together to celebrate this holy holiday. Bless Ella and John as they move forward in their life together. Bless Sara for the many sacrifices she has endured in her quest to provide her daughters and the daughters of others a better future. Bless Thaddeus and his military journey. Help us all to learn to love each other more each day. Bless this food we are about to receive and keep us all safe in your love. Amen."

Everyone added their Amen, and the chatter began while they passed the dishes.

"What are we going to do today?" Thaddeus asked.

"Well," said Henry, "I thought we could go ice skating. I didn't buy those skates to sit on a shelf."

Ella, Thaddeus, and Liz all chimed their approvals.

John turned to Ella and said coyly, "I don't want to embarrass you, but it has been at least ten years since I've put on skates."

"Don't worry, John, Ella will teach you," Thaddeus said, patting him on the back.

"Mother and I spent most of our courtship on skates," Henry revealed, and Sara couldn't help but flush. "She is quite the master."

"Henry, I am afraid I am a bit rusty, too. I haven't skated since before Adam was born." As soon as the words left her mouth, a wave of sadness flooded over her and the rest of the family.

There was a nervous moment of silence for Adam, and then Thaddeus broke it by challenging Liz to a race on skates.

Liz accepted the challenge with a grin.

***

They allowed what they felt was sufficient time for the rink caretakers to get the ice cleared, but took shovels as a backup, just in case. They headed off for the pond where the family had always skated in by gone years.

A few children were there, but the ice was far from being crowded. Sara and her family sat on the benches and put on their skates.

The gentlemen helped the ladies with their bindings, and soon they were off.

John was a bit shaky at first, but he soon got the hang of it. Ella helped him feel his way around the rink.

Liz and Thaddeus were on a mission to be the best. They had laid out plans to skate the perimeter of the pond two times. The winner would be the first person returning to the starting point after two laps. They were off almost before anyone else was able to get on their feet, and Sara chuckled warmly at their cheer.

Henry and Sara were the last on the ice. Sara was a little nervous but didn't hesitate. She skated out to the center and made a few quick turns, then ended up skating backwards in a large circle.

Henry watched proudly and Sara gave him a warm smile.

He skated behind her and placed his hand at her waist, and they skated around the pond together. The second round was a waltz type move, with Sara skating backward and Henry twirling her around in his arms at various intervals. Sara liked the feel of Henry's strong arms around her waist, and it was obvious he enjoyed it also. Neither spoke.

They returned to the bench breathless and sat next to each other, enjoying the sight of their children in playful exercise. Henry slipped one arm around Sara's shoulders as he pointed out the lessons being taught to John by Ella, and Sara let him. "Remember when that was us?" Henry asked.

They watched as Ella and John took several more turns around the ice.

"I have an idea," Sara said. "Follow me." She and Henry skated out to them, and they intermittently changed partners.

Meanwhile, Thaddeus and Liz delighted everyone with their expert performances on the ice.

Then Thaddeus challenged everyone to a game of crack the whip. Ella led the line-up, with John holding tight onto her waist. Sara was next, with Henry close behind her.

At first, he was so close she could almost feel his warm breath on her neck, making her shiver. Liz and Thaddeus were at the end of the whip and commanded, "Faster, faster."

Soon on a vicious turn, Liz broke away from her father.

She and Thaddeus went sailing across the ice, barely able to stay standing up, but neither willing to fall.

Henry reached back to catch Liz, but in the process, pulled Sara away from John.

She landed in Henry's arms. The moment changed; the game forgotten. Henry grabbed Sara tight around the waist, and they spun round and round with her back against his chest and his cheek pressed on her rosy cheek.

Once they had control of themselves, he spun her around to face him.

He pulled her tightly to him and gave her a warm kiss. She wanted to resist but was helpless in his arms for a moment. Eventually, she released herself and skated to the bench, face on fire, panicking.

Henry followed her. "Sara, I am sorry. I looked in your eyes and twenty years melted away. You were nineteen and I was twenty-one."

"It's okay, Henry. It was a mistake," Sara lied, knowing full well that she felt the same, but also sure that this couldn't happen, shouldn't happen...at least not yet.

***

Over the next several months, Sara spent a lot of time with the family. They spent the rest of the winter playing Monopoly and ice skating. They had dinners together and long talks.

Sara spent time with just her girls, too. Liz was learning how to knit. Ella was planning a wedding. It was three years away, but there was a lot to do.

Sara continued her part in the suffragette movement, but did it mostly from Tillie's home, writing letters to everyone she could think of with political clout. She took part in the local activities of the Milwaukee division, and helped in planning rallies and speaking to Wisconsin legislators. Occasionally, she received a request to speak to a group outside the state, but rarely went beyond Chicago or Minneapolis. She could not leave her children for long.

John and Ella decided to wait for marriage. Ella was busy with her studies at Downer, and John had moved into a dormitory in Madison. Thaddeus was back at West Point.

Sara spent as much time as she could with Liz. It was their chance to make up for time lost. Liz had quickly adapted to the mother she barely remembered, and in the early days of 1919, their bond grew stronger and stronger.

As for Henry, he was so much like the man Sara had married—but with one big exception. He was now a believer in her cause. He had listened patiently to her beliefs and ideas and realized the unfairness of the system, becoming her number one supporter.

She wondered if it would last. Everything indicated that he was sincere.

Sara wanted him, not only for the sake of family and security, but also because she felt a burning desire for him as a man, as a lover.

But Sara also knew if she succumbed to that desire, she would no longer control her destiny. Control was important. No, control was imperative. Control was what kept her focused and dedicated to go on— for herself, for her daughters, and for the future of women everywhere. It would be so easy to be swept off her feet by passion. She had already sacrificed so much, and she could almost feel the culmination of all their efforts within their grasp.

Chapter Fifty-nine

On February 10, 1919, the Nineteenth Amendment was again voted upon but failed by only one vote. Sara made pleas to each of the senators opposing the bill. She could taste victory. If they could only change the minds of two more senators, they would have passage. She knew it in her heart and decided this would be a good time to revisit Washington, even if it meant losing a few weeks with her children.

In early April of 1919, Sara arrived by train in Washington, D.C. Cherry blossoms were in full bloom. This was her favorite time of year in the nation's capital. Catherine and James met her at the train station. Sara had planned a two-week visit—plenty of time to take care of business and spend time with her old friend, Catherine.

Sara went to dinner with James and Catherine that evening. They decided on Gadsby's Tavern. James drove, and as they crossed the Potomac to Alexandria, Virginia, where this historic restaurant had stood since the 1700s, Sara took a moment to marvel. It was a favorite gathering place to conduct business, carry on political conversations, and rub elbows with the Washington elite. It was also a place to get a splendid meal. On the way, Sara was delighted in the sights and smell the blossoms' fragrance in the air.

James proudly entered the restaurant with a beautiful lady on each arm. Heads turned, and guests nodded to the familiar James Morgenson. A few took the opportunity to greet them personally.

"James, I do say you travel in beautiful company...and who may I ask is this delightful lady?" the senator from North Dakota inquired.

"This, my dear friend, is Sara Dewberry. You may have heard of her from your discussions regarding the suffragette movement. Mrs. Dewberry is a firm advocate for the suffragettes' cause and is here to meet and enlighten several senators regarding the issue." James smiled slyly, and Sara tried not to chuckle.

"Porter McCumber, if I am not mistaken." Sara offered her hand. "I have contacted you by letter. Could you possibly spare a few minutes later this week so we can talk?"

The senator stiffened. "Ah yes, Mrs. Dewberry. Contact my aide and he will set up an appointment. Very nice meeting you, Mrs. Dewberry, Mrs. Morgenson, James." Senator McCumber nodded and quickly took his leave.

"Guess you caught him off guard," Catherine whispered, poking Sara in the side with a grin. "Don't waste any time—call from the telephone in our apartment tomorrow first thing. Don't let the opportunity slip by."

"I certainly will do that." Sara was pleased with the opportunities presented at this venue. Later, James introduced her to two more senators, who were equally taken by surprise but agreed to a meeting.

The three enjoyed a delightful meal of Virginia smoked ham, crab cakes, and roasted vegetables. They were quite satisfied but found room to share a plum cake for dessert. When they returned to the apartment, it was late, and Sara was exhausted. She retired for the evening, deciding to spend the following day with Catherine, catching up on news and reminiscing.

The next morning, a jangling noise startled Sara. Catherine rose and went to the telephone to see who was calling.

It was James. He wanted to tell Sara that the senator from Tennessee would be in his office the following morning, if Sara wished to set up an appointment.

Sara was definitely interested and soon had an appointment with the senator for ten o'clock the next morning.

Catherine brought out tea. "I want to hear everything about your life. Don't leave out anything."

"I will, Catherine, and please, you tell me about my girls. I understand they did turn to you for guidance on occasion. They have grown up so wonderfully."

The women shared the stories of accomplishments and challenges. Ella had reached puberty about the time Sara had left, so she had leaned on Catherine for advice.

Catherine chuckled at the memory. "Oh my. I didn't think, having no

299

children of my own, that I would be the one explaining the birds and the bees to a young girl on the brink of womanhood. But I must say, it was a bonding experience," Catherine said proudly. "Both girls are delightful, Sara. I feel in a way like they are my own."

Sara took her hands. "I knew you would step into my shoes. I thank you, Catherine. I will always be indebted to you."

"No, Sara, I thank you. It was an experience I wouldn't give up for anything," Catherine replied. "But now, I need to know the real gossip. What is happening between you and Henry?"

Sara sighed, her feelings bubbling up inside her. "We have known each other for over twenty years. You know me better than anyone. Since we met, we have confided in each other, and you were always the one to make sense of everything. I need your wisdom now."

"Lay it out for me, sister," Catherine commanded. "You were always the one to overanalyze things. Let's see if we can keep it simple."

"I love Henry. I always have." Sara hesitated. "I was very angry with him, as I should have been. I didn't think I would ever be able to forgive him for the pain he inflicted on me. He is a good man, but very misguided in his beliefs...or at least, the beliefs he had a few years ago."

"Believe me, Sara. He was an...I can't say it. He was a donkey's buttocks. That is as simple as I can make it. I don't think I could forgive him, either. I liked him before he went berserk, but I am not sure if I could have ever forgiven him." Catherine's voice was firm.

"I know, but he has changed. So have I. We are different people, but somehow, I still find him attractive and interesting. I find it difficult to be angry with him since he has changed. He is supportive of my cause. He has apologized over and over again, but it is hard to rebuild trust when it has been so horribly broken. There is a part of me that wonders if it could happen again."

"Trust is a very important issue, probably one step above love, and it takes time. How are you feeling about that issue?" Catherine poured more tea.

"When I am with him, I trust him completely. When we are apart, I think more clearly, and I am not sure," Sara confessed. "Over Christmas, I spent the night at the house, and I felt..."

"Whoa, whoa, whoa! You spent the night with Henry?" Catherine gasped.

Sara flushed. "No, no nothing like that. We had a horrible blizzard and my car was snowed in. I slept in Henry's bed and he slept in the guest room," she explained.

"Well, how did that feel?"

"It was very strange at first. You know, Catherine, he has never removed any of my things from the room. All my clothes were still there. In fact, I dressed in some of them the next morning. It felt strange for a while, but then it felt right. It felt good. I didn't want it to end."

"Until?" Catherine encouraged Sara to go on.

"I spent the weekend with the family. We had a wonderful time and it seemed like we belonged together. It was so nice." There was a moment of silence while Sara reflected. "When I finally had to leave, I felt a deep sadness and a pain in the pit of my stomach. I quickly said my good-byes and cried all the way home."

"And you didn't, you know, uhm, get intimate?" Catherine asked with a wink.

"No, but I don't think it would have taken a lot of encouragement for it to happen. I wanted him so much, and I am sure he felt the same but didn't want to alarm me." There was another brief silence, and Sara felt her face grow even hotter. "We kissed."

"You kissed?" Catherine encouraged her to go on.

"Yes, it was on the ice rink. He caught me from falling and we were face to face, with his arms around my waist. I turned away and he apologized, but Catherine, I wanted him to kiss me again."

"Do you worry that he may become the domineering person he was?" Catherine pressed.

"Oh no," Sara quickly said. "Not the way he was."

"Well then, what is the hesitation?"

"I don't know. I just don't want him to become some other maniac that I haven't met yet." Sara laughed nervously.

Catherine squeezed Sara's hands, her eyes sincere. "Honey, we all change. We all make mistakes—and I must admit the one he made was a doozy. We can't live our lives wondering about things we have no control over, and things that probably won't happen anyway. You miss out on a lot of life that way."

"The girls want us back together and I think Thaddeus would like it, too," Sara rationalized.

"Forget the girls and Thaddeus. They will soon be building lives of their own. You need to follow your heart. Girl, what are you waiting for?"

Sara trembled with nervous excitement. "Catherine, you always make things so clear. I know Henry wants me back, the rest of the family does, and I guess it is what I want, too."

"Go get your man, and if he gets out of line again, you show him where the line is!" Catherine hugged her, and for the first time since she had left Milwaukee, Sara felt sure of where her heart lay.

Chapter Sixty

Sara had secured appointments with several senators and congressmen for the following day.

That morning, she began her rounds, knowing that her work was cut out for her. These legislators were her biggest challenge. They were the force of opposition. The senator from North Dakota listened to her politely, but Sara left feeling that she could have been talking to the chair.

Her next meeting was with the representative from Tennessee. Tennessee had been one of the biggest holdouts, and this would be a difficult vote to win over. But Sara would not back down.

The congressman had a trimmed beard and a belly paunch, with a full head of white hair and the look of a southern gentleman. His looks defied his true character.

"My dear, ya'll are a lovely lady. Why are ya'll gettin' yerself so involved in this mess? It isn't right. Your place is in your home with your children. It is the God-given natural order of things." He patted her hand in a patronizing way. "Go on home and ferget this nonsense."

Sara gave a placid smile, but was direct. "My dear Congressman, this mess, as you call it, has been created by persons like yourself who refuse to look into the twentieth century. Women understand the issues more than most men because they must struggle day after day in fields beside their husbands, in factories when men are off to war—war that was created by man. Mess you say. It is a mess created by men. Men will not even give women a voice to be heard in the form of a vote. We need a few women to straighten out this mess."

The congressman stiffened and cleared his throat. "Ahem, ahem," he choked. "Madam, I can see that you are passionate about this issue, but why do ya'll want to worry your pretty head over such matters? If your husband is a good man, he will take care of these things for you."

Sara lifted her chin. "And what, Congressman, do you tell women who do not have a husband, or who has a husband who is a louse? A husband who flits around with concubines and harlots, or a husband who imbibes in alcohol until he is no longer coherent and beats his wife and children? Those women have no recourse, they have no voice. They could not even leave penniless and take the children with them. What, Congressman, do you say to those women?"

"Ah." He stroked his beard. "So, that is your problem. A pretty thing like ya'all should have no problem finding another man. One who would treat you well." He reached out his hand to touch her cheek.

Sara recoiled from his touch. "No, Congressman. I believe this discussion is over. It is clear to me that you are a letch and an imbecile. I have nothing further to say." Sara picked up her bag and stomped out of the room.

We will never win them all.

Next, Sara met with a few legislators, pleading her cause. Some seemed supportive, but she wasn't sure if their comments were sincere. She had hopes that at least one or two would see things in a different light.

Finally, as she hurried to meet with her final appointment of the day, she hoped at least one congressman would respond in a way that made her feel that she had won him over. Her last stop was a senator from Kentucky.

From the moment she stepped into his office, she felt the cool reception.

"Come in, come in. I am very busy," he said gruffly. "I agreed to see you as a favor to one of my colleagues, but I must tell ya'll, yer wastin yer time!"

He stood and his six-foot-two frame towered above Sara. But behind this gruff exterior, Sara felt there was a man who would call a spade a spade and that is something she could deal with…a man of reason.

"Senator, I will take as little time as possible. You are aware of my mission, so perhaps we can save some time if you will tell me why you are objecting to this amendment."

"Simple. Temperance!"

Sara could tell he was a man of few words. She stayed patient.

"Temperance?"

"Temperance. It seems to me that the women are all fired up about alcohol and want to put an end to it. They are bashing in saloons and picketing inns that serve alcohol. They are trying to get the ratification vote to put an end to it. And Madam, I like a shot of good Kentucky bourbon on occasion and enjoy a good Bordeaux with my dinner. I don't want to give it up." He shuffled papers on his desk.

"It is true that there is a faction of the women's movement that is concerned with that issue," Sara said. "There are no controls over the content in the bottles of alcohol sold and there is some mighty wicked stuff out there. Some of it has gasoline and horse rubbing alcohol in it." Sara challenged his position on a level that perhaps he might consider.

"Rot gut!" he said, disgusted. "Personally, I would like to see that done away with, but it isn't for me to dictate what my fellow man chooses to drink. I don't want anyone telling me what I can or cannot drink." He scratched his balding head.

"Well, if it makes you feel any better, I like a glass of sherry on occasion myself."

The senator looked at her quizzically, obviously trying to decide if she was telling the truth or trying to butter him up. Being a man who occasionally indulged in a game of poker, she saw the moment when he decided to call her bluff.

He went to the cabinet behind his desk and pulled out a bottle. He held it up and said, "Ah, 1884, a good year." He poured two glasses of fine sherry and handed a glass to her. His eyes twinkled.

Sara smiled, swished it in the glass, and took a generous sip, letting the fine wine flow over her tongue. She swallowed and nodded in agreement. "Yes, 1884 was a good year."

He laughed heartily and took a sip himself. "So, what do you want?"

"I would like you to consider this amendment on its merits, not dwelling on the consequences of votes any more than you would a man. The Nineteenth Amendment simply states, 'The right of citizens of the United States to vote shall not be denied or abridged by the United States or by any state because of sex. Congress shall have power to enforce this article by appropriate legislation.'"

She set down her glass and put her business face back on. "You are a wise man, why would you want to deny the many votes you would gain in your election if the support of women was behind you? You have heard the many arguments for supporting the amendment. If a man proposes a bad idea, intelligence prevails, and we defeat it. It would be no different if a woman makes such a proposal. All women want is a vote, a voice."

The senator smiled. "I don't agree with some of the issues the suffragettes have backed, but I do believe in their right to be heard. If truth be told, I would welcome you in the seat of some of my colleagues. We have partisan voices and they don't always make sense. You, my friend, make sense."

Sara took a last sip of her sherry and thanked the senator with a smile. "I will stop wasting your time now and be on my way. Thank you for your time and for the wonderful sherry." She raised her glass to him, and he showed her out.

Sara heard him mumble, "Quite a lady, quite a lady," as she made her way out. She could not help but celebrate on the way home. Perhaps, she had changed a mind today and brought the cause one step closer to victory.

The days had quickly passed, and Sara had one more day to spend with Catherine. She was sad to see their time end, but anxious to get back to her girls. And yes, she admitted, was anxious to see Henry again.

Sara was pleased with her time in Washington. She felt sure that the amendment would soon be passed. President Woodrow Wilson, it appeared, had recently once again become a strong advocate for the cause, and his operatives worked diligently to see it passed. Word in Washington was that the amendment would come up for vote again in May.

But despite it all, on the train home, Sara could think of little else than her moving back into her home and sharing it with her family.

Chapter Sixty-one

Sara's train arrived in Milwaukee at four in the afternoon. Henry was on the boardwalk waiting for her arrival. He stood anxiously by the passenger car as she stepped off the train. In her nervousness at the sight of him, she missed a step and fell into his arms.

"Looks like I was here right on time." He gazed into her eyes, grinning.

"That was clumsy of me." She rolled her eyes.

He still had his arms around her. Her eyes met his and she melted into his arms. He placed a quick gentle kiss on her lips, then stood back to see how she responded.

Sara looked at him with acceptance in her face. She put her arms around his neck and pulled him to her in a passionate kiss. *Scandalous.* It brought a blush to her face.

"Washington bodes well with you, my lady." He gave her his arm as they went to fetch her luggage.

Sara was enthusiastic about the possibility of another vote coming up soon, and especially excited about her future with Henry in a world where she had a voice.

"You must be tired and hungry. Do you feel up to dinner tonight?" he asked.

"I'm not tired, but I am starved. I need to go to Tillie's house to freshen up, but I would be delighted to have dinner with you." Sara wanted to share her newfound confidence with Henry.

Henry dropped her off at Tillie's house. "I will be back to pick you up at seven. We can go to Mader's Restaurant, if you'd like."

"I can't wait." Sara was thrilled. It had been years since she had been at Maders. It had been their favorite restaurant for as long as she could remember.

She bathed and put on an ivory satin dress with a cowl neckline and low-cut waist. She had purchased the dress in Washington one day with Catherine. It was the latest fashion.

Sara put her hair up and placed a lovely hat on top of her auburn curls, letting ringlets trail around her ears. She completed the outfit with emerald earrings and an emerald pendant on a gold chain. She slipped on bone heels and admired herself in the mirror. "Perfect," she said as she checked her makeup and ruby lips.

At seven, she was ready and patiently waiting for Henry's arrival. There was a chill in the evening air, so Sara grabbed a fox stole that she found in Tillie's closet. James had instructed her to do as she pleased with Tillie's things, but she couldn't bear to dispose of anything just yet. With his permission, she had on occasion worn some of Tillie's jewelry, but never the stole. As she put it on, she smiled. It felt good. It *looked* good.

She was jarred from her thoughts of Tillie by a rap at the door. She grabbed her bag and went directly to answer the door. Henry took her arm and led her to his vehicle.

"You look marvelous," he said. "Please allow me to assist you into your carriage and whisk you off to the ball."

"Oh," Sara teased, "I thought we were going to Maders."

"Your wish is my command." Henry bowed deeply and rushed around to the driver's seat.

Maders was crowded, but they were shown to a table in a far corner near the fireplace. Henry ordered a bottle of fine house wine, and their choice of entrée was wiener schnitzel, a very thin, breaded, deep-fried schnitzel from veal. It was the national dish of Austria, and a house specialty at Maders.

Sara could not believe the taste—it was as delicious as she remembered.

As they dined, Henry wanted to know more about Sara's trip to Washington.

She filled him in on her discussions with the legislators and spoke about her hopes for the next vote on the amendment.

Henry seemed completely enthralled and praised her for her work.

"Tell me about Catherine and James," Henry encouraged her next.

"They are so happy." Sara smiled. "They are planning a trip to Paris soon. James works a lot of hours, so Catherine spends a great deal of time alone, but she is extremely outgoing and that keeps her busy with the wives of many of his colleagues, attending social events, charity events, and afternoon teas. Washington is a whirlwind of activity. They have been invited to two dinners at the White House, and one day, she said to me, 'Imagine me, Catherine Morgenson from Wisconsin, dining with the First Lady at the White House.'" Sara laughed.

"Mrs. Wilson held a luncheon and invited several women who are involved in a project to help the poor. Poor houses are so full, Henry, and the conditions are deplorable. They are making great progress in that area. She also attended a luncheon focused on education. Catherine is so good with children. She should have been a teacher." Sara smiled fondly at the thought.

"Perhaps one day she will be a mother," Henry suggested.

"We talked about that. She thinks she is too old. She is my age, and I think I understand. I would not want to go through infancy and child rearing of toddlers at my age. Even if she is still able, by the time her child is out of high school, she will be an old lady of sixty. We vowed to grow old together, and I told her I would be as old as Tillie when the Lord calls me, so we have many years to look forward to." Sara chuckled.

Sara and Henry chatted through dinner. The meal was delicious, and they passed on dessert. Both were more than sufficiently filled.

"My, my," Sara stated. "I don't know when I last ate so much, but it was so delicious I couldn't stop. Thank you, Henry, for such an enjoyable evening."

Henry was hesitant for a moment, then said, "The evening is just beginning, my dear. We could do some high stepping, a little tango, a little two-step, maybe even a little ragtime. I am sure the maître d' can tell us which ballroom is lit up tonight."

"If it is all the same to you, perhaps you could wind up the Victrola and play a bit of Irving Berlin, and we can continue our conversation at home. I have had a long day and it would be nice to relax for a few hours before I need to retire for the evening." Sara didn't want the evening to end quite yet. She had so much she wanted to share with Henry, but not in a crowded ballroom.

"Whatever you wish, my lady. That sounds like a wonderful idea to me." Henry led her back to the automobile and assisted her into the seat.

They were soon back at the home on Astor Street.

It was very quiet inside as Henry held the door open for her. "Where are the girls?" Sara inquired, kicking off the new shoes killing her feet.

"I meant to tell you," Henry said. "Edith planned an overnight trip to Chicago with several girls from Downer College. They are visiting the museums there. Ella was very interested in visiting the Field Museum. Remember? We went there before the children were born, only then it was called the Columbian Museum of Chicago. Marshall Field was a major benefactor, so with the money came naming rights."

"Oh, yes, a fantastic museum. I know Ella will find it fascinating with its archaeological and natural science exhibits. Liz would have liked it even more. Where is Liz?" Sara asked.

"Well, that is the interesting thing. One of the Downer students became ill, and they had her train ticket and museum admission already purchased. They didn't have another Downer student available and Liz wanted to go. Edith checked with me first, then the school and they approved it, so Liz got to go with them."

"That is amazing. I can just see Liz. She will have fun."

"We couldn't quiet her for two days." Henry laughed. Then his voice grew sly. "Of course, you know what that means, don't you?"

"I imagine she will be feeding us all facts about various creatures for months to come," Sara surmised.

"No, my dear, that means that we have the house entirely to ourselves." Henry winked.

Suddenly it hit Sara, and she blushed. "Henry, you are incorrigible. You tricked me."

Henry laughed harder. "No, love, you were the one that suggested we come here and listen to Irving Berlin on the Victrola. You tricked me!"

Henry wound the Victrola and placed one of Berlin's newest songs on it. "Would you like some coffee?" he inquired. "I've gotten quite good at brewing it."

"That would be lovely," Sara said, and Henry made his way to the kitchen.

Sara tried to get comfortable on the chair in front of the fireplace, but her corset was stabbing her. She fidgeted to find a good position, suddenly nervous for the first time that night.

Sara could hear Henry clattering utensils in the kitchen.

The sounds of Irving Berlin filled the air, the mood soft and relaxing. "I Love You More Each Day," and then "A Pretty Girl is Like a Melody" played. Sara tried to ignore the music.

Henry placed the coffee pot on the table in front of the fireplace and gave her a mug filled with steaming, nutty-flavored coffee.

As she took the mug, their hands touched and lingered a moment.

Henry sat on the rug in front of the fireplace where he could look directly up into Sara's eyes.

She continued an upbeat conversation with Henry as her face warmed. "That's a new rug," Sara observed as she pointed to the huge bearskin rug in front of the fireplace. "Are you a bear hunter now?"

"No, actually, we gave a loan to a hunter who couldn't pay his debt. He owed two hundred dollars, so some of us at the bank purchased his wares. Fred got a bearskin rug with the head intact. I couldn't quite handle that, but this one is quite comfortable. Come sit by me." He patted the space beside him on the rug.

"Well, I am sure glad you didn't take up hunting; I would hate to see you with a gun." Sara laughed.

Henry took her by the hand and pulled her beside him. Sara saw how he tried to maintain a casual atmosphere, but his intentions were written all over his face. "Sara." He put his hands on her shoulders and gazed deep into her eyes. "I want you to come home. I love you. We all love you, and we want you back with us."

Her conversation with Catherine came flooding into her mind. "I want to come home, too," she whispered, meeting his gaze.

He drew her into his arms and kissed her softly on the lips. His mouth travelled across her eyelids, brushing them gently.

He kissed her again.

She clung to him, not wanting to let go.

His lips traveled down her neck. His hand cupped her face, his fingers caressing the back of her neck and behind her ears.

Her lips searched for his hungrily. Her head spun as he reached behind her and unzipped her dress from neck to hips. The dress slid off her shoulders, and Sara let it fall, no longer unsure.

His hands searched for her breasts, still covered in her undergarments.

He undid the laces of her corset as she grappled with the buttons on his shirt. He had long since removed his jacket and tie.

She stripped his suspenders from his trousers and unsnapped them at the same time he released her from her undergarments. She felt beautiful under his stare.

His tongue tickled the tips of her breast, causing her nipples to stand upright. She was drunk from his kisses. How the rest of the clothing was removed, she hadn't a clue, but her body ached for his.

He pulled the comb from her hair and her long tresses dropped over her shoulders. He laid her back on the rug, and their bodies molded together. She could feel the hardness of his manhood slide between her legs, and she raised her hips, begging him to enter her. It was slow and gentle as their bodies moved as one.

At first, they moved as the gentle waves of the ocean, but soon she wrapped her legs around him, and he responded with the passion of an unleashed storm. Their breaths came loud and fast.

Sara moaned as their bodies shuddered and they lay exhausted in each other's arms.

They spent time basking in the magic of the moment and in the pleasure of each other's company, sharing relaxed lazy caresses as they laid there until the fire turned to glowing embers, much like their passion for each other.

Sara felt she would never stop glowing, so long as Henry was back in her life.

The room had started to get a bit of a chill when Henry said, "Sara, please stay the night."

Sara nodded.

They climbed the stairs together. And she relished the glow of renewed love.

Henry went to the washroom as she turned back the bed and found her old bathrobe. She sat on the vanity bench brushing her hair when Henry entered the room wrapped in a towel.

She stood, and he tangled his fingers in hers and led her to their bed. With a nudge from him, her bathrobe slipped to the floor, and he picked her up and laid her on the bed.

"I love you, Mrs. Dewberry," he said passionately.

"I love you, Mr. Dewberry," she replied.

Chapter Sixty-two

The next morning, Sara awoke early and made her way to the kitchen. She fried potatoes in a skillet and got a bowl with eggs ready to be scrambled. The aroma of fresh brewed coffee filled the air. She was about to place freshly made biscuits into the oven when Henry entered the room, yawning.

She poured a cup of coffee and handed it to him. "Good morning."

He smiled before he placed a gentle kiss on her cheek, taking the mug of steaming coffee from her hands.

"That the best you can do?"

"You know better than that," he said and laughed. "I'm afraid if I allow more than a mere peck, we will be in bed the rest of the day."

Sara sat down at the table with Henry while the biscuits were baking. "Henry, we need to talk about my moving in," she said, a bit of anxiety in her voice. "First, we need to tell the girls. I am sure they will be fine with it, but I don't want to shock them with the news."

"And second?"

"Second, I need to wait a couple of weeks," she said hesitantly.

"And why is that?" Henry's face showed his insecurity, and he took her hand.

"I need to go back to Washington in a couple of days. I came home to tell you that I want to move back home, but I wanted to make sure that you felt the same. I still have some unfinished business to take care of."

"Oh? A scorned lover?" he teased.

"Not exactly," Sara continued seriously, "but it is a love, or at least a passion. President Wilson has finally focused on the women's movement and he would like to see the Nineteenth Amendment passed soon. He is calling a special session of congress. I want to be there the day the amendment passes. I believe this vote will be it."

"How long will you be?" he asked.

"I don't have to leave until after the weekend. I believe this will come to a vote about the middle of May…possibly sooner. This is an important, historic day and I don't want to miss it. It is the culmination of all of the work Tillie and I have poured into this project in the past five years or more," Sara explained. She hoped he would understand.

Henry's eyes were warm and loving as he looked at her. "I have waited five years for you to come back home. I don't know how, but I guess I can wait a few more weeks."

Sara got up to check the biscuits and fry the eggs.

Henry rose to refill his coffee mug, and as he moved past her, he playfully slapped Sara on the behind with a dish towel. "Just hurry back. I understand…but I will miss you."

With the snap of the towel, she squealed and turned quickly, almost bumping into him.

He placed his hands on her waist. "Dearest, I am proud of you. Sincerely, I am. I don't know why I didn't see it earlier, but it makes perfect sense that women should have equal rights, especially the right to vote. I would be right there by your side, but there is important business at the bank that I need to tend to."

Henry sighed. "I always thought of you as a smart but frail, quiet girl that needed to be guided and taken care of. You have opened my eyes to a courageous, beautiful woman who is intelligent and competent and strong. I guess I thought the world out there would scare you back to me, so I wanted to make it as scary as possible. I will always regret that. It is the one thing that will haunt me until the day I die. I have changed, and I love you more now than ever."

"My one fear, Henry…was that you would not be able to accept me for the woman I have become. I have changed, too, and I like the person I am." Sara gazed into his eyes. "And Mr. Dewberry, I like the man you have become."

Just then, Sara smelled the smoky aroma of burning biscuits. "Oh no."

She grabbed a towel and quickly rescued the biscuits from the oven. "We will have to cut off the bottoms, but at least some of them can be salvaged."

"Well, at least your culinary skills have not changed." Henry ducked and turned as Sara spun around, leaving his derriere in perfect position for her to return the smack with the towel in her hand.

He chased her around the table and caught her in his arms, planting a big kiss on her lips.

She melted like the butter on his biscuits, and he tweaked her nose with his index finger. "Don't ever change again, Sara. You are perfect just the way you are."

"Eat your breakfast," Sara commanded, red-faced but smiling.

Henry pulled out her chair and they lingered over breakfast for the next two hours, discussing what to tell the girls, plans for her trip back to Washington, how they would manage the move, what would happen to Tillie's house, and what Sara would do after the amendment was passed. Time passed swiftly.

They would have loved to lull the day away, but Henry needed to get to work and Sara needed time to pack her things for her trip to Washington. Packing her things for the move back home could wait until her return.

The girls were due to return that evening. Sara and Henry had agreed to meet Ella and Liz at the train station together. The train wasn't due until seven-fifteen, and the girls would be excited and full of delight in telling their stories. They would have eaten in the dining car, so plans for dinner would be soup and biscuits—new biscuits that would not be burned.

***

Henry and Sara were waiting when the locomotive chugged into the station. A loud toot of the whistle announced their arrival. True to their expectations, the girls were full of excited chatter with tales of the amazing city, the interesting displays in the museums, their experiences riding the train and eating in the dining car, and friends they had met. The chatter went on non-stop throughout the evening.

Eventually, Liz fell asleep on the chaise and Ella began to yawn.

"I am going to leave, but I will see you tomorrow," Sara said. "Your father and I will be taking you out for dinner. Perhaps we can go shopping in the afternoon to get you some fashionable outfits. Your father has done a very good job of keeping you clothed, but I am afraid his fashion savvy is a bit dated. Tomorrow's dinner will be a celebration, and I want everyone to be dressed for it. We will be dining

315

at the Commodore Hotel."

"Woo-hoo! Ritzy." Ella approved.

Liz began to stir as Sara prepared to leave. She opened an eye. "Goodnight, Mother," she managed to say through a yawn. "See you tomorrow."

Sara gave her youngest daughter a hug.

"Goodnight, Ella." Sara hugged Ella next. "I will be back early in the afternoon."

"Night, Mother. I can't wait. You can stay, you know," Ella offered.

"I know, dear, but I need to change my clothes and take care of a few things," Sara explained.

Henry followed Sara to her car and assisted her into it, closing the door. "You know, you really can stay."

"Soon, Henry...soon," Sara promised.

Henry hopped onto the running board and leaned far into the vehicle, taking her face in his hands. "Promise?" he asked, nose to nose.

"Promise," she whispered as his lips met hers, sealing their promise.

***

On Saturday afternoon, Sara arrived to pick up two eager, young ladies. They had searched the Sears Roebuck catalogue earlier and were anxious to find the perfect outfit for dinner that evening. Sara had anticipated being bombarded with questions about the celebration, but when they inquired, she stated, "It is a surprise." And they dropped the subject.

They shopped for hours. Their first stop was at the beauty shop. Liz wanted her dark hair cut into the now-fashionable bob.

Sara agreed that it would look great on her. Her shoulder-length hair was soon lying in a mass on the floor. Her long eyelashes and dark eyes were a perfect compliment.

Ella didn't want to lose her long auburn tresses but chose to have the upper portion braided and placed in a crown around her head. The remainder tumbled to her shoulders and down her back.

Sara decided the sophisticated look of a chignon was right for her. The silver streaks in her hair only highlighted the look.

They left the parlor pleased with their makeovers. Then, the serious shopping began.

When they came home with their bundles of purchases, Liz had a pink scoop-neck chemise with a white hip sash and matching accessories. The trend was to coordinate colors as much as possible, and with the accent of Liz's dark hair and eyes, she was stunning.

Ella chose a purple knee-length chemise with a silver belt that fastened at her hips, alongside silver jewelry and a perky triangular purple hat. She also purchased a silver evening bag on a long silver chain.

Sara had found a rich, royal blue dress with scoop neck and matching jacket trimmed in fur. She remembered her diamond stud earrings at Henry's house. She had seen them in the jewelry box when she had gotten dressed the morning before.

They had plenty of time to get ready for dinner. Sara sat at her vanity in the master suite, checking out her appearance. She hoped Henry would be pleased.

Someone knocked at the bedroom door. Sara, expecting it to be one of the girls, called out, "Come in."

Henry opened the door. "Oh dear, too late." He looked disappointed.

"Too late for what?" Sara asked, puzzled.

"Too late to help you get dressed," he teased. "But I see you haven't finished yet." He sat at the end of the bed. "I hope it fits." He handed her a blue box from Tiffany's.

She smiled at him coyly. "What have we here?" She pulled the ribbon from the box.

As she opened the box, her jaw dropped. "Henry, it's beautiful." She took a striking diamond necklace from the box. The pendant was a deep blue sapphire with diamonds surrounding it.

He took it from her hands and fastened it around her neck.

"Oh, Henry," she said as she admired it in the mirror. "I have never seen anything so stunning."

"It isn't the necklace that is stunning; it is the lady wearing it." He pulled her up into his arms, took her left hand in his, and caressed her ring. "I couldn't replace this ring, 'til death do us part,' but this necklace is a mere token of the love I give with it."

Sara fell into his embrace. "I am the happiest woman alive right now."

***

They arrived at the Commodore precisely at seven. They were ushered to their table. Henry held Sara's chair, and the maître d' held the chairs for each of the young ladies.

Henry asked for a bottle of champagne for Sara and himself and ordered lemonade for the girls.

"So, what are we celebrating?" Liz couldn't wait to know. "Are we taking a trip?" Liz had told them her recent expedition to Chicago was a taste of the world to be discovered, and she had decided she wanted to see all of it.

"Well, perhaps," Henry said thoughtfully. "Maybe next summer we could all go to Paris…but that is not the surprise."

"Did the amendment pass?" Ella asked, curious. "Did I miss it?" She smiled in anticipation at Sara.

"Hopefully very soon." Sara patted Ella's hand. "But that's not it."

"What is it?" both girls asked in unison.

"The best news ever." Henry took Sara's hand and looked into her eyes.

"Oh my gosh," Liz blurted out. "They're getting married."

Sara and Henry laughed. "Liz, we are already married. Your mother is coming home."

"To our house, to live with us?" Ella asked.

Sara smiled and nodded at the girls.

They both screamed and ran to their mother and hugged her.

Patrons at the other tables looked to see what the commotion was about. Seeing it was a wonderful celebration, they nodded, smiled, and went about their own business.

The girls could hardly contain themselves long enough to check the menu and make their choices. Dinner seemed irrelevant.

"When, Mother? Tonight?" Ella asked.

"No, girls, it will be a little while. I will be going back to Washington tomorrow. I have to pack, and I will be leaving in the morning."

"How long will you be gone?" Liz wanted to know.

Sara thought of the road ahead with a smile. "Perhaps a week. Maybe a bit longer. I will be there until the amendment comes up for a vote. We anticipate it will be voted on next week. I will return immediately after the vote, and it is our hope Wisconsin will ratify it soon after. Then my work will be done. Women will continue the fight for equality, but at least they will have a voice. I will have to tie up some loose ends with Tillie's estate, and then I will be all yours, no strings attached."

"There will be strings attached," Liz stated firmly. "We will be attached to your apron strings. You won't ever be able to leave again."

"We'll drink to that," Henry said as he raised the glass. "To Mother… may she live a long and happy life in our home, never to separate again."

The following morning at ten a.m., Sara boarded the train back to Washington, D.C. As she thought about the evening before, she couldn't help but smile. Moving home felt right.

Chapter Sixty-three

In May of 1919, Congress was not in session. Normally, special sessions of congress were only called when the country had to deal with a dire emergency. However, since Congress was not in session more often than it was in session, President Wilson deemed the matter of the Nineteenth Amendment to be of significant importance. 1920 was an election year, and he was relying on the women's vote to elect a Democratic president for the next term. Wilson would not be seeking a third term, and hoped the women's vote would tip the scales to the relatively unknown Governor Cox.

Harding chose to ignore Cox, and ran his campaign against Wilson, the president who was elected on an anti-war theme but eventually took the country into the Great War. Wounds were still festering about the war, and the one-hundred-ten-thousand Americans who gave their lives. Wilson needed some issue to generate votes for his party. He called the special session to do just that.

An order was sent out to congress leaders to convene in June to debate and vote on the Nineteenth Amendment to the Constitution.

Sara had arrived on May twenty-eighth. She immediately went to Catherine's home.

Catherine had invited her to be a house guest for as long as necessary. At first, there was nothing noteworthy happening on the political scene, which was normal for a time when Congress was not in session. Thus, Sara and Catherine had plenty of time to talk.

"So, tell me, Sara, how are things with you and Henry?" Catherine wasted no time getting to the point.

"Oh Catherine, amazing, simply amazing," Sara confided, feeling giddy. "He took me to dinner at Maders and…"

"Ah, Maders your favorite restaurant, and…"

"Well, we talked for hours and he wanted to go dancing, but I told him I would prefer to listen to the Victrola and relax."

Catherine's eyebrows rose. "You vixen."

Sara smiled. "You don't know the half of it. The girls were gone to Chicago overnight. I didn't know it when I suggested an evening at home. I thought they would be home."

"You stick to that story." Catherine grinned.

"No, no." Sara pushed her friend on the arm. "I really didn't know."

"Okay, now that you are in the lion's den, what happened? Don't spare any details."

"We had coffee and listened to the Victrola by firelight. We talked for hours, and well..."

"Well, what? Don't keep me in suspense." Catherine wiggled in her seat.

"I spent the night," Sara blurted out, turning red at the thought.

"Sara, you are blushing. Not like Christmas, you spent the night. Together?"

"Together...in the same bed. We are still married, you know." Sara justified her actions.

Catherine let out a squeal. "You didn't!"

"I did."

"And was it...good?" Catherine prompted.

"It was better than ever. It was the fourth of July and Christmas rolled into one. It was fantastic." Sara let loose, confiding in her best friend like they were schoolgirls.

"Oh my gosh. That is wonderful. Did you stay?"

"Yes...well, no. I stayed until noon the next day. Henry had to go to work; I needed to pack to come here. We agreed to tell the girls over dinner on Saturday. I took them shopping for some stylish clothes for our celebration dinner. We shopped Saturday afternoon and then dined at the Commodore on Saturday evening."

"What did you wear? What did you eat? I told you, don't leave anything out," Catherine prompted.

Sara told her, adding in the part about the necklace from Tiffany's, which made Catherine squeal again.

"How did the girls take the news?" Catherine asked, continuing the interrogation.

"They were elated. I told them when I return I would tie up some loose ends, and then I would be moving back into our home," Sara said, full of excited anticipation. "James will have to decide what to do with Tillie's house. I should be out by mid-June."

"Since our last conversation in April, I told James I thought it would be only a matter of time for you to make this decision, so he is prepared. I must say, you came to this conclusion much sooner than I expected— but I should know by now, when you make up your mind, you do not dally." Catherine's face was filled with sincerity, and Sara squeezed her hand in gratitude.

Sara and Catherine spent the next few days exploring Washington DC, walking the mall, and visiting the Capitol, the Washington Monument, and the Smithsonian.

Sara was very relaxed. This was the first time she enjoyed Washington and its splendor. Her previous visits were confrontational and intense. Now, she saw Washington through new eyes, filled with awe.

"When Congress convenes, do you think the amendment will pass this time?" Catherine asked.

"I feel very good about it," said Sara. "The president is backing it. I think we have enough congressmen and senators open to it, and I am hoping nothing stands in our way."

"Well, only a few months ago, it failed by two votes. Has much changed?" Catherine frowned.

"We have been rallying constituents throughout the country. The popular vote is in favor of the amendment. Of course, there are some radical opponents, and they can exert a lot of influence; particularly the churches. The Roman Catholic Church is vehemently opposed. The Wisconsin Synod Lutheran faction is opposed, too, and there are a number of Protestant religions that could go either way." Sara had some apprehensions, too.

"But church and state are separate," Catherine analyzed.

"True, but that doesn't mean they don't carry a lot of weight with their parishioners, and ultimately their voice is heard by the Representatives." Sara made a concerned face, kneading her fingers together. "I hope that reason will prevail, and this is the vote that will pass."

"I hope you are right."

***

In June, Congress convened, and discussions were underway. Sara stayed close to the phone at Catherine's house, anticipating the call from James to alert them that a vote was underway.

The call came on June 4, 1919. The phone rang, and James, his voice filled with joy, said, "Sara, I am sending an automobile for you and Catherine. The Speaker has called for a vote. We should know the result within the hour."

Sara rushed for her transportation. She quickly made her way to the front gate, and an automobile arrived within minutes to whisk her away to the Capitol, where a podium was set up outside. There were no gallery passes available to this event; however, it was arranged for an aide to pass the information on to Sara and the delegation as soon as it was made available. It was up to Congress to pass the deciding vote.

With fifty-six ayes and twenty-five nays, the amendment was passed that very day. As soon as she heard, Sara nearly fell to her knees in tears of relief, but managed to stay standing, because she had never felt so strong. At last, after years of sacrifice and suffering, they had done it. Tillie would've been thrilled.

Several representatives of the Women's Suffrage Movement were given the right to speak. The crowd cheered, and there was dancing in the streets.

After several notable suffragettes spoke, the spokesperson announced, "This all would not have been possible except for the tireless work of Tillie Morgenson, who recently passed away, and her protégé, Sara Dewberry. Sara is here today. Sara, can you share with us your thoughts?"

Sara took the megaphone, her entire body trembling with joy. She looked to the sky and saw it cloudless and beautiful on this unforgettable day. "Women of America. This is an historic day. This is a day to rejoice. However, our work is not done. We need to have every state in the union ratify this amendment before it becomes official. I urge you to not give up yet. Go home and convince your legislatures that this amendment must be the law of the land. We will continue to fight beside you and support you in any way we can until the amendment is ratified by every state and every woman has a voice."

Sara left the podium to cheers. Catherine was in tears. They knew the fight was not over, but it was well within reach of total ratification.

After, Sara went back to Catherine's home and gathered her things together. She would leave for home first thing in the morning, and she couldn't wait.

***

Before Sara left Washington, she spoke with James about the house. James intended to keep the townhouse in New York, but he would sell the home in Wisconsin. He was well-rooted in the Washington scene, and his primary residence would remain there. Catherine loved the bustle of New York, and she invited Sara and the girls to come to New York right after Thanksgiving to begin holiday shopping. Sara agreed it would be a delightful trip, but she did not commit the girls, since they would be in school.

James told Sara to feel free to remove any of Tillie's personal property for herself.

Sara was not interested in the monetary value of her choices, but she had decided on two items. The first was the andirons and fireplace tools in Tillie's parlor. They had claw feet and lion's head handles. Tillie had always been cold and enjoyed a roaring fire. They had often laughed that the lions helped to make the fire roar.

The second item she chose was an attractive dragonfly table lamp, which stood on the table by Tillie's favorite reading place. She would tell James when she took them. They would help remind her of Tillie and all that they had shared.

Sara arrived in Milwaukee on the seventh of June. It was a beautiful summer day in Wisconsin. She was scheduled to meet with Senator Robert LaFollette on the ninth. He had returned from Washington and addressed several members of the Wisconsin Legislature. He informed Sara that a vote would be coming any time, making Wisconsin the very first state to ratify this Constitutional amendment.

After speaking with Bob LaFolllette, Sara met Henry for dinner.

"Oh, Henry, Senator LaFollette informed me that the vote to ratify the amendment will occur on Friday. I have been so busy, I haven't had time to gather my things, but I assure you right after the vote, we will gather at the library for a victory celebration and I'll get my bags packed. I will be home immediately after. We can get the rest of my things on the weekend." Sara felt the end of the journey near and took Henry's hands as her eyes watered. This was it.

Henry squeezed her fingers in his own. "Sara, Sara, finally, you will be home at last. I can't wait a moment longer. In fact, why don't you come tonight?"

Sara smiled. "Patience, my love, it will be just one more day. I have a speech to write and my clothes to ready for tomorrow. I want my first night home to be special. Tell the girls, and we will go immediately from the gathering to our home. I can't wait, either."

Chapter Sixty-four

On the tenth of July, Sara gathered with members of the Wisconsin Suffragette movement at the library. The event was publicized, and since the vote was imminent, a large group had gathered outside the library, awaiting the results. The excitement was building. Edith would receive the information as soon as the vote was determined.

At two in the afternoon, word finally came that Wisconsin was indeed the first state to ratify the Nineteenth Amendment.

Edith had received the call from Madison, and she walked to the podium with a grin from ear to ear. "Ladies and gentlemen. The Nineteenth Amendment to the Constitution of the United States of America has been ratified by the great state of Wisconsin. Wisconsin is the first state in the union to ratify it. Be proud, be strong, and be counted." She lifted a fist, and a loud, lengthy cheer went up from the elated crowd.

Sara cheered as loud as she could and felt the support of all her friends around her. There were hugs and tears of joy all around. She wished Catherine was there with her.

When the noise subsided somewhat, Edith continued, "Tillie Morgenson would be so proud. She is no longer with us except in spirit, but we do have with us Sara Dewberry, who stepped into Mrs. Morgenson's shoes and continued valiantly and vigilantly to see this mission accomplished. Please welcome and thank Mrs. Sara Dewberry for her tireless efforts to see this through. Sara Dewberry!"

Thunderous applause greeted her.

Sara stepped to the podium at the top of the library stairs, her heart fuller than it had ever been.

"Today is a glorious day," Sara said. "Be proud, ladies and gentlemen of Wisconsin, for you are the very first to ratify the Nineteenth

Amendment which gives women the right to vote. Ladies, for the first time in the history of this great nation, your voice will be heard."

Applause and cheers rang out.

"Many women have worked long and hard for this day. Since the convention of 1848 in Seneca Falls, New York, where Elizabeth Cady Stanton wrote and delivered the Women's Bill of Rights, women have been rallying to the cause. They have paid enormous prices for their convictions, but we have this very day ushered in the new era. This does not mean we are finished. Wisconsin took the first step in making it a reality. There are forty-seven more states to win over. We only need thirty, but hopefully we will have the support of all forty-eight states."

Sara cleared her throat and looked out over the crowd. So many familiar faces smiled back at her and urged her on. "We know it will be the beginning of many new and wonderful things. Women will one day have equal rights with men. They will hold property in their own name. They will have a right to keep and raise their children in the event of a marital breakup, and they will be able to claim the wages of their labor as their own. The right to vote will pave the road to those successes." Sara thought of her own family at home, the faces of Ella and Liz, and lifted her chin higher.

"We must move forward and go to the polls and cast our ballots for issues that will support the agenda of women. We must vote for candidates who will make us not superior, but equal to every other citizen of these United States. We must go to the polls for the women who went before us in the past half century, those who paid a big price for us to be heard. We must go to the polls for our daughters who follow us, who will have a brighter future because of the accomplishments of this vote today.

"Raise your voices and educate those who are narrow-minded and who wish to hold onto the idea of male superiority and domination. Speak up in your churches, in your communities. Speak up, ladies. You have a voice."

Applause and cheers rang out once again.

Sara received congratulations and praise from her colleagues on the podium and felt shaky as the weight of the past five years lifted just an inch off her shoulders. She couldn't stop smiling, despite the work still to be done.

The crowd rang out her name and reached out to shake her hand. She saw Henry in the crowd and blew him a kiss. He had tears in his eyes and clapped louder than anyone. She held the rail as she descended the steps to the welcoming crowd.

A well-dressed gentleman stood at the foot of the steps and reached out to assist her down the stairway. She took his hand and smiled into his face as he pulled her closer to him, his left hand holding hers, his right hand in his pocket. She was directly in front of him when he pulled a Derringer from his pocket and a shot rang out.

Sara's face went blank as she dropped to the ground.

The crowd gasped.

Chaos erupted.

The crowd immediately pounced on the man, who was screaming, "God has spoken! Damnation to the suffragettes!"

The constables pulled the man out of the crowd and took him off to jail.

Medics soon arrived on the scene.

Henry cradled Sara in his arms, tears streaming down his cheeks as he cried, "Sara, Sara, my love. Come back."

But Sara was dead.

She had sacrificed so much to have her daughters' voices be heard, and now, her voice had been silenced forever. But never forgotten.

Epilogue

One hundred years later.

Melissa Cartwright was seated in the old bentwood rocker next to the fireplace on Astor Street in Milwaukee. Her daughter, Vanessa stood in front of the fireplace with a cup of coffee in her hand.

"So, Vanessa, that is the story of your great, great-grandmother Sara Dewberry. I wish women would understand the sacrifice women like Sara paid so they could have a voice, so they can vote."

"Yes, so many have taken that right for granted and many choose not to exercise their gift," Vanessa agreed. "But Mom, what happened to Grandpa Henry and the children?"

Melissa sighed, time rewinding in her mind as she remembered her own mother's stories. "Henry was a broken man. He never quite recovered from the shock of Sara's death. He lived the rest of his life a recluse and died of heart failure five years later at the age of forty-eight. Some say of a broken heart. The children grew up. Thaddeus had a career in the military and Liz became a nurse. Ella, as you know, was your great grandmother."

"Did Grandma Ella vote in the 1920 election?" Vanessa asked.

"The amendment was fully ratified August 18, 1920. Ella was just eighteen when her mother died. She had to be twenty-one to vote. However, in 1924, the next presidential election, she proudly cast her ballot."

"Tell me about Grandma Ella. I hear she was quite a firecracker," Vanessa said, encouraging the story to go on.

"Ah, your Grandma Ella was pretty amazing in her own right. But it is late. Let's save that story for tomorrow," Melissa suggested. "Reliving Sara's sacrifice is quite enough for one day."

If you enjoyed *Sara's Sacrifice* **by Flo Parfitt, you may enjoy her next book in the Daughters of Evolution Series,** *Ella Endures* **to be released in 2020.**

Sara Dewberry's daughter, Ella, was born into the Greatest Generation. She lived through Prohibition, the Great Depression, and World War II. Ella witnessed firsthand the heartbreak of suffering, the poor houses, and the orphanages.

Like her mother, she wasn't afraid of danger. She persevered and gave her all to give comfort and healing to all she encountered. She worked in the factories and did her part during the war effort. She fixed what she could and endured the pain of others through their trials until finally, she encountered the one obstacle she could not survive.

Acknowledgements

I wish to acknowledge the following people who were a part in making this book possible. First, my son, Jim Parfitt for his work in building my media platform and Heidi Gillis, who was my first beta reader and corrected many of my errors. She told me she cried through one chapter and got up during the night to read another, which made me realize I hit a chord.

Thank you to award-winning author, Jim Rubart, whose professional eye and encouragement made me never give up, and to my Monday morning Writers Group who put the critical eye to this story and called my attention to tiny little things that were a big help. My editor and publisher, Brittiany Koren, who made it all happen on a timely basis. Thank you, guys. I couldn't have done it without you.

About the Author

Flo Parfitt is a lifelong student, attending seminars, workshops, and other educational programs throughout her life. She attended Northeast Wisconsin Technical College and Downer College. Most recently, she completed a program at Rubart Writing Academy and enrolled in the Lifelong Learning Institute at University of WI-Green Bay. Throughout her career, she has worked as a business manager at Everson, Whitney, Everson & Brehm, S.C. law offices, Seering & Company Advertising Agency, and Warner Bros Television.

She was published in several trade journals, including the Wisconsin Bar Journal, Callaghan's Law Office Management, Integrated Office Technologies "The Word" and others. She has worked with Court Appointed Special Advocates (CASA) for abused and neglected children and various charitable causes. She is a member of the League of Women Voters, the Green Bay Area Writers Guild and Writers Group. She lives in Wisconsin.

CPSIA information can be obtained
at www.ICGtesting.com
Printed in the USA
BVHW082350171219
566946BV00001B/8/P